CHARLES CANDENNING WAS STARING AT THE MUZZLE OF A VERY UGLY WALTHER MILITARY MODEL AUTOMATIC . . .

At the forward end of the car, Karen was still kneeling beside her valise blocking the aisle. Candenning saw the second German lean over, grab her by one arm, and drag her to her feet. Domingo Portes also saw the movement. *"Momento!"* he called to the German.

The rest was almost a blur. Portes threw his right fist into the German's nose. Arms flaying wildly, the man staggered, but did not go down. Blood now drenched his upper lip and mouth. His eyes were wide with pain and fury, his voice inchoate as he, too, drew a pistol and leveled it at Portes . . .

IMPERIAL EXPRESS

JAMES BELLAH

A JOVE BOOK

IMPERIAL EXPRESS

First Jove edition published February 1982

First printing

Printed in the United States of America

Jove books are published by Jove Publications, Inc.,
200 Madison Avenue, New York, NY 10016

This book is for all of those unfortunates who have, at one time or another, been spattered, soaked or drowned by the tides of Government.

It could never have been written without the kindness, courtesy and cooperation of:

Damaris Rowland, a delightful semantic engineer;
Lt. Col. Larry E. Joyce, Chief, News Branch, Public Information Division, United States Army;
Frederick J. Kling, attorney at law;
Celeste Mitchell, one of the world's greatest typists;
Mary S. Pratt, Principal Librarian, History Dept., Los Angeles Public Library;
Charles G. Worman, chief, Research Division, United States Air Force Museum; and
Albert Zuckerman, D.F.A., a man of great faith and ability.

Withall, it is still for G. H., née L., for reasons which she and I shall keep to ourselves.

CONTENTS

Book V: DURANGO

Book VI: CHIHUAHUA

Let us have faith that right makes might; and in that faith let us to the end, dare to do our duty as we understand it.

—ABRAHAM LINCOLN

Sir, there are rascals in all countries.

—SAMUEL JOHNSON

Prologue

AFTER THE ROBBERY, they left San Cristóbal. They urged the animals throughout the night. The tiny, muscular man led them toward the higher mountains. The slender blond rode in the rear, constantly searching the darkness for possible pursuers.

By dawn they were already in the highlands. Finally confident that they had not been followed, they stopped at a clearing.

Exhausted, excited, William Scofield slid from the lead burro. With the arrogant grace of the very short, he walked several paces across the clearing, dug a cigarette from its crumpled pack, and lit it. He took a deep pull, held the richness of the smoke in his lungs for as long as he could, then exhaled. He looked over the lush, savage jungle washed now by the first glow of tropical sunlight. Satisfaction rested in him like the heaviness of a delicious meal. Lazy and perfect, it was now part of his very soul.

William Scofield nodded to the roseate glow of awakening sun and waved his cigarette grandiloquently. "Crime of the century," he whispered to the sweating wilderness. "Crime of the goddamned century."

Tall, dour and by now almost oblivious to the constant and murderous humidity, Ian Conrad finished tethering the burros and walked to where Scofield stood. He took a pipe from one pocket of his perspiration-soaked shirt and a tobacco pouch from the other.

Alone in the remote wilderness, the two men stared downhill over the thick foliage which seemed almost pastel in day's first illusive light. They had done what they had set out to do and they had escaped. For the first time in many hours the adrenalin had ceased to flow. Their blood pressures were returning to normal.

"Christ!" Scofield sucked on his cigarette again. "Must be two—maybe three million worth there."

1

"Aye." The Welshman glanced to the twelve heavily laden burros standing vacuously where he had tethered them.

"We're rich," Scofield spoke, as if to the jungle itself. "More goddamned rich than we'd ever have been with the mine."

"Aye." Conrad finished loading his pipe. He struck a match and began to puff the tobacco alive.

Scofield took a final long suck of his cigarette, then flicked it away. It hissed faintly as it hit the wet jungle undergrowth. As he looked to his partner, the smile on his lips was contradicted by his lowered brows. He inspected Conrad's thin, enigmatic face, then shook his head. "Well," he said, "the least you can do is smile."

The Welshman continued to look at the animals and beyond to the thick, forbidding foliage. "It won't do no good," he said.

"What won't?"

"That." Conrad nodded toward the burros. "The gold."

"You silly son of a bitch," Scofield said. "Goddamned jungle's made you crazy. You know whoever hid that stuff was hiding it from the government. You think for one minute they're going to squeal? Hell's bells, man, the whole goddamned church is against the law!"

"It's not that—"

"Oh? Maybe you think some wild-eyed priest or friar or monk or something is going to come out of hiding and climb up here gunning for us?"

Conrad breathed easily on his pipe. "You're bold, Bill," he said. "I'll give you that. But you don't understand. Sure, you sniffed out the gold. Sure, we got it, and we've got clean away as well—"

"So, what's wrong then?"

Conrad took the pipe from his mouth and inspected it as though some particularly offensive insect had made the smoldering tobacco its funeral pyre. "Should have thought of it before," he mused, "but we were working too fast—getting the animals, getting into that house, loading the stuff. Should have known it wouldn't work."

"Goddamn it, Ian, we've got the gold!" Scofield waved in the direction of the animals. "What more proof do you need? The priests won't come. Hell, what difference does it make if they do? There're probably no more than ten of them left in

2

the whole stinking country. And even so, priests don't carry guns."

"Not the point."

"You think some bishop is going to run straight to President Cárdenas and tell how he's been squirreling gold from the state, and then expect the government's help in getting it back?"

"Not the point."

"All right." Scofield pulled the flattened pack of cigarettes from his shirt pocket, dug for the last one and thrust it almost viciously between his lips. "All right," he said again. "So I don't see the point. So maybe your almighty limey wisdom can explain the goddamned point."

Conrad nodded. "We've neglected the hard political facts. We've not reckoned on Cárdenas."

"Screw Cárdenas. Screw the whole goddamned government."

"It's true," Conrad went on, "there's a fortune here. But you can see for yourself, Bill, there's no place to spend it—no place to melt it down."

"So what?" Scofield demanded. "I don't plan to stay in this pisspot country forever."

"No. But we can't get out. Not with that."

"Who'll stop us? The church? Shit, man, there is no church."

"Somebody hoarded that gold."

"So, maybe a priest or two is left in the whole stinking state of Chiapas. But they'll never tell. You going to tell? Me?"

"No," Conrad sighed. "They'll get us at the border. If some smart Mexican doesn't do it, some smart American will. Sure, we're high on a mountain watching the bloody poetry of dawn over Chiapas, and we've possession of a fortune, but we'll never get it north to America or over the sea to anywhere else."

"Goddamn it!" Scofield drew himself up to his full five feet three inches and looked pugnaciously at the much taller man. "Conrad, you're a pain in the ass—a royal pain in the goddamned ass." He walked across the clearing until he came to a rocky ledge overlooking the jungle and valleys below. There he finally reached into his trouser pockets for matches and lit the dank cigarette dangling from his lips.

All his life William Scofield had wanted only two things.

3

Bastard son of an illiterate farm girl and a drummer in dry goods, his first childhood desires were to leave forever the parochial and actual chill of Minnesota. Even more than that, he had wanted a fortune. Now that fortune was his, but Conrad, with his damned pedantic practicality, was trying to tell him it was worthless.

He sucked on the cigarette and gazed into the great ball of molten fire which had just peeked over the eastern ridges.

"Well, it's not worthless," he said aloud. "Not by a goddamned sight."

Whatever he may have lacked in physical stature, Bill Scofield had always made up for in dogged determination and a capacity for being utterly ruthless when his own interests were at stake. It was the fury of his fists which had put him through the Colorado School of Mines at Golden, and had supported him as Kid Scofield in tank fight after tank fight as he wandered farther and farther south after that unpromising graduation day in 1930. It was his larcenous awareness that had discovered the gold in the first place. That awareness, coupled with the ruthless, long-standing war between Church and State in Mexico, and his own purely gut-level feeling, had all combined to make him rich beyond any dreams he may have had. Now, here, isolated in the stinking, humid highlands of southern Mexico, Ian Conrad was throwing a wooden shoe into the machinery of all his dreams.

It annoyed him. It infuriated him.

He cleared the phlegm from his throat and spat over the ledge on which he stood. He had never been able to understand Conrad. They had worked well together at the mine until the labor racketeers had come down from Mexico City to organize the Indian workers and ruin the venture. All the while Conrad had been an enigma. Even when they had found the gold in the basement of that house, the Welshman had only grunted. True, they had made a good team. Conrad might be silent and dull, but he had known where to get burros and he had known how to load them fast and well. Still, he was about as dreary and annoying as a man could be.

Scofield looked absently over the vast and verdant jungle panorama washed now by the dawn's partial light. "Pain in the ass," he whispered. He took a long and thoughtful drag of his cigarette.

Then, although his flat eyes did not change expression, he smiled. Very deliberately, he turned around.

4

He looked at Conrad, who was still sucking thoughtfully on his pipe. "I know how we'll get it out," he lied. "I know exactly how we'll get it out."

Conrad looked up. A flicker of interest sparked, then disappeared in his blue eyes. "Oh?"

"Of course!" Scofield assured him. "Come here. I want to show you something."

Slowly, very deliberately, Ian Conrad walked to where his partner stood.

Scofield looked up to the older man and smiled disarmingly. "You know, Ian . . ." He took a last sensuously long suck of the cigarette, then flicked it far out over the ledge. "You really are a pain in the ass."

Conrad didn't reply.

Scofield's hard left jab caught him just under the pipe. The right cross that followed broke the Welshman's jaw and sent the Canadian briar spinning out over the ledge.

Ian Conrad dropped like a sack of coffee beans.

Scofield looked down at his unconscious partner. Absently it occurred to him that mere seconds before, he had been a wealthy man, but that now—now—he had the chance to be far more wealthy.

He looked over the mountainous ledge.

It would look like an accident. Stupid gringo slipped and—*adios muchacho, no mas*.

He bent over, slipped his hands under the older man's armpits, and then pulled him almost erect. With a gentle but deliberate pressure, he pushed Ian Conrad over the ledge.

He heard the first damp thud, then another, and one more. He looked down but could only see one grotesquely twisted leg. The foliage and heavy shadows obscured the rest of Conrad's broken form.

The limey would be a pain no more. Even if the fall had not killed him, it would only be a matter of days, perhaps no more than hours, before the insects and other feral things of the jungle would.

Now Bill Scofield alone was rich. Still, he had a problem. Ian Conrad might have been dour, dreary, enigmatic and boring, but he had never been stupid. The gold might very well be worth an emperor's ransom, but here, now, in its present form, it was absolutely worthless.

He simply couldn't leave one country and cross into another carrying millions of dollars or pesos worth of gold artifacts. In his case, such a journey would be particularly difficult, for the country he was leaving was Mexico, where the government had, only months before, reaffirmed its legal right to confiscate any private property for the public welfare, and the country he would be entering was the United States, where the president had seen fit four years earlier to recall all gold from circulation and impose a $10,000 fine on anyone hoarding it.

The gold had to be disguised—melted or ruined somehow—without having its real value changed.

He looked at the animals, twelve burros, and the twenty-four crates, each filled with objects of pure gold. His partner might be out of the way, but Bill Scofield still faced what could very likely prove an insurmountable problem.

"Pain in the ass," he muttered as he walked across the clearing. "Pain in the goddamned ass."

Book I

CHIAPAS

1
Helios

THE COURIER WAS young. He was eager and quite obviously impressed by the importance of his particular mission in the Great Scheme of Things.

Luther Mannas, Colonel, United States Army Intelligence Corps, was no longer impressed by much of anything. After twenty-one years of regular service, many missions and many dead comrades, cynicism had, if not consumed him utterly, at least scorched the perimeters of his soul. At a glance, he noted the perfection of the boy's salute, the frail masculinity of his cornsilk mustache, and the exact cut of his tunic and Lobb boots. The young man standing before him was like thousands of other junior officers in every army of every nation of the world—good family, backbone of society, leadership potential and, in the event of war, easily slaughtered. This one was fresh from school and bound now for dubious glory in the bleakness of west Texas, 1937.

Mannas returned the parade-ground perfection of the courier's salute with a gesture somewhat less exacting. He didn't speak. His eyes alone questioned.

"Dispatch, sir." The young man was obviously excited. "From Washington. I came from the airfield as soon as—"

"Yes, yes." Mannas reached across the desk.

The boy took a step forward, fumbled with the straps of the dispatch case, and finally handed Col. Mannas the envelope. He then fell back to a perfect attention. "The pilot's waiting for your reply." He seemed suddenly embarrassed. "That is, Sir, if there is one."

Luther Mannas again inspected the young man standing rigidly before him. "Lieutenant . . . ." He took a deep breath, then let it out. "Go across the hall and have a cup of coffee, will you."

"Sir?"

"Dismissed, goddamn it. Dismissed. I'll send for you if there's a reply."

With a weary lack of enthusiasm, Luther Mannas slit the envelope open and extracted the single sheet of paper. As soon as he saw the word *Helios*, nineteen years of accumulated cynicism vanished. Soldiering was no longer a dreary, peacetime game. In the opening of a single communiqué, it had again become a very deadly, vital business.

He read the dispatch through twice before calling his first sergeant.

Nathan Banners was that most perfected of creatures, a top soldier of twenty years' service. After the Great War, while his comrades had ached to get home or died of the influenza epidemic of '18, Banners had re-enlisted. Over the years, his individual talents and animal cleverness had carried him to the top enlisted rank.

He stepped easily, but without presumption, into the office and closed the door behind him. "Sir?"

"Banners . . ." Colonel Mannas tapped the dispatch lying on the desk before him. "This is not the usual run of the fuck-up communiqué. There'll be a man coming up from Mexico in a week or so—a German Jew headed east. He's to be met and escorted."

"Sir."

"Trouble is, no one knows what route he'll take. Most likely he'll fly up to Brownsville, but if he's followed, if he thinks he's in any trouble, he could try to come up any way, cross in anywhere—Laredo, even Nogales, if he can make it overland."

"Sir."

"Check through personnel, Banners. I want to know of every officer you can find who's capable of meeting this man. I want Intelligence Corps men with absolutely top clearances. They have to be experts in small arms and self-defense and thoroughly fluent in German. And, Sergeant—this is real. Not a word to anyone."

"Sir."

"Oh, yes, tell Jack Armstrong across the hall that he can go home. No message. I'll handle the rest by phone."

Luther Mannas stared at the single sheet of paper for some moments after Sergeant Banners left. Then, very deliberately, he lifted it from the desk, flicked his cigarette lighter alive, and touched flame to one corner. One-half minute later, the

9

letter personally signed by Secretary of State Cordell Hull was no more than ashes in a government-issued waste bin.

If the slender man was trying to be inconspicuous, he was failing utterly. Still, no one cared. He was just another foreigner in a city that attracted foreigners the year around with its timeless gardens, colonial architecture, and huge continent-famous Indian market, representing over a millennium of man's fiscal intercourse.

The man was not a *tourista* in the strictest sense, although he was quite obviously alien. His sombrero did not entirely hide the blond of his hair laced at the temples by a faint wash of gray and his blue eyes belonged anywhere but among the Mixtec or Zapotec tribes, which made up almost the entire resident population of the provincial town and broad valley beyond.

Charles Candenning adjusted his easel to command a more aesthetic view of the magnificent church, which was now no more than a monument to past ecclesiastical glories. He wanted, if possible, to capture both the extravagant baroque opulence of a bygone era and the spiritual emptiness of his own time. Finally satisfied, he opened the folding stool he had brought from the hotel and placed it near the wrought-iron fence, then inspected his canvas. He had already sketched in the outline of Santo Domingo with charcoal the previous day. Now he sat down and set about mixing colors which would reflect not merely the arid glare of semitropical sunlight but also the very texture of the ancient city. He wanted to create in paint the unique pastel quality of Oaxaca—the faded rainbow illusion of Hernán Cortés's ancient estate.

He was content—at absolute peace with God and men. For the first time in years—specifically since the repeal of the Volstead Act in '33—he was exactly where he wanted to be, doing exactly what he wanted to do. Putting the palette aside for a moment, he opened the bottle of El Minero mescal he had brought with him. He drank deeply before resuming his work.

The taste of freedom was sweet, and here he could savor it absolutely, at least until the end of the month. He had come to Mexico in search of himself and a small slice of the Eternal Truth and he intended to find them both, no matter what.

At forty years of age, Charles Candenning was at once successful by the world's standards and a self-styled failure.

His illustrations had appeared in all the major magazines—the *Post*, *Colliers*, *Liberty*. The depression had never touched him. He owned a large house and had married a beautiful woman, yet he had been miserable with both. After five years of the questionable joys of matrimony, he simply had to get away—to be by himself if only for a short while.

Divorce, of course, was out of the question. There was a certain honor to such matters and Charles Candenning, though not necessarily a rigid man, was a believer in the correctness of things. Despite his career in art, there was still a trace of his early years in Pennsylvania—still a bit of the Old School Tie, the Republican Party, and a number of other abstractions that always seem to cling like diaphanous but imperishable gauze to members of Fine Old Families.

Still, he had needed time to think, to be, to experience a reality of self long buried under the commercialism of his work. The whole thing had been so much easier than he had imagined. Elizabeth had been the soul of cooperation. She actually had seemed to understand for the first time in years.

As a result, he was in the mountainous country of southern Mexico where the valleys opened southward to Zaachila and the Pacific, and southeast to Tehuantepec and then Chiapas. It was a land without clocks—a place of ancient ruins and the slumbering gods of yesteryear. Time had stopped. Elizabeth, the marriage, the house in Connecticut all seemed as unreal as the land of Oz. He didn't care about Fireside Chats or President Roosevelt's battles with the Supreme Court. The war in Spain might have been no more than an ugly rumor. Even here in Mexico President Cárdenas's consolidation of absolute power—his appropriation of property and sweeping programs of reform—mattered not at all.

Neither did the fact that miles to the north, First Sergeant Nathan Banners was, at that very moment, extremely frustrated. He had combed personnel files for regular officers with the qualifications Col. Mannas had mentioned, but he had found no suitable candidates. There were enough airport personnel to be on the lookout for a man flying in from Mexico and also enough qualified officers to watch for him on the ground at Brownsville, Laredo, and even Eagle Pass, but the remaining two railheads would be left unwatched if the job had to be done by career men.

So Banners had abandoned the regular lists.

In Oaxaca, Charles Candenning took another swig from the

11

El Minero bottle and touched his brush to a subtle mixture of yellow and red oxide caressed by a dot of raw sienna. He squinted slightly against the morning glare, then quietly attacked the canvas.

Miles to the north, First Sergeant Nathan Banners scanned a roster of reservists. He stopped at Candenning's name and remembered him kindly as a young lieutenant attached to division staff in France some twenty years before—an officer who had been an exceptional pistol shot and who spoke fluent German.

That spring the tiny fishing settlement was still asleep. Taxis were not yet running tourists over the bumpy road from Salina Cruz, and the beach at Ventosa was still virginal and magnificently isolated.

Karen Tait stopped her bicycle and extended her long legs like shapely bronzed props. She was absolutely alone. There might have been nothing in the world but the infinite expanse of near-purple Pacific to the south and the steaming tropics behind her. Here she could escape the humidity and rid herself, albeit briefly, of gritty perspiration. She could even forget the lingering sounds of Tehuantepec's spring fiesta which, despite the miles, still seemed to hang in the heavy air.

She brushed a damp wisp of strawberry hair from her cheek and slid off the bicycle. It had been almost a year. She had noted and written, sketched and taken hundreds of pictures. Now her study of the Zapotec Indians was finished. All it needed was a final typing.

Far more important, she had forgotten. The pain of betrayal, even the trauma of the divorce itself, was almost gone. So, unfortunately, was her money. She barely had enough left to last through the summer and then pay her way back to New York in the fall.

She laid the bicycle on its side and looked over the deceptively calm waters of the Pacific for a moment before unbuttoning her blouse and lifting her slender legs out of her shorts and underwear. She tossed her perspiration-soaked clothes unceremoniously on her bicycle, then stood erect to enjoy the ocean breeze caressing her naked flesh.

Lean, healthy, and still possessed of that wonderfully intangible freshness which the mystical thirtieth year can never quite erase, Karen Tait would still probably not have attracted

12

the attention of Sandro Botticelli as she stood naked at the water's edge. A tall, well-proportioned woman, she would have been infinitely more attractive in a purely artistic sense if, over the last several months, she had devoted some attention to the evenness of her suntan.

She hadn't. Except for cleanliness and the dictates of personal hygiene, she had given no thought whatsoever to any form of purely feminine vanity. The result was a dark, almost chocolate-colored face dotted with incongruous azure eyes. Her calves and forearms, constantly exposed to the searing heat of the tropical sun, were the color of polished mahogany, but tapering inwardly from them to the torso of her athletic body were many different shades of complexion ending with the stark and shocking white of her hips, the paleness of which made the punctuation of pink pubic triangle quite brutal by contrast.

Almost regally unconcerned, she crossed the strand and stepped into the ocean. She bent to cup water in both hands and splashed its soothing coolness on forearms, stomach, and breasts. Then, she filled her lungs with humid air and made a long, flat dive into the water.

She was still splashing happily over a half hour later, looking more like a long-haired Huckleberry Finn than a onetime sweetheart of Sigma Chi, when she heard her name called.

At first, countered by the much nearer sounds of the moving ocean, the cries of birds overhead, and the fullness caused by a drop of water lodged in her right ear, the sound came only as an auditory illusion.

"Señora Karen! Señora Karen!"

She lifted her head from the water, shook it from side to side, then smoothed her hair back with her palms. Some twenty yards away, just beside the bicycle, stood a young woman dressed in the colorful, almost oriental costume of the Tehuanas. She was waving something white in her right hand.

"Señora Karen!" Her voice had a note of urgency quite out of place on the otherwise serene tropical beach.

Karen blinked, focused, then frowned. The girl was Juana López, one of the five daughters of the Indian family with which she had been staying for the past several months. The girl should have been miles away tending to her chores.

13

Obviously a matter of some urgency had sent her alone this far from her daily routine.

Karen swam a few strokes toward shore until she was able to stand, then waded the rest of the way to the beach. The ocean breeze had increased to the point where her face and torso were almost completely dry by the time she reached the strand.

Juana, graceful and almost radiantly beautiful despite her long journey, was obviously quite upset about the paper she had been waving. She thrust it into Karen's hand.

"It's evil, Señora Karen. I know. It was brought especially to the house—especially to you. Trouble for sure. I ran to find you so you would be warned."

Karen controlled an urge to smile. *Desconfianza!* The entire Zapotec society—the population of the entire isthmus—seemed to be built on a foundation of absolute and total distrust. Even if the letter contained good news, she knew Juana would insist it was only some form of deceptive illusion.

She looked at the envelope. The arms and motto of Vassar College were printed in the upper left-hand corner, her name and mailing address in the center. She slit the envelope open with her thumbnail and pulled the letter out.

"It *is* trouble." Juana was frowning. "Isn't it?"

Karen read the brief message, then shook her head. She refolded and replaced the note in the envelope.

"But I see it—in your face."

The wind from the sea was stinging bits of sand against her calves and thighs. Dry now, she reached for her clothing.

"It's not bad news," she told the girl. "But I am sad. I can't help that." She stepped into her shorts and fastened the side. "They want me to start teaching this summer instead of fall. It means I must leave sooner than I planned."

She slipped her arms into her blouse and started to button it.

"I am ashamed," the girl said. "It is my fault."

"Yours? Don't be silly."

"I brought you the message."

"But you didn't write it."

"We have a saying . . ." There were the beginnings of tears in Juana's eyes. "An old proverb . . . 'it is the best friend who is the worst traitor.' "

Karen turned and laid her palms gently on the girl's shoulders. "You have been a good friend, Juana, and you are not a

14

traitor. I love you—you, your family, everyone here. But I couldn't stay forever. You knew I would have to leave one day."

The girl lowered her head for a moment; then, almost compulsively, she twined her arms around Karen's slender torso. "I know." She was trying desperately to hold back her tears. "You have been good to us and good can never last. Please, Señora Karen, let me go with you. I could help you."

"I can't, Juana. This is your home. Your family—"

"Then to Oaxaca. Please. I have never been to the capital."

"I can't do that, Juana. You know I can't."

The girl relaxed the grip of her arms and moved away. Her face, desperately sad a moment before, now held an expression of absolute resignation. "I know," she said. "There is only so much goodness and much more evil. Here . . ." Abruptly, she unfastened the necklace of gold and gold-washed silver coins she had been wearing. "Take this with you, Señora Karen—for good luck."

Karen stared at the necklace crumpled in the girl's outstretched hand. Some of the coins were undoubtedly quite valuable but, more importantly, they represented the tokens of many admirers, many generations of them.

"I can't take that, Juana. It's from your mother . . . your grandmother . . ."

The girl still held the necklace in her hand.

Embarrassed, Karen turned away. She picked up the bicycle and started to push it toward the sandy road leading to Salina Cruz.

Juana followed, the necklace still in her hand.

"Besides," Karen insisted. "I already have good luck. I've met you, haven't I? And your family, your people? And what could possibly happen on the trip north?"

Jakob Pelzig was afraid. Fear was an emotion with which he was now intimate. It was like the dull, ever-present ache of arthritis—constantly there, inseparable as a shadow—a thing one accepted and lived with for lack of an alternative.

Very deliberately, he struck a match, watched as it leapt to flame, then touched it to the end of his cigar. He puffed it alive, inhaled deeply, then jetted smoke toward the ceiling of the room.

The irony of his situation was too appallingly unreal. He was a doctor of physics—holder of the Copley Medal of the

15

Royal Society and the Franklin Institute's Gold Medal. He had taught and researched at the Kaiser Wilhelm Institute and the Prussian Academy of Sciences. Yet he was a fugitive.

He took another suck of the cigar and shook his head. Once he had been an honored and respected member of the German academic community. Now he was a criminal. He and his wife were both criminals. They had committed the unpardonable crime. They were Jewish.

He glanced at the frail woman still asleep in the room's single bed. To him she was still the beautiful, lithely slender girl from Ulm he had first met almost thirty years before. She was the healthy, raven-haired Hannah Mann, the most wonderful thing that could ever happen to a graduate student at the University of Prague. For him the streaks of gray in her hair, the pallor of her complexion, and her sick, labored breathing did not—could not—exist. He loved her utterly and, because he saw perhaps more, was willing to see less. He only knew that she must be protected, must be taken from here—from this hotel and this city and this country.

Suddenly the mild, scholarly Jakob Pelzig was seized by bitter anger. He turned from the bed and began to pace the room.

A somewhat shorter than average man, Dr. Pelzig had not yet shaved or combed his very thin gray hair. He wore a long bathrobe and leather slippers and held his cigar clamped tightly between his lower teeth and upper plate. He turned to glance out the window and abruptly stopped. Behind their spectacles, his gray eyes took on an expression of resigned sadness mingled with cynical bemusement.

Beyond the window, the storm-beaten palms swayed over the Plaza de la Constitución like drunken soldiers at uncertain attention, but he did not focus on them. Instead, he saw the bird. Like Edgar Allen Poe's raven of yore, it stood on the outer ledge of the hotel's open window. Except for an occasional blink, it did not move.

Pelzig inhaled another lungful of smoke and stared back. A vulture! Vera Cruz was thick with them. They roosted on the bell tower of Our Lady of the Assumption and when it became too crowded, they clawed for more space on the cross itself. They waddled arrogantly down the main streets, ignoring traffic, for they were sacred to the city. They were the official sanitation department, protected both by centuries of tradition and the law itself.

16

To Pelzig the bird was symbolic and insulting as well. He was blinking, thinking—perhaps considering that Jakob and Hannah Pelzig might be his next meal.

He leaned toward the window and blew a jet of cigar smoke in the bird's face.

Arrogant to the last, the vulture blinked once more before soaring from the ledge.

Pelzig lifted his eyes over the palms, followed the bird, and marveled at how one creature could be so repulsively ugly on the ground, yet so gracefully beautiful in flight.

Then, as suddenly as the thought had come, it vanished. He had to think and think carefully. He had to get out of Vera Cruz.

Jakob Pelzig had no real proof that he and his wife had been followed since leaving Germany. It was intuition alone which had whispered to him that hostile eyes had been watching him for months. He had tried to tell himself that he was only suffering some mild form of paranoia, but that did not ease his suspicions. That's why he had taken every possible precaution. That's why he had left Berlin so suddenly and taken such a circuitous route to Lisbon; why he had come to Mexico instead of going directly to the United States; and why, the day before, after they had passed through customs in Vera Cruz, he had suddenly grabbed Hannah and dragged her into the crowd of passengers, greeters, hawkers, and beggars at the pier.

She could hardly breathe after that. As the taxi had carried them through the somber streets, her coughing had made his very soul ache. Still, he had insisted on an involuted rather than a direct route to the hotel and had made absolutely sure no car had followed them.

Perhaps he actually had eluded them, he thought. Then he admonished himself for being overconfident. The Nazis would never give up. He knew that. Someone at the Institute had hinted to them of the magnitude of his work. Whoever had listened, he was sure, had taken the hint seriously. It was only logical. Otherwise, he would have been treated like other Jews. His property would have been confiscated. He would have been "relocated"—or worse. None of that had happened. He had been allowed to continue with his work. That—that alone—had made him suspicious.

Even a fool could understand that Hitler was not playing games by letting his *Luftwaffe* practice in Spain. The man was a maniac who, by some dark charismatic miracle of the obscene, had captured the national psychosis of the entire German people. A barely intelligent child could see that Spain wasn't enough for him. He wanted a real war—a big and totally destructive holocaust. Anyone who had taken the effort to wade through the literary elephantiasis of *Mein Kampf* could see exactly what the man was planning. If that same reader had even a hint of the specific knowledge Dr. Jakob Pelzig possessed, he would also understand why the physicist had fled without obvious provocation.

Jakob Pelzig was one of three men on earth who understood one tiny germ of knowledge sufficiently to be able to cultivate it into that which held the power of the sun itself.

For the moment he was safe, but he could not afford a false sense of confidence in his security. He hated his position. He hated the city itself. There was something heavy and evil in the dank heat of Vera Cruz. The harbor was seething with sharks, the winds that swayed the palms over the Plaza de la Constitución were contained but evil. There was a barely harnessed cruelty in them. Even the cobbled streets and the barred windows with their drawn blinds were forbidding. The vulture on the ledge had become the ultimate symbol.

He puffed again. Thank God for the smoke. The only redeeming quality to the entire city was its tobacco. Vera Cruz, he admitted silently, did have excellent cigars.

Jakob Pelzig set his mind to his task. He sat down at the room's small desk and stared at the map lying there. The simplest route was straight up the east coast of Mexico and over the American border at Brownsville. There were regular flights daily, but air travel was too risky. He was sure all possible flights had been watched ever since he left Berlin. There was no reason to believe they were not still under surveillance. It would have been nice if he could take a train north through Tampico, then Matamoros, and over the border. The only trouble was that despite President Cárdenas's sweeping programs to improve the Mexican transportation system, no railroad ran along the coast.

His first practical choice was to take the scenic route through the mountains and jungles up to Mexico City, then swing north to Laredo or transfer at Monterrey and take the train east to Brownsville.

He shook his head. It would be too obvious. It was the route they would expect him to take. They at least suspected

18

the nature of his work at the Kaiser Wilhelm Institute. It was obvious that if they knew anything about it, anything at all, they also knew his ultimate destination in the United States. He had to camouflage his route. He simply could not risk trying to enter in the east either at Brownsville or Laredo. He would have to travel in directions completely different from those he preferred. His index finger tapped the map, gently tracing, from one junction to another, the route on which he decided: east to Puerto Mexico. South from there over the Isthmus of Tehuantepec to Salina Cruz. He and Hannah would follow the route along the Pacific to Puerto Escondido, then turn north at Oaxaca. Unfortunately, as in ancient Rome, all roads led to the capital. Still, he might confuse them there. Instead of taking a train from Mexico City directly north, he could go all the way west to Nogales.

He looked at the map again. It wouldn't work. There were no tracks going the entire distance. He would have to go overland from Guadalajara to the line coming down from Mazatlan. It would be too exhausting for Hannah. No, he decided. They would go south and around to Mexico City, then plan from there. It was long and roundabout, but it offered the maximum safety. Furthermore, it was the only way he could think of to throw them completely off his trail. The Nazis might be clever and powerful, he thought, but they surely would not consider the planned route as one taken by a man in a hurry to reach Princeton, New Jersey, there to renew both an old friendship and a working partnership with Albert Einstein.

Very slowly and deliberately, Jakob Pelzig folded the map. He crossed the room to where his wife slept, then leaned over and touched her shoulder.

"Hannah," he said very softly. "Hannah, *Liebchen*, we must go now."

She opened her soft brown eyes, filled with both sleep and pain. She focused on him, then nodded. In the simple movement of eyes and head an immensity of love was expressed.

"Escaped! What exactly do you mean, 'escaped'?" *Schutzstaffel Standartenführer* Frederick Hiller rose to his full six and a quarter feet and stood, the incarnation of all Teutonic fury, staring down at *Oberleutnant* Dichter.

Even in the black uniform with the ominous death's head insignia, Ernst Dichter would never look more prepossessing than the myopic clerk which he in fact was. Uniforms and regimes might change men like Hiller from louts to something close to soldiers, but Ernst Dichter would always remain meek, mild, slightly (but never completely) bald, and pedantically efficient, despite his weak eyesight. "I have the cable here, *Standartenführer*. Apparently they both escaped in Vera Cruz."

"Apparently! Apparently! What the devil do you mean, 'apparently'?" Hiller rounded the huge desk and snatched the cablegram from Dichter's hand. He read it, then crumpled it in one huge hand. "Damn him!" It was almost a whisper. "Clever little Jew and his scrawny wife!"

He turned from Dichter and walked to the huge window overlooking the length of the Kurfurstendamm and stood, apparently doing no more than appreciating the architecture of the Emperor Wilhelm Church in the distance to his right.

Dichter blinked as he waited for orders he knew would soon come.

"Ten thousand kilometers, Dichter." Hiller's voice was barely audible. "We've followed that *Scheisskerl* across half a continent and an ocean as well. Now, he's lost. Well, *Oberleutnant* . . ." He turned abruptly and took a step forward so that he towered over the diminutive Dichter. "He's not going to remain lost. I can assure you of *that*! Get me a map of Mexico, Dichter, the most detailed you can find—roads, railroads, every bicycle route and cow path out of Vera Cruz. I'm going to find Mister Doctor Jakob Pelzig if I have to do it personally. He may be a slippery little Jew, but he's not *that* slippery. Believe me, he's never going to get near the United States, let alone New Jersey."

"Of course, *Standartenführer*."

"Well?"

"I merely thought, *Standartenführer*, that it might save a great deal of effort if, when we did relocate Dr. Pelzig—and, of course, I'm sure we shall—. . . After all, a German—rather a Jew and his wife—traveling in Mexico will hardly be inconspicuous. What I'm getting at, *Standartenführer*, is the possibility of, shall I say, losing Dr. Pelzig entirely. After all, he has been quite a nuisance ever since he left."

"*That*, Dichter, is summing the matter up as mildly as possible."

"Well then . . ."

"If *Reichsführer* Himmler ever intended to make my task easy, I would have had both Pelzig and his wife pushed overboard long ago. No. My orders are quite clear, Dichter. He is to be apprehended. He is to be brought back to Germany. Whatever that man knows, whatever he took with him, must be returned."

"Yes, *Standartenführer*."

"Now go, Dichter. Get the maps."

"Yes, *Standartenführer*."

Frederic Hiller turned to the window again.

An observer would have thought the huge man was merely contemplating the shape and form of the Emperor Wilhelm Church. In fact, he was not even aware of the building or of the traffic on the broad avenue below him. He was silently damning both a Jewish doctor of physics, lately of the Kaiser Wilhelm Institute, and his own superiors, who insisted that the man be returned to Germany alive—regardless of the cost in lives or *Reichsmarks*.

2
Politics

LIKE ERNST DICHTER thousands of miles to the northeast, Victoriano Felix, was a clerk. There, however, all similarity between the two men ended. Whereas the German was absolutely subservient to the regime which commanded his life, and altogether lacking in an ability to daydream, the Mexican was a man of entirely different character.

Victoriano Felix was outwardly loyal and obedient. He was as methodical as necessary for the performance of his job, but by far his most conspicuous trait was his ability to imagine huge and succulent pies falling from the sky.

Until the previous February, Victoriano had worked for the National Bank of Mexico in their main offices. Then he had been transferred to this new assignment. He was a trusted clerk, charged with guarding and cataloguing certain valuables which the state had been confiscating since President Cárdenas had issued a fiat the previous November authorizing seizure of private property for the public welfare.

Victoriano's place of work was a barren alcove overlooking a vault, the walls of which were lined with safe deposit boxes of various sizes. He had been entrusted with the key to the vault itself, but the boxes within could be opened only by three men: the president himself; Narciso Bassols, the minister of finance; and Jesús Guerrero, the president's close personal friend and aide.

On this particular morning, while idling at his work, Victoriano happened to look up from his ledger and gaze blankly at the vault ten feet in front of him. From where he sat, he could not be sure, but it seemed to him that one of the boxes was slightly out of line.

Conscientiously, he rose from his seat, unlocked the iron gate, and entered the vault. When he reached the wall, he found that, indeed, the box was slightly open—a fraction just sufficient to prevent the lock from catching.

Curious, Victoriano pulled it open.

The contents were unprepossessing. The box contained four once-white, but now filthy, bags, each approximately the size of a man's fist.

He lifted one bag and again, merely curious, untied the string securing it.

For years Victoriano Felix had been losing on lottery tickets and cockfights, and in innumerable other ways dealing with millions of pesos in the abstract. Now the abstract vanished. The small bag was full of cut diamonds! He could not possibly imagine the worth of the bag as a whole. Certainly any one of the stones could buy far more than his own monthly salary.

Victoriano retied the bag, replaced it in the steel drawer, and closed it again—but only as far as it had been shut before.

He needed time to think.

He left the vault, relocked the gate, and returned to his desk. There he tried to think of his wife and children. He tried to think of his mistress. He even tried, however briefly, to concentrate on the open ledger before him. Nothing worked. All he could think of was exactly how he could steal the diamonds.

The plan that formed in his mind was both grandiose and conservative. It was designed to secure maximum wealth while generating a minimum of suspicion.

The diamonds had been catalogued in his ledger by someone else. Strangely, their value was not stated. Whereas other

22

boxes containing gold or easily evaluated items had been listed in terms of their value in pesos, this particular drawer's notation was merely: *"Diamantes—quatro sacos."*

Obviously whoever originally catalogued the bags had intended to remove at least some of their contents himself. That person therefore was a thief, and to steal from a thief was hardly a crime.

Slowly, as he pondered and sorted alternatives, Victoriano began to see that there *was* a way whereby he could have his cake and eat it too. He decided to steal of the treasure *partially*. He would take only four—no, five or perhaps six—stones only from each bag. No one would notice such a difference.

He went over the plan step by step, thought out exactly how he would proceed, then, just before he closed his ledger, he made one almost insignificant modification. Six, he realized, would not be enough for a man of his stature. After all, the blood of Aztec princes flowed in his veins along with that of noble Castilians.

Yes. He could not escape the necessity. He would have to take at least eight—possibly even ten—stones from each bag.

Col. Luther Mannas looked at the papers which First Sergeant Banners had handed him. He shook his head, then glanced up. "This won't do," he said. "There must be more."

"I'm afraid not, Sir. These are the only regular officers with the qualifications you mentioned."

"Shit!" Mannas pushed his chair back. "Well, Sergeant . . ." He took the last cigarette from the package on his desk, crumpled the green paper and foil, and tossed it into the wastebasket. "We can't meet a man at every airport and railhead up from Mexico with an escort of two officers if we have only three officers to begin with."

He turned from the desk and glanced out the window to the military exactness of Fort Bliss.

"Sir . . ." As ever, Nathan Banners' tone maintained a perfect balance between the obsequious subservience of a man of lesser rank and the inner self-confidence of one indispensible to the running of the machine. "If I may make a suggestion?"

Mannas flicked his cigarette lighter to the tip of his Lucky, inhaled deeply, and spun his swivel chair around. "Christ, yes, Sergeant. At this point, any suggestion's welcome."

Banners walked to the map of Mexico, Texas, Arizona, and California that dominated one wall of the otherwise spartan office. "Initially, Sir, when we discussed this man, you mentioned that he was heading east. It would seem, in that case, that his best entry would be from Matamoros over to Brownsville. That's the regular Pan Am run."

Mannas nodded.

"Of course, there could be a number of secondary considerations, reasons why he might prefer to alter his route or even avoid flying entirely. Foremost, I think, is the logical assumption that he has something or knows something that makes him important. Furthermore, the German authorities undoubtedly know about it, just as we do, otherwise why the necessity for the escort? They probably want him apprehended or done away with entirely, but, it occurs to me that if he has proved smart enough to get out of Germany and get as far as Mexico—undoubtedly Vera Cruz—he's also smart enough to play fox and hounds with any pursuers."

"Stop showing off, Banners. What's your suggestion?"

The sergeant almost smiled. Again his slight facial movement was a perfect mixture of subservience and condescension. "I offer these assumptions, Sir, simply to preface a proposal."

"All right, all right, go on."

"Well, Sir, we have three regular officers, and you want this man met by at least one, preferably two. I suggest we alert the authorities at the airfields and save our men for the ground. Frankly, I don't think he'll fly. Too conspicuous. Too dangerous. If we stay on the ground, we can put our most qualified man at Brownsville. He would, on the basis of those records . . ." He nodded toward the colonel's desk, "be Captain Schilling. He can play tourist in Matamoros, as long as he meets every train arriving there."

"Fine." The cynical expression on Mannas's lips seemed even more pronounced than usual. "That's Brownsville," he said. "What about the rest of the border?"

"We can assign Lieutenant Muller to Laredo. He can meet incoming trains there and maintain periodic telephone contact with the airport and Captain Schilling in Brownsville. Lieutenant Hoppe can do the same thing at Eagle Pass and Piedras Negras. This way we'll have the entire border covered in

24

terms of air entry, and at least the eastern part secured by rail. If this man comes through by plane or train, he can be met by at least one officer who can contact a second, the one nearest him, almost immediately. A double escort can be formed within hours.''

"Commendable, Banners. Fucking commendable. It only lacks two things.''

"Sir?''

"First, it leaves almost a thousand miles of border unwatched, and second, it completely neglects the two railheads at Juárez and Nogales.''

"Not quite, Sir.''

"Oh?''

"Obviously, because of the political situation, we can't send a man into Mexico to meet him—''

"Jesus Christ, Banners! The way things stand between all the American business interests and this Cárdenas fellow we'd be asking for a catastrophe!''

"I know, Sir, but the army doesn't actually have—how shall I say—an option on this man. We could simply notify the border authorities. Let their men keep an eye out for him at their regular highway checkpoints and bridges. If they spot him, they can detain him until we have sufficient time to pull our officers in and form the proper escort. As for El Paso, I believe our only logical choice is to recall a reservist to active duty—temporarily, of course—and place him there. I've taken the liberty of pulling this file, Sir.'' He crossed to the desk and handed the colonel a manila folder. "His name's Candenning. I served with him in the war. He might be a hair past his prime now, but other than that, he's an excellent man for the job—fluent German, crack shot.''

Mannas opened the records jacket, looked casually at the papers, and grunted, "Personal commendation, Purple Heart . . .'' He pursed his lips and let his eyes scan the page.

"As for Nogales, Sir, frankly, it's the least likely place for this man to cross. To get from Vera Cruz overland to Matzatlán is a hell of a trip. If he's important, he's probably also in a hurry. My guess is he'll head for Brownsville, though he *might* vary his route as far west as El Paso. But that's it. Still . . .''

"Yes.'' Mannas inhaled thoughtfully. "Still, we can't afford to let Nogales go unwatched.''

"No. Of course not, Sir. But we could put our least qualified man there, just in case."

"It would appear, Sergeant, that you've already run out of men. We have three regulars and you've pulled a reservist out of a cocked hat. Now, what's your suggestion for Nogales?"

This time Banners actually did smile. His sense of superiority managed to get the better of his military subservience, albeit for only a moment. His eyes flashed like those of a small boy awaiting the effect of a perfectly planned hotfoot. Almost immediately, they became military and somber again. "Well, Sir, when you asked me to dismiss the courier, I took the liberty of talking to the young gentleman. He's not a graduate of the Point but of Virginia Military—"

"What the hell does that—"

"Where he seems to have shown a somewhat amazing aptitude for Teutonic languages, specifically German."

Mannas frowned.

"Incidentally, Sir, he was also captain of the pistol team."

Incongruously, the frown darkening the colonel's eyes was gradually overcome by a smile that slowly began to rise upward across his face.

"I took the liberty of suggesting he go over to the BOQ—that you might have some sort of a reply for him after all."

"Banners, sometimes you are a fucking genius."

"Yes, Sir." There was neither pride nor humility in the statement. It was merely an acknowledgment of fact.

Colonel Mannas rose from his chair and crossed to the map. His eyes scanned the major border-crossing spots from Brownsville in the extreme east to Nogales on the Arizona border. He grunted once, nodded his head, then turned to face his first sergeant. "We could, of course, move our all-American boy east to El Paso and put this fellow Candenning in Nogales. After all, the lieutenant is here and the reservist—"

"I had thought of that, Sir, but the fact is . . . With all due respect, Sir . . . the courier is just a bit wet, if I may say so, behind the—"

"He's fucking dripping, Banners. You know that. Goddamned placenta's still sticking to his ass."

"Yes, Sir."

"No. You're right. We'll put him in Nogales and pray that nothing shows up there. As for this reservist, this Candenning—"

"I can personally vouch for him, Sir."

Mannas walked to the desk. He ground his cigarette out almost brutally, then propped himself by the pressure of his fists on the desk and again glanced to the open records jacket. "Lives in Connecticut—Pomphret. Never heard of it." He turned to Sgt. Banners. "Have orders cut on him right now. There's no time to mail them. I'll telephone direct. He can report here and then pick them up. I'll get a plane for him. Pomphret? Where the fuck is Pomphret?"

"It's about midway between Providence and Hartford."

"Money country, eh?"

"I would think so, Sir."

"All right, you can also cut orders on your other three. As for the boy wonder, just send him back to me."

"Yes, Sir."

Nathan Banners had not quite closed the door when Col. Mannas grabbed the telephone in what appeared to be a strangle grip. It took him almost five full minutes with both the long distance and information operators before the telephone in Charles Candenning's home actually began to ring.

It rang four times.

"Hello . . ."

The female voice carried with it not merely the tone and culture of its owner, but a hint of finishing school, a slight peevishness, and the affectation of a somewhat insecure woman as well. In it Luther Mannas could detect the anxiety of a young woman concerned about her inescapable movement through her middle thirties and a hint of her house as well. He visualized a white clapboard dwelling with rooms furnished in antiques. There was undoubtedly a huge fireplace—stone, not brick. The beautiful rolling countryside of spring-washed Connecticut was perhaps visible through French doors overlooking a terrace, on which a wrought-iron table probably stood.

"Hello—Mrs. Candenning?"

"Yes."

"Colonel Mannas, United States Army. Is your husband in?"

"Charles?" The way she pronounced the word gave Mannas the impression that from time to time she actually did forget her husband's name. "Why, no. Didn't you know? He's in Mexico."

"Mexico!"

"Oh, yes. He went down to some horrid little place there—

27

Ochacka or something like that. Won't be back for—oh, I should say, the better part of a month. Wanted to paint, you know. He was down there as a boy—before the revolution. Says it's simply teeming with ruins and churches, something to do with the Dominicans, I believe. I really could never understand that sort of thing. It's baroque. Yes, I think he did say it was baroque."

"Would that be Oaxaca?"

"Why yes, I do believe that's the place."

"Oaxaca," he repeated. "Of course. The Mitla ruins and Santo Domingo."

"Oh!" Now her voice seemed somewhat distant, almost peevish. "Are you a painter, too?"

"No." With an effort he controlled his fraying temper and urge to slip into profanity. "Just a friend," he said. "I wonder, do you happen to have his address there? I mean his exact address, the hotel . . ."

"Why . . ." There was a long pause. "I don't . . . let me just think for a moment."

"It's quite important," Mannas said.

"I think it was the mount or monty something or other. Really, I'm not quite sure at all."

"How would *you* reach him if you needed him?"

"I?"

"Yes."

"Why—do you know—I've never given that much thought, really."

Luther Mannas glanced to the ceiling of his office and bit his lower lip. With an almost supreme effort of will, he contained his more florid vocabulary. He simply said, "Thank you, Mrs. Candenning," and hung up.

He stood for a moment holding the shaft of the telephone in his left hand, then finally replaced it on his desk and turned again to the map.

"Oaxaca," he said aloud. "Mount monty something or other—"

He reached out and touched the map, allowing his index finger to tap lightly against the star marking the city of Oaxaca. His eyes caught the smaller notation to the southwest of the city: *Ruins of Monte Albán*.

It was a long shot but a definite possibility.

"Banners!"

The sergeant might have been standing just outside the door.

"Yes, Sir."

"Get a telegram off to this Candenning fellow—Monte Albán Hotel in Oaxaca. Send the same wire to American Express if they have an office there. 'Report active duty immediately.' Hell, you can word the damned thing. Just get the son of a bitch up here and on the fucking double!"

"Yes, Sir."

The president of the Republic of Mexico was a man of deceptive appearance. Massive, gray-clad, with a military stiffness to his back, he still appeared somehow ineffectual as he sat behind the desk in his small, somber office. His enormous head was reminiscent of the bas-relief sculpture of the Mayan priests in the temples of Copan and Palenque. The full-lipped mouth and slightly receding chin disappearing into fleshy jowls might have given one the impression of weakness, but as Jesús Guerrero inspected the full mustache and determined hazel eyes, he marveled at the contrast that was Lázaro Cárdenas. The president might look like an oversized sales clerk, but he was possibly the strongest and, to Guerrero, the most dangerous leader Mexico had had throughout the revolution. As always of late, he wondered just exactly how much President Cárdenas actually knew of his, Guerrero's, real loyalties.

"I have heard," Cárdenas said significantly, "of a treasure."

"Oh?"

"Yes. Religious items, Mayan relics, tools, utensils and such. It's a rumor, of course," the president said. "Still, experience has shown that most rumors have at least some basis in fact."

Guerrero nodded.

"Several millions of pesos worth of gold."

"Really?"

"Yes. Dating back to the days when Bartolomé de las Casas was the first bishop of Chiapas and all the Church's wealth was secretly held by the Jesuits."

"Jesuits!" Guerrero almost laughed. "Impossible."

"Nothing, my dear Jesús, is impossible. I know the Church is illegal. I know General Calles crushed the Cristeros a decade ago. But I also know Catholicism is far from dead."

"But millions—"

"Faith, Jesús, can accomplish anything. I have faith in the destiny of my country. Someone down south has had faith enough to hide a treasure."

"But the Church—"

"We cannot change convictions with bullets. I'm tired of closing churches and finding them full. The people must be educated without superstition. Only then can I open the churches and have them remain empty. This treasure will accomplish much."

"If it actually exists."

"I hear many things, my friend. All are true—in part. Now this rumor. Supposedly it concerns all the gold ever owned by the Church in Chiapas."

"Chiapas! But the churches are closed there. Even the bishop's in exile."

"I know. I know. Supposedly all the churches are destroyed in Tabasco, too. But we still have one priest for every ten thousand Mexicans, and the people still believe. If they believe, they can do anything—even amass millions in gold."

Guerrero shook his head. "Impossible. Why, the State's been confiscating Church property for over a century. Mother of God! If anything wasn't taken before, General Calles certainly would have gotten it in '27. And what of your own order of appropriation last November?"

"I don't question rumors, Jesús. I'm a soldier. I prove them. They are either true of false. But, even when they're false, there's always at least some truth. If this treasure does exist—even if it only exists in part—it's vital to Mexico. There is much to be accomplished and little time. I want you personally to go to Chiapas."

"Chiapas!"

"You can start in San Cristóbal. That's where it's supposed to be. But I want every church, secret or not, every monastery, every square centimeter of any property even faintly associated with the Church—inspected. This gold could be absolutely vital, particularly in terms of my plans for transportation."

"Yes. Yes, of course." Jesús Guerrero had walked directly into a trap. Everything he had planned for months was being destroyed by the very man he intended to usurp.

"Good!" the president said. "How soon can you leave?"

The situation was unreal—almost like a dream. How could an intelligent man even entertain the thought of a treasure secretly held by Jesuit priests—and in Chiapas of all places? The Church couldn't possibly have concealed the gold of a tooth filling, let alone a treasure worth millions of pesos. Every Mexican government for over a century had systematically raped the Church of money and power and prestige until there was nothing left. Plutarco Calles had dealt the final blow in 1927! Yet now Cárdenas, a supposedly sensible man, was ordering him to go south, to disrupt all his carefully laid plans, in order to chase a wild and obviously fictional goose.

"Well?" the president demanded. "How soon?"

He had to fight for time. "I do have some unfinished business—" Guerrero stalled. "Perhaps a week—"

"A week! No!" The president was adamant. "Out of the question. If I know about this, they know that I know. Speed is our only ally. The land must be distributed. You know as well as I that the priests and the landlords are allied. Once the peasants have the land and the government schools, they can be freed from the yoke of superstition. But I can't wait for railroads and schools to build themselves."

Jesús Guerrero struggled to think of some way he could make Cárdenas countermand or forget the order for him to go south. Desperately, he grasped at the very straw the president himself had offered—mention of the railroads. If he could somehow get the president more interested in the very real problems of Mexico's woefully inadequate transportation system, he might be able to dispel the absolutely ridiculous notion of a Church-held fortune.

"It has occurred to me, Mr. President," he ventured, "that the Americans—"

"Damn the Americans!" Cárdenas snapped. "Smiling, friendly. They know there's war coming and they won't be able to get out of it for too long. They're trying to gobble all our oil so they can defend themselves with the last drop of Mexican blood. No. I will not even think of dealing with the Americans."

"Then perhaps," Guerrero appeared almost timid, "it might be beneficial to act on the Rodríguez Proposal."

Cárdenas looked up. "Nationalize the debt?"

"Why not?" *Maybe he had an advantage. The president did seem interested.* "Make them all cooperative. Turn them over to the workers themselves."

"Drastic, I should think. But still, a possibility."

31

"It worked when you were a boy, didn't it? Didn't you do something like that with a business?"

"Yes, but that was printing, not railroads. Besides, it was before the revolution."

"Revolution . . . before, after . . ." He could feel victory almost within his grasp. "It's still going on. It's been going on for over twenty years."

Cárdenas looked up. "You don't believe I've finally brought peace?"

"Peace?" Guerrero echoed. "You just finished crushing a strike. Only last year you exiled the very man responsible for your presidency. You have bandits operating all over the country—Tallarin in Morelos and Almidero in Durango."

"Ah, the Scorpion. There's another problem. I personally intend to crush Almidero."

"There'll always be another self-styled counterrevolutionary general. Perhaps I presume on our friendship, Mr. President, but if this is peace, it's tenuous at best."

"Still, Jesús . . ." The president's hazel eyes appeared cloudy and dark behind their jet black lashes. They were very direct and almost hard. ". . . it *is* peace. And still, my friend . . ." His gaze was very even. "Still, I want you to go south. I want this rumor of Church gold explored to the limit."

Guerrero felt as if he'd been hit in the solar plexis with an ax handle. It would be a miracle, he thought, if his expression remained at all calm.

"I would go myself," the president said. "Unfortunately, this Scorpion, Marcos Almidero, is becoming entirely too bold. I must personally go to Durango and destroy him. You know, I trust very few men, Jesús. You're one of the few. I want you to act as my eyes, as my right arm. The treasure may not amount to millions and it may not even exist, but somewhere there's a basis in fact. Find that basis and bring it back to me. Then, with luck, we shall have our railroads. I'll discuss the Rodriguez Proposal when we return."

He had lost. As usual, Lázaro Cárdenas never for an instant lost sight of his goal. Jesús Guerrero turned from the president and walked across the executive office. Although his almost theatrically handsome face remained absolutely expressionless, his thoughts churned in frustrated fury. Silently he damned Lázaro Cárdenas and his socialistic administration. Hero of the people, the workers' champion, idol of the

32

mestizo . . . To Guerrero, the president was no more than a Communist—a mad Bolshevist dedicated to breaking the very backbone of his country. Lázaro Cárdenas was systematically destroying everything that Guerrero and Plutarco Calles had labored so long and secretly to form. Unchecked, he would alienate every nation on earth, particularly those with large sums of investment capital. Mexico might take its place with the world's nations under President General Cárdenas, but what of Jesús Guerrero's rightful place? He'd end his days a peon, starving on the crumbs of an oft-divided estate.

With one request, Cárdenas had destroyed months of secret planning. Guerrero had been plotting to travel north, there to ally himself with the exiled former president, Plutarco Calles, then to return to Mexico to overthrow Cárdenas once and for all. Now he had no choice. He could either go south or expose himself as the traitor which, in fact, he was.

He opened the door.

A man could not travel in two directions at once. It couldn't be done.

He closed the door behind him, turned to walk down the hall, then stopped.

Or could it?

The groundwork had already been laid. It wasn't as if Cárdenas actually had discovered the plot. Perhaps, he thought, the presidential order was not a catastrophe after all, but an unforeseen stimulus. Maybe it should be considered a blessing in disguise—as a cause for accelerating his own plan.

His well-formed features, contained for so long in expressionless placidity, finally relaxed into a broad smile. His pace was brisk as he walked down the long corridor.

Jesús Guerrero suddenly realized that he actually could travel south and, by so doing, arrive north. Furthermore, such a trip would prove a wonderful mask with which to hide his real purposes.

Victoriano Felix spent his afternoon quietly performing his functions while pondering how he would go about changing the diamonds into more easily negotiable pesos. At the end of his working day, he closed his ledger and stepped around his desk to the vault. He took the key from his pocket and was about to insert it in the lock when the pressure of his left hand on the gate eased it slightly open.

33

Victoriano frowned. He was sure he had locked it before leaving for his midday meal.

He pushed the gate slightly forward to allow himself entrance, and stepped into the vault. The drawer was exactly as he had left it—open just enough to prevent the lock from catching. He walked to it and pulled it open all the way.

It was empty!

The diamonds—*his* diamonds—were gone.

Only three people could possibly have betrayed him: the president himself, the minister of finance, or the presidential aide, Jesús Guerrero. One of them—highly placed and highly trusted—had stolen a fortune. If that man was the president, he would, of course, have had a good reason for his action. Still, he could not help but respect and admire Victoriano's loyalty in reporting the loss. If, however, Narciso Bassols or Jesús Guerrero had stolen the stones, President Cárdenas would undoubtedly want to know.

Victoriano decided to go directly to the president. Naturally, General Cárdenas would be so grateful that he would offer Victoriano a very substantial reward—one which undoubtedly would be worth as much or even more than the diamonds he had just lost.

Victoriano rose from his desk. He locked the gate to the vault and turned toward the stairs. It would be easy. After all, hadn't General Cárdenas publicly announced on numerous occasions that he would personally hear the complaints of his people?

They met in Valencia, once the paradise of the Moors, then the country of El Cid. It was a city of ancient citadels and churches which, despite the civil war, was trying to devote itself wholeheartedly to modernization.

Unfortunately, little of the contemporary was evident in the darkened hotel room. The blinds had been drawn against the glare of Mediterranean sun. There was no view of the ocean to the west, no view of the fertile agricultural country to the east.

Julio Móndez had bathed less than a half hour before, then dressed in a loose shirt and linen trousers, yet perspiration had already flattened his clothes to his body and made his hair dank. He felt sticky. The oppressive heat was not only on his flesh, but in his viscera as well.

34

Julio Móndez was, through no fault of his own, in a serious situation.

Despite his recent journey, the major appeared completely unaffected. He was a man whose body chemistry could accept extremes of heat without apparent reaction. He was also that fortunate type of soldier who invariably emerges a hero from his war. He was a staff officer: a man who served close enough to combat to be able to cover himself with a certain patina of glory without, in fact, experiencing any real danger.

He was also intent upon his mission and had no qualms about using a sadistic sense of the melodramatic to build to his ultimate point.

"The new government was formed yesterday." He spoke in a soft voice shaded with a Castillian lisp.

"Oh?" Móndez knew the government was not at issue.

"Yes. Juan Negrín has replaced Caballero."

"With your permission, Major, one government is much like another."

The major unbuttoned the left breast pocket of his immaculate tunic, extracted a silver cigarette case and snapped it open. "I don't think so," he said. "This time all the defense ministries have been unified."

"Oh?" Julio Móndez wished it weren't so unbearably hot. The room should at least have had a fan.

"Yes." The major snapped the case shut and tapped his cigarette several times on it. "Under Indalecio Prieto. He is, you know, a man attentive to details."

"I know."

"He is aware of the order placed last February after the capture of Malaga."

The major's innuendo was unnecessary, if not actually childish. "Should I be surprised?" Móndez said.

"He is aware that the guns have not arrived."

Móndez shrugged. "What shall I do, Major? I have already cabled my man in Mexico. Shall I now summon a magician? Shall I have him conjure weapons from the air itself?"

"I don't think you understand the seriousness of this situation, Señor." The major lit his cigarette, then replaced the silver case, and fastidiously rebuttoned his tunic pocket. "It's not simply a matter of small arms."

"Time then? Is that it?"

"Not quite, Señor. Granted they were ordered months ago,

35

but the real issue is, I believe, that you were, at that time, paid in full.''

"I have always been paid beforehand, Sir. That is my method of business. If you and your general and Señor Prieto don't like—''

"Frankly, if it hadn't been for the defeat of the Italians and the capture of all those supplies at Brihuega, we would have been in a very serious position. The question of your loyalty . . .''

Móndez stood up. He almost took a step toward the major but controlled himself. "My loyalty, Sir, cannot be questioned. This is a matter of geography—of politics—not patriotism. The Portuguese are openly siding with the insurgents. General Franco holds the north—''

"Señor Móndez—a favor. Calm yourself. I am merely suggesting that Señor Prieto and my general are somewhat— how can I put it kindly, Señor?—disappointed. It has even been suggested that it cannot possibly be a question of loyalty. After all, an arms runner is not really expected to have honor. He is merely a smuggler—''

"Smuggling, Sir, has always been an honored profession here in Valencia.''

"That, I'm afraid, is a purely philosophic consideration.'' He took a long pull of his cigarette and exhaled through his nostrils. "The hard facts are that we have paid good money for guns, but have, in truth, received no weapons. Your reputation, if you care to call it that, appears—mind you, I said appears—to be honest and loyal, but your man in Mexico— this Neil Oberon—is quite suspect.''

"Ridiculous!'' Móndez snapped. "It can't be Oberon. It's something to do with the political situation there—Mexico can't be too open in cooperation. After all, Roosevelt is still in control—still insisting on nonintervention.''

"How much . . .'' The major leaned forward. ". . . do you really know of Oberon?''

"He's a good man,'' Móndez insisted. "Why, he's like a son to me.''

"A son, *Señor*?'' The major lifted his eyebrows theatrically. "Am I to consider you an indulgent parent?''

"I resent that, Sir. In fact, Major, I resent you.''

The major waved his cigarette as if to brush away an imaginary insect. "We have done some investigating. We

36

know a bit about your 'son'—your supposedly honest weapons buyer in Mexico and the United States.''

''Oh?''

''Yes. First of all, he enjoys large sums of money.''

''A human weakness, is it not?''

The major shrugged. ''You knew his father was destroyed by the American financial disaster of 1929?''

''So were many men. The Americans are childish. They don't understand money.''

''Your man, Oberon, knew enough about it to get into the liquor business.''

''And you fault him for that?'' For the first time Móndez smiled. ''Prohibition is the law of an idiot. Neil is an intelligent young man. He has expensive tastes. Why not enter a profitable business?''

''The issue is not that he is intelligent, *Señor*. The issue is that he acted against the law. The issue, *Señor*, is also that he has apparently lied to you. He is a man on the run. He cannot enter the United States.''

''What?''

''Senator Dossier's daughter *is* dead. Neil Oberon was not only escorting her, but was at the party where that unfortunate incident occurred.''

''There's never been any proof,'' Móndez snapped. ''Never!''

''There doesn't *have* to be proof.'' The major took a last pull of his cigarette and slowly ground it to extinction. ''Senator Dossier is an extremely important man. He's quite friendly, so I'm told, not merely with President Roosevelt, but with this man Hoover as well.''

''Hoover?''

''J. Edgar Hoover. He's head of an organization called the Federal Bureau of Investigation. Neil Oberon is on Hoover's list of wanted men. He cannot risk returning to the United States.''

''That's absurd!''

''Of course, he may not in fact be a criminal, but what difference does it make? The point is that he is not—as he led you to believe—in Mexico through choice. He's hiding there.''

''No.'' Móndez shook his head. ''He would not have lied to me. Besides, he's always managed to get the weapons we wanted.''

''Until now!''

"I tell you, Major, it is not Oberon. It is something else, something unforeseen."

"Señor Móndez, you and I both know that Mexico is barely alive after almost thirty years of civil war. Lázaro Cárdenas may be a dedicated president, but one man, regardless of his energy and patriotism, cannot make Mexico an industrial giant—certainly not overnight. The Mexicans may sympathize with us, but they just don't have the money. The weapons we want *must* come from the United States and Neil Oberon cannot risk going there to get them."

"No. I trust him. You cannot weaken my trust."

"It is rumored, Señor Móndez, that he has recently lost heavily at gambling—so heavily, in fact, that he no longer has the money which we gave you and which you sent on to him."

"I cannot believe—"

"Believe!" The major's low, condescending tone was now quite military. He was obviously tired of his own game. "We have documented the fact. It is quite clear. Oberon is a traitor."

"No."

"Then the traitor must be you." The major's smile lacked any trace of humor.

"You know that's not true."

"Then Oberon is our man, isn't he? He's a traitor and must pay for his betrayal. He must be destroyed."

Julio Móndez looked at the major. He could not believe what he had just heard, yet the other man's eyes were absolutely level and totally lacking in emotion. "You don't suggest that I—"

"He *is* your employee, isn't he?"

"I've told you," Móndez said. "He's like a son to me."

"We are at war, *Señor*. You selected your business. You were aware of the risks and the demands. You knew the devotion your people would have to show. It's ruthless, true, but life itself is—I'm afraid—ruthless. The man may, as you say, be like a son to you, but he has betrayed you. He has not only betrayed you, he has betrayed the loyal forces of Spain and, most of all, he has betrayed Spain herself."

"I can't," Móndez said.

"Very well." The major rose from the overstuffed chair in which he had been sitting. Meticulously, he smoothed the skirts of his tunic. "If you can't deal with him directly, we

38

will. We have, as you know, other men in Mexico—men who *will* follow orders.''

"Mother of God," Julio Móndez sighed. "Do you know what you ask?"

"Of course." The major's voice was again quite calm. "I ask your loyalty. It has been questioned. Look at this as an opportunity to prove yourself."

"But, in the name of God—"

"I believe it was another American—can't remember who precisely—who suggested that war is hell." He walked to the door and opened it.

Outside, the hall was somewhat brighter and, if anything, even hotter.

The major stepped into the narrow corridor, then turned, and almost smiled as he held out his hand. "Until we meet again."

Julio Móndez took the hand automatically. "Go with God," he said, but it was just an expression. He didn't mean it. It felt empty on his lips and very heavy in his soul.

3
Alchemy

WILLIAM SCOFIELD RAN thick and filthy fingers through his matted brown hair, then rubbed the back of his hand over the grimy stubble of his beard. He sighed as he looked across the oppressive single room of the makeshift shed he had built in the foothills of Chiapas' central highlands.

The humidity and the stench were almost overpowering, but Scofield was barely aware of either.

As he smiled in absolute contentment, his face, except for the flat eyes, took on an expression of almost childlike bemusement. He shook a cigarette from a crumpled pack and lit it. The shed, the jungle beyond—Scofield's diminutive stature and youthful appearance—all these created the illusion of a young boy sneaking his first smoke in some isolated utility shed.

Bill Scofield let the inhaled smoke settle in his lungs. This part of his work was done. For the first time in over four months, he could afford the luxury of relaxation and, with it, a touch of nostalgic reverie.

Lady Luck, he was sure, had promised to be his steady girl. Certainly, she had been right beside him just after last Christmas. If she hadn't pointed the way, he would have done no more than wander idly by the arcaded palaces and red-tiled buildings of San Cristóbal or perhaps inspect the wares of the Tzotzil or Chamulan Indians who came to town to market them.

But that day she had pushed him. Otherwise, why would he have climbed the steps of that house, let alone opened the door?

"Goddamned right," he said aloud. "Pure, undiluted luck."

Scofield had peeked into the house just in time to see a man genuflect, then remove two candlesticks from a table, which had obviously been used as an altar. The movement had not been made in a surreptitious or guilty way, yet Scofield had experienced a purely visceral feeling. The simple act, he had been sure, had far-reaching ramifications. The house, he realized, was one of scores, perhaps even hundreds, of secret places of worship that had been established after the slaughter of almost the entire priesthood and the Church Herself ten years before. It represented man's refusal to surrender his conscience. The mass house, tiny and humble, was proof of a sustained belief in the Supreme Being.

Scofield had stood on the steps, had watched the man genuflect a second time before carrying the candlesticks into another part of the house—and somehow he had just known. It had been pure luck, nothing else.

It had taken a while to convince Conrad, but he had finally managed. They had watched the house, noted the timing of the visits by little groups of men and women, then, by joining one group, had posed as worshipers. Once inside the house, they had concealed themselves and waited for the faithful to leave. In the darkness, they had explored the building and found the door leading to the basement. There, Lady Luck had almost literally pointed the way. It had taken less than a half hour of snooping and probing to find the alcove with the false wall and, behind it, the gold itself.

It was a treasure beyond the furthest bounds of the imagination. It was also a miracle. Somehow the Church not only had succeeded in keeping itself alive but, throughout government after government and administration after administration, had denied Caesar his due.

Scofield finished his cigarette, dropped it on the dirt floor and ground it flat under his boot. "Pain in the ass," he said aloud, but he was still smiling.

It had taken him over four months, but now he was finished. He had everything he had ever wanted and was about to get out of Mexico as fast and easy as sand through a rat hole.

After brutally dissolving his partnership with Ian Conrad, Scofield had spent some days pondering his problem. Finally, he had hidden the gold in the mountains while he made several trips to different towns in the valleys of Chiapas. He had collected vats and batteries and quantities of copper and nickel. He had build an isolated shed to hide his activities and had collected many wooden packing crates which he had just finished stenciling appropriately.

When all was in readiness, he had spent long weeks electroplating every object which made up the treasure. Each one had been plated with copper and then a second time with nickel. Now he had just finished anodizing the last chalice in a cheap, yellow-colored "gold" which, for the most part, was made of magnesium.

The millions of dollars worth of utensils, art objects, and *sacramenti* looked like little more than hundreds of cheap reproductions of Mayan artifacts and Spanish religious trinkets—the kinds of things tourists bought for a peso or two from street vendors.

William Scofield was pleased with himself. Kid Scofield had come a long way from the icy poverty of Minnesota. He might still be illegitimate but, by God, he was really a rich bastard now.

Even if someone did suspect—some Mexican official or American customs inspector—he would never be caught. If the outer plate happened to be scratched, only nickel would show. A deeper scratch would only reveal the cheapness of copper. No one but an expert with an exact sense of weight and access to nitric acid and/or a sharp file could possibly guess that Bill Scofield had successfully camouflaged gold that was worth millions.

Now there remained only one thing left to do. He had to pack the treasure on his burros, then journey downhill to the nearest river. There he would shave, wash weeks of slime

41

from his sticky flesh, then journey southwest to Tuxtla Gutiérrez to buy clothing befitting his new profession. Finally, he planned to travel over the Isthmus of Tehuantepec to Oaxaca, and there board the first train headed north.

Very carefully, William Scofield began to pack his fortune into the stenciled wooden crates. He had ceased entirely to be a mining engineer. He was now a soon-to-be-retired businessman. He represented W. S. SCOFIELD CO.—IMPORTS & EXPORTS, a dealer in cheap art reproductions—a man headed for a life of warmth and ease.

The provincial looked exactly as one would imagine an officer of the Society to look. He was tall, very lean and quite fit. His hands were those of a man who had labored hard and who appreciated the soil. They were hands that in youth had even killed.

His shoulders were wide, his jaw clean shaven and his entire bearing quite military, if not actually militant. Yet, it was his eyes alone that gripped the attention of his listener.

As Domingo Portes looked into the eyes of his superior, he realized without surprise that they did not register the compassion of a purely spiritual man. They were eyes worthy of an El Greco—eyes that had seen at firsthand the horrors of life— that had witnessed almost thirty years of revolution and civil war and, with them, the rape and maiming of a beloved motherland and an even more beloved mother, the Church itself.

Father Portes decided that the provincial's eyes were perhaps the very color of the nails used to affix his Savior to the cross. They were the eyes of a soldier leading a never-ending frontal attack against the hordes of Satan. They belonged to a man of absolutely unflagging determination, of unrelenting devotion to the *Compañía de Jesús*, the Ignatian doctrine, and the Church—but most importantly, to one who would never— who could never—forgive.

"I have summoned you," the provincial said very deliberately, "to entrust you with the future of the Church and the Society here in Chiapas. Perhaps in all of Mexico as well."

Father Portes frowned. It was not like the provincial to be melodramatic.

"Some months ago," the older man continued, "two men entered a house here in San Cristóbal. Unfortunately, they found what I and my predecessors had succeeded in hiding

42

for over a century." The frown deepened. "I'll tell you the details later," the provincial went on. "What matters now is that you understand the complexity of the situation. We are at war. That's no secret. We'll always be at war until the secular regime recognizes the true authority of the Church."

Portes watched the older man turn. He appeared to be struggling against a massive urge to do physical violence or perhaps even a scream. The impression lasted but a moment. The provincial regained self-mastery and turned back as abruptly as he had turned away. His iron black eyes bore into Domingo Portes.

"We had succeeded in hiding a substantial treasure," he said. "Originally, of course, it was quite legal, quite permissible, in terms of the temporal authorities. Bartolomé de las Cassas began collecting it from the Indians here. He always paid the king's fifth and used the gold for the betterment of the Indians and the glory of the Church. It began as a fund for education and for the needy. Subsequent bishops added to it until, due to the troubled situation surrounding Maximilian, the responsibility of guardianship fell to the Society."

"It's hard to believe."

"I know," the provincial almost allowed himself the luxury of a smile. "That we could hide millions of pesos worth of gold objects from the thieves and murderers who have ravished Mexico for so long. The point is, however, that we did it. We were able to thwart the pawns of Satan—Diaz and that antichrist Calles!"

"But how?"

The provincial's eyes were no longer just hard. They actually seemed to reflect some unearthly fire. "Do not trouble yourself with the whys and hows of the Society's right to guardianship or even the stratagems we used to keep this treasure secret. Suffice it to say that we approached this task as the nuns in the Convent of Santa Monica in Puebla. Just as they remained hidden from the government for two hundred years, we were able to conceal the gold. We succeeded in this as in every other task appointed us—through discipline, unaltering devotion, and unflagging determination."

"Yes, Father."

"The gold was in a mass house here in San Cristóbal. It was, I thought, well concealed in an alcove behind a false wall. I was wrong. It's gone. It has been gone since January and, quite obviously, with government policy being what it is, my inquiries as to the thieves and their whereabouts have had to be extremely guarded and discreet. As you well know, the priesthood today is not known for the longevity of its members. Fortunately, however, there are still a few loyal Christians left in Mexico.''

Domingo Portes watched silently as the provincial paced the length of the spartan room, then turned, and walked back. The older man seemed to be collecting his thoughts for the clearest, most succinct presentation possible.

"The day of the robbery," he began, "two men—English or American—bought burros. Burros are scarce here in Chiapas. You know that. Labor here is for oxen. Men who buy burros are not planters, not lumbermen.''

Portes nodded.

"Later, one man—a foreigner—was seen leading a train of burros into the central highlands. That was some months ago. From what I can judge of the timing of that report, he was spotted just about a week after the robbery. Now, today, I received other news. I have heard that this same man was seen—again leading loaded burros—in the Grijalva Valley.''

"Can we be sure?"

"Have *faith*, Father Portes! I have very strong reason to believe that two men stole the treasure. I am convinced that the man in the Grijalva Valley is one of them. A foreigner, leading burros, hiding for no apparent reason in the mountains— all these things clearly indicate that he is one of the men.''

"I am not being frivolous," Portes ventured, "but if indeed this man does have the gold, there seems little we can do." His tone became quite sarcastic. "Certainly, we can't notify the civil authorities.''

"Of course," the provincial snapped. "He's already nationalized everything else. Cárdenas wouldn't blink an eye before grabbing this, and killing us both in the bargain. They'll all pay in hell, but that doesn't help now. Now there is only one point to remember. That gold, that treasure, must not be stolen by the state! I don't care what kind of insane laws are passed. They are temporal laws! The Church is the instrument of God, not of General Lázaro Cárdenas. It cannot be broken or intimidated by worldly politicians. That gold belongs to the Church alone. It *must* be brought back to where it belongs.''

"Surely, Father, if the man is in fact one of the thieves, I hardly think he will surrender.''

44

The provincial ignored Portes's suggestion. He was like an officer of the line, singlemindedly planning his assault. "My report today indicates that he is traveling west. There is strong reason to believe he is heading for Tuxtla Gutiérrez, possibly to rendezvous with his partner. There is absolutely no doubt in my mind that the two men will try to flee the country. That, as you know, can be a boon. They will be as careful to avoid representatives of the state as we must be."

Again he looked directly at Portes. The fire in his eyes cooled slightly, but did not subside entirely. "You will apprehend the thieves," he said. "You will reclaim the treasure."

"You flatter me, Father."

"Humility is an admirable trait, Father Portes. Now, however, is not the time for its display. You are here because I specifically requested you. I am not a fool, Portes. I would not reach into a hat, grab for any man, then entrust him to regain millions of pesos worth of gold."

"No, Father."

"You have been a member of the Society for six years. Before that you fought with the *Cristeros*. You have been wounded twice. You have killed in the name of Christ. You're intelligent, Portes. You're resourceful and—yes, heroic. In short, Father Portes, you embody exactly what Saint Ignatius envisioned for all of us. Your Superior tells me you are an exceptional man—completely obedient yet quite capable of acting independently when circumstances demand."

Domingo Portes did not speak. All of what his provincial had said was true. What the older man could not know was what Portes himself barely knew. Inwardly some of his early religious fire and singleminded dedication to the principles of service laid down by Inigo de Loyola had, if not turned to ashes, at least lost a few degrees of heat. Portes's very intelligence and resourcefulness had, over the last several months, been nudging him subtly away from totally spiritual considerations. More and more, he had found himself questioning his behavior, seeking more purely temporal answers to his questions.

"You have fought for the independence of the Church in worldly battle. You have sworn vows to our Lord and Savior and have proven yourself worthy of the Society. Now you are to regain the property of the Church."

"But, Father—with all due respect—I do not see how one man, no matter how high your kind opinion of him . . ."

"We are very few, Portes. We are hunted, forced to hide. Frankly, I have only one man—you. And, may I remind you . . ." The provincial's voice was very low. His eyes were once again those of a man absolutely and irrevocably committed to the annihilation of evil, no matter what the cost. "You are a soldier of the Cross. I am your provincial. I order you to regain that gold and I authorize you, in the name of God and the Virgin Mother, to use *any* measures necessary to accomplish that end."

"Father . . ."

"It is God's gold!" The provincial's voice expressed absolute finality.

"Yes, Father." Domingo Portes knelt before his provincial.

The older man made the sign of the cross above him, then laid his hand on Portes's head in blessing.

The illusion was momentary but very powerful. To Domingo Portes, the provincial's hand was cold—cold as honed and tempered steel. He rose and, without further word, left the simply furnished room and walked into the oppressive heat of San Cristóbal.

A few yards in front of him, he noticed the open door of a church. How, he wondered, could one man, armed only with faith and determination, overcome two ruthless thieves and reclaim a fortune?

He stared at the church. It would be nice, he thought, if he could go there, kneel within, and offer his problem to the Almighty for solution or, at very least, guidance. However, the building was no longer a church. On the steps, under the El Minero sign, several soldiers were lounging. They were smoking and making suggestive remarks to passing women. From within, Portes could hear the sound of a guitar and behind it, the faint occasional click of billiard balls.

He shook his head almost sadly, then walked away from the ancient building.

The blond man with the scarred and concave right cheek under the dead gray of a once-blue eye slid from the mule very slowly. Silently, he tied the animal to a tree, then removed his pistol from its holster. He cocked the weapon and looked across the small clearing.

There was no sign of movement, no hint of other life.

Painfully, he dragged his deformed leg as he moved toward the flimsy shed. His ears were alert for any threatening

46

sound. His good eye moved this way and that, anticipating any hostile movement.

He reached the door and stopped. He took a deep breath, then pushed the door in.

It fell with a sickening, flat sound to the damp floor.

Pistol at the ready, Ian Conrad limped into the ovenlike confinement of the shed. His good eye scanned the room, carefully noting the tanks and batteries and other evidence of his onetime partner's work.

Something feral scampered across the room and dug its way out under the far wall. The cabin now belonged to the jungle. It was obvious that Scofield had abandoned it.

Conrad holstered his pistol and sat on a five-gallon container that had been used to haul much-needed water from the lowlands.

Scofield was gone. Still, he could not have gone far. This project, Conrad knew, had taken some time. While he had lain broken and unconscious, then been treated by the Lacandone Indians who had found him halfway through death's door, his onetime partner had been obliged to do a lot of scurrying around. In order not to be caught, he had probably gathered his equipment from various sources. While he was collecting it—while Conrad was being nursed back to some semblance of health by primitive medicine and mind-warping drugs—months had passed. During this time Scofield had been up here disguising their treasure. To look like what?

He glanced around the room. Scofield had spent the time during Conrad's convalescence altering the appearance of the treasure somehow so that he could get it out of the country.

With pain and difficulty, Conrad rose and limped outside. The heat was dank and oppressive. It made the badly set bones of his crippled leg ache the more. The ground beneath his feet was soft—easily impressionable. His good foot sank slightly with each step. The other dragged dead foliage with it as he pulled it through each agonized pace.

About four yards from the shed he noticed tracks. They had clearly been left both by burros and by very small human feet. If he didn't know better, he would have thought the boot prints belonged to a young boy.

Near the hoof and boot prints were the unmistakable marks of things that had been dragged. Some boxes or crates must have been so heavy it had proved easier to drag than to carry them. The important thing about the marks on the jungle floor was their freshness. Conrad was sure they could not be more than a few days old.

He followed the pattern of the tracks from the cabin for several yards before satisfying himself absolutely that they led in a clear and easily followed path downhill. Then, dragging his crippled leg in a grotesque limp, he returned to his mule. With slow and painful exactitude, he untied the animal and remounted. He neck-reined and started downhill, following the burro tracks. They led, he was sure, to the Grijalva Valley, probably to Tuxtla Gutiérrez.

Ian Conrad glanced up through the heavy jungle foliage to an overcast sky. It looked like rain, but rain or not, he intended to accomplish what he had set out to do. No one—nothing—could stop him.

William Scofield would die. He'd die even if every one else in Mexico—in the entire world—had to die with him.

Book II

OAXACA

1
Diamonds

JESÚS GUERRERO HELD the telephone as if, in some obscenely perverted way, it was a love object. His voice, already low, was further muffled by the cupped palm of his right hand. Still, its tone of urgency was quite evident.

"Never mind that," he insisted. "It's all changed. You can't risk being seen at the airport. You'll have to mingle with the peasants, take the bus south."

As he reached for the cigarette smoldering in the ashtray before him, his near-beautiful features appeared strained to the point of annoyance. He nodded impatiently, sucked a deep breath of tobacco fumes then snuffed the cigarette amid the broken corpses of several others.

"Vida mia," he whispered, "how can I predict? He's planning to launch a campaign against General Almidero in Durango. There's no telling what he'll do when he gets back—with the railroads, the oil companies, or anything else. You just be there." He kissed the mouthpiece. "We'll meet in Oaxaca." He kissed it one more time. "Until soon." He shook his head and recradled the telephone.

What a pity. He reached absently for another cigarette. He loved her. That was the whole trouble. He loved them all.

He lit the cigarette, leaned back in the chair, then blew a long jet of smoke toward the beamed ceiling. He had made his final telephone call. His plans and his route to Texas had been adjusted to make it appear that he was carrying out the president's order. Now there was nothing left but a war against time. It was a total, ultimate risk. Still, he was confident. His wife and children would be ready to leave within the hour. If time proved cooperative, he could rendezvous with General Calles in a matter of days.

He opened the top drawer of the desk, removed what appeared to be no more than a tangled mass of straps, and laid it before him. Squinting in order to see through the cigarette's smoke, he studied his creation one last time.

It was a device meant to buckle around a woman's waist like a garter belt. This particular garment, however, was far less alluring but infinitely more practical. It was made of unstained leather and had four vertical straps, two on each side. Each contained a pouch the flap of which could be secured to prevent loss of its contents. These pouches had been positioned so that, when the wearer stood erect, one would hang on the inside of each thigh and the other set against the back of each leg, sufficiently below the curve of the buttocks to allow for moderate comfort. Two other belts, these horizontally, were stitched to the bottoms of the pouches to hold them securely to the wearer's legs.

Looking at his invention, Jesús Guerrero imagined it being worn first by his wife, then by his mistress. Then, following an ever-widening path of sexual fantasy, he visualized the slender, naked hips of a pale-skinned blonde—a European tourist or one of the thousands of long-limbed beauties who inhabited the state of Texas.

As so often happened, his fantasies got the better of him. Sitting in the sparsely furnished room and looking at the belt, which was in no way alluring, Jesús Roberto Martinas Diego O'Neil Guerrero was suddenly overwhelmed by sexual desire. Almost viciously, he rose, picked up the belt and left.

His heels clicked with authority on the tiled floor of the long corridor leading to the rear of the villa. The walls of the huge house, now stripped of the more valuable oils and sconces, picked up his demanding rhythm as he walked to the master bedroom.

He stopped at the heavy door and knocked punctiliously, but without waiting for a reply, slipped the belt behind his back and walked in.

The room was large and airy. Although modern in terms of convenience, it had been designed to create an illusion of having been occupied by *conquistadores* and their well-born, imported ladies. If nothing else, it was a chamber to be used by the very rich or the highly-placed. Still, like the small office Guerrero had just left and the corridor leading from it, the room was singularly lacking in decorative items. The only pieces of furniture were a large bed and an armoire. There were no rugs, paintings, or other accoutrements of any sort.

Leaving the door open behind him, he took a step into the

51

room. There were two women standing beside the bed. They looked up but did not speak.

He too was silent as he waved dismissal to the older one, a servant who had been packing a suitcase lying open on the bed.

The Indian woman glanced briefly at her mistress, curtsied almost imperceptibly, then slipped silently behind Señor Guerrero. As she left the room, she closed the door behind her.

Jesús Guerrero stood looking into his wife's huge eyes for some moments before he crossed the room and bent to kiss her forehead in what appeared to be an almost dispassionate manner.

"Elodia, *vida mia*," he said. "I have brought you a present."

Her slender brows knitted, momentarily etching two shallow lines on either side of the top of her nose.

"Ah yes, *Amada*, but you must do me the honor of removing your clothing first."

"My clothing? But, it is the middle of the day."

"Time, *Querida*—what is time?" He lowered his face to hers, gently lifting her chin with a gentle upward pressure of his right hand. His lips covered her mouth with a very tender, yet undeniably insistent pressure.

For what seemed a sliver of eternity, he moved his mouth over hers, savoring the ever-new joy of physical contact with a female as the pressure of his torso on hers forced her closer to the bed.

Finally he removed his mouth and with casual presumption began to unbutton her chemise.

"Please, Jesús . . ." Her tone lacked any real commitment. "The servants . . ."

His fingers continued their downward journey. "What of them, *Amada*? They know nothing of love."

Obediently, she allowed him to unbutton the last button of her chemise and to loosen her skirt sufficiently so that it fell in a puddle of fabric at her feet. Then, she sighed with what appeared to be helpless resignation.

Elodia Guerrero was used to her husband. Her protestations were token sounds uttered to satisfy the demands of a God supposedly critical of carnal sensuality. She pulled her slip over her head and removed the rest of her underclothing. She stood before her husband completely naked, save for her high-heeled shoes and silk stockings, held in place by ruffled garters.

He sat down on the bed and let his eyes nibble at the beauty of his wife's slender form. Unlike so many other women, she had not allowed her two pregnancies to scar her abdominal flesh or warp and puff her youthful figure. There was a pride in Elodia Guerrero which traced its way back to the time of Rodrigo Diaz de Bivar and to the nobility of his bygone age. At thirty-one, she was a strikingly beautiful woman possessed of a richly healthy complexion and a sensual yet noble elegance of face and form which was particularly captivating as she stood almost totally naked a mere foot or two before him.

Her hair, coiffed in the latest European fashion, was cut short and waved tightly to her head. Her breasts, although smaller than average, were remarkably firm and high despite having nursed two children. Their long ruby nipples appeared to be pointing to something over his head and behind him.

Jesús savored his wife's beauty, slowly lowering his eyes to her smooth abdomen punctuated by a teardrop of navel, then down to the soft ebon triangle below.

"Don't, Jesús." She sounded almost plaintive. "You embarrass me."

"Still?" His voice had an absent, far-away quality. His eyes relished every detail of her mons while his mind imagined parts unseen. The reality of her beauty mingled in his mind with his fantasies like the ingredients of a succulent feast soon to be savored. He could not help smiling in anticipation.

"Please, Jesús . . ."

"Very well." He drew his left hand from behind his back and let her see the belt.

Although she had allowed herself to be measured and fitted on two previous occasions, her eyes widened in an expression close to alarm when she saw the finished product. Her lips parted, then pursed. Her alarm changed abruptly to disgust.

"It's ugly," she said.

"It may be ugly, my darling, but it is still our passport to a far more rewarding future."

"Won't it be uncomfortable?"

"Elodia . . ." He drew a deep breath. "What is a minor discomfort? I have slaved and lied and played the pawn to that goat Cárdenas until I have no choice left. It's little enough to ask for the sake of the future. Once we're in the United States—once General Calles is ready to return again—I

53

shall be the second most powerful man in Mexico. Then—in time—the president himself.''

She did not answer, although her expression of repugnance softened slightly as he bent foward, looped the belt behind her, and very slowly buckled it in place around her slender waist. He then secured each of the smaller belts around her thighs and leaned back to consider the fit.

The spectacle was exactly as he had imagined it. He inspected the belt, let his eyes move from the pouches and straps to her red garters, the tops of her rolled silk stockings, then back to her mons. Slowly, very deliberately, he slipped his hands under the rear straps then over her buttocks. He drew her body toward him.

"Oh, don't," she whispered. "Jesús . . . a favor . . . It's not . . .''

"Not what, my darling?'' His eyes remained fixed on her triangle of raven hair.

"It's . . . It's not right.''

He leaned back slightly and chuckled. "You say that for God to hear, *Amada*. Well, *vida mia*, let your lips be with God. Mine seek a sweeter heaven.''

As he pulled her toward him, he did not see her clenched teeth or the hard outline of her jaw muscles clamped against her revulsion. Indeed, if he had, it would have made no difference. Jesús Guerrero could not possibly imagine that his wife no longer loved him. Such a notion was not only unthinkable—it was absolutely impossible.

That afternoon in the Palacio Nacional had been a preview of hell. It had culminated shortly before three o'clock in an office on the comparatively new third floor of the huge building, which was occupied by one Señor Miguárdez. The guard had introduced Victoriano, then taken a step backward as though trying to disappear.

Juan Miguárdez was not only a short man but one who had been denied the descent of one testicle. Constantly aware of his diminutive stature, as well as the bad joke Fate had made of his masculinity, he had, throughout his life, sought to compensate for his physical deficiencies by the exercise of power over others. Aide and secretary to President Cárdenas, he had become master of that peculiar brand of psychological sadism so common to civil servants everywhere.

He listened attentively as Victoriano told his story. When

54

the clerk finished, Miguárdez fixed him with a penetrating, very cold stare. "A matter, you say, of great national importance?"

"Yes, Señor."

"One which must be shared only with General Cárdenas?"

Felix bowed slightly, his eyes downcast. "I mean no disrespect, Señor. You see" he lowered his voice to a conspiratorial tone, "it is of a highly confidential nature, highly personal."

"Ah." Señor Miguárdez tilted his head back, then pursed his full lips very deliberately. Finally he nodded several times. "You know, of course—" His thick mustache appeared about to fall from his lips. "—that General Cárdenas is a very busy man."

"Of course, but he has said on many occasions that he will listen personally . . ."

"That's true, that's true," Miguárdez said. "It's only that at the moment he is planning a very important strategy."

"But what I have to say is also quite important."

When Miguárdez smiled, he looked as though he was about to snap his tongue out to catch a fly. "He has given me the personal responsibility to determine just exactly what is important enough to be heard and what he must be spared."

"I assure you, Señor . . ."

"Let me be candid with you, Señor Felix. You may have come here to talk to the president, but it is I who shall determine if, in fact, you do so. Now, tell me, what precisely is this urgent matter?"

"I mean no disrespect."

"Of course not."

"I assure you I am only acting as a loyal citizen."

"Señor, I too intend no disrespect, but how can I be sure? Can you assure me that you are not, in fact, a maniac—a criminal—a would-be assassin?"

"I'm only trying . . ."

"You are trying, Señor, to circumvent authority. You are, in fact, breaking the law."

"No."

"Oh yes. Yes, very certainly. And, Señor Felix, if you don't explain your business to me very clearly and quickly, I shall have you escorted directly from this office to jail where, I might add, you will assuredly remain until you become more communicative."

Victoriano Felix had walked into a trap. More furious with

himself than with Miguárdez, he bit his lower lip and tried desperately to think of any loophole or crack through which he could scurry away from the office and the Palacio Nacional itself.

There were none.

Looking like a complaisant linen-clad toad, Miguárdez sat at the huge desk in front of him while behind him, at the door, the guard still stood wearing a very large and undoubtedly loaded North American .45-caliber revolver.

Victoriano had no choice but to explain to the presidential secretary what he had hoped to communicate strictly to General Cárdenas. Still, he refused to be cowed completely. He took a step forward, his hat held before his genitals like a shield and, in a whisper, begged Señor Miguárdez to dismiss the guard.

The official waved his hand.

Victoriano waited until the guard had left and closed the door. Then slowly, deliberately, he told his story.

Loyalty to the government, he insisted throughout, was his only motivation for coming to the Palacio Nacional. He could not, of course, be certain that the president himself had not taken the diamonds, but, he was quick to point out, if this proved to be the case, he was absolutely confident that General Cárdenas had unselfish and patriotic reasons for doing so.

What bothered him, he confided, was an uneasy feeling that perhaps someone else might have appropriated the property of the Mexican people. Naturally, he was not one to accuse his superiors, but the facts were that only three other men in the entire Republic even knew of the vault, and only two of them had any real knowledge of its contents.

The Minister of Finance, Narciso Bassols, had known about it and the president's aide, Jesús Guerrero, had also been privy to the secret. Victoriano was absolutely convinced that his own superior in the Banco Nacional knew only of the vault, not of the enormity of its contents.

As he told his story, he tried to study Miguárdez's expression. It remained an enigma. The small man had propped his elbows on his polished marble desk top and throughout Victoriano's monologue had done no more than nod several times over his tinted fingers.

His report finished, Victoriano heaved a long and, he hoped, very emotional sigh. "Of course," he said finally, "I seek no reward for this information. It is, Señor, simply a matter of duty, of patriotism to Mexico, and belief in the principles of the revolution.''

"Of course." Miguárdez continued to nod several times as he stared absently at Victoriano. Finally he leaned far back, looked to the ceiling a moment, and again pursed his thick lips. He remained in that posture for some moments before turning to face Victoriano.

"If what you say is true, Señor . . ." His eyes were as expressionless as those of an iguana. "The president may very well be grateful. However . . ." He lifted the ear-piece from his telephone. "I doubt if he would be so pleased with unfounded accusations."

"With your permission, Señor—"

Miguárdez raised the palm of his left hand to silence him then lifted the telephone. "Ministry of Finance," he said. A moment later, the connection made, he asked to speak to a Señor Gómez, waited again then began to ask very direct and pointed questions regarding the activities of Señor Bassols over the previous week. Apparently satisfied, he clicked the telephone's cradle down with his finger and placed a second call, this time to the office of Señor Guerrero. Again he asked for an informant, identified himself, and began to ask similar questions.

"South?" He appeared puzzled. "Ah," he said at length, "I see . . . I see . . ."

He recradled the telephone and stared at the desk top for a moment before lifting his eyes to Victoriano again. "You have acted correctly in this matter," he said. "Unfortunately, your suspicions are unfounded. The Minister of Finance has been confined to his bed for almost a week and Señor Guerrero is on a mission to Chiapas. We do, however, appreciate your report."

"Naturally," Victoriano leaned slightly forward, "I seek no reward for this information."

"Naturally," Miguárdez echoed. "We all wish to help Mexico as much as possible." He nodded in dismissal.

"Yes." This time Victoriano also nodded, but his teeth were tightly clenched. "Of course, Señor Secretary." He took two paces backward before turning to open the door.

The uniformed guard accompanied a very quiet, almost maniacally furious Victoriano Felix down three flights of stairs and into the afternoon sunlight outside the Palacio Nacional. There the clerk stood for some time staring blindly across the trolley tracks to Zacola Square. Finally he became aware of the pain his tightly clenched jaws were causing him.

"*Cabrones,*" he muttered through still clenched teeth as he started to cross to the park. "*Cabrones politicos. Hijos de sus Chingada madre!*"

The map of Mexico was sprawled over the president's desk, completely covering everything on its surface. Consequently, when the telephone rang, Lázaro Cárdenas was forced to lift the entire eastern seaboard from Chetumal to Matamoros before he could pick up the instrument.

As ever, Juan Miguárdez was calm and respectful. Still, his voice contained the barest hint of urgency as he requested an immediate audience.

Affairs of state were never easy. Time for thought and planning was never entirely free of interruption. General Cárdenas gave permission, recradled the telephone, and again pulled the map out so that he could study the topography of the state of Durango. He had just picked up a magnifying glass the better to inspect the Nazas Valley region when Miguárdez knocked on the door.

The president laid the glass on the map. "Enter."

Juan Miguárdez opened the door abruptly, slipped through, and closed it just as fast. There was in his movements something surreptitious. He might have been a part of some deadly, secret conspiracy. Almost at a trot he crossed the room to the president's desk.

"Mr. President . . ." His voice was scarcely more than a whisper. "I am sorry for the necessity of troubling you, but I have received a report which may have far-reaching significance."

He went on to explain all that Victoriano Felix had told him, adding that his two telephone calls had done nothing to ease his suspicions. The Minister of Finance had supposedly been sick all week, but there was no proof. He could have been anywhere. Señor Guerrero had supposedly left the capital, but from what little information he had been able to gather, he was sure one of the two men had, in fact, stolen the diamonds.

The president listened quietly to the entire report. When Miguárdez finished, General Cárdenas' serious mouth almost broke into a smile. "My first consideration," he said, "would be that this clerk, this Señor Felix who came to you, has tried to erase suspicion from himself. After all, Juan, he is the most likely and certainly the most needy suspect. Think, if you were in his position, would you not see an advantage in possessing millions? And after stealing them, would it not seem an intelligent ruse to report the matter simply to exonerate yourself?''

"I don't think so, General. Not in this case. I studied the man. His posture is subservient and though there is some animal cleverness in him, his most obvious emotion is anger.''

"Anger?''

"Fury might be a better word. He is an extremely bitter man, Mr. President. I'm sure he only wanted to see you to make sure you had not taken the diamonds yourself. My guess is that he may have considered taking the stones, but that someone else got there first.''

"Ah!''

"I believe he's convinced himself that the diamonds are his. I'm sure he only came to us in hopes of some financial compensation for what he actually considers his personal loss.''

"I see.''

"It's a very serious situation, Mr. President.''

"Yes,'' Cárdenas conceded. "Bassols or Guerrero.''

"Exactly,'' Miguárdez said. "But it's not simply the theft, General. I'm sure you realize the possibility of treason as well.''

The president's smile was almost wistful. "It may sound foolish to you, Juan, but the threat of treason is something I find almost easy to live with. It's always there, you know. And it's always considered by those closest to the seat of power. Still, I have known Bassols for some time and Jesús Guerrero is like a brother to me. Why, I personally ordered him to Chiapas.''

"Still, Mr. President, this matter cannot be ignored.''

"No. You are right. No one is ever entirely above suspicion. More important, those diamonds could be of great value to the government. We have very little time and even less money. Good. I'll leave this matter in your hands. Solve the crime, Juan. Find the offender and when I return, I'll take action. Meanwhile,'' the president looked to the map again, "I have a scorpion to crush.''

* * *

The large room had already absorbed the first chill of evening. Although the lights were on, their illumination was not sufficient to erase a sense of gloom due almost entirely to the great size of the office. It had an ominous quality that counterpoint to the warmth of the polished wooden paneling and smiling rococo cherubims lining the ceiling.

The atmosphere perfectly complemented the mood of the single occupant.

Juan Miguárdez sat at his huge desk studying once again the reports given him earlier that afternoon. They were the results of several days of guarded research, observation, and questioning regarding Narcols Bassols and Jesús Guerrero.

Of the two, Bassols was more likely the man to be considered a thief and traitor. Everyone aware of the inner workings of the administration knew that Bassols frequently considered his personal wants when discharging the needs of the state. Ever since he had first been appointed to high office under President Rubio, he had proved to be a hard and competent worker but a man with a dagger as well. He had turned on General Calles. He would be just as willing to turn on Cárdenas if it suited his purposes.

Still, he hardly needed to steal four bags of diamonds. As Minister of Finance, he was in a position to embezzle the entire treasury. Furthermore, at the time the diamonds were supposedly removed from the vault, Narcols Bassols had been confined to bed. Too many witnesses—doctors, family members, close associates—had seen him there.

Miguárdez closed the folder, set it aside, and opened the report on Guerrero. He had always detested the younger man. Purely from a political point of view, he envied Guerrero's closeness to the president; what was more, he hated his charm and virtually effortless power over women. Guerrero was everything Miguárdez was not. He was handsome, athletic, and very obviously aware of his seductive charisma.

One glance at the photograph of Guerrero, which was lying on top of the carefully typed report, made the presidential secretary painfully aware of his own diminutive stature and undescended testicle. Bitterly he reminded himself that the same Fate, which had stunted and malformed him, had endowed Jesús Guerrero with all the attributes of an Adonis.

"Pimp!" he whispered to the photograph before turning it over. "Better in a whorehouse than government."

Juan Miguárdez had reviewed the report several times that afternoon and, with each reading, had sensed something which didn't quite ring true. As a result, two men had been waiting outside his office for the past hour. They were Rafael Estrada, Guerrero's private secretary, and Louis Robles, one of Miguárdez's own employees.

The first page of the report contained an interview with Estrada, who had verified that on the day the diamonds had supposedly been stolen, his superior had been summoned by the president. Supposedly, that was the first time Guerrero had any indication that he would have to leave the capital. Yet Estrada claimed the trip had been planned for some time.

Juan Miguárdez stared across the huge room. He remained motionless—lips pursed, eyes vaguely focused—for a moment. Then, almost viciously, he rang for the guard.

The door opened. "Señor Secretary?"

"Send Señor Estrada in."

Rafael Estrada was a man in his late fifties who had seen too much of revolutionary government to be awed by anything. His manner was subservient enough to be mistaken for politeness, but it was immediately obvious to Miguárdez that the older man could not be intimidated. He was neither impressed nor fearful. If anything, he was thinking of nothing more than the inconvenience of having his dinner delayed.

Miguárdez studied the balding, bespectacled Estrada for some time before deciding he thoroughly disliked the man. He tapped the report with the knuckles of his right hand. "Earlier this week you suggested that, even before his last audience with the president, Señor Guerrero was planning to leave the city."

"Yes."

"He told you that?"

"He didn't have to."

"Didn't have to?"

"With due respect, Mr. Secretary, I have been with the government many years. One gets a feel for such things. A change in working schedules . . . missing files . . ."

"Files? What missing files?"

Estrada remained placid. "Nothing vital, Señor. Information anyone would take on a trip."

"Such as?"

"Names of places and people to visit."

61

"What places? Who?"

"I don't remember everything, of course, but I recall some details—locations of confiscated funds, men retired from government, military garrisons—information like that."

"Like that, eh?" He realized that he was speaking through clenched teeth. "You wait outside," he snapped. "I may want a word with you later."

Obediently, Rafael Estrada allowed himself to be ushered out.

Miguárdez again returned his attention to the report. He needed more information. Unfortunately, it just wasn't there.

He had sent Louis Robles to Guerrero's home some days before. Robles had simply verified the fact that Guerrero had gone. His report consisted of no more than two short paragraphs.

Again he rang for the guard.

Louis Robles was young, eager, and fundamentally nervous. His taste in clothing was slightly gauche of center, and he wore entirely too much Vitalis. A man who could not possibly conceal his desire for advancement, he also could not hide the fact that he was both self-seeking and unworthy of too much trust. There was to Louis Robles much in common with the weasel.

Again Miguárdez tapped the report with his knuckles. "This is all—half a page?"

"There was nothing else."

"You did talk to the servants?"

"Yes, Señor."

"All of them?"

"There were only two."

"A villa that size? Don't you think that's odd?"

"The family was gone. There was nothing to do, just a little dusting."

"How much did they take with them?"

"How would I know, Señor? The usual things, I would imagine—trunks, suitcases, whatever would fit into a touring car. That and the wheelchair."

"Someone was injured—sick?"

"No. Señora Guerrero's girl said her employer insisted on the wheelchair. She didn't know why."

Miguárdez nodded several times. He leaned back, looked for a moment at the elaborately paneled ceiling, then turned back to Robles. "You know, of course, that Señor Guerrero is a collector of statuary and fine art."

"No. What difference—"

"Did you see any in the house?"

"No. There was very little. Just furniture."

"What about souvenirs of the bull ring?"

"Bull ring?"

"He's an *aficionado*, idiot. Everyone in Mexico knows that. Bulls' heads, hoofs, portraits of *toreros*—they should have been quite conspicuous."

Robles shook his head. "No," he said. "Nothing like that."

"And you don't think it worth mentioning that a high government official leaves with a healthy family, takes along a wheelchair, and that everything he values—art, statuary, mementos of many *corridas*—is all missing from his villa?"

"But—"

Miguárdez waved his arm in a loose gesture of contempt. "Go," he said. "Get out, imbecile."

He turned Robles' statement over and glanced at a third report. On the highway from Puebla, just north of Tehuacán, local police had aided in repairing a flat tire. It was an unusual service, but the car repaired belonged to an unusual man. The terse, officially worded account mentioned Señor Guerrero's destination as Chiapas. It listed his wife and two children as passengers and noted date, time, and services performed. Conspicuously absent was any mention of a chauffeur or wheelchair.

Juan Miguárdez leaned back. Solid evidence of guilt was simply not there. Still, one simply did not rob one's own files or strip a huge villa of hundreds of objets d'art without reason. One did not pack a wheelchair only to discard it within a few hundred kilometers. Finally, one did not summon police to repair flat tires.

Miguárdez nodded his toadlike head. He was sure Jesús Guerrero was heading south only to be seen on the road. Thus the police report. He was sure the man's ultimate destination lay not in Chiapas, but north in the United States.

Guerrero was defecting. He intended to make contact with the exiled Plutarco Calles, then return to overthrow the present government.

Still, there was no tangible evidence Miguárdez could present to President Cárdenas. He leaned forward, replaced the various reports in the folder, and again looked at the photograph of the almost pretty Guerrero. He thought again of the man's easy way with women and was again aware of his own masculine deficiency.

He shook his head almost sadly. "This time, *bastardo*," he said very quietly, "I will scramble *your* eggs."

2
Strategy

THE HUGE MAP covered almost the entire desk. *Standartenführer* Hiller leaned over it, supporting his massive torso on the prop of his left arm. He grunted occasionally and, from time to time, his right index finger made a small arc over the chart, then stopped abruptly before outlining another curve. His hand might have been that of a senile conductor who had perhaps forgotten the music entirely. There was, however, no hint of absentmindedness in Hiller's features. They were intense. His heavy brows were drawn tightly over his hard, contemplative eyes.

Standing on the opposite side of the desk, Ernst Dichter was the personification of absolute patience. He watched his superior without motion or expression.

"Vera Cruz," Hiller mused. He straightened his back and stared over Dichter's head to the opposite wall of the huge office. "He sailed on the *Prince Umberto* from Lisbon. We know that. He docked in Vera Cruz on the fifth. He doesn't speak Spanish. That could be to our advantage, but not in Vera Cruz. Too international. It wouldn't matter."

Suddenly he lowered his eyes and focused on Dichter.

The *Oberleutnant* blinked behind his thick-lensed glasses. He made no other move.

"Well?" Hiller demanded.

"He was, in fact, on the *Prince Umberto*, *Standartenführer*. He and his wife dashed into the crowd immediately after clearing customs."

Hiller looked again at the map. "But, would he . . .? No. His whole behavior pattern is that of a man alone. A contact in Mexico is out of the question."

"Unless . . ."

"Unless what?"

"I'm merely supposing, *Standartenführer*. After all, we are fairly certain that his ultimate destination is New Jersey. All logic points to it. He has worked with this Einstein person before. He could be following a pattern."

"Pattern? Nonsense."

"We cannot discount the Americans."

"Degenerates."

"I agree, but they're not blind to the potential of this man's knowledge—particularly if he and Einstein meet again. Roosevelt may be a bumbling dreamer, but he's not a complete fool. Even he should know that war is written on the wall. Despite all this current business difficulty with Mexico, he's going to bend very far to keep the Good Neighbor Policy in effect."

Hiller grunted, then looked absently at the map. "Scientists!" He almost spat the word. "The devil alone knows what they cook in their damned beakers! All right. There is a possibility—a possibility, mind you—that he has been met in Vera Cruz. Still, I doubt it. Roosevelt's a coward. He's faced with enough internal problems without asking for more trouble with Mexico. No. I'm sure of it. Mister Doctor Jakob Pelzig was not met in Vera Cruz."

"Do you really believe the Americans are so ignorant?"

"Ah, Dichter! *That* is an entirely different matter. Of course they know. They knew when he boarded the *Prince Umberto* in Lisbon. They probably even had a man on board, and there's no doubt they were watching the landing. But if our men lost him, their men did too. The point is, the Americans don't want any sort of incident. They're afraid of Cárdenas, don't you understand? The man's telling them to go to hell in a basket, and he's getting away with it because if there is a war, the Americans want the Mexicans to do their fighting for them. No. My guess is they're watching Pelzig and that's all. They're trembling on their own side of the border, scared completely shitless. It's typical."

"Yes, Sir."

"Which, of course, puts Pelzig on his own—in Vera Cruz— lost—probably intelligent enough to know we've had our men on him all along, and probably scared enough to realize that, even if he has dodged them once, he's far from free.''

"Yes, *Standartenführer*."

"So . . ." Again he looked directly at Dichter. "He's in a hurry. But he also has to be careful. Let us suppose, Dichter, that you are a Jew on the run—in Vera Cruz."

Dichter stepped to the desk and leaned over the map. "The obvious choice would be to fly up the coast over Matamoros and enter here, at Brownsville. However, I seriously doubt if he'll take the plane. He hasn't flown yet, and I'm sure he's intelligent enough to realize we have the airports watched. Besides, almost all the flights north from this area are completely filled with American oil company employees. Cárdenas is giving them too much trouble. They're all leaving the sinking ship."

"True," Hiller conceded.

"As far as ground transportation along the coast, it's primitive in the extreme. Pelzig alone might just try that route, but he's wearing a chain."

"His wife."

"Yes. I don't think we can overlook their devotion when it comes to choosing a route. Frankly, I think he'll take the train right here in Vera Cruz, go through the jungle, up to the plateau of Mexico City. From the capital, he can go directly north to any point of entry he likes."

Hiller nodded his huge head. "It's the obvious choice," he conceded. "That's exactly why he won't take it. He's too slippery. Remember how he got out of Berlin, how he managed to get into Switzerland, then back to France, and finally down to Portugal? No. Pelzig never goes in the direction he's headed. He's a clever man, Dichter—and a desperate one. If he's going to Mexico City, and you see . . . look here. He *has* to go to Mexico City. All the roads meet there. He won't travel there directly."

Dichter frowned slightly while at the same time nodding agreement.

"He could, of course, rent a car," Hiller said. "Or take a bus perhaps. No. He won't do that either. The train. It offers maximum comfort for his wife. But he won't go directly."

"South?"

"Yes. South or east. He might cross the Tehuantepec Isthmus to Salina Cruz. He might come here to Oaxaca—anyplace. But . . ."

"All roads lead to Rome?"

"Exactly."

"You intend to abduct him in Mexico City?"

"No. I don't want an incident any more than the Americans. Pelzig has consistently gone in the wrong direction and then turned back. We know he intends to go north, so pragmatism indicates he will first go south. But look, Dichter—here. Before he gets to the capital, this is where his train must stop."

"Puebla."

"Exactly. A few good men boarding the northbound train in Puebla will surely encounter Mister Doctor Jakob Pelzig and his wife. If not, he'll be on the next train, or the next."

"A rather difficult situation, *Standartenführer*. The Americans—"

"Don't worry about the Americans, Dichter. They are a race of sheep. Despite this depression, they think only in terms of creature comforts. They are physically and morally weak and certainly do not want any sort of incident. Besides, our task became somewhat more simple as of this morning."

"Oh?"

"Yes. I have talked to *Reichsführer* Himmler. Ideally, Pelzig should be returned to Germany. However, if that cannot be accomplished, our mission is simply to prevent contact with Professor Einstein."

Hiller began to fold the map. "After all, Dichter . . ." His expression was almost benign. "What's one Jew more or less to the Reich?"

Because she lacked confidence in the pilots of the erratically scheduled planes to Mexico City, and because she found the employees of the nearest rail line involved in one of their frequent strikes, Karen Tait had been forced to endure the ultimate horror—a Mexican bus.

It was Friday, and both the road and the vehicle were packed with all manner of people carrying all manner of merchandise to market for sale the following day. The trip was a jerking, honking, sweating agony which Karen survived only through the exercise of uncompromising stoicism.

Finally, like a creature in the throes of St. Vitus's dance, the bus ground to a shuddering halt on the rim of Oaxaca's huge central market and dislodged itself of its motley cargo.

Filthy, exhausted, and covered with perspiration, Karen

ignored everything but her quest for a taxi, relaxed in a state bordering on catatonia during the short ride to the hotel and there, still almost in a trance, followed the driver into the lobby and, more like a robot than a human, paid, and tipped him.

She was so preoccupied with her own fatigue and filth that she paid little attention to the people around her. As she approached the desk, she might have been a pearl diver moving under several oppressive fathoms or an athlete on screen slowed in motion by an over-cranked camera.

Almost completely unaware of the man standing before her, she leaned over to let her heavy valise drop. In that position—slightly bent, her hand on the suitcase—she heard the man's voice.

"Bastards!" He spoke English and was obviously surprised as well as annoyed. The hostility of his tone was contained, as though he were speaking to himself. "Damned bastards!"

She released the grip of her case and started to straighten up. It was when she was exactly halfway up that she saw a blur of movement and, before she could react defensively to it, was hit with sufficient force to send her small bag and package flying across the lobby and to knock her off her feet.

It was the last straw. She wasn't physically injured, but as she lay on the floor of the Monte Albán Hotel, she almost wished she had been. If she had been knocked unconscious, she would at least have been transported from the misery which had composed the entire day.

She squeezed her eyes tightly shut to contain the tears that had been threatening to erupt for hours. A second later, when she opened them, she was looking up to a slender blond man with very concerned blue eyes. He was holding her right wrist in what seemed like a professional manner.

"*Lo siento,*" he said, frowning slightly as he looked at her more closely. "I'm afraid I didn't look. I just turned and . . ."

Strangely, her only thought was not of injury but of feminine modesty. Her dress had leapt well above her knees. She allowed the man to help her to a sitting position then smoothed the fabric over her legs.

"I really am sorry." His smile was almost fey. "I mean, I don't make a practice of knocking down stray young ladies in hotel lobbies."

68

She was numb. The misery of the day had now been compounded. The man's accidental move might have been the final emotional humiliation, but when she saw that the package which had contained her notes and manuscript—her rolls of undeveloped film and sketch pads—had broken and scattered its contents over several yards of hotel lobby, that became the ultimate handful of salt rubbed into the raw lacerations of her frayed emotions.

The final wire of control pulled past its elastic limit. She covered her grimy face with her hands and began to sob convulsively into her palms.

The man knelt beside her and put one arm gently around her shoulders. It was not a presumptuous move—merely one of attempted understanding. "I really am terribly sorry," he said again. "So very foolish. I should have looked."

Frustration and humiliation—exhaustion and physical discomfort—all bubbled over the pot of her containment and, by some strange alchemy, changed her emotions from what they actually were into something new and totally dishonest—hysterical fury.

"Oh, go away!" she sobbed. She shook his arm from her shoulders and struggled awkwardly to her feet. "Go to hell for all I care! Just go away!"

He was standing beside her now, a slender, quite good-looking and genuinely sympathetic man. "I really am . . ."

"You really are an awkward son of a bitch!" She was sobbing through clenched teeth. "Oh, God *damn* you! Go away! I never want to see you again!"

Despite the fury of her outburst and the murk her tears made of her vision, she was somehow able to gather her scattered papers, rolls of film, and sketch books and repackage them sufficiently to get to the desk. There, she almost begged for a room with its own bath.

By the time she had signed the register and allowed one of the bellboys to lift her valise, the blond man was gone.

Infrequently a sleeping car was attached to the Vera Cruz–Guatemala Border train, but experienced travelers never counted on it. They took their chances on the wooden or black leather seats and tried to make the best of whatever was available. That spring only the railroads in the northern half of Mexico were acceptable to outsiders. The southern lines were not yet ready for an invasion of foreigners.

Before he boarded the first train, Jakob Pelzig bought cigars. Long before he arrived in Puerto México, he was more than happy that he had. They were insufficient but still he tried to fool himself into believing he could bury some of the odor of Lysol which the porter seemed constantly to be splashing on the aisle from a huge bucket.

The layover in Puerto México might have been enacted from a script by Dante Alighieri. It seemed to be a punishment designed exclusively for fleeing Jewish scientists and their sick wives.

Hannah slumped beside him in the crowded, evil-smelling terminal until the second train arrived. It was quite late by the time they boarded and found seats.

Throughout the night the train stopped, then started again. Passengers bumped and slid against Pelzig, and their belongings buffeted his head and shoulders.

Finally it was over. They arrived in Salina Cruz, the shabby, bleak, sand-scoured terminus of the Trans-Isthmus Railroad.

Hannah had slept through almost the entire journey. Sick though she was, she appeared more refreshed than he as they climbed from the ancient train and looked over the unappealing town. On the platform her hand slipped easily into his and he looked at her fondly.

Somehow she was again Hannah Mann, the beautiful slender girl from Ulm. The circles vanished from under her dark eyes and there was color in her cheeks again. Thirty years dissipated in a breeze from the sea, and he knew the worst was over.

He put his arm around her and squeezed her very gently before releasing her to pick up both their suitcases. When he spoke, however, his tone was precise and determined.

"Come love," he said. "We must hurry to Oaxaca."

Karen Tait awoke to the sounds of market day. A dull cacophony of animal and human noises clattered in the morning air. Far away *mariachis* sighed; nearer, to the east, the cathedral's bell did penance. Long years before, as legend had it, it had consorted with the devil. The Inquisition in Toledo had exiled it to Oaxaca, there to be struck by hammers every fifteen minutes *in perpetuum*.

She rolled on her side to fight against waking, but the heat of the morning and her own hunger could not be denied. She rose, sighed, and, for the sheer luxury of it, bathed before dressing. She would enjoy a leisurely breakfast, then make arrangements to take a train north.

She was crossing the hotel's lobby when the first jiggle of earthquake startled her. It was followed immediately by a more insistent seismic jolt which almost knocked her off her feet. It was both unexpected and deceptive—an illusion of ultimate, eternal violence. It seemed to begin slowly, as though Nature had desired to give at least some warning, then abruptly had changed Her mind. The shaking became increasingly violent—an intangible force possessed of horrid fury.

In fact, the quake lasted only a few seconds. It was one of many that occur frequently in the area. Still, as inevitably happens with such tremors, it brought with it a painful awareness of one's own personal insignificance.

It was as though the world were being buffeted by infuriated gods. She, the hotel, Mexico, the entire earthly sphere— all seemed reduced to the helplessness of a mouse being snapped back and forth by a particularly sadistic cat.

The quake struck so suddenly that it overwhelmed both her physical and spiritual equilibrium. She was hardly aware of being jerked toward the hotel's dining room.

The world was still heaving as she looked up to see the blond man who had knocked her down the previous evening.

Again his smile was almost fey. "It's safer in a doorway," he said.

The earth convulsed. The hotel jerked and pitched like a flimsy carton adrift on a tempestuous sea. In the dining room, glasses broke and flatware clattered to the floor. Outside, a child screamed. There was the horrible, high-pitched sawing of frightened burros and, beyond all, the unrepentant clanging of the condemned bell again consorting with the devil.

"Apparently . . ." He was still smiling, "I'm being punished for last night."

It was as if his remark was a panacea for whatever powers had taken such magnificent offense, for the shaking stopped as abruptly as it had started. The earth shuddered twice and then lay still.

She was standing in the doorway of the dining room of the Hotel Monte Albán, looking at a very handsome blond man who still had his arm curled protectively around her waist.

Suddenly she was overwhelmed with embarrassment. Her behavior the previous evening had been inexcusable. She had been so exhausted, so completely unstrung by an irritability

71

compounded of a thousand elements other than being accidentally knocked down that she had been unspeakably rude.

"I'm afraid I was awful," she confessed. "I should be apologizing to you."

"Nonsense." His smile widened. "Let me introduce myself. I'm Charles Candenning."

She might have been twelve years old and in dancing school again—an awkward, skinny girl whose hands and feet were too big, and who never seemed to know the right things to say. Still, she managed to extend her hand and take his in a friendly grip.

"Charles Candenning?" she repeated. There was something vaguely familiar about the name which didn't quite fall into place until she glanced beyond him to the hotel's lobby. There, by the main door, stood a man's suitcase. In addition, there was an artist's paint box and easel. "Not the illustrator?"

Now it was he who seemed embarrassed. "I'm afraid so. I hope I don't have to apologize for that as well."

Embarrassment flowed away through a suddenly opened drain, and, for an instant, she relaxed completely. He was charming and protective and really quite nice. But, just as suddenly as her embarrassment yielded to a sense of security, that too vanished, swept aside by something close to terror.

He was entirely too likable. Attractive men were spoiled and selfish. Hadn't she spent four years married to one, only to wake up to his embezzlement of corporate funds and subsequent flight to Canada with his secretary?

"Not at all." Even she could hear the defensive coldness in her voice. "I've admired your work."

His expression did not quite have time to become a puzzled frown. The man behind the hotel desk rushed to where they stood.

"*Lo siento, Señor—Señorita, no tenga miedo. Hay muchos temblores de tierra aqui.*"

"*No importa,*" Candenning said. "We're fine. *Gracias.*"

"For the hotel, Señor . . . Señorita . . . I am very sorry. These things . . . it is unfortunate. They happen very often in Oaxaca."

"You mean," Candenning looked at the man with mock seriousness, "we cannot hold you personally responsible?"

"Señor, I . . ."

"*No es nada.* No trouble at all." Candenning was smiling now. "We're quite alright. *Ya se acabó.*"

Obviously somewhat puzzled by his guest, the clerk returned to the desk.

"It would appear," Candenning ventured, "that the management lacks a sense of humor. Also, we are probably the only Americans within miles. On the basis of that common denominator, would you care to join me for breakfast?"

"I really don't think—"

"As a peace offering?" he said. "No strings." He held up his left hand. "See? I'm married. Besides, I'm leaving within the hour."

There was something of both boyish honesty and pique in his tone. She struggled to maintain an aloof reserve.

"That's probably why I wasn't looking last night. I simply read the telegram, turned around like an oaf and . . ." He shrugged his shoulders to complete the sentence.

She must have been frowning.

"I've been recalled, you see. No reason. No rhyme. First real vacation I've had in years and the army wants me to report to Fort Bliss immediately, if not yesterday."

"I'm afraid I don't understand."

"Frankly, Miss—?"

"Tait. Karen Tait."

"Frankly, Miss Tait, neither do I. That's why I'm offering breakfast. No strings. All I want is unadulterated motherly commiseration."

There was something in his manner so totally disarming that she couldn't help but smile. She even felt a touch of genuine compassion.

She followed him to a table, and ordered eggs and coffee.

Without looking at the menu, he simply asked for Scotch and, noting her expression of surprise, merely shrugged. "After all," he assured her, "it is five o'clock somewhere."

Despite the earliness of her companion's cocktail hour, he proved pleasant and unthreatening. He reminded her of the Arrow shirt man, or of pictures she had seen of Scott Fitzgerald. It was his contained politeness, however, which impressed her most. Beyond his reserve, she was sure, lay some annoyance that stemmed from something more important than military recall.

"Really," he told her, "it's quite exasperating. I haven't been down here since I was a boy—before the revolution. It was just a visit, but I fell in love with the place. Now, for the first time in years I've had a chance to break away, do some decent work for a change, and the army wants me back."

"There must be *some* reason."

"None." He took a long pull of his drink. "Absolutely none whatsoever. I've no military skills at all. Just a reserve officer. Thing to do, you know. I mean, we're not at war. What would the army possibly want with magazine covers?"

He started to lift his glass again but was interrupted by the hotel clerk, who had come to the table.

"I am very sorry, Señor," the man said. "I have distressing news. I have received a telephone message. The earthquake has done some damage, very minor, but the tracks must be repaired. There will be a delay."

Candenning set his glass on the table. His expression was a mixture of resignation and relief. "How long?" he asked.

"Oh, today, certainly, Señor. This afternoon for certain."

Candenning nodded. "That means by Tuesday, right?"

The clerk shrugged. "Perhaps, Señor."

Candenning chuckled. *"Asi es la vida,"* he said. "Earthquake in Oaxaca, tracks warped. National security in the north and your usual, run-of-the-mill catastrophe in Mexico."

"I suppose we could fly up." She really intended it as a question.

"I am *not* going to fly!"

She frowned at the intensity of his tone.

"First vacation in years and I'm not going to soar out of here thousands of feet in the air unable to see anything. The army can damned well wait!" Suddenly he became almost peevish. "I'm sorry," he said. Then he shrugged. "At least there's one consolation."

"Oh?"

"Of course. Now there's time for another drink. Call it one for the railroads."

She frowned slightly as he beckoned the waiter. Then she was suddenly annoyed at herself for feeling concern at all.

3
Gold

TUXTLA GUTIÉRREZ, CAPITAL of Chiapas, is an ancient city. It enjoys a certain distinction as headquarters for the local coffee trade, but it has never held any great appeal for visitors. In the spring of 1937 the population was still well under 10,000. The Mayan ruins of Bonampak had not, as yet, been discovered and El Sumidero would remain virtually unexplored for another twenty-three years.

El Sumidero translates somewhat unromantically as "the sink" or "drain," or even "the sewer." In fact, it is a spectacular natural phenomenon. One of the most formidable in the entire Republic of Mexico, this magnificent canyon lies just northeast of Tuxtla, where its sheer walls soar thousands of feet above the channel of the Rio Girjalva.

That spring those walls were covered with lush verdure. Tropical birds cawed to one another through the lazy humidity and the sound of flowing water was like an endless kiss. El Sumidero could have been Eden transplanted, for it was almost stupifying in its naked, primeval grandeur.

All of which was completely lost upon the lone white man who had already made his treacherous way along some twenty-five miles of the canyon. That he might be the first of his entire race to view and hear, to feel and experience, the grandeur of El Sumidero never once occurred to him. He was a man consumed by a passion that gnawed at his soul with the insatiable squirming of a termite army.

There was now to Ian Conrad an absolute directness of purpose which blinded him to everything but his ultimate goal. Drugs, a basic tenacity of character, and his now constant physical pain had allied themselves into a horrible confederation dedicated to the absolute annihilation of another man.

He had spoken not merely to one, but three, Indians in the hills. Each had confirmed his suspicions. There had been another foreigner. He had come from the highlands—a small man leading many burros, each carrying two crates with strange markings on them. The Indians could not, of course, know the man's name or destination, but how many foreigners traveled through Chiapas and where would one go in country like this?

The man could only be William Scofield.

His destination could only be Tuxtla Gutiérrez.

Ian Conrad had been raised in the rugged Cornish country near Land's End. Like so many others from that area, his character had been formed by rigid parents, the unyielding dictates of stern schoolmasters, and employers bereft of compassion. The Bible had been the cornerstone of his education, but the lessons therein had proved bipolar when applied to the practical issues of temporal life.

In the tropical paradise of El Sumidor Canyon, the laws of the Israelites came to him again in fragmented, pulsating rhythm. An unheard drum hammered his consciousness. It throbbed against his crippled leg and snapped stinging perspiration into the sightless orb of his dead eye.

As he made his way south, from time to time he would mumble snatches from the twenty-first chapter of Exodus; and, as he did so, he could fairly taste the feast of revenge soon to be his.

And if men strive together, and one smite another with a stone, or with his fist . . .

An eye for an eye . . . foot for foot. . . .

And . . . then . . .

thou shalt give life for life. . . .

Miles to the east, also journeying toward the state capital, another man sought solace in scripture. His instructions had been clear, but as Domingo Portes traveled the road from San Cristóbal Las Cassas, doubt rode with him.

In the city itself, William Scofield had already sold the burros. He had bought a suit of clothes, sought out and negotiated with an independent teamster, and had personally overseen the loading of his crates aboard the rented truck.

He stood now smoking a cigarette, glancing from the truck to the capital building in the distance, then to the truck's owner, a tall, cadaverous man engaged in conversation with two other Mexicans some ten yards away.

The tobacco was vile. He would never get used to Mexican cigarettes. He snuffed deeply, then cleared his throat. He snapped the cigarette into the street and followed it with a great wad of phlegm.

Juchitán lay some 125 miles to the west over a rough and unpleasant road. There he might be able to catch a train north. What troubled him was yesterday's earthquake. Such annoyances were common in the area. Still, he had heard that a certain amount of damage had been done.

He glanced to his watch.

It wasn't wise to rely on rumors, particularly in southern Mexico, but he had heard not once, but several times of impassable roads and warped railroad tracks.

10:42. Christ! He wanted to get out—get north to Texas or California and start to live for a change.

He fumbled in his pocket for a cigarette pack, touched it, then remembered the taste, and withdrew his fingers. He had some money left. He had also managed to get a good price for the burros. If worse came to worst, he might have to pay the truck's owner to take him all the way to Oaxaca. Still, he didnt't like the idea. He didn't like much of anything this morning.

Again, he glanced to where the driver was talking to his friends.

"Hey *Hombre*," he called. *"Vamonos!"* Then, in muttered English, "Goddamned greaser." He waved his hand. "Come on," he yelled. *"Vamonos* for Christ's sake. *Vamonos!"*

The driver turned from his friends. He stared for a moment at Scofield as though he had never seen him before. Then a glow of understanding appeared to illuminate his features. A matizo Ichabod Crane, he shrugged his shoulders and, bidding farewell to his companions, crossed the street, rounded the hood of the truck, and climbed into the cab.

Scofield pulled himself up afterward and, because he had nothing better to do, lit another cigarette.

The vehicle sputtered to life, then began the journey west.

The following morning, a cripple with almost white hair dragged himself into Tuxtla Gutiérrez. In cantina after cantina, he asked about a tiny man who might have come to the capital with several loaded burros. Late that afternoon, by a stroke of good fortune, he came upon two men who had spoken to William Scofield's driver.

He interrogated them about the crates, their markings, and the destination of the rented truck. Then he asked them to find him some sort of motorized vehicle and driver to take him to Juchitán.

There was about the stranger something to be avoided—a plague of the spirit—a contamination of the soul. As with animals, some ancient sense within both men whispered that the purpose of the cripple was evil. They refused to help him.

Far beyond any thought of capitulation, Ian Conrad was now a fanged tortoise racing an unsuspecting hare. He left Tuxtla to begin the slow, agonized trek in search of the one who had almost killed him.

The two men he had questioned watched and were thankful for his departure. Later they spoke to another stranger of their experience. They told him of the intensity in the cripple's single eye and of his strangely accented speech. Although they were both sure he was not an American, neither would essay an opinion of his true nationality.

"His name?" Portes asked. "Did he give his name?"

"No, friend—neither his own nor that of the man he was seeking. He was possessed. He spoke of burros, then cursed the city."

"It is true," said the other. "Then he mentioned Juchitán and muttered in his own tongue."

"He is following the other man then?"

"Oh yes, and he means no good. He is evil."

"And the other, the one who rented the truck, what of him?"

"Nervous, friend. He smoked a great deal. He was anxious to go to Juchitán."

"Juchitán." Portes savored the word. Juchitán was both the gateway to the Pacific and an important terminal of the railroad north to Vera Cruz. Suddenly he realized the enormity of his problem. He had been thrust into a desperate race against time. The first man, whatever his name or nationality, had severed his partnership. He alone had the gold and was obviously fleeing the country.

He turned to the two men. "In the name of God," he said, "you must help me. I must find this man before he leaves Mexico."

The two men exchanged glances. "God?" one said. "What can God do? God is but a superstition."

* * *

Charles Candenning was standing outside the hotel, idly staring across Avenida Hidalgo, when the car clattered up. It stopped, coughed, wheezed, and coughed again. Then, with a great and final sigh, it slumped to silence. By any standards, it was ancient. The right front fender and running board were missing, as was half of the engine's hood. It looked much like the crippled vehicles which had littered France during the last muddy days of the war—a wounded veteran of many miles, many accidents, and many repairs.

He looked at it with the casual indifference of one not particularly interested in anything. The weather was too hot. He was bored—tired of waiting in the hotel, playing an inane game of hurry-up-and-wait with the Mexican railroad system. For two full days, his life had conformed to a thankless schedule of constant inquiries on the progress of track repair, broken only by trips to the bar.

He didn't feel well. He had been drinking entirely too much. Completely packed now, he didn't want to risk a trip through the market to continue painting the church. His recall to military service bothered him as much by its actuality as by the mystery surrounding it and, on top of everything, was the nagging, constant knowledge that at age forty his career, his marriage, his very life could be summed up by only one word—failure.

In this disillusioned state of self-recrimination, the automobile, mundane as it was, offered something close to much needed solace. Still, as he glanced at it, his senses were not, at first, fully operative. They might have been attached to some form of dimmer which initially allowed only a small percentage of receptivity. He looked at the vehicle without actually seeing it, and heard without actually thinking, until something long-forgotten suddenly snapped into aural focus. He frowned and listened again, then realized he was hearing German.

He looked at the ancient car with new interest as a short, bespectacled man with thin, gray hair opened the back door. He was perhaps as unprepossessing as any middle-aged man. He wore a rumpled, perspiration-soaked shirt and linen trousers from which the crease had long since been erased. Yet there was about him an illusion of dynamic intensity as he leaned inside the vehicle and spoke to someone there.

A woman's voice—very soft and quite gentle—replied. Candenning could not hear the exact words, yet the tone

79

alone sent a sting of nostalgia through him. For an instant he was a little boy again, hearing his mother's voice.

The illusion was broken by the slamming of the driver's door. A very round Mexican passed in front of the car and, in Spanish, demanded payment from his passenger. Candenning could not help but find the scene amusing. It was obvious that the German spoke only a few feeble words of Spanish, while the driver understood absolutely no German. The scene might have been offered on a vaudeville stage.

Charles Candenning continued to listen to the bilingual exchange and watched the various inept hand gestures for several seconds before walking the few paces to the car.

"Guten Tag," he said to the shorter man. "It seems you need some help."

The man might have been stabbed with a cattle prod. He spun around, his eyes wide with terror, his mouth half open as he stared at Candenning. He gasped once, then, with a supreme effort, regained his control. *"Sie sind Deutcher!"* There was a definite tremble in his voice.

"Nein." Candenning smiled. *"Ich bin Amerikaner."*

"Oh?" The older man studied Candenning's face. There was an almost hostile suspicion in his gray eyes. "You speak remarkably well."

"My mother . . ." He let it hang.

"Ah." The man was still obviously on his guard.

"If I can be of assistance?" He nodded toward the driver. "It's fairly obvious he doesn't recite Goethe in his spare moments."

The older man did not smile. He continued to stare at Candenning, his eyes darting back and forth, seeking some clue to the American's motives. Finally he sighed. "I don't understand him," he said. "There was a Frenchman in Salina Cruz. He helped us hire . . ." He seemed almost totally beaten by some unseen hand, yet somehow desperately determined, if not actually driven, to go on.

"It's alright," Candenning assured him. "I'm your local Boy Scout."

The situation, which originally appeared to have all the elements of hysteria vital to any Latin altercation, was simply unraveled. The driver wanted his fare, which his passenger was willing and able to pay. Monetary transactions finished, Candenning helped the couple carry their luggage into the hotel.

80

In the lobby he held out his hand. "I'm Charles Candenning," he offered.

The man was still suspicious. He took Candenning's hand, nodded curtly, but did not speak.

"Jakob," the woman admonished. "Please, Jakob . . . we must trust someone."

"I am Jakob Heinrich," Doctor Pelzig said. "This is my wife."

"Herr Heinrich." Candenning was sure the man was lying. "Frau Heinrich." He nodded to the woman. "Shall you be in Oaxaca long?"

"We are tourists . . ." Pelzig groped for an answer. "No. We are going to . . . to Tehuacán."

Candenning allowed his eyebrows to lift slightly. "In that case," he said, "you might as well take a room. You probably won't get there for a while."

The little man's eyes narrowed behind his glasses. He seemed exactly like a tiny animal, cornered but about to make a last, desperate dash for freedom. "What do you mean?"

"There's a train forming now for the trip north. Unfortunately, the situation with the railroads is somewhat—how shall I put it?—unstable."

"Unstable?"

"First of all, Herr Heinrich, the earthquake did some damage to the tracks. On top of that, there's talk that President Cárdenas is about to do something drastic to the entire transportation system."

"Drastic?" Pelzig said. "How?"

"In Mexico," Candenning shrugged, "who knows?"

"He's not going to stop the trains."

"They're already stopped," Candenning said. "That earthquake was just God's last straw thrown in for symbolic effect. The workers have been striking off and on for months. The whole transportation system here is a mess. Part of the local charm, really. Don't you think?"

"I'm afraid," Pelzig admitted, "I would prefer a bit more order."

"Well, at least Cárdenas is on your side. From what I hear, he's sick of simple nationalization. It's just not working. The story is he plans to hand the railroads—all of them—over to the workers. The theory, of course, is that people don't strike against themselves."

"And this train north?"

"It may very well be the last one. That is, if it gets formed at all. If Cárdenas does act on this Rodríguez Proposal—if he does give the railraods to the workers—there's no telling how long the confusion could last."

"We'll be trapped."

"It's a nice town, really." Candenning smiled. "Besides, I don't charge for translation."

The little man turned to his wife. His whisper was almost feral. "We can't stay, Hannah. We can't."

"I'm afraid," Candenning offered, "you have no real choice."

Again, the little man whirled on the artist. For the briefest instant, it seemed that he might even do him bodily harm.

Hannah Pelzig laid her hand on her husband's arm. "He's an American, Jakob—an American."

"Not only that," Candenning said, "I'll be happy to buy you both a drink. If we are trapped in Oaxaca, we might just as well make the confinement palatable. Besides, I'm getting regular reports on the situation. You see, Herr Heinrich, I, too, must go north."

"Oh?" Again the eyes narrowed behind the spectacles.

"Yes. I have the unique misfortune of being recalled to military service."

"You?" Apparently the notion struck Pelzig as preposterous. "You are a soldier?"

"A reservist. Actually, I'm an illustrator."

"In the American army?"

"Of course. I really am an American."

Somehow the confession finally broke through the barrier of doubt the physicist had erected. For the first time since their meeting, Dr. Pelzig essayed a smile. He and his wife exchanged glances, apparently making a silent agreement if not to trust Candenning entirely, at least to tolerate him with a more cordial politeness. Almost at ease, the three turned toward the hotel's bar.

They remained there for almost a half hour during which the conversation, although apparently casual, was still somewhat defensive. Candenning was convinced that the man had lied about his name. There was something surreptitious about him which seemed contrary to his personality. He was like someone unused to crime who, for some inexplicable reason, had been forced to steal. He was also a man who was obviously used to thinking in terms of details, but was now apparently overwhelmed by some huge conglomerate totality.

His wife's sickness was a part of that totality, but above and beyond that, Candenning speculated, was some compulsive desire to do something or get somewhere very fast.

The Pelzigs in turn discovered that their companion was married but childless, that he had served in the Great War, and that he was drinking entirely too much. They also realized that he was invaluable. No matter what his faults, Charles Candenning was the only person they had met since docking in Vera Cruz who spoke both German and Spanish.

His third drink had just been placed before him when the hotel clerk entered the room and walked directly to Candenning.

"Buenas noticias, Señor."

"Oh?"

"Si. Las rejas se han reparado. El tren esta listo. Saldrá entre una hora."

"Gracias." He took another tug at his drink, then turned to the Pelzigs. "It appears," he said in German, "that I was wrong. The train is ready, Herr Heinrich." He drained his glass. "It leaves within the hour."

Karen Tait spent that morning in the Mercado, savoring the mingled aromas of flowers and fruits, luxuriating in the myriad colors of fabric, pottery, and other merchandise. Although every square foot seemed crammed with goods and vendors, the crowds were thinner than on the weekend. She was able to wander for blocks without undue jostling.

Because she knew it would be her last visit to Mexico for many years, she allowed herself the luxury of buying more than she could afford. In a matter of days, she would be in New York starting a new job as well as organizing her notes to finish her Master's thesis. The work would do her good. Certainly it would ease the agony of her past.

It would also clear her mind of the tall American who had insisted upon breakfast after Saturday's earthquake.

For two days he had been constantly on her mind, not as an actual part of her thoughts, but rather like a prowler lurking outside the window of consciousness. He was there. She knew it. Yet he was never clearly visible simply because she had refused to focus on him.

She hated the feeling—had made every effort to fight it. She had even gone out of her way to avoid meeting him again.

83

Since Saturday's breakfast, her behavior had been akin to blind, almost hysterical flight.

Now, away from the hotel, she finally tried to analyze her feelings. Certainly there was nothing threatening about Mr. Candenning. He had made no overt gesture or proposal. He had acted exactly like what he claimed to be—a married man on vacation, baffled and annoyed about his recall to active duty.

Still, since the moment he had pulled her into the hotel's doorway, Charles Candenning had been a specter. He *was* attractive. She couldn't deny it. And how long had she been in Mexico?

Ten months! Almost a full year of absolutely celibate dedication to research. In Ventosa, Salina Cruz and Juchitán she had subjugated her entire being to her work. She had been able to push all other thoughts—all other feelings—from her mind. She had almost forgotten the embezzlement and the divorce. She had stuffed herself into a protective sack and sewed herself in.

Now, with the request to begin at Vassar earlier than she had expected, with the change of pace offered by travel, combined with the train's unforeseen delay, some of her carefully stitched seams were straining, if not actually broken.

A complete stranger had pulled her into a doorway. For him, she was sure, the gesture was one of simple courtesy. Everyone knew doorways were the safest places during an earthquake.

But she wasn't a nun. She was a healthy woman who had denied herself for so long that she had lost her ability to be selective.

She was annoyed at the man. He may not have intended it, but he had awakened long-buried feelings. He might be married and he might be polite, but Charles Candenning *was* a threat.

She felt trapped by him. More than that, she was infuriated with herself.

She stopped in front of San Juan de Dios embedded in the very heart of the market. *You're acting like a bitch in heat*, she told herself. Then, aloud, directly to the closed, almost ugly church facade, "No, by God! Pull yourself together, Karen."

She took a deep breath, turned abruptly and, more like a

84

soldier on a forced march than a leisurely shopper, walked back to the hotel.

In the lobby, the clerk told her that the train was ready.

"And the gentleman?" *Damn! Why had she even asked?*

"He and the European couple have already gone."

"European couple?"

"They arrived after you left."

"Good," she said in English. "They'll keep him company." She turned again to the clerk. "I'll take the next train."

"With your permission," he said, "there may not be another. There have been rumors. Who knows what the president will do?"

"Damn!" she said. "Damn, damn, damn!"

The train was a great, wheezing dragon huffing impotently, apparently unsure of its appointed mission. Karen struggled her luggage aboard, then swung through the vestibule into the car. A few people were already scattered in the seats. The first one she saw was a small man sitting to her right.

Although he was dressed in a suit, the collar of his shirt was open. He had pulled the knot of his tie away from his neck. She noted casually that his hair was quite short and uncombed, then that he was staring at her with a complete lack of expression in his flat brown eyes.

"Bet you're American." His voice was not quite a drawl. It had something of a Scandinavian lilt to it.

She stopped, feeling somewhat like a bird being hypnotized by a snake. "Why, yes," she told him. "I am."

"So am I." He patted the seat beside him. "Been saving this just for you."

"Thanks, I—"

"Might as well sit with your own kind." His flat, somewhat reptilian stare was almost frightening.

"Really, I—"

"These *frijoles* can get mighty rancid on long trips."

"*Frijoles*?"

"Greasers . . . chili pickers . . . call 'em what you like."

"The passengers?" She felt personally insulted. "I call them people." She started to move along the aisle again, but before she could take her first full step, he reached over and grabbed her wrist.

"Come on, kid," he urged. "We Yanks should stick together. I'm just trying to be friendly." His grip was remarkably firm, his jaw pugnacious, and his eyes, despite the wide smile below them, quite unnerving.

"No!" With an effort, she pulled her arm free. Immediately, she regretted her abruptness. "I'm . . . I'm with friends." Again she started along the aisle.

"Suit yourself," she heard him say. "It's a free country . . . so they tell me."

At the far end of the car on the right, she noticed the middle-aged couple. The woman was quite frail and apparently sick. The man was obviously nervous. Behind his spectacles, his eyes darted back and forth as if, at any moment, he expected to be leapt upon by some horrid monster or power that would simply materialize from nothing.

Sitting with the couple, his back toward her, his blond hair meticulously combed, was the unmistakable form of Charles Candenning. Although she could only see his shoulders and the back of his head, the view was unsettling.

A little flurry of interest scampered through her, making her very conscious of her femininity. The realization made her almost viciously annoyed at herself.

She glanced around the car. On her left, about midway through, sat a lone young woman. She was staring very intently out the open window, a frown almost scarring her otherwise quite beautiful face.

Karen dragged her luggage to her. "Do you mind if I sit here?"

The woman continued looking out the window. She appeared quite tense, perhaps even afraid.

"Miss . . ."

She jerked her head as though pulled abruptly from a reverie. "Oh! I'm sorry. Please . . . Sit."

Karen placed her luggage on the overhead rack and introduced herself.

The younger woman, although polite, was obviously far more interested in the mundane activities taking place outside the train than in conversation.

At the terminal, visitors, vendors, and passengers were milling about as the train continued its meaningless huffings and wheezings. Nothing seemed even to be faintly out of the ordinary. The Oaxaca station could have been any of a thousand others in any part of Mexico.

Still, something of great importance, was obviously happening or about to happen out there, which was vital to the young woman. Her remarkably beautiful features were drawn into a tight-lipped scowl indicative of both hurt and annoyance. It was an expression of pique, perhaps even of rejection.

Suddenly she relaxed. She sighed, leaned back, closed her dark eyes, and allowed a tiny, very satisfied smile to play over her full lips. The expression was so worldly—so overtly sensual—that, in spite of herself, Karen turned around and looked out the window.

The station was still remarkably ordinary. The only thing vaguely unusual was that a young man in dark glasses was urging two little boys toward the train as he pushed a woman in a wheelchair. He was strikingly handsome and dressed more expensively than men usually are in southern Mexico, but other than that, the scene was quite commonplace.

She turned back and again inspected her traveling companion. The woman's eyes were still closed and the smile, although now almost imperceptible, was still quite smug on her lips. She was obviously very content, even satisfied.

Karen frowned. She had chosen, she decided, a rather strange traveling companion.

Abruptly, the train shuddered, wheezed, and groaned. With five very rapid puffs, almost like blows from an annoyed hammer, it jerked backward for several yards, then stopped and, like an athlete about to essay a particularly hazardous stunt, drew a deep, almost profound, breath.

Slowly, meticulously—a great inanimate thing about to discharge a vital function—it started inching its way from Oaxaca.

It was still moving at a very slow rate when she heard a cry from the station. A man in a cheap and rumpled suit stood there waving frantically and shouting inarticulate syllables, as though he thought the mechanized dragon would heed his bidding.

The train's speed increased. The man cried out once more, then dashed forward.

Karen lost sight of him as the train moved away from the station. Gradually, the movements of the train became more regular, more rhythmic and soothing. She closed her eyes and settled into her seat, expecting a completely uneventful journey north.

4
Guns

THEY MET IN Sanborn's near the recently renovated Palacio Iturbide. A monument to the rape of tradition, the completely Americanized drugstore catered to tourists, casual visitors, and the sort of people least interested in the history of the blue tiles or the legends of the ancient building. Here, it was quite unlikely that they would be recognized, let alone reported. Still, they were conspicuous, if only as an incongruous, contradictory pair.

The taller one appeared completely at ease and quite cosmopolitan. He was obviously of pure Caucasian stock. The other was almost fascinating in his resemblance to a mustached toad. He represented an hereditary potpourri of races from Spain, Phoenicia, and North Africa, mixed with those of a score of different Indian tribes. If any single bond linked them in any way, it was an innate ability to accept and use naked ruthlessness as one of life's necessities.

Nicholas Markoff was meticulously dressed as well as cloaked in mystery. He invariably seemed about to whisper of intimate connections with powerful people, or to lash some unfortunate lackey across the cheek with a pair of paper-thin kid gloves clenched in one patrician fist. In Mexico City that spring he was one of hundreds who were members of a group aptly called "coyotes."

In fact, Nicholas Markoff was a gentleman, not merely as a result of education, but by breeding and birth itself. He had, at the moment, no obvious means of support, yet had managed to keep himself moderately solvent by performing, from time to time, certain politically oriented chores. Although many of his intimate connections with those in power had been severed by the Bolshevik revolution of '17, he had managed to make certain new contacts in Mexico where, due to governmental fluctuations, the services of amoral gentlemen were frequently in demand by one faction or another.

The ex-colonel of Imperial Russian cavalry looked exactly like what he was—a professional soldier without a command—an aristocrat without a social order or, for that matter, a country. His suave charm and impeccably tailored clothes were completely out of place across the table from Juan Miguárdez. Indeed, he was only there as a matter of fiscal necessity. It was socially unfortunate, but the diminutive presidential secretary represented a connection which, although crude, had just outlined an opportunity which could form the cornerstone of a completely new existence.

Markoff fingered his coffee cup and looked across the bridge of his magnificently aristocratic nose with an expression of barely concealed disdain. He arrested a sigh with a slight smack of his thin lips. "It is gratifying, Señor Miguárdez, to feel necessary."

"You understand . . ." The little man darted his eyes right and left before looking at Markoff again. "You realize how delicate this situation is?"

For a brief moment Markoff had the impression that his companion might leap from his chair, as though from a lily pad. "Of course," he said. "That is precisely why your offer is so woefully inadequate."

"You've worked before . . ."

The Russian leaned back in his chair and looked very deliberately at Miguárdez for several annoying seconds. "I am, of course, a foreigner, but I am hardly an ostrich."

"It's just another assignment."

"With certain unique features, you will admit."

"I grant you, he's close to the president."

"He's like the man's brother."

"An exaggeration."

"And enormously popular with the people."

"Perhaps."

"Come now, Señor Secretary, with his death, half the women in Mexico and Guatemala will go into mourning."

"That's preposterous!"

Markoff could see he had gone too far. The smaller man was genuinely annoyed. He decided to press his cause more directly. "Perhaps not," he agreed. "But the fact is there's not another man in Mexico who can do this for you."

"With your permission, Señor, that's absurd."

"Oh?" Markoff cocked his leonine head to one side. His faint smile barely moved his lips. "Hire a Mexican then.

Even if he doesn't botch the job completely, there's a strong likelihood of capture.''

''Nonsense.''

''Just imagine what kind of furor *that* would bring. If not revolution again, at least the great Lázaro Cárdenas will be swaying dangerously on his pedestal. Heads would roll like spilled apples. Think of where your own would be.''

''Your humor is offensive.''

''It is not humor, I assure you. I said I was not an ostrich. I'm not a fool either. The shooting may have stopped momentarily, but this Cárdenas fellow is sitting on a powder keg. It's all very well to picture him as an idealistic patriot of the highest order, but I wasn't born Friday afternoon. The fact is, he's just another tyrant—benign, I grant, but still a tyrant—and smart enough to know that power is a tenuous thing. It must be guarded jealously.''

''The revolution is finished. You know that. General Calles is in exile. The government is stable.''

Markoff smiled. ''The winds blow many ways in your country. Don't forget, I read the Spanish, not the English, newspapers. You're still killing priests on sight. The Jesuits might just as well be a fifth column movement. As for the rest of society, no one ever knows where anyone else stands politically. You can't even risk talking to a Mexican about this. He might just take your money and run right to Cárdenas himself. After all, he has offered to hear all people personally.''

''I screen the petitioners.''

''Not entirely, and you know it. Cárdenas is a suspicious man. He likes to get to the truth of everything.''

''It hardly matters. He's going out of town. What really matters is your own position.''

''I have already proven myself.''

''Only as far as a peso will carry you.''

''Ultimately, there is no other transportation. Gold is, after all, the supreme authority.''

''You know, Colonel Markoff, I have certain power. You could find yourself in a great deal of trouble.''

''Nonsense.'' The Russian almost chuckled. ''Even you wouldn't cut off the hand that wipes your ass.''

''You're not indispensible.''

''No one is indispensible.'' Markoff took another sip of his coffee. Immediately he was sorry. In the restaurant-drugstore of the brothers Sanborn, which profaned an artistic palace, everything tasted the same. Chocolate smelled like soda water, soda water smelled like chocolate, and the coffee was merely unpleasant.

"There are Americans," Miguárdez offered.

"Ludicrous! Cárdenas has already pressed them about as far as they'll go. If Roosevelt wasn't such a pacifistic coward, you wouldn't have a country at all. Go—hire an American. Let Cárdenas find out and he really will go too far. General Pershing may be one thing but, as I recall, the last time the Americans were *really* annoyed, you lost a few acres."

"They would never—"

"On the political chessboard, all moves are possible. You of all people should know that. You should also know that is precisely why I require a substantially larger retainer than usual."

Miguárdez blinked his huge eyes but remained silent.

When the Russian spoke, his voice was absolutely level. He might have been doing no more than mentioning the time of day. "Half a million pesos."

"Half a million!"

"There's always the likelihood of being caught."

"And, if you are?"

"My nationality is no threat. After all, Imperial Russia—"

"You'll talk."

"I consider myself a professional. A professional is loyal to his clients."

"Half a million pesos is an enormous sum."

"Not for one as highly placed as you, Señor Secretary."

"Still . . ."

The Russian shrugged. "Either you want this man eliminated or you don't. After all, he does seem to pose a certain threat to Mexico and . . ." He leaned over the table in a burlesque of conspiracy. "He is *very* close to the president. Who can tell what kind of damage a man like that might do, both politically and . . ." He lowered his voice almost to a whisper. "Think of it, Señor Secretary, personally?"

Again Miguárdez blinked. Markoff could see that he had hit home. The Mexican sighed. "There is a possibility," he said, "only a possibility, mind you, that I can get the money, but with a matter of this importance . . ."

"And when the deed is done, I shall need another half million."

"A million pesos!"

"And safe conduct."

"A million pesos!"

"Oh, don't be so melodramatic. Five—even ten million—what's the difference? You don't give any more of a damn for Mexico than I do. The whole stinking country is just a tool to lever your own ambition. And now with Cárdenas about to leave the capital on one of his little cross-country jaunts, you'll have a perfect opportunity. This man's a thorn in your side. He's influential. More than that, the ladies love him. Everyone knows that. You'll get the money because it's a personal matter. You'd have done it long ago if you'd only had an excuse."

Miguárdez blinked again. He seemed incapable of speech.

"Come, Señor Secretary, be honest with yourself. Of course I'll kill him. What difference the reason—defection, treason, overly active virility . . ."

"All right! Enough!"

"Good." The Russian leaned back and fingered his coffee cup again. "You say he's traveling south?"

Miguárdez regained his outward composure with some difficulty. "He was," he said at length. "I'm having him watched—not followed, mind you—just reported on from time to time. Right now, he's on a train traveling north from Oaxaca."

"North?"

"He was planning it all along. I'm sure of it. He only went south to make things look like he was following the presidential order. The point is, he's headed for Texas. I'm convinced he intends either to join General Calles there or travel west and rendezvous in San Diego."

"But he has to come back here to the capital?"

"Exactly."

"You want him killed here?"

"That would be easiest."

The Russian shrugged. "One place is as good as another. The door to eternity can open anywhere."

"Incidentally, he's traveling with his wife and children."

"You want them killed as well?"

"I leave that entirely to you."

The Russian pushed his chair back. He rose and, the picture of ultimate aristocratic arrogance, looked down to Juan Miguárdez. "I shall be ready as soon as I receive my retainer. If our man is on the train now, he should arrive quite soon.''

Miguárdez sighed heavily and pushed his own chair back. ''I'll have the money for you this afternoon.''

''Good.'' Markoff glanced from the Mexican to the table, then back again. The smile on his thin lips was condescending but somehow ingratiating as well. When he spoke, he might have been speaking to a beautiful woman instead of the man who had just hired him as an assassin. ''You will take care of the check?''

He didn't wait for a reply. As though on parade and still in the uniform of a colonel in his Tsar's service, Nicholas Markoff turned and left.

Some claimed God was an Englishman. Margaret Whitley agreed—in part. The Almighty's nationality could not, of course, be disputed, but they were wrong about Her gender.

As she stepped from the tub and wrapped herself in the luxurious softness of a huge towel, Margaret was not, however, pondering things spiritual. Her thoughts were on purely temporal matters, which she had finally decided to subdue to her own purposes.

As she considered the exact tactics she would employ, she finished drying herself, tossed the towel aside, and turned to inspect her naked form in the bathroom's floor-length mirror. Except for three abdominal scars, the permanent reminders of a ruptured appendix and subsequent cohesions at age nine, she was completely satisfied—even compelled to agree that she had indeed been created exactly in the voluptuous image of her English goddess.

Margaret Whitley possessed a body which defied the rules of proportion. No single part conformed to any other as it was supposed to in a sketching class. Her legs were too long, her hips too wide, her waist too narrow, and her breasts too large. Still, Amedeo Modigliani might well have given up drink to sculpt her face and neck, and Charles Gibson undoubtedly would have agreed that she was the living embodiment of his ideal woman, for it was in the totality of her anatomy that her form became so exceptional. Margaret Whitley had been blessed with a body uniquely suited to both the most delicate nuances and wildest extravagances of the world's oldest profession.

She had also been blessed with sufficient intelligence to

realize that the best whore does not sell her valuables piece-meal, but rather allies herself to that one man who can benefit her most completely at the moment. Currently, that man was Neil Oberon, a young American, in whose opulent Mexico City apartment she had been living for some months. Her intent had, upon moving there, involved the hope of marriage which, in turn, would lead to cinematic stardom in the United States. Unfortunately, her lover had not proposed and, because of her own somewhat tenuous position, she had not pressed the issue.

Beautiful, intelligent, and talented, Margaret Whitley earnestly believed that she was English. To her sorrow and sometimes fury, the United States did not. This difference of opinion made her chances of reaching Hollywood infinitesimally small.

The sun never set on the British empire. Unfortunately, it did set on the Cape of Good Hope and, in that particular twilight, Margaret Whitley's dream had been obscured. Despite the policies of Prime Minister Hertzog, and despite parliamentary domination by an English minority, the population of the Union of South Africa was still predominantly Asiatic and Negroid.

As a democratic nation, the United States welcomed immigrants. American hospitality and fair play in the matter had been spelled out in the New Quota Act of 1924. It was unfortunate perhaps that this law, reinforced by Presidential Proclamation Number 2048 of 1933, seriously affected individuals emigrating from "colored" areas.

Although she had every genetic and logical right to consider herself English, Margaret Whitley had, in fact, been born in Capetown. Statistically, therefore, she was directly comparable to any Bantu, Kaffir, or Zulu. In 1937 the United States allowed only one hundred immigrants from the Union of South Africa. Waiting lists were long. Margaret had not even bothered to place her name on one.

As one raised to endorse the necessity for racial separation and white supremacy, Margaret understood the logic behind the new Quota Act. Purely on an emotional level, however, she considered it distinctly unfair. The situation was one which she was now determined to change.

She slipped her slender arms into the caressing softness of a silken kimono—a gift from a previous lover who had been instrumental in getting her several high-paying singing engagements—looped the sash casually around her waist and, pausing only for a final inspection of her cinnamon hair and exquisite form, left the bathroom.

The cablegram was on the night table where she had left it. She had noticed it two days before in Neil's wastebasket, and an inexplicable urge had compelled her to pick it out and read it. At the time she had not quite understood the message. Still, something visceral had whispered that somehow it was vital.

She lifted a cigarette from an open silver case beside the cablegram, lit it, and again inspected the single sheet of paper as she had numerous times before. The terse Spanish translated simply and directly.

SITUATION EXTREME STOP MUST HAVE
MERCHANDISE STOP LAST REQUEST
M

She had known for some time that her paramour was involved in an import-export venture, but it wasn't until the day before that she realized the exact nature of his business, as well as the seriousness of his present situation. A stranger had come to the apartment. Apparently neither he nor Oberon had realized Margaret was there. She had not intended to eavesdrop. It had just happened.

Neil wanted the man to go to Durango and contact General Almidero, *El Escorpión*. He himself would follow later. He had to supply weapons to a Spaniard named Móndez. Apparently the Scorpion owed him a favor. Neil intended to travel north to collect payment.

Everyone in Mexico knew *El Escorpión*. Posing as a counterrevolutionary, Marcos Almidero had terrorized Durango and Chihuahua since before the Calles Administration. He led the most brutal and feared private army since the heyday of Pancho Villa. Móndez was clearly the "M" who had signed the cablegram.

Neil Oberon was in trouble. That was obvious. Apparently, the only way he could clear the matter was to ally himself to an outlaw in order to get guns from the United States to Móndez in Spain.

Another woman might have felt a certain sympathy toward her lover's plight. Margaret Whitley, however, saw Oberon's misfortune as distinctly to her own advantage. She would be twenty-eight in another month. Time was running against the current of her ambition.

She savored the cigarette, sucking deeply then exhaling in long, almost melodramatic jets across the expensively furnished room. Neil Oberon was planning to cross the American border. When he did, she intended to be with him as his wife. He could return to Mexico if he liked. That was of no concern to her. Once she was accepted as a citizen of the United States, a divorce could be easily arranged.

She took one last pull of the cigarette and was just grinding it out when she heard the door of the apartment open. She exhaled, took a clean breath and, filling her voice with maximum sensuality, called, "That you, darling?"

Neil Oberon was, as ever, meticulously dressed, combed, and manicured. At a distance, he had frequently been confused with the actor Leslie Howard. In fact, he was somewhat shorter than the Englishman and his hair was quite a bit darker. More important perhaps, his features were at once less kind and less strong. As he closed the door and crossed the huge living room, he was obviously preoccupied almost to the point of nervousness. He slipped out of his suit coat, tossed it on the ottoman and, in a mock attempt at casual banter, called to the bedroom, "Who were you expecting?"

"Oh, darling!" Margaret came into the room, crossed to where he stood, and entwined her arms around his neck. She made sure he could feel the full warm pressure of her breasts on his chest. "You know I love you."

He kissed her absently, then untwined her arms. "Sure," he said, "for the moment." There was no sarcasm in his tone. It was simply a statement of honest belief. He turned from her and walked to the bar. There he poured himself a liberal tumbler of Berreteaga and splashed a dash of soda on top of it.

She waited a moment before moving to him and laying one hand on his shoulder. "What's the matter, darling?" she purred.

"Nothing," he lied. "Just some business problems."

Her hazel eyes were quite level and disarming. "I know about the cablegram from Móndez."

"What?"

"And the message to Almidero."

"Don't be silly."

"You're going north, aren't you?"

96

He gulped at his drink. "Maybe." He sounded like a sulking child.

"And you were thinking of leaving me."

He fumbled a cigarette from the open pack on the bar and lit it. "All right, Maggi, I'll level with you. I've had some—well—business problems. Nothing really earthshaking, mind you, but problems just the same. I just have to leave the city for a few days, that's all."

"You're going to the United States, aren't you?"

"Don't be silly."

"Well, I want to get married."

"Married? What brought that on?"

"Oh, my darling, I do hate blackmail so."

He sipped his brandy again and frowned at her. "What the hell *are* you talking about?"

"You're going to the United States and I'm going with you as Mrs. Neil Oberon—signed, sealed, and legal."

"Now wait a minute—"

"Otherwise, my dearest, I'm afraid the American authorities in San Antonio will find out about you and your friend the Scorpion and your wonderful plan to steal their rifles."

As he stared at her, his expression was at first incredulous, then slowly changed to one of open admiration. Finally his features relaxed completely, and he moved his mouth in a smile of infinite charm. "All right," he chuckled, "you win."

"You'll do it?"

"Not only that," he told her, "I'd do you one better. After I talk with Almidero, we'll get you a visitor's permit and I'll even marry you on the American side. Then you'll really get what you want. What do you think about *that*?"

"Oh, darling!" She literally leapt into his arms and entwined herself around him. At last she was on her way to Hollywood, but the truly amazing part of it all was that it hadn't been difficult at all! In fact, it had been ever so much easier than she could have possibly imagined.

As she squirmed her breasts and abdomen against him, Margaret Whitley could not see her lover's face. Indeed, if she had, she probably would have thought nothing amiss in Oberon's expression. He was what a later generation would call "cool"—a professional confidence man of the highest echelon. Charming, handsome, and disarming, Neil Oberon had outlied and outcheated some of the very best.

97

This particular minor victory, in postponing a marriage which would never take place, was almost incidental to him. He was, however, subtly pleased by Margaret's desire to go north with him. She might not be able to help him directly with Móndez in Valencia, but Marcos Almidero had, he knew, a weakness for women. It was quite possible that the bartering strength embodied in one very beautiful, cinnamon-haired blonde might just make the difference between success and failure or, more importantly, between his own life and death.

The raid had been easy. The train's military escort only offered a token resistance. The crew was quite respectful of *El Escorpión*'s armed efficiency. The cars had all been stripped of valuables within less than five minutes. The depot and storage warehouse took barely a quarter of an hour more. Now the pack horses and wagons were loaded.

Passengers, soldiers, and crew huddled in terror. They had been separated into two groups. The more attractive, younger women stood near the wagons, many sobbing openly, or crying out to the Holy Mother, or a favored saint. The others, less fit for the pleasures of sexual abandon, remained near the train. They stood in quiet, near catatonic shock, refusing to understand what the next few minutes would bring.

The Scorpion inspected the scene from the doorway of the telegraph office. Marcos Almidero was a large man in his late thirties who enjoyed the luxuries of plentiful food and drink. Despite his inclination toward dissipation, he was still in outwardly good physical condition, due undoubtedly to days spent almost entirely in the saddle. Only the beginning of a debauched paunch was evident above his gun belt. Only the yellowing of his eyes hinted at the somewhat less than perfect condition of his liver.

" *'Sta Sta bueno.'* " He spoke absently to the various elements of the panorama before him. Then he addressed the man to his right. "Load the women into the wagons," he said. "Kill the rest."

He turned to look inside the small building which served as a telegraph-relaying point. The only occupant was a young man wearing an open-collared white shirt. He sat at a paper-cluttered desk on which rested a telegraph key and a mug wherein several pencils stood at uncertain attention. He stared with wide, terror-filled eyes at the Scorpion.

The bandit looked from the young man's ashen face to the telegraph key, then turned again to call outside. "A moment."

His second in command stopped.

"Cut the wires as well." The Scorpion returned inside. There, very deliberately, he drew the American-made .45-caliber revolver from its holster and cocked the hammer with his thumb.

"No!" the young man cried. "A favor! Mother of—"

The first shot smashed into him just below the Adam's apple. The impact of the bullet made him leap from the chair as it pulverized three of his cervical vertebrae and splashed blood and flesh on his previously immaculate shirt front and the wall behind him.

He died instantly, but before he fell, the Scorpion shot him again, this time lower in the body. The second bullet jerked him sideways. As he fell to the floor, his dead left arm dragged across the desk and pulled a scrap of paper with it.

The single sheet fluttered like a glider out of control to the dirty floor. It settled just beside the pool of blood oozing from the young man's chest and neck.

Outside, the shots and screams—the cries of physical and emotional agony—lasted only a few moments longer. The women destined for rape were herded into the wagons. Some still begged for the Virgin's intervention. Most covered their eyes and breasts in stunned resignation to the dictates of a vicious Fate.

El Escorpión inspected the young man he had just killed. He was satisfied. He left the building without looking at the sheet of paper on the floor. It was only a telegram which would never be relayed. It had come from Oaxaca and was addressed to a man named Mannas in Fort Bliss north of the border.

"TAKING NEXT TRAIN," it said. It was signed "CANDENNING, C.L., 1ST LT."

Satisfied with a day's work well done, *El Escorpión* stepped into the sunlight of Durango and mounted his horse.

Almost 6,000 miles to the east, another cablegram was, in fact, being relayed. It had originated in Valencia and would ultimately reach a man named Kemp in Mexico City.

"FIND OBERON," it said. "ELIMINATE."

It was signed only with the initial "M."

Book III

PUEBLA

1
Treasure

ALTHOUGH ONLY ONE very pungent and truculent goat was standing, the car was filled with passengers and parcels. Some of the latter had been placed on the overhead luggage racks, but most of the parcels littered the narrow aisle, making passage perilous if not potentially lethal.

Domingo Portes stood at the extreme rear of the car sucking his lungs full of fetid air, which combined the stenches of Lysol, burning tobacco, stale food and hot, unwashed bodies. He squinted through a heavy cloud of humid cigar and cigarette smoke to study the passengers seated before him.

Since leaving Tuxtla Gutiérrez, the Jesuit had followed both honest reports and rumors about a foreigner and his cargo. He had traveled through Juchitán and over the Rio Tehuanatepec, through El Camaron and past Totolapan, pursuing stories of a truck hauling several wooden crates. The reports had finally led him to the railhead at Oaxaca. There he had talked to the station master.

"Yes," the official had told him, "a foreigner did pay to have some boxes loaded aboard the northbound train."

Portes had pressed for details, but the station master had only shrugged. "A foreigner . . . How can I say? They are all the same—arrogant, willing to pay too much for everything."

Portes had been about to ask more specific questions, but had been interrupted by a great sigh from the train which had been wheezing outside. Suddenly it jerked backward as though retreating from several heavy blows to the front of its engine. It stopped as suddenly as it had started, then began a slow, almost agonized forward acceleration.

The train, he realized, might contain nothing of value. It could be no more than a straw of flotsam in a sea of rumors and speculations. Then again, it could in fact be carrying the treasure of Bishop Las Casas. He couldn't risk the luxury of doubt or the time necessary for more questions.

Portes had rushed outside and cried out, hoping to attract the attention of the engineer, but his screams had been drowned by the puffs and wheezes of the struggling train.

In desperate frustration, he had finally started to run the train down. The effort had proved almost futile. Although apparently moving quite slowly, the train had already placed considerable distance between itself and the sprinter and was gaining momentum. Portes, although hardly an old man, was still not in the physical trim he had enjoyed while fighting for the *Cristeros* a decade before. Also, the leg wound he had received in the revolt of '27 greatly reduced the speed which he otherwise might have attained.

Still, he had forced himself to a supreme effort of mind and body by compelling every sinew and tendon—every nerve and centimeter of muscle fiber—beyond even maximum potential. With a near maniacal intensity, he had literally willed a fanaticism into his aching legs, making them pump faster and stretch longer than their own extreme capabilities.

Finally, in a last Herculean surge of energy, he had made an almost suicidal leap from beside the tracks and had managed to clutch the rear car—at first with no more than his fingertips, then with a grip sufficiently strong to pull himself aboard.

For some time he stood in a state of utter exhaustion, trying to fill his aching lungs with air that was seemingly devoid of oxygen. His left leg and arm hurt from old wounds. His right side might have been in the grip of a huge and unrelenting dog, and his heart hammered inside his rib cage with a force nearly sufficient to break through.

Exhausted almost to the point of dementia, Domingo Portes felt like a complete fool. Even if the gold and the thief were on the train, his search would be difficult at best. He knew nothing about the man he sought other than that he was a foreigner who smoked. In Tuxtla, he had been told that the man's partner was not an American. Chances were, then, that the man himself was probably European. It was precious little information on which to base any sort of apprehension.

As he made his way slowly through the train, he scanned each car in search of both a foreign face and an empty seat. In the third car he stopped. He was still panting heavily and now feeling very frustrated and infuriated—both with himself and his mission.

Immediately to his left, next to a woman casually breast-feeding a naked infant, sat a tall blond man of about forty. He was smoking a cigarette and drinking from a bottle of Moctezuma beer as he talked to the couple before him. Except for the nursing mother, they were all obviously foreigners. They were speaking German or Dutch or one of the Scandinavian tongues.

He started to inch his way along the cluttered aisle. As he did so, he glanced this way and that to study the other passengers. Most were local Indians riding the three or four miles from one village to another to visit friends or sell their wares. About halfway down, however, he saw a young woman with strawberry hair and serious blue eyes. He also noticed her stunningly beautiful companion and felt a slight sense of disturbance. There was something hauntingly familiar about her. He was sure he had seen, perhaps even met, her before. He did not, however, make the mental effort necessary to remember where, for almost at the far end of the car, he spied a man sitting next to what appeared to be an unoccupied seat.

Portes made his way over spittoons and parcels, sleeping animals and sandaled feet extended into the aisle until he reached the empty seat. Briefly, he inspected the man next to the open window. He was round-faced and shorter than average, dressed in what appeared to be a new suit. He was calmly smoking a cigarette and looking out toward the almost grim mountains in the distance.

He could be another foreigner, Portes speculated, but it would be impossible to tell without hearing him speak. He sat down.

Apparently jarred from some minor reverie by the pressure of Portes' weight next to him, the stranger turned from the window. He waved his cigarette in a small circle. "Hope you don't mind?" he said. The Spanish was good, but the accent was definitely American.

"Not at all." Portes studied his traveling companion. The little man had a disarming smile, but there was something very hard and inflexible in his eyes.

"Scofield's the name." He extended a surprisingly large right hand with very thick fingers.

"Domingo Portes." He took the offered hand. "You're a visitor to Mexico?"

"Merchant," Scofield said. "I come down here maybe twice a year. Business, y'know."

"Oh?"

"Yeah. Maybe a week or so at a time, no more." He snapped the remains of his cigarette out the window where a single, heavily loaded burro, the epitome of cynicism, stared at the smoldering butt until the train passed.

Portes leaned back against the seat. He would have to be absolutely sure before making any move. Were he to arouse suspicion in the real thief, his man might escape again. Conversely, if the wrong man were accosted, he might go directly to the secular authorities. Either way, the gold would be lost and he himself would undoubtedly be exposed. Despite the supposed leniency and toleration of the Cárdenas Administration, the likelihood of facing a firing squad was almost a certainty.

Again he looked down the jerking, swaying length of railroad car and again was arrested by a certain uneasiness when, for an instant, his eyes met those of the woman he had noticed earlier. She was one of the most striking, sensuously beautiful women he had ever seen. Embarrassed, he turned to his traveling companion. "You're from the United States, then?"

"Yeah."

"You know," Portes lied, "I've always wanted to travel to the United States. I hear it's a very wealthy country."

"You do?"

"Oh, I know the streets are not actually paved with gold."

Scofield chuckled. "Most of them are not paved with much of anything right now. Depression, y'know."

Abruptly, the train jerked to a stop. Almost half a minute went by before a hand car passed on the double track opposite the two men. Another several seconds passed before the engine gave a great wheeze of satisfaction and jerked forward again.

Domingo Portes looked up the aisle and again rested his eyes on the woman. This time she did not look up. He was able to remain unembarrassed and analytical. She was, somehow, a contradiction. Although dressed in Indian costume, she was quite obviously not a member of any of the local tribes. Indeed, her features, although dark, were almost purely Latin. Portes knew he had seen her before and was quite upset with his own inability to remember where or when.

He turned back to Scofield. "They tell me your President Roosevelt is doing amazing things for the economy."

Scofield stared at Portes. The hard thing in his eyes seemed, if possible, even more bitter than before.

"Franklin Roosevelt," he said, "*es un* pain in the ass *grande*."

"Pain in the ass?" Portes had never heard the expression.

"That son of a bitch has already done more to destroy the United States than a thousand Hoovers could do in a thousand years. Pain in the ass, I say. Him and his whole New God Damned Deal."

Regretting that he had inadvertently stepped on a political sore toe, Portes once more looked up the aisle.

Although the young woman was talking to her red-headed companion in the opposite seat, her thoughts were quite obviously elsewhere. Her eyes kept darting one way and then another in what seemed now to be no more than nervousness while then very serious embarrassment. She seemed at once humiliated as well as thoroughly afraid. She would speak a few words, then abruptly look out the window, then, just as suddenly, glance down the aisle to the car forward.

As he studied her, Portes suddenly realized what had disturbed him about her in the first place. It wasn't her striking beauty, although such ravishing good looks were certainly not common. It wasn't even the contradiction posed by her physiognomy and costume. Rather, it was the fact that she was traveling without the large number of parcels and wares usually brought on trains by Indian women. Further, she was traveling with a foreign woman and—he noticed it now for the first time—she was wearing around her neck, not the usual Indian jewelry, but a cross.

As Domingo Portes quietly pondered the mystery of the woman, she turned from her red-headed companion, rose, and started to negotiate her way down the aisle toward the rear of the train. Portes was immediately suspicious. The fact that she had been traveling with a foreigner, that she was dressed in a contradictory manner, and was behaving very suspiciously all told him that somehow she had been connected with the robbery in San Cristóbal. He was almost positive that the two women could very well be the wives or concubines of the thieves.

Entirely forgetting his companion's bitterness toward Franklin Roosevelt and the New Deal policies in effect far to the north, Portes rose and again started along the cluttered aisle, this time in pursuit of the woman.

Despite trying to muster a yogi's determined fatalism, Karen Tait had found it impossible to sleep. The train slowed, then accelerated. It jerked and rolled and stopped for anything larger than a chicken. The bumpy, irregular movements made any attempt at relaxation absolutely impossible.

Beside her, a man with a sombrero over his face snored softly. Another man in the opposite seat chewed tobacco, a vacuous expression in his dull eyes. Occasionally he would spit in the aisle, each time missing the cuspidor there.

Karen had exchanged a few words with the woman sitting opposite her, but her companion had obviously been more concerned with matters other than conversation. She seemed quite nervous and troubled.

When the train had stopped to allow the handcar to pass, Karen had looked out to inspect the scenery. Just beyond the tracks was a clay bank. Two little boys were digging there. At first, they looked like well-fed children who were merely playing. Then she saw them eating great wads of dirt—a desperate method to relieve the agony of worms.

She turned away as the train jerked forward again. She started to say something but held her tongue. Mexico was an ancient land. Some things would never change.

The woman opposite glanced from the open window to the next car forward, then back again. Finally, she rose, stepped over the tobacco chewer and started to make her way toward the rear of the train.

Karen wondered if she might need some help or perhaps just feminine companionship. She seemed so upset and, yes—lost. She considered following her to offer what little assistance she could, but decided not to interfere. She settled back just as the man who had chased the train stumbled up the littered aisle.

She was looking out the window in a mood of near hypnotic somnambulance when an unpleasantly familiar voice drew her attention back to the car.

"Hi, kid."

She turned to see the short man who had first accosted her when she boarded the train. He had settled into the seat vacated by the young woman and was staring at her with his peculiarly flat, expressionless eyes.

"I saw the other dame leave." He was smiling. "Thought we could get acquainted. Birds of a feather, y'know, should stick together. 'Specially in Mexico. No telling what could happen to a pretty girl in a place like this."

"I'm sure I can take care of myself." She tried to control the edge that had crept into her voice.

"Oh, I'll bet you can, kid. I'm just trying to be friendly, that's all."

The train slowed and she turned away from him. Outside, it seemed that the entire population of the next village had assembled along the sides of the tracks. Scores of women towed their naked children to see the train. Others held infant sons aloft, apparently eager to show their masculinity to the passengers. People were selling everything imaginable—food, lottery tickets, cigars, baskets.

One little boy rushed across the southbound tracks and trotted beside her window waving a small, two-headed statue in one hand and what looked like a stone phallus in the other.

"Very old, Señorita. Dug from the ruins. Only fifty *centavos*!"

Even before the train stopped with a final sigh, the car had become a turmoil of jostling humanity. Boys from the village skipped easily along the crowded aisle offering their services as luggage guards to those who wanted to go outside. People moved to get on and off, others hawked their wares, and one young man, aged approximately ten, stood at the extreme rear, chanting a doleful ballad in a very sad alto.

"The name's Scofield," the little man said above the din. "Bill Scofield."

Karen glanced at him, then looked across the aisle to where a newly arrived passenger was hanging a brace of birds by their necks. He seemed unconcerned that occasional drops of blood fell on the shoulder of the woman sleeping below them.

"What's yours?"

She turned back to face him. "What?"

"Your name?"

Through the mass of people jostling this way and that in the crowded aisle, she managed to get an occasional glimpse of the middle-aged European couple and Charles Candenning's back at the very rear of the car. Beside the tall American, an Indian woman suckling a child rose and started to leave.

At that instant, Karen was suddenly aware of how thoroughly annoying Bill Scofield was. There was nothing about the man or his behavior which she could isolate, except perhaps his air of almost arrogant presumption and the frighteningly cold depthlessness in his eyes. Still, she felt decidedly uncomfortable with him. It was almost as though his presence actually did constitute a very real and serious danger.

As though Scofield was, in fact, a vicious enemy and Candenning her only possible ally, she fairly leapt up, stepped over the man still snoring beside her, and struggled through the teeming aisle to the rear of the car.

There she leaned over the recently vacated seat and spoke to Candenning. "Do you mind?"

He turned from the window and inspected her with a very calm and, she thought, kind expression that was such a contrast to the flat, almost saurian stare she had just left. His smile was quite genuine. "I'd be delighted," he said. "Absolutely delighted."

An annoying, warm shiver scurried through her lower torso. Again, she was aware of how very attractive he was and again felt ashamed of herself for noticing it. She was also stabbed by a certain regret for her rudeness to Scofield. She had been presumptuous and brazen and thoroughly unfeminine.

Feeling like the gawky, inept school girl she had once been, she sat down. Away from the indefinable annoyance of Bill Scofield, she now felt only a deep sense of embarrassment at having presumed to intrude. She was afraid that even her heavy tan might be insufficient to mask the flush of blood which had rushed to her cheeks.

If he was at all aware of her feelings, Charles Candenning gave no sign. The personification of social grace, he indicated the couple sitting opposite her. "Miss Tait . . ." he was at once absolutely at ease, yet somehow formal as well. "I'd like you to meet Herr Heinrich and his wife. Unfortunately they don't speak English."

Karen nodded meekly as Candenning addressed the Pelzigs. "*Herr Heinrich, Frau Heinrich, das ist Fraulein Tait. Sie ist Amerikaner auch.*"

The Pelzigs nodded.

Karen tried to essay a smile, but felt numb—embarrassed beyond words. It was with an actual sense of relief that she endured the first forward jerk of the train, even though it snapped her neck and almost knocked several standing passengers from their feet.

In the struggling mass of people cluttering the train and clogging the station, Domingo Portes had lost sight of the woman he was following. With the first, almost brutal, jerk of acceleration, he had thought that perhaps she had slipped away through the crowds. Still, he had forced his way backward sufficiently so that by the time the train was moving normally again, he had made his way into the last car.

She was standing at the extreme rear, her back toward him, looking out to the receding tracks. He could not see her face or the expression it bore. He didn't need to. Her posture alone spoke of total hopelessness. Each railroad tie, which appeared to shrink as it flew into the distance, might have been an unsaid bead in a ghostly rosary—a lost month of youth's abandon never to be lived again.

He was not quite sure how to approach her or what to say. Still, he kept moving closer, swaying this way and that through the car until he stood directly behind her.

He paused, took a breath, then tapped her on the shoulder. "Good day."

She gave a startled gasp as she turned.

Again, he was actually awed by the startling beauty of her features. Now, however, it was countered by sorrow in her eyes and the drawn line of her otherwise sensuous mouth. In her total expression, he saw something beyond mere melancholy. It was, in fact, something quite close to terror.

"I know this sounds foolish," he began. "Quite presumptuous, in fact. But I'm sure we have met before."

She smiled. It was no more than a half-lifting of her mouth to acknowledge his remark. "I think not."

"No," he countered. "I'm sure of it."

Then he knew. He had not in fact met her, yet had seen her many times.

"Of course," he said. "You're the actress—Teresa Inez!"

Had she acknowledged or denied the fact, Domingo Portes might have been better prepared than he was for what happened.

She simply turned away from him and again looked over the receding ribbon of track. Huge tears filled her eyes, swelled to great puddles there, then flowed in shining rivers down her cheeks. Her body shuddered slightly as she sobbed, but she made no sound.

It was so completely unexpected that Portes could not even react to it. He was so stunned, so emotionally and socially impotent, that he did the only thing he was capable of doing. He waited beside her, neither speaking nor gesturing in any way, until she cried herself dry.

She took a deep breath, sniffed almost indelicately, and then turned to face him. "Please . . ." Still shining with spent tears, her eyes were impossibly large, very black, and overwhelmingly beautiful. "Please leave me alone."

Portes did not consider the danger. He merely knew that he was facing a human being in trouble, and it might be within his power to help her. "You wear a cross," he said. "You are a Christian."

She nodded.

"These are troubled times for the faithful."

"Please . . ." she said again.

"Perhaps I can help." He glanced toward the front of the train. They were alone. "My name is Domingo Portes. I'm a Jesuit—a priest."

"A priest!"

"For a favor," he cautioned. "Not so loud, my child."

"I'm sorry. I never thought." She seemed quite pensive for a moment, then looked up to him. "Oh, Father," she said. "Please help me."

Now he thought again of the treasure and the chance that she might be in some way involved with the thieves. "I cannot help you—" He looked at her directly. "—unless I know your trouble." He reached out and placed both his palms on her shoulders. Holding her at arm's length, he stared at her as though trying to fathom her very soul. "Have you been involved in some—crime?"

She lifted her chin, then let it drop. She stared at the train's floor for a long moment before raising her head again. "Crime?" This time he saw total resignation in her features. "Crimes without number, Father." She gasped a faint, very sarcastic chuckle. "For me to wear this . . ." She lifted the cross from her bosom. "It's a miracle God doesn't strike me dead on the spot."

He still held her shoulders. "God is not so cruel, child."

"He thought we could hide—that no one would suspect."

"He?"

"You won't believe me, Father. You can't help."

111

"What crime, child? Have you stolen something?"

She nodded.

"Something of value"

"The greatest."

"And where?"

"I'm pregnant, Father."

"Pregnant?" He was baffled. What could an unborn child have to do with the treasure of Las Casas?

"I'm not married. Isn't that crime enough? To steal another woman's husband then to carry his bastard child?"

His bewilderment now mingled with a certain sympathetic embarrassment. She was telling him anything but what he had hoped for or expected.

"Don't you see, Father? I'm pregnant—running away. But we'll get caught. I know it. They'll kill him."

"Kill? Who?"

"Jesús."

"Jesús!" Surely, he now thought, the woman was completely mad.

For the first time her fear and sorrow vanished and she smiled. "Oh, no," she chuckled. "Not Jesús. Not the real Jesús. My Jesús. Jesús Guerrero."

"The politician?"

She nodded. "We're leaving Mexico together."

"Together?"

"They'll find out, I know. They'll kill him, Father. And I . . . the child. Oh, please, Father, in the name of God, help me! Forgive me!"

The treasure of Las Casas—millions upon millions of pesos worth of pre-Columbian and ecclesiastical artifacts—might, at that moment, have been no more than the dusty Zuni pueblos once mistaken for the seven cities of Cibola. Domingo Portes still held the woman by the shoulders but was himself gripped by a very deep and sincere human compassion. "Of course," he said. "I'll do what I can."

Again tears filled her exquisite eyes as her single sob was countered by a wide smile of gratitude. She stepped forward, embraced him, and pressed her wet cheek to his chest.

Through the fabric of his clothing, he could feel the warmth of her softly feminine body against him. He heard the mumbled tones of her inchoate thanks and breathed a gentle bouquet mixed of expensive soap and womanly fragrance. He patted her lightly on the back because he thought the gesture might somehow be the Christian thing to do. Yet at that moment the feelings stirring within him were hardly religious. Parts of the Sermon on the Mount rang in his ears: *But I say unto you, That whosoever looketh on a woman to lust after her hath committed adultery with her already in his heart. . . .*

He tried to free himself but could not. Instead, he embraced her and, as he did, felt a quiet joy, the like of which he had never before known.

In the switching center at Tehuacán, the telegraph operator handed the station master a message.

The latter read it, crumpled it in his fist, then threw it to the floor. "Damn," he said. "Is there no way we can contact the northbound from Oaxaca?"

"No, Sir. There's no radio on board. We're the nearest telegraph right here."

"*Maldito sea!*" he said again. "They may have fixed the damage from that last earthquake, but if this rain does come and we do get a flash flood, that's one train we'll never see here."

"No, Sir."

The station master walked outside the small building. He looked up to a very bleak and forbidding sky, then down again. In front of him, a mere meter and a half away, the first huge raindrop splattered itself to death. Another followed almost instantly.

"God be with you," he muttered. He looked again to the dull sky as the raindrops falling from it increased in number. "You will surely need Him now."

Madness is a cannibal. It devours its own festering flesh. As it feeds itself, it gains size and strength from the ghastly repast, for insanity alone is its own nutriment. Like a horrid phoenix, it consumes itself only to rise, renewed and intact, from the unholy feast. It licks its dripping jowls in arrogant satisfaction, for each meal makes it stronger, more confident, and more complete.

So it was with Ian Conrad.

As he rode west, he appeared outwardly calm, even though somewhat preoccupied. Within, he was chewing the remains of his last maniacal feast. The trains had been stopped by an earthquake. Repairs to the tracks were taking time and time delayed flight. He had also heard rumors that President Cárdenas was not satisfied with the nationalization of the railroads. He intended some political move—some change. He might even give the railroads to the workers.

No matter what the president did, Conrad knew that Bill Scofield would ultimately have to depend on the railroads. At one time he had thought his ex-partner might try to leave Mexico from Juchitán and sail across the Pacific. It had been a short-lived consideration. He recalled Scofield's telling him of a swimming accident in Minnesota when he was a boy. He knew the little man was deathly afraid of drowning. He would never sail from Juchitán or Vera Cruz. He would try to leave Mexico by land.

Whatever he had done to the gold, it still occupied twenty-four crates. One man could never carry them alone. Scofield had already given up burros for a truck, but Conrad knew he would give up the truck as well. A truck was expensive. More importantly, it would be thoroughly inspected at the border. A shipment on a train, coming to the United States with many other shipments would not be so carefully scrutinized.

Ian Conrad had been in Mexico for many years. He knew the ways into and out of the country. He was convinced that Scofield was, at that very moment, on a train headed north. He also knew that all tracks rose to the central plateau—all trains eventually went through the capital.

From Mexico City Scofield's choices were limited. He could travel north but only to one of three terminals: Nuevo Laredo, Ciudad Juárez, or Nogales. There were no other rails.

Bill Scofield was alone on a Mexican train with twenty-four crates of stolen gold, but Ian Conrad had many allies. Trains here were slow, erratic, and virtually unscheduled. Politics, at least according to the rumors, were about to join his vendetta, and even nature herself was with him. The earthquake had disrupted many miles of track. Now, with the advent of rain, he was more confident than ever.

In Mexico City Conrad would be able to determine the route his ex-partner had decided upon. By aeroplane, he could travel that route much faster than any Mexican train.

The mule sloughed through the heavy slime underfoot, but Ian Conrad, though drenched with the glucose paste of his own sweat, appeared unconcerned. He was a man possessed of ultimate surfeit. He had fed on his own madness. Now, he could actually taste the retribution to come.

In Mexico City he would buy certain supplies. Then, somewhere in Sonora, or Chihuahua, or Nuevo León revenge would be sweet—and easy—and thorough.

William Scofield—the gold, the train, and all aboard—could not escape.

2
Pursuit

DURING THE HUMILIATING interview with Juan Miguárdez in the Palacio Nacional, the wings of Victoriano Felix's *machismo* had been painfully clipped. Not only had his diamonds been stolen, but when he had reported the matter in the logical expectation of a reward, he had been dismissed without so much as a *gracias*!

Victoriano Felix, a man whose greatest single talent lay in his ability to believe in instant wealth, began to hate. He continued to go about his work with quiet efficiency, but as he did so, a metamorphosis took place. The hatred within him grew and transformed him from a slow, prodding burro of a man to a lythe and muscular beast of prey absolutely dedicated to finding the thief and, regardless of his station, bringing him to justice.

He dismissed General Cárdenas as a suspect almost immediately. As a man, Cárdenas was too direct. As president, he had no need to steal.

Like Juan Miguárdez before him, Victoriano called the Ministry of Finance and talked to Señor Gómez there. Posing as an aide for Miguárdez, he found out merely that Señor Bassols had in fact been bed-ridden before, during, and after the theft.

At the Guerrero home, however, Victoriano proved to be a much better detective than had Louis Robles. Returning from the huge villa to his own far more shabby quarters, he was able gradually to fit the pieces of the puzzle together so as to arrive at the same conclusion as had Juan Miguárdez.

Jesús Guerrero had traveled south with his family only far enough to erase suspicion. He had probably already turned back toward the capital and would have to come through the city before continuing north.

Cat and mouse! It was an exciting game.

Victoriano Felix was no longer a minor bank employee. He was a stalking feline while the handsome, powerful Jesús Guerrero was really no more than a scurrying rodent.

As he waited in the railroad station for the arrival of trains coming from the south, Victoriano Felix occasionally smiled. The dream of instant wealth was still very much alive, and the straight razor in his coat pocket felt very reassuring.

By slow and painful increments, much like the tightening of an emotional thumbscrew, the journey had become increasingly intolerable for Jesús Guerrero. Spoiled by the trappings of privilege, his initial mistake had been the simple assumption that a first-class or sleeper car would, as a matter of course, be on the train from Oaxaca. At first he had accepted the lack for it had not seemed to matter. From the station he had seen that Teresa Inez was already aboard and dressed as he had suggested. The escape was progressing as planned.

The prospect of riding a coach had, at the beginning, offered what had appeared to be the elements of an adventure. He and his family would be able to experience the quainter aspects of southern railroad travel while amusing themselves by studying a variety of whimsical passengers.

The wheelchair, however, had proved a serious liability. The illusion of a crippled wife, which was necessary to conceal the outline of the belt she wore, had forced Guerrero, on several occasions, to enlist the aid of others in lifting and negotiating the chair. Finally it had been pulled up the steps of the train and maneuvered into the aisle. It had remained there, jostled and bumped by every passing passenger, animal, and parcel.

Initially, Elodia had seemed almost stoic. For the first several jolting, rocking miles, she had remained in the cumbersome wheelchair without uttering a single verbal complaint. When bumped or otherwise inconvenienced, she had only sighed her displeasure or simply gritted her teeth in annoyed frustration. It wasn't until after leaving the third small village that she had begun to attack her husband as the person directly responsible for the filth of the passengers, the annoyance of their animals, and the bits of food occasionally dropped into her lap.

The children, too, had begun the trip in what had appeared to be a spirit of pleasant anticipation. Now it had completely exhausted itself. The stench of the car, the burden of humidity so slimy one could almost color it green, and the jerking, jolting irregularity of the train's progress had all taken a heavy toll. For a time, the boys had proved themselves quite adaptable. Now, they were two small monsters, bickering with each other and whining to him and Elodia.

Guerrero had peeled out of his coat and removed his dark glasses. Although his first disguise was gone, nature had created another. His hair was plastered to his head with perspiration, as was his shirt to his body. A glaze of physical and emotional exhaustion lay in his eyes and his mouth hung slightly open like that of a sun-struck dog. Jesús Guerrero looked totally unlike the strikingly handsome presidential aide who had left Mexico City a few days before. He felt as though he had been encased in a great wad of dawk flour dough about to be rolled into a monstrous tortilla. He was infuriated at the train and all its passengers. Most of all, he was sick of his immediate family.

Although he had not planned to make any contact whatsoever with his mistress until after arriving in Mexico City, exasperation now fairly compelled him to see her. He ordered his sons to remain with their mother, told the three of them that he wanted to stretch his legs and pulled himself away from the amalgam of perspiration that had glued him to the seat.

He slid past the wheelchair and started to make his way slowly up the aisle, avoiding packages, feet, and spittoons as he went. The next car to the rear, he was sure, was the one in which he had seen Teresa.

She should have been about halfway down the east side of the car, but she was gone. Although it was packed with people, the only person who was in any way distinctive was a small man sitting in the seat where he had expected to find Teresa.

As he passed, he and the man exchanged a brief glance. In it, Guerrero detected a very acute sense of being despised. The man's eyes were flat. In their depths was an animal's passion, without moral constraint. There could be no reason

117

for the hatred, yet it was there and, apparently, directed toward him.

Beyond, at the end of the car, sat a middle-aged couple, very obviously European. Facing them, their backs to Guerrero, were a blond man and a woman with almost pink hair.

There was no sign of Teresa.

A little nagging fear began to tug at him like a beggar boy pulling his coattail. Teresa might have considered the risk too great or the masquerade too dangerous. She could very easily have left the train at any one of the villages where it had stopped. Doubt gripped him as he swayed through the car looking at the faces to his right and left.

The sky was overcast and, if possible, the humidity had increased. Most of the passengers seemed almost comatose. The atmosphere of the packed car was insufferable. The only hint of relief came from the current of warm air oozing through the open windows.

Guerrero pressed his way into the last car. He was more than halfway through it before he finally saw her. She stood at the extreme rear of the train facing a sloppily dressed man whose hands were on her shoulders.

At first he was simply baffled, but when she leaned forward to embrace the stranger and he, in turn, entwined both arms around her, a fury of jealousy swept through him.

He renewed his efforts to negotiate the cluttered aisle and, after much difficulty, reached the place where they were standing. By that time they had separated.

She spoke before he could lash out at them. "Darling." She sounded as she always had after making love—exhausted, yet very content. "This is Domingo Portes. He knows—"

"Knows!" Jealousy was replaced by a panic that stabbed him in the solar plexus. *The diamonds, the plot to overthrow Cárdenas!* Visions of a firing squad danced in his mind.

"About us, darling."

The terror must have shown like a naked thing in his face, for the man laid a reassuring hand on his arm. "Be at ease," Portes said. "I have more important concerns than two lovers."

Guerrero studied the man. He was slightly taller than he and apparently in good physical shape. Although hardly handsome, his face had a distinct masculine strength. In the line of his jaw and the confident expression of his eyes, Guerrero saw not so much an ordinary traveler but a soldier thoroughly dedicated to the cause he served. More than that, he realized that Portes knew and understood the impression he had made.

"Oh?" he challenged. "And what might they be?"

"There is no need to fence," Portes said. "Affairs of state hold no interest for me. Teresa has merely suggested that, because of your political importance, there might be some difficulty—"

"There is no difficulty!" Guerrero lied. He grabbed his mistress by the wrist and would have dragged her back through the car had Portes not clutched his arm in a remarkably stern grip.

Infuriated, Guerrero turned. Again he looked into the eyes of a man who was intimately familiar with, and quite willing to use, physical violence.

"I only thought . . ." Portes's voice was calm to the point of gentleness. He might have been talking to a child. "It might be a bit conspicuous for a presidential aide to drag a woman through a train."

Guerrero released Teresa's wrist. He looked from her to Portes then back again. "Yes," he said at length. "Of course."

"I will watch her," Portes said. "You need have no worry."

As if the words had been a cue to the Almighty, the entire sky seemed to open. Rain, which had only bluffed and threatened a moment before, abruptly showered the world. The sound of it hammering on the train's roof was nearly deafening. The myriad spots it made in the quickly formed puddles beside the track leapt like geysers caused by machine gun fire.

Jesús Guerrero looked from Teresa Inez to Domingo Portes, then outside to the violence of the downpour. He was puzzled and close to awe.

Without speaking, he turned and started back to his family.

Nicholas Markoff left the Estación de los Ferrocarriles Nacionales and turned east. Except for one minor concern, he considered himself among the most fortunate of men. He had money, he had time, and, because he felt in a contemplative mood, he decided to walk rather than hail a taxi.

He headed in a leisurely way toward a favorite haunt, a little leftover bit of garden just at the corner of Venustiano Carranza and Bolívar. It was over a mile away, but the thin air was fairly snapping with vitality, and he enjoyed both the exercise and the opportunity to savor the city.

Ciudad de México was to him unlike any other place he had ever lived. Moscow, Paris, Berlin—all had charm and character, but Mexico combined them all. It was at once ancient and modern, full of mystery and music, haunted by ghosts of yesteryear and cajoled by promises of centuries to come. A friend had once called it an Aztec princess—a merciless beauty in a Parisian gown—stepping with delicate disdain over pools of blood shed by the thousands of men who had fought for her.

It was a description he particularly liked—a perfect woman to symbolize the perfect city. He had enjoyed Mexico. He would miss her when he left. Departure, however, would be absolutely necessary. Within a day he might very well be one of the most sought-after men in history.

He had expected far more negotiation and bargaining with Juan Miguárdez than, in fact, had taken place. He had also felt that his assignment would prove far more complicated. Instead, it had all been remarkably simple.

He turned south on Salgado, then east again on Orozco y Berra. The city was drenched with memories of blood—Montezuma and Cortés; Iturbide and Maximilian. Soon Jesús Guerrero would join them.

Juan Miguárdez had been as good as his word. The money had arrived a few hours after their luncheon in Sanborn's. More than that, the presidential secretary had been able to supply him with reports on Guerrero's progress. His own final check at the railroad station had shown that the train was just south of Tehuacán. There were reports of rain and the possibility of delay due to flash floods. Even without that, it could not possibly arrive in the capital for another six hours.

Markoff would meet it. Despite any possible attempts at disguise, a man traveling with two children and a wife in a wheelchair would hardly be inconspicuous. He would be very easy to spot—and to kill.

The best part of the assignment, however, was that he would not be forced to commit an amateur assassination in public. Miguárdez had given him one bit of information which, if factual, would make this killing one of his easiest.

Guerrero would probably be delayed in Mexico City for at least a day. Miguárdez had mentioned the president's decision to act on the Rodriguez Proposal—to give the railroads to the workers in the hope of eliminating further labor disputes. No matter how skillfully the move was handled, it would mean a disruption of schedules, perhaps even a complete interruption of rail travel for days.

Nicholas Markoff took a deep breath of mountainous air as he left the Paseo de la Reforma behind. To his right a long row of open booths lined the edge of the Alameda. He passed pottery, iguana shoes, blankets, and a circus of fleas each dressed quite correctly in a tiny *traje de luces*. He kept a leisurely pace, slowing now and then to inspect a bit of leatherwork or a tiny clay *vaquero* with a head no bigger than that of a match. Outwardly, he appeared to be a man without a care in the world. Within, he was pondering the exact execution of his assignment as well as what could prove to be a *sabot* about to be tossed into the machinery of the job.

At the railroad station he had noted the various faces of people moving here and there or lolling in sleep. Most belonged to men and women awaiting the arrival or departure of some train or person. They were faces and expressions to be seen in any terminal in any major city of the world.

One, however, had bothered him. It belonged to a very ordinary man who had also asked about trains coming from the south. Despite the time involved, he had obviously decided to remain in the station until the train actually arrived. What bothered Markoff was that the man, although fundamentally nondescript, had been conspicuous. As he walked along Avenido Hidalgo he tried to analyze why.

The man had been dressed in a cheap suit of unprepossessing cut and fabric. His shoes, although polished, were worn. His shirt was white, obviously hand-ironed, and his tie was of an insignificant pattern. His face was hardly one which should have stood out in a crowd, yet it had.

Nicholas Markoff was a man whose very existence had frequently depended on an ability to analyze character at a glance. As a political errand boy and professional assassin, he had honed his powers of observation to the point where he was seldom in error.

The man was nondescript, yet he possessed one very conspicuous quality. There was a hungry determination in his eyes. Markoff was sure he was some form of government employee, perhaps even a plainclothed policeman. It occurred to him that Miguárdez might even have hired the man to make sure Markoff would not escape after killing Guerrero.

He dismissed the thought as he turned down Bolivar. Although the eyes of the man in the station had been strangely determined, they lacked that curious hard quality of the police. Markoff tried to recall more. Several times he had noticed the man slip his right hand into the side pocket of his coat as though reassuring himself by touching something there.

Almost to the intersection of Venustiano Carranza, it occurred to him that the nondescript man was on a mission similar to his own. He was waiting for that train in order to steal from, or kill, or kidnap one of its passengers.

The speculation was disconcerting. In fact it was quite frightening, because it was apparent that the man was an amateur. It was this that worried the Russian most as he stepped into his little garden. He knew from experience that simple ineptitude frequently produced monumental catastrophes.

The garden was empty except for a few flower sellers and bootblacks gathered around a little fountain in which a jaunty green frog played a red mandolin.

Nicholas Markoff removed a cigarette case from an inside pocket, extracted a cigarette, and lit it. As he inhaled, he contemplated the statue.

It looked remarkably like Juan Miguárdez.

He exhaled a long jet of smoke toward the fountain. "So, my very ugly employer . . ." He spoke very quietly in Russian. "You shall have your Guerrero." He took another pull of the cigarette. "Unfortunately, I may have to bring you another as well."

Thomas Kemp had read the cablegram and, as a matter of course, burned it. Now, he slipped the clip easily into the Luger and snugged it home with the palm of his left hand. He pulled the receiver up and back to lodge one bullet in the chamber, then casually flicked the safety down with his right thumb. Almost absently, he stared at the word *Gesichert* now exposed on the side of the weapon.

An American, Kemp had fought in Spain because, when the civil war broke out, he had thought he believed in human dignity, the rights of free men and the evils of Fascism. All that had changed quite radically the previous August during the siege of Alcazar fortress when an errant sliver of shrapnel had removed exactly one-half of his penis.

Very bitter and no longer involved with concepts of human

dignity because he no longer felt that he himself had any, Thomas Kemp left Spain. Unwilling to return to the United States, he had wandered to Mexico. He knew the language and understood the people. Furthermore, the political situation gave him an opportunity to utilize his newfound hatred against a world responsible for his mutilation.

He slipped the pistol into a specially designed shoulder holster, buttoned his coat, and inspected himself in the bathroom mirror. There was no telltale bulge. The young man staring back at him might have been a tourist, a college student, or even an employee of one of the many foreign companies with offices in Mexico City. His face looked open and apparently quite sincere. The scattered pepper of freckles over the bridge of his nose gave it the look of a Tom Sawyer grown up. It was, on the whole, a remarkably deceptive face, for there was little if any of the all-American boy left to Thomas Kemp. Like Nicholas Markoff, he was a professional assassin. There was, however, a basic difference between the two men. The Russian killed for necessity—quickly, cleanly, and strictly for the money. Kemp, on the other hand, enjoyed his work.

Whenever possible, he would prolong the agonies of his victims in order to savor their screams and impassioned pleas for mercy. Somehow, that was the only thing left that made life worthwhile, for only through the torture of others could he obtain the pleasure denied him by a sliver of Spanish shrapnel.

Thomas Kemp adjusted his tie. He turned from the mirror and crossed the hotel room.

Neil Oberon's apartment was only a few blocks away. There was plenty of time. He decided to walk.

3
Asylum

RAIN DRENCHED OAXACA and Puebla. It lashed the mountains, peeling away great shreds and whipping them into kinetic slime. Like a million wet hammers, it pounded the hills, smashing away clay and foliage, rocks and animals. It made rivers where none had existed before and, with greedy, splashing fingers, tore silt and stones from the highlands and threw them down to the fertile valleys. What stood before the oozing mire of rock-studded sludge was devoured.

The train slogged on. Tehuacán was less than ten kilometers away.

Over a thousand miles northwest, Col. Luther Mannas was unconcerned with meteorology. Although outwardly angry, even bellicose, he was actually feeling quite sorry for himself. Like thousands before him, he suffered a common soldier's agony: He was torn between his duty to his country, and his unbridled contempt for the policies of the particular government under which he served.

From the window of his office he could look over the sun-drenched exactitude of Fort Bliss. The precise, military orderliness might have inspired a certain sense of security. In it, he should have known emotionally that all was well with the world and would continue to be well. Order is an absolute thing. Because it is absolute, everything should conform to it, and, when everything conforms the machinery of life will run with maximum efficiency.

Mannas was not impressed by the view. Government, he was convinced, was a system devised by geniuses for the perpetuation of idiots. He paced the office in long strides, his boot heels clicking angrily on the wooden floor. Occasionally, he would look to the huge map that occupied one wall, and as he passed might glance out the window without actually focusing on anything there. He puffed his cigarette, gritted his teeth, frowned, pursed his lips, and puffed again. The ashtray on the desk was already filled with butts. One crumpled green and red pack lay beside it, another, freshly opened, was on the blotter.

Fury was building in Luther Mannas. Along with it, he experienced a growing desire to destroy, controllable only by years of military and personal discipline. When the door of the office opened, he whirled as if intent upon murder.

A man other than Nathan Banners might have been terrified by Mannas' appearance. The sergeant, however, was inured to both facial expressions and overly explicit vocabulary.

"Well?" Mannas demanded.

"Nothing, Sir," Banners said. "I've checked with the Message Center at least every hour. Nothing from Mexico at all."

"Son of a bitch!" Mannas took a final drag on his cigarette, ground it in the already heaped ashtray, then immediately reached for another.

"Perhaps the telegram never got to him."

" 'Perhaps'—bullshit. In that goddamned country the variety of fuck-up is infinite. The fact is our man is on his way up from Vera Cruz and without this Candenning fellow of yours, we can't even do half the job. Hell, even with him we'd still be screwed."

"Yes, Sir."

Mannas turned again to the window and stared across the post for a long, contemplative moment. Finally, he lit the cigarette jutting pugnaciously from his lips and turned back to Banners. "It's absolutely impossible," he said, "to step high enough and wide enough to get over the mountain of shit coming from Washington. Goddamned president's giving handouts to every incompetent goldbrick—secretary of state's more interested in reciprocal fucking trade and nonintervention than our own security. Christ! Mexico's walking all over us with this Cárdenas Bolshevik. War in Spain, the Japanese about to walk into China, and the goddamned Democrats have their thumbs up their ass as usual."

"Yes, Sir."

"All right—" Mannas drew a deep breath, coughed, then looked at Banners again. "Forget the screed. Get some civilian clothes for that courier and put him in Juárez."

"Sir?"

"I know. I'll take full responsibility. You just make sure

125

he's not alone. The kid may speak kraut and shoot, but he still needs all the help he can get.''

"If I may say so, Sir, you're risking—''

"I'm *serving*, Banners. I'm serving my country—not a yellow-spined administration. Just get him across the border and make sure he has a good man with him.''

"Yes, Sir.''

"We've got the airports alerted.'' Mannas sounded almost helpless. "It's the goddamned ground routes that are going to screw us.'' He turned and looked out the window for a moment, then snapped around to face Banners again. "All right,'' he said. "Put anyone who's even faintly qualified in Nogales. Same thing—civilian clothes and on the Mexican side. It's all we can do until the administration decides to grow some balls.''

"Yes, Sir.'' Sergeant Banners waited a polite four seconds in possible anticipation of another order. When it didn't come, he left the office as silently as he had entered.

Mannas stood looking at the wall-sized map for some time until, with a sigh of resignation, he turned back to his desk. He sat down, dropped the cigarette into the loaded ashtray and, very slowly, unlocked the desk's center drawer. He lifted his personal book of telephone listings and placed it on the blotter.

There were 500 miles between Vera Cruz and the nearest point on the American border—1,300 to Nogales. Anything could happen in an area that size, yet all he had been allowed to do was place men at the border. He was risking his career even to have them in civilian clothes watching the railheads.

Helios was big. How big, he didn't really know. He had been told only that it was something of a weapon—the greatest thing since the Roman short sword. One man traveling in Mexico with a sick woman had the secret to an ultimate weapon, and just because the Roosevelt Administration was torn between Lázaro Cárdenas and a few oil and railroad interests, the full power of the United States of America had to sit on the border.

Didn't it occur to Washington, he wondered, that if Helios actually was as big as it seemed, someone else might want it? The Spaniards were blowing their guts all over Iberia, Hitler was building to no good, the Japanese were just aching to get into China, but Washington was going to wait quietly

126

while one man made his safe and easy way from Vera Cruz to some unknown place on the Texas or Arizona border.

He opened the book, wondering why he had chosen the career he had for, as had happened so many times before, he was ultimately disappointed with the men who ran his country. They sat safely in their Washington offices and trembled in fear because a Mexican president had suddenly decided to howl at the moon about how important his second-rate country was.

"Christ!" he said aloud. "Bandits still running around Sonora—no fucking phones, no radios, no trains or planes on schedule—and the son of a bitch is dictating to Washington!" He reached for the telephone. "Shit!" He pulled it toward him, dialed the operator, and asked for long distance.

His connection finally made, the call was answered by a very soft yet very efficient southern voice. In it he could almost smell the aroma of magnolias and see the young lady's flirtatious eyes.

"This is Colonel Mannas at Bliss," he said. "I have to speak to the secretary."

"I'm sorry, Colonel . . ." The voice might have belonged to Scarlet O'Hara herself. "Mr. Hull's in a meeting right now. I just can't—"

"Listen," he announced, "you just go right on in to that li'l ole meetin' and you tell Mr. Hull that I'm callin' about sweet li'l ole Project Helios. You tell him that Helios is about to be a first-class, top-drawer snafu."

"Snafu?"

"Yes, sweetheart. The situation here is very normal, all f——. Never mind. Just tell him I can't handle it properly without more cooperation."

He waited several seconds, lit another cigarette, and was exhaling the first puff when the gently southern voice of Cordell Hull came on the line.

"Mannas?"

"Yes, Sir."

"What's the problem?"

"Frankly, Sir, I'm afraid you've put me in a ringer. On this Helios thing, we only know the point of landing. I have men placed at all the major crossing points and I've notified the border authorities in case this man tries to come in over open ground. Of course the logical thing is for him to take the Pan Am flight to Brownsville, and I have the airport there alerted, but there's been no sign of him yet. Frankly, Sir, it's just not enough. The question is whether he's going to be logical or just goddamned slippery. He could be anywhere—on a plane, train, on the highway to El Paso. Hell, he might even be riding a burro up for all I know. If you want him, I don't think we should handle it only from this side. After all, anything can happen between here and Vera Cruz.''

The other end of the line was absolutely silent for so long that Mannas finally asked, ''Mr. Hull?''

''I'm here, Colonel.'' Another long pause followed. When the secretary of state spoke, there was a definite touch of resignation in his voice. ''Mannas . . .''

''Yes, Sir?''

''You do what you can, but make absolutely sure your men don't cross that border. Our relations with General Cárdenas are entirely too delicate. We simply cannot afford to have military personnel on any mission in Mexico.''

''Yes, Sir.''

Well, Mannas thought, *there go twenty-one years right down the old patriotic rat hole*.

Cordell Hull replaced the telephone's receiver on its cradle, rose from his desk, and walked to the anteroom where his secretary sat. He spoke to her almost in a whisper.

''Call the president,'' he said. ''Tell him I must see him immediately. Have the car brought around and . . .'' He nodded toward the conference room in which he had just been. ''Tell those gentlemen I've been summoned by a higher authority.''

She smiled. ''Like God?''

He did not return the smile. His face was quite serious, even drawn, as he walked to the door. ''Yes,'' he told her. ''Like God Himself.''

The man sitting behind the huge desk, long cigarette holder jutting arrogantly from his mouth, was the picture of confident strength. In his eyes, however, there was an expression of speculative doubt. He had listened to his secretary of state with keen attention. As a result, he was faced with one of the most important decisions of his life.

He leaned back in his wheelchair, removed his spectacles, and rubbed the bridge of his nose. He replaced his glasses with care, then looked up and smiled. "You sum it up splendidly, Cordell," he said. "Horns of a dilemma."

"This sort of situation is never easy."

"Exactly," the president said. "Dr. Pelzig must be brought here safely. If that cannot be done, he must be prevented from going elsewhere. From what you say, it amounts to the expedients of abduction or assassination."

"Hard words, Franklin. Unfortunately, it's the doing—"

"Anything can be done," the president said. "The interests of the United States are far more important than the manner in which they are served. It's not what we do that counts, Cordell. It's only what people think we do. After all . . ." He laid his cigarette holder across the edge of an ashtray on the desk. "Public opinion is an elephant. If you prod it correctly, it goes where you want it to and there's not much of anything big enough to stop it."

He rolled his chair away from the desk, spun it deftly to the right, and pushed himself to the office's window. "We both know war's inevitable." He spoke to the capital, sweltering in the summer heat beyond the glass. "The question is only when and where. I simply cannot afford to make any of Wilson's mistakes in something like this. You've done a splendid job with nonintervention in Spain, but Mexico's still involved—at least emotionally. Also, there's Italy—there's Japan—and we can never forget Hitler. Cordell . . ." The president spun the chair around and faced his secretary of state. "Just exactly how big is Helios?"

"It's big, Franklin—monstrous, really. I simply don't know how monstrous. From what I can gather, the only people who do are Dr. Pelzig and Albert Einstein at Princeton, and an Italian named Fermi. We might call New Jersey—"

"No," the president said. "With Pelzig already in Mexico, it's too much of a risk. The fewer people aware of this, the better. Who knows now?"

"You and I. Colonel Mannas at Fort Bliss has some idea. He knows Helios is a weapon."

"Sumner Wells? The Chief of Staff?"

"No. No one else. Even the people involved know only enough to do their individual jobs. Those have all involved tracking Dr. Pelzig. Unfortunately, he eluded our men in Vera Cruz."

"And suspicion?" the president asked. "Who suspects?"

"Anyone. The Germans, of course. The Italians might have heard something, perhaps the Spaniards, even the Japanese."

The president sighed. Again he turned the wheelchair slightly so he could glance over his right shoulder to the panorama of Washington beyond the window. "Cárdenas is tooting a toy horn," he almost mumbled. "The trouble is we still must dance to his tune. There are just too many American business interests in Mexico, too much American money. This trouble with the oil companies is a tinderbox. If he starts exercising his appropriative powers, the repercussions could throw us back five years."

"Also, we're rushing hell-bent toward war. When it comes, we'll need a southern ally."

The president smiled again. "Yes," he chuckled without humor. "And that *must* be Mexico. We can't arm any faster than we are already. An attack here would cripple us. Mexico would give us time. Do you realize, Cordell, the destruction of Mexico could very well be the only thing capable of saving us in the event of land attack?"

The secretary of state's features were quite serious, but in his eyes there was an expression almost of appreciation. "You know, Franklin," he said after a moment's silence, "you're very much like him."

"Cárdenas?"

"Yes."

"I have never thought any one man had an option on love for his own country."

Hull cleared his throat. When he spoke, his tone was completely businesslike again. "I think our only real worry is Germany," he said. "Dr. Pelzig is German. He's been working in Berlin. A leak in security, a chance remark . . ."

"We know," the president said. "If we know, anyone could know." He turned the wheelchair again so that he was facing the southerner. "Horns of a dilemma," he said.

"Yes, Sir."

"That's one of your favorite expressions."

"In the State Department, Franklin, it's one of my most frequent positions."

The president tilted his head back and enjoyed a short laugh. Again he was a man of supreme confidence, outwardly in control not only of this situation, but of all problems, great and small. His laughter done, however, he again looked directly and seriously at his secretary of state. "The army

130

mustn't handle this. You've done what you could with Mannas and his people. Let him meet Doctor Pelzig at the border, but we can't afford any military personnel on the other side. Cárdenas is flexing his biceps. He's showing off to his own people and everyone else in Latin America. Any overt move on our part could ruin everything we accomplished in Buenos Aires last year—everything Joe Daniels is working for now. It might even shatter the Good Neighbor Policy entirely."

"Still, we simply can't afford not to go in there and get him out."

"I know," the president said. "But make haste slowly. Appearances are vital. I'll know nothing about this. If you're caught or implicated in any way, I'll disown you. He may be strong-willed and he may even be a communist, but I'm going to need Cárdenas and I can't predict how soon. The world's going to explode, Cordell."

"I know."

"And if this Pelzig man has the knowledge, I want to make damned sure we push the plunger—not someone else."

"Yes, Mr. President."

"You get Pelzig out of there any way you can."

"Yes, Mr. President." The secretary of state turned to the door. His hand was on the knob when he was interrupted by the president's voice."

"And, Cordell . . ."

He turned to see his old friend, one hand slightly raised in a characteristic gesture, a warm smile on his confident face.

"Yes, Franklin?"

"Don't get caught. I'm going to need you in days to come."

San Antonio was the largest city in Texas. Famous for its historic shrines, commemorating some 245 years of life and often violent death under six different flags, it was also proud of its modernity. It called itself "Santone, the place where sunshine spends the winter," and was host to the nation's largest military installation. A cavalry post and the headquarters of the 8th Corps were located at Fort Sam Houston on Government Hill. In addition, there was a motor transport camp, an artillery camp, arsenals, and various rifle and big gun ranges.

There were also two flying schools and three airports, the most prominent of which was Randolph Field. For Randolph, known as the West Point of the Air, the government had selected some 2,300 acres and had already spent ten million dollars toward making it a model air base. Randolph Field had a continuing population of some 4,000 men, including flyers, instructors, and cadets. From this installation, at any time, several hundred armed ships could take to the air.

"Santone" was also a port of entry covering a customs district doing some 65 million dollars worth of yearly trade with Mexico. That June the customs district occupied all or part of several buildings, some of them newly built by the Works Progress Administration. In one of these, Sidney Desmond had offices.

Although he now considered himself as good a Texan as anyone, Desmond had originally come from Clay County, Tennessee where, in the spring of 1898, he had joined H Company of the 4th Regiment of Tennessee Volunteer Infantry.

His hope of seeing combat in Cuba was never realized, for by the time his unit sailed for Havana, the war with Spain was over. Thus, his few months of military service were spent on garrison duty in Santa Clara where he was assigned as striker to the company's young captain, Cordell Hull.

Despite their differences in rank, the two men formed a strong friendship. Desmond respected and admired Hull's brilliance. Hull, on the other hand, was somewhat awed by Desmond's uncanny cleverness. The striker was a man whose character balanced between the clearly honest and the unquestionably criminal. Sidney Desmond always seemed able, no matter what the situation, to find the nonexistent, to achieve the unreachable or secure the unobtainable.

After being mustered out of the service in May of '99, the two men pursued their different careers. Hull practiced law, then went into politics. Desmond tried his hand at a variety of endeavors, one of which involved promotion of a wild-West show. It was while managing Cherokee Gordon's Frontier Scouts that he had the misfortune of losing his right eye while trying to separate a less-than-honest ticket vendor from an enraged patron carrying an umbrella.

In April of 1917, when he again attempted to enlist in the service of his country, he was told that one-eyed men in their middle thirties were not exactly what the army wanted. Still, he genuinely believed he could be of some service, so contacted his former commanding officer who was, at the time, a congressman.

Within a week, Sidney Desmond was in the employ of the United States Government.

Since 1917 he had done many things for his country. Unfortunately for any would-be biographers, most of Desmond's achievements lay under the rose of political discretion. His accomplishments were invariably entombed in a moral no-man's land, simply because the various issues and situations involved could never have been approached or solved by direct or purely honorable methods.

That June in San Antonio, Sidney Desmond was officially involved with certain minor aspects of trade between the United States and various Latin American countries. He had learned Spanish in Cuba, had spent some time traveling in the south and, at an apparently lazy, indifferent and slightly overweight fifty-seven years of age, seemed to be as good a choice for such a non-taxing, routine job as anyone.

In fact, Sidney Desmond was one of the State Department's very elite, confidential functionaries stationed in various parts of the world to assure that the interests of the United States were not interfered with or, if they were, such interference would not last long. There are many names for these men. They have been called spies, agents, scouts. Desmond himself preferred the label "trouble-shooter."

When the telephone rang, it broke the indolent monotony of an insufferably hot day. He reached for it with apparent indifference and lifted the receiver to his ear. "Desmond." There was still a heavy Tennessee drawl in his voice.

He was both pleased and surprised to hear his onetime company commander's voice at the other end of a less than perfect connection.

The secretary of state wasted no time on amenities. "Sidney, listen very carefully. This is vital. Absolutely vital. There's a man named Jakob Pelzig somewhere in Mexico. He's about five-eight—gray hair, balding, wears glasses. He's with his wife. She's sick—tuberculosis. Landed in Vera Cruz on the fifth. Came in on the *Prince Umberto* from Lisbon. He's headed north. Find him."

"Find him! Sweet Jesus!"

"This is absolutely imperative, Sidney."

"I suppose you know Mexico has a few goddamn square miles."

"I didn't say it would be easy. Just do it. Find Pelzig and

133

get him across the border. Use any methods, any people you want as long as you don't jar the Mexican government.''

"Somewhere in Mexico?" Desmond said. "It's a big goddamn country down there.''

"He's a German with a sick wife.''

"Swell.''

"You're the only man I know who can do this, Sidney. I'll give you *carte blanche*. I'll be behind you one hundred percent.''

"Thanks a hell of a lot.''

"Just one thing.''

"And?''

"If you're caught—if the Mexicans suspect anything, anything at all—we don't know you exist.''

"Story of my goddamn life.''

"I can't tell you how very crucial this is.''

"Somewhere in Mexico. Jesus Christ! That's a needle in a goddamn cactus patch.''

"This needle can puncture the world.''

"No shit?''

"Not one bit.''

"Well . . . hell," Desmond said. "I guess it's better'n sitting here watching haircuts.''

"Thank you," Hull said. "I knew I could rely on you.''

Desmond recradled the telephone and stared across the almost barren room to the open window and the clear Texas sky beyond. "Shit," he said. In the profundity of his tone, the single word contained two syllables.

He took a deep breath, heaved it out in a monumental sigh, and reached again for the phone.

The rain stopped as suddenly as it had started. Still, she was completely drenched. The German and Charles Candenning had tried without success to close the train's window and shield the two women from the downpour that lashed into the car. Their efforts had been quixotically disastrous. She and the older woman were as completely saturated as the two men.

Karen had thought she was getting used to such things and was now, if anything, as close as she could bring herself to a state of stoic indifference. The German woman, too, seemed able to accept the inconvenience as part of an inevitable pattern of travel in Mexico. Her husband was less complacent. Obviously one who respected order and assumed that inanimate objects would perform as they had been designed to, he was quite irritated by the window, his own inability to close it and, worst of all, his wife's dripping discomfort.

Only Charles Candenning seemed unconcerned, if not actually amused by the spontaneity of the shower, the completeness of his own saturation, and the suddenness of the rain's cessation. As the train ground to a squealing, protesting stop in Tehuacán, the illustrator was actually chuckling.

Karen turned to him, a puzzled expression on her face.

He smiled almost apologetically. "There're just two ways to approach this country," he said. "Either you read Frances Toor's guidebook like the Bible, and become terrified of the food and water, complain about windows that don't open on the hot days and don't close when it rains, or . . ." He shrugged his shoulders. "You just relax and accept the—how shall I say it?—the unique charm of a very unique country."

His attitude, his entire manner and tone of voice, had an infectious quality. She felt herself smiling. The wet dress plastered to her body, the drops of water running from her hair along the back of her neck and down between her breasts were almost forgotten.

He said something in German which must have had the same effect, for the frail woman smiled and the man, who looked like something recently drowned, appeared, if not actually happy, at least far less irritated.

"Care to stretch?" Candenning stood up and reached for her hand. It was a gesture of easy presumption, but she did not mind. There was a quality to the man that was almost gallant. Somehow, despite the filth of the train, the evil stench of the food and animals, and people, and the unpleasant saturation of hair and clothing, he was able to transcend the misery of their surroundings. He might have been the ghost of Renaissance elegance—cruelly transported, yet completely unbroken.

She took his hand and let him help her to her feet. His eyes, she noticed, were very blue and almost sad. His smile, faint and cynical as ever, was still quite sincere.

Their wet shoes made almost disgusting sounds as they walked the few paces to the car's vestibule then down the steps.

Over Tehuacán, the sun was struggling to push through the last bit of overcast sky. Buildings and damp ground were already steaming under its evaporative power. The roofs of the town might have been the undamaged, yet smoldering, hearth for some celestial fire.

Candenning took a cigarette case from his shirt pocket, snapped it open, and offered her one.

She shook her head.

He tapped his cigarette several times on the case the more firmly to pack its tobacco, then lit it as the German couple slowly descended from the train.

As when she had first been introduced to him, Karen thought the man unusually nervous and apprehensive. He constantly looked this way and that apparently in an effort to seek out some hidden motive in each person leaving the train as well as soon to become a passenger. No one seemed above suspicion. The little man had all the behavior patterns of a desperate animal running from something he knew had him completely at its mercy.

Candenning apparently noticed it too, for he began an easy conversation in German. Although Karen didn't understand the words, there was a reassuring quality to his voice. The woman smiled several times and, albeit gradually, the man appeared to relax.

Karen was looking along the length of the train just as William Scofield stepped down. Hoping he would not see her and perhaps try to join the group, she turned away and, in doing so, almost bumped into the man in the ill-fitting suit, who had run after the train as they left Oaxaca.

"Forgive me . . ." He bowed to the group. "It may be presumptuous, but you are apparently strangers to Mexico. I am Domingo Portes. If I can be of service . . ."

"Why, yes." Candenning looked directly at him. There was a very serious, almost stern, expression on his face.

"I'm at your orders."

"Could you . . ." The serious expression fluttered away for just an instant, then returned. "I mean, do you suppose you could get the trains on schedule?"

As she glanced from the Mexican to Candenning then back again, Karen saw both the twinkle of humor in the artist's eyes as well as the perplexed expression on the other's face. Charles Candenning had barely met the man but was already presuming to tease him. Karen tried, but couldn't control her laughter.

Portes, who had apparently taken the remark seriously at

first, turned to her then accepted the joke with an easy smile. "I'm afraid," he said almost sadly, "there are some miracles even the Almighty cannot perform."

"Ah," Candenning grunted. "What about beer that's cold?"

Portes shook his head. "You ask for impossible things, Señor. There is, however, the water, Tehuacán is famous for its mineral water."

"No." Candenning was quite serious again. "As a favor, no water."

Portes frowned. "You are not German." His voice was quite casual, but Karen saw a strange intensity in his eyes.

"No," the artist told him. "I only speak it. Unfortunately, the Heinrichs here speak neither Spanish nor English. Makes it all very amusing, don't you think?"

"But, you speak Spanish so well." The unwavering fire never left Portes' eyes.

Candenning shrugged.

"You have been here some long time?"

"No, worse luck."

Now Portes shrugged. It might have been a badly rehearsed gesture in an amateur theatrical. "Mine is an amazing country," he said. "It has many beauties, many treasures. I have traveled from San Cristóbal. Do you know San Cristóbal?"

"Never been that far south." Candenning shook his head. "Only to Oaxaca. Precious little time there either."

"Ah." Portes drew in his lower lip and seemed to suck on it a moment. "And your friend, the German gentleman? Perhaps he knows of Chiapas—of San Cristóbal?"

Candenning turned to the German couple and spoke a few words. They, in turn, held a brief exchange. Finally, the American turned back to Portes. "Unfortunately, they've never even heard of it."

"It's fascinating country," Portes said. "Very green—very rich."

Before Candenning could reply, a railroad employee near the forward end of the train cried out "*Vamonos*!" and waved his arm to signal the passengers aboard. The engine's bell rang several times, indicating an intention to move at some future time. Candenning and Portes nodded politely as they turned back toward their separate cars.

As Karen walked the few steps back to the train, she watched the Mexican return to the young woman with whom he was now apparently traveling. She also noticed the extremely handsome man standing with two small boys. He was looking directly at her with an almost arrogant expression, which left no doubt as to his thoughts.

Embarrassed, she climbed rapidly aboard and returned to her damp seat just as the train made its first forward lurch.

The German couple now seemed almost completely relaxed. The woman rested her head on her husband's shoulder and he stroked her hair very gently. His eyes no longer darted this way and that in feral anticipation of disaster. In them now, she noticed only love and a deep concern for his wife's comfort.

She too was beginning to feel almost completely at ease next to Charles Candenning. Despite his cynicism and rather strange sense of humor, there was something genuinely warm and almost protective about him.

The train increased its speed.

"Curious fellow." Candenning snapped his case open and withdrew a cigarette.

"Señor Portes?"

"Yes."

"I have a funny feeling," she said. "He's not just traveling. I don't really know how to say it, but he's looking for something—something very important."

He nodded, lit the cigarette, and exhaled out the window. "Me too." He took another deep drag, then sighed. "Probably a railroad detective," he said, "or some sort of governmental somebody. Oh well, whatever it is, I hope he finds it."

He remained silent, almost pensive for some time, before turning to her. "There's only one major stop between here and the capital," he said. "Puebla. If I had the time, I'd get off and paint the cathedral. That's the whole damned trouble. I'd expected a whole month down here and then the damned army . . ."

There was something almost childish in his manner. He might have been a ten-year-old who couldn't quite understand a stroke of bad luck. Without thinking, she reached out and, in an effort to reassure that little boy, laid her hand on his.

He placed his free palm over it and turned. Still, he was the little boy but now, instead of wistful sadness, he was possessed of an almost wild enthusiasm. "Damn the army," he said. "They can wait one more day. I want to see the capital, do a tour—Chapultepec, the Almeda, the Palace of Fine Arts, the works. Would you come along with me?"

She had misjudged. Her unthinking plunge had ended in a belly flop. Reality slapped her. With it came all the fear, all the caution, of a once-hurt female. She pulled her hand free.

"Oh, come on." he pleaded. "I've had my whole vacation ruined. You've been stuck in the tropics for God knows how long. We're the only two Americans within miles. Please . . ."

"Really, I—"

"Look," he said. "I've never seen Mexico. Just been through. I was so eager to get to Oaxaca. I remembered it as a boy, before all the shooting started. My father took me down there. Fantastic town, beautiful churches—but the capital— Mexico . . ."

The little boy was back, and looking at him—seeing again the wild innocence of his eyes, the almost mendicant expression on his face—her fear dissipated. Caution remained, but she no longer felt the urge to flee. Like a fawn, she looked at him and cocked her head to one side. "You're a strange man," she said.

"Oh?"

"An artist—a soldier."

"I'm afraid I'm not much of a soldier."

"There must be some reason for calling you back."

"I'm sure I don't know what."

"Some special talent?"

"I paint magazine covers." He smiled. "But that's not the point. Please come along with me. I mean, it won't be any good unless I can share it."

She looked at him for a long moment before releasing a sigh of resignation. "Oh, all right," she said.

Somehow, even then, she knew it was the right decision.

The ride northeast to Puebla was scenic and the atmosphere relaxed. As the train climbed, the climate became more comfortable. She even began to accept the discomfort of dank clothing and the unpleasant aromas of the train.

The German couple slept most of the way, while she and Charles Candenning chatted impersonally about Mexico, Spanish architecture, and her work with the Indians. By the time the train hissed into the station at Puebla, she felt so at ease that she had no desire to descend to the platform.

Passengers milled back and forth along the crowded aisle. Vendors hawked their wares and people and animals shuffled this way and that. The stopping was absolutely normal in every way until she heard the German gasp, "*Oh Gott!*"

She looked up to see him staring over her shoulder and down the length of the car. He looked like a man who had just been hit in the solar plexis.

"What is it?" she asked.

The older man turned to Candenning. He spoke very softly, but urgently and rapidly for a few seconds.

"What is it?" she said again.

"Nothing," Candenning said.

"Nothing! He looks like he's had a stroke." She started to turn to look down the length of the car.

Gently, but firmly, he placed his left palm against her cheek. "Don't," he said. His voice was very soft.

"Don't be silly."

The pressure of his palm increased, forcing her to turn back toward him.

"Miss Tait . . ." His tone was absolutely serious. "We may be in a somewhat awkward situation. Our friend here has just told me of some new passengers."

"Well—what of it?"

"Apparently they intend to harm him."

"That's ridicul—"

"Frankly, I'm inclined to believe him."

"But—"

"But," he echoed, "relax." He smiled. "Try to think of it as just another aspect of travel in Mexico."

The train wheezed, then suddenly jerked forward.

"Oh, my God," she said. "You're serious."

Candenning nodded. "Deadly serious," he said.

"Oh, my God," she said again.

Book IV

MEXICO CITY

1
Suspicion

THE BUILDING HAD once been the modest palace of a distant cousin to Maximilian. Subsequently, it had been occupied by various functionaries, mistresses, or favorites of those in power until, during the short-lived puppet administration of Portes Gil, it had been completely renovated and redecorated.

Now, although still apparently the single residence of someone favored or powerful, it was in fact an apartment complex tenanted by five Americans who, for varying reasons, did not care to live in their own national residential district in the southwest section of the city. Four of the tenants housed their wives and children with them. The fifth, although polite and affable, had been consigned to Coventry by the others, because he lived openly with a woman to whom he was not married. It was commonly known, at least by North Americans, that such behavior constituted a threat to people more decently inclined.

The building itself boasted all the modern amenities and conveniences available to those of taste and solvency north of the border. Water ran hot or cold at any hour, pilot lights burned constantly on the stoves, and there was electricity throughout. The rooms all had radiators, as well as overhead fans, and security was assured both by the decorative iron grillwork over the windows and a man named Alfredo.

Alfredo was a tall and imposing veteran of the confrontation with General Pershing's expeditionary force in 1916. That year, at Carrizal, four machine-gun bullets had smashed into his left arm, shattering his elbow and the lower humerus so thoroughly that amputation had been necessary. He accepted the loss with a certain cynical irony, for the Americans responsible for crippling him then were the very people responsible for supporting him now.

Alfredo acted as doorman, security guard, and general factotum for the apartment building. The tenants all knew and respected him yet rarely called him by name. All seemed far more comfortable referring to him simply as *El Portero*.

That afternoon Thomas Kemp encountered the porter outside the building, where he was skillfully cultivating a small flower garden with a hoe.

"With your permission . . ." Kemp pursed his lips in what he hoped would look like a completely innocent, perhaps even naive, facsimile of Huckleberry Finn's smile. "I wonder if this is the home of the American, Mr. Oberon?"

"Ah." *El Portero* stood erect, looked at Kemp for a moment, then sighed luxuriously. "Yes," he said. "The young gentleman with the English woman."

"That would be the man." Kemp smiled again. "And—in which apartment?"

El Portero sighed again. "Unfortunately, Sir . . ." He lifted the stump of his missing arm in what was perhaps intended as a gesture of resignation. The result was only grotesque. "Mr. Oberon is not in the house."

"Oh?"

"No, Sir. He and Miss Whitley have gone."

"Gone? Where?"

He scratched his stump almost thoughtfully for a moment. "A very good question, Sir, but I don't know the answer. I only know they have gone to a hotel."

"But he has an apartment here."

"It's true. But the ladies—you know how they can be, Sir. Living in adultery . . ."

"That's ridiculous!" Kemp snapped. "A man doesn't leave an apartment and go to a hotel—unless—" he said in English. "Damn it!" He turned to Alfredo and, in Spanish again, asked, "Which one?"

"Ah, Sir, unfortunately, I cannot answer that either."

"You know he's at a hotel, but you don't know which?"

"You see, I was here when the taxi came. I myself said farewell to Mr. Oberon and the lady. You understand, Sir, he put her into the taxi first and then followed her. I heard him say, 'hotel,' but then he slammed the door on the very name. Sir, I am only a porter. It is not my business to spy."

Kemp tried to mask his growing fury. He was as angry with himself as with Oberon. Obviously, he had misjudged his quarry. There could be only two possible reasons for Oberon to leave the security of his apartment and go to a hotel. Either someone had told him he was a marked man, or he was on his way to some assignation that might help him get out of the mess which he had managed to get himself into.

Kemp tried to put himself in the other man's position. He could either hide in Mexico City until he smoothed over the situation with Móndez—that would surely mean an accomplice of some sort—or he could try to flee the country entirely. If he made a run for it, it would either be north to the United States or east out of Vera Cruz.

All of which was pure speculation. The hard and annoying fact was that, on an overcast summer afternoon, Mr. Neil Oberon was in only one of the scores of hotels in Mexico City, and Thomas Kemp had been assigned the unfortunate task of finding him.

He asked Alfredo to get him a taxi, and while he waited for it to arrive, he tried to outguess or at least guess in the first place Oberon's moves. The man was used to luxury; that he knew. He would want the very best in accommodations—unless he planned to flee. In that case, he might want to get as close as possible either to the railroad station or the airport.

The taxi stopped in front of the building. *El Portero* opened the door. "Good luck, Sir."

Kemp grunted as he slid into the vehicle.

"To where?" the driver asked.

Thomas Kemp pursed his lips. It might be a mistake, but he decided to start at the top. "Hotel Reforma," he said.

He settled back in the seat. It was going to be a long afternoon, he was sure. It might even become an unpleasantly long night as well.

As the taxi negotiated busy traffic on noisy streets, Kemp allowed his anger the luxury of growth. He was furious at this inconvenience, insulted by having been outsmarted by his intended prey. Yet behind his bitterness—there glowed a single consolation: Kemp knew that his quarry had indeed bought a few hours, perhaps even a day or so. He also knew that, for all practical purposes, Neil Oberon was, in fact, already a dead man.

Supposedly precious *per se*, human life is never quite so valuable as when considered subjectively. Suspicious, intuitive and precociously wise in the ways of survival, Oberon had selected a hiding place far less prepossessing than the Hotel Reforma. In an attempt to be at once inconspicuous while still moderately comfortable, as well as near his intended spot of departure from the capital, he had taken a room in the Biltmore. It was not a particularly large hotel, and the accommodations were hardly as luxurious as those of the Reforma or the Ritz, but the room was clean, there was a bath, and the charge was only five pesos. Most important, however, was the fact that it was so close to the railroad terminal.

Oberon was sure that if, in fact, he was being stalked, his would-be assassin would expect him either to follow an established pattern of luxurious living, or break that pattern entirely by hiding in one of the small, purely Mexican hotels completely disassociated from American or European clientele. The Biltmore, located where it was and being neither elegant nor popular for roof garden, cocktail lounge, or other amenity, had seemed a perfect choice. He was confident that, posing as Mr. and Mrs. John Noyes, honeymooners on their way to Buenos Aires, he and Margaret could remain safely there for a day or perhaps two before actually leaving the city.

Ideally, he would have flown to Durango. That way, he could have left rapidly and made much faster contact with Marcos Almidero. Flying, however, had too many drawbacks. The man he had sent north to make initial contact with the bandit had insisted upon motoring. His car would be much slower than any aeroplane and, once arrived, he would need time to locate the elusive Scorpion.

It was not timing, however, but Oberon's basic instinct for survival that had kept him on the ground. Julio Móndez's final cablegram had been terse—precise as a surgeon's incision. The two words, LAST REQUEST, had spoken volumes. Oberon knew he either had to get the long overdue rifles or end his days along with the scores of others who were found murdered each day in a supposedly peaceful, yet politically turbulent, Mexico.

He had absolutely no doubt that the airport was being watched. His chances of boarding a flight out of Mexico were perhaps one in ten. Even if he could get safely aboard a plane, he would only be moving into a trap. Destinations were always known, and fast as flight was, radio, telephone, and telegraph were still faster. The FBI would be waiting for him at any American airport. A machete or bullet would surely greet him in Vera Cruz, Guatemala, or anywhere else to the south.

His one hope lay now in hiding for a day or perhaps

145

two—hoping to convince any pursuers that he had already left the capital—then trying to get lost in the crowds at the railroad station. If spotted, he could always jump from a train. He could always vanish into a crowd at some obscure station.

He was standing at the hotel room's window, absently looking down at the traffic crawling along Ramos Arizpe, when Margaret came from behind and snaked her arms easily around his torso. She nuzzled her cheek against his back and sighed seductively.

"I'll get the tickets tonight." He spoke to the street below. "We'll get out on the first possible train."

"It's all right," she said. "I rather like hotel rooms. There's something quite sensual—clandestined really—about them. Don't you think?"

"I hadn't given it much thought."

"Well then, how about honeymoonish?"

He only grunted.

"Oh, darling," she purred. "Don't be such a frightful bear."

"We're going to have to stay here," he told her. "Not go out for anything."

When she spoke, her voice was no longer playful. "You really are in trouble, aren't you? This hotel—hiding here like some gangster . . ."

He turned to face her. "It's just best to lay low for a while, that's all."

"What you mean is we're trapped—probably even being watched."

"Oh, come on, Maggi. Don't be so damned melodramatic."

"All right." She lifted her chin and feigned a slight pout. "I'll be perfectly serious then. Explain it any way you like, but you don't want to leave the room. And if I can't leave the room either, I'd like to do something interesting."

"Such as?"

"Well, after all, darling, we *are* supposed to be honey mooners."

"So?"

"Oh, darling, don't be so impossibly dense."

"Oh." He was hardly in a mood for romance.

He tried to glance noncommittally over her head, but she pulled his lips almost to hers. "Now, dear heart . . ." She spoke almost into his mouth. "Do be nice to me, won't you? After all, if you're nice to me, I shall be ever so nice to you."

"You know, Maggi . . ." His sigh was almost one of hopelessness. "Beneath all the glitter and charm, you really are basically a tramp."

"Of course, darling." She pushed her hips forward and ground herself provocatively against him. "That's exactly why you love me, isn't it? After all, how many of your precious four hundred Meadowbrook or Wellesley girls would treat you as nicely as I?"

He merely grunted.

"Besides, we *are* going to get married."

"Sure."

"And practice, they tell me, makes perfect."

"All right," he said. "You've made your point."

Although he lacked any real enthusiasm for what was about to happen, he started to unbutton her blouse. They would be confined to the room for several hours, and he had brought no cards or reading matter. Besides, he told himself, Margaret was, despite her fundamental vulgarity, a woman who genuinely liked to give and take sexual pleasure.

Still, as his fingers worked their way to the second button, he knew that at the moment he would just as soon have smoked a cigarette.

With Teresa Inez, Domingo Portes had again descended to the station platform to stretch his legs at Puebla. He had wanted to question the German and the tall American further, but he had not seen either the man or the women with whom they had talked at Tehuacán. He had, however, encountered the short man who disliked President Roosevelt's policies and, in an attempt to make amends for his earlier social ineptness, had asked him about his business.

Scofield was obviously quite self-satisfied. "Imports," he told Portes. "Y'know, all these phony tidbits the boys are selling down here for five, maybe six, *centavos*. Once I get them up across the border, I make six—seven hundred percent profit."

"Interesting," Portes conceded. "You deal in artifacts then?"

"Phony stuff—trinkets. Stuff like that. Very cheap."

"And you have a shipment with you?"

147

"Hell yes! Twenty-four cases. Right in there." He nodded toward the train.

Twenty-four cases!

"Really?" Portes tried to sound unemotionally impressed.

Twelve burros—two cases each!

"That's a large cargo."

Scofield continued looking at Teresa. "Yes," he said. "It's true. I'll make a few dollars this trip."

Portes did not like the flat expression in Scofield's eyes. He did not like the way the man looked at the actress. Was he jealous, he wondered? He refused to answer his own question for fear he might have to admit its very existence. He returned his concentration to his mission. The truth had almost been stripped bare now. The tall American and the German were only what they had appeared to be—travelers. It was this overconfident little man who was unquestionably one of the thieves. Portes was almost sure of it. Scofield, with his flat eyes and ill-concealed lust, was the man he had followed from the mountains of Chiapas. He was also the man someone else had followed through Tuxtla Gutiérrez and Juchitán. That second someone could only be the other thief—obviously a betrayed accomplice.

"I'm happy for you," Portes said. "Here in Mexico such huge profits are not often possible."

He wanted to press Scofield to say more about his business. He wanted to see the man's merchandise, but as a priest—an outlawed member of the dreaded Society of Jesus—he had to move carefully. He was alone, trapped between an obviously ruthless criminal and a hostile secular authority.

Trying to appear absolutely casual, he glanced forward along the length of train. Several members of the military escort were leaning on their rifles, smoking and chatting. As had happened several times before, he was about to kill a man for the sake of the Church. This time, however, it would not be in armed rebellion against heretics. This time it would not be in combat with a hot desire for revenge in his soul, and the image of the martyred father Miguel Pro kneeling by a bullet-pitted wall etched indelibly in his mind's eye.

This time it would be a very cold and precise assassination—premeditated murder for the greater glory of God, in the name of Christ the King. He had to be utterly sure, beyond even the hint of a doubt, of the little man's guilt.

"Yes, sir," Scofield said. "A tidy little profit."

"We will be in the capital soon," Portes said. It was patently obvious that Scofield wanted Teresa. Portes thought he might just as well try to dangle the actress before the arrogant little man. After all, ends always justified the means. Wasn't that the secret of all strength? "Perhaps when we arrive, you might like to join Miss Inez and me for dinner in the city?"

"Sure," Scofield said. He looked as though he was literally unable to tear his eyes away from the young woman. He might have been the victim of some sexual rather than metallic Midas touch. Then, slowly, reluctantly, he turned away and sighed. A man torn between two objects of lust, he was forced to make a monumentally painful choice. "I'd like to go," he said. "Just can't neglect business. Got to make sure my merchandise is transferred right to the next train."

Portes was more convinced than ever. "Yes," he said. "I understand."

The engine clanged its bell several times. The soldiers tossed their cigarettes away and clambered aboard. With the other passengers who had decided to exercise their legs, Portes, the young actress, and Bill Scofield turned back to the train. Scofield reached the steps first. He climbed two of them, then turned and looked down to Portes.

"Say," he said, "I forgot to ask. What line of business're you in?"

"I?" The Jesuit smiled. "I'm a soldier."

"On leave, eh?"

"Not really." He looked the little man directly in the flat, reptilian eyes and allowed himself an even broader smile. "I retired for a time. I've just been recalled."

Apparently unimpressed, Scofield only grunted before turning, scampering up the final step, and turning into the car.

As Portes waited with one foot still on the lowest step, he could almost feel Teresa's look on him. He turned and saw her questioning frown.

"Don't worry," he assured her. "It's a game I sometimes play. After all, a priest can't be too careful these days."

"But a soldier?"

" 'What's in a name?' " he quoted. " 'That which we call a rose . . .' "

"You know Shakespeare?"

Her undisguised enthusiasm was somehow quite unnerving.

He turned, climbed the stairs and, at the top, turned to offer her his hand. "After all," he said, "we are allowed to read more than the Gospels."

She was standing beside him now in the vestibule. Her black eyes were very sincere and almost hypnotic. "I'm glad you did not lie to me."

Her hand was still in his. It was very soft and delicately smooth. He forced himself to release its warmth and turn away from the magnet of her eyes.

In the car William Scofield was just paying a few *centavos* to the boy who had guarded their seats. Portes and the actress sat down across from the tiny man just as the train gave a mighty sigh and heaved itself forward.

Domingo Portes tried to erase the perfumed presence of the woman next to him. He forced himself to return to his mission.

"How long have you been in the import business, Mr. Scofield?"

He could barely hear his own voice. He found it difficult to concentrate on his prey. He was too aware of Teresa's presence—her warmth, the sheer magnitude of her person. He did not even notice the two men in the seat almost directly opposite him.

They were dressed in conservative business suits. Both wore hats. They sat facing the rear of the train. Neither spoke. They were quite obviously foreigners. Just as obviously they were not Americans. They sat too stiffly, as though physically unable to relax their spines.

Both men had light blond hair and blue eyes. Had Domingo Portes noticed the two—had he looked into their eyes and tried to describe them—he would have been carried back to the time of the *Cristeros* and to the rebellion of '27.

He would have called them, *ojos de los ametralladoreros*—machine gunners' eyes.

At the very rear of the car, Charles Candenning appeared to be the picture of absolute relaxation. He leaned back on an angle so that his left shoulder pressed into the seat, while his right rested against the side of the train next to the window.

"What do they look like?" He might have been asking the time of day.

Dr. Pelzig was also attempting to appear as casual as possible. "They look exactly as Mr. Hitler would wish them to look. They are blond and athletic. Believe me, there is no question, Mr. Candenning. We are in very serious danger."

"It is somewhat difficult to understand, Mr. Heinrich."

Hannah Pelzig turned to her husband. "Oh, Jakob—tell him. He is the only one we can trust. We will never get off the train! Your work . . . all these years . . ."

Jakob Pelzig sighed. "All right." He raised the palm of his left hand slightly off his knee. "All right," he said again. "Listen to me, Mr. Candenning. We have little time before reaching Mexico City. I cannot tell you everything, but my name is not Heinrich."

"Somehow, I gathered that in Oaxaca."

"I am not good at this, really. I feel almost like a criminal. I am a professor of physics. My name is Jakob Pelzig."

"And in the middle of Mexico two men intend to kill you? You must be very hard on your students."

"Don't joke, please. We had to leave Germany. I don't know how, but I simply knew. The Nazis—they want what I have. If they cannot have it, I know they will kill me. They will kill us both—perhaps you and the young lady as well."

"Physics is obviously more exciting in Europe than when I went to school."

"Please . . ." Pelzig glanced furtively over Karen's shoulder, then back to Candenning. "Don't ask me any more." He seemed worried that the two men at the far end of the railway car might even hear him. "I know something. It is not perfect yet, but believe me, it is just a matter of time. Hitler is going to war. Any thinking man knows that. I and two other men may know how to stop him. Those men down there know it. They intend to force me back to Germany or to kill me."

Candenning nodded but did not speak.

"What is it?" Karen asked. "What's he saying?"

"He's saying," Candenning told her, "that we're not really on a train. We're in an Alfred Hitchcock movie."

"I don't—"

"Naturally," Pelzig went on, "we are safe as long as we sit here with passengers around us. But if we try to change cars when we get to Mexico City . . ."

Candenning nodded again. "Right," he said. "I understand." Then, almost abruptly, "Have you ever played football?"

"Football?"

"Yes."

"What has football to do—"

"Never mind," Candenning said. "You get off the train as fast as you can. Just up and out the vestibule behind you. We'll see what we can do to help." He turned to Karen. "And you . . ." he said in English. "How do you like football?"

"What?" She was annoyed at her own inability to understand German.

Charles Candenning smiled. "Or perhaps I should say Christmas shopping at Macy's?"

"I do wish you'd make sense."

"Apparently, Miss Tait, we have fallen into an adventure. If you're willing, I'd like you to help me do Doctor Pelzig a favor."

"Doctor Pelzig? Who is—"

"I'll explain later," he said. "Right now let's you and I choreograph an international incident."

Despite the ever-treacherous winds over Vera Cruz, the Taylor J2 Cub made an almost poetically perfect landing. It taxied to the end of the runway, then turned back for the necessary inspection of passengers and cargo. Although it had actually come from Randolf Field and had flown east before turning south, the light aircraft, apparently owned by the Mexican Eagle Oil Company, had Brownsville, Texas listed on its log as its point of origin.

Cargo was limited to four leather suitcases containing little more than men's clothing and toilet articles. In addition, there were several packs of Chesterfield cigarettes and a flask of whiskey. Such items were to be expected in American luggage.

The two passengers and the pilot carried passports and visas which were in order. All three men had papers identifying themselves as employees of Mexican Eagle, a subsidiary of the Royal Dutch Shell combination. The pilot's name was Henderson. A man in his middle forties, he was obviously a veteran of more than one dog fight. His posture, the quiet authority of his voice, and the easy, almost arrogant way he held his cigarette were all unmistakable marks of a man not merely used to fighting, but inured to winning as well.

The two passengers had been cut from an entirely different mold. They were both inconspicuous men of a new generation, and were apparently consumed by an aspiration for security rather than a lust for adventure. Their papers identified them as brothers who had interrupted vacations in the United States due to a minor family crisis. They had decided to travel north precisely when, unknown to them, their parents had left Europe to surprise them by a visit to Mexico.

The two young men were quite convincing at the customs office, where they explained that they had lost track of their father and mother, who had been on the *Prince Umberto* which had arrived several days earlier.

"An elderly man . . . gray . . . wearing glasses . . . And mother . . . a frail woman. Sometimes she coughs . . ."

"*Ay, si. Si, recordo!*" A customs officer did remember such a couple. They had passed through inspection, but then had run for a taxi. "Yes," he told them. He did remember because of the other men—the two young Germans who had caused the disturbance trying to follow them. Apparently they were with the old couple, but did not wish to be inspected. It was an unfortunate incident.

The two young men found sympathy wherever they went. Family was important and they had lost their parents. The people to whom they talked commiserated with them, but could offer little help. The older Pelzigs had not been seen at the airport or the bus terminal. One railroad porter, however, did remember the couple taking the train to Guatemala.

At the airport again, the two younger men conferred with their pilot. In the cabin of the small plane, they sorted the scant bits of information given them by Sidney Desmond.

"He has no reason to go south," Henderson said. "He's trying to get north, isn't he?"

"He knows they're after him," said one of the younger "Pelzigs," who was actually a young man named McMillan, a graduate of West Point now working not for an American oil company but for the State Department. "He's dodging—trying to confuse them."

"But Guatemala?"

"He doesn't have to go all the way," said the second of the younger "Pelzigs." He was, in reality, named Klein, a graduate of Harvard's Law School also working for the Department.

"Train south." McMillan tapped the map. "Then—maybe a plane over the isthmus."

"No. No planes," Henderson told them. "If he dodged them here at customs like you said, he would have taken the regular Pan Am flight out then. He's not flying. You can bet on it."

153

"A train?" Klein speculated. "He'll be on a train or bus."

"Train," said McMillan. "He wouldn't put his wife on a bus—not in Mexico. Yeah . . ." He tapped a long, well-manicured finger on the map. "He got off that Guatemala train, then swung south. He's heading north from the Pacific instead of the Atlantic coast."

"There," his partner said. "Right there. Our man's in Oaxaca. I'll bet my ass on it."

"Yeah?" McMillan countered. "And if you're wrong?"

"I'm not. If he's not there now, he's been there, and if we're right—if he won't fly—there's only one way out—the train up to the capital."

He turned to Henderson, but the pilot had already anticipated him. The thirty-seven horsepower Continental A 40-3 engine was already spinning the propeller. Within a matter of minutes the tiny craft had headed into the wind then risen from Vera Cruz. At two thousand feet it banked south and headed over the mountains toward Oaxaca.

2
The Station

IN LATER YEARS Charles Candenning would occasionally claim that, as a choreographer, he had once shown some little promise, even though his career as an arranger of dance patterns had been both short-lived and near-catastrophic. In fact, it had almost been responsible for taking his own and at least one other life.

At the time, however, he considered his aptitude for planning actual movements as good as his ability to illustrate the interactions of imaginary people in short stories. Although outwardly casual and cynically uncaring, there was to Candenning's character an exactitude which, in the final analysis, was probably responsible not only for his success as a commercial artist, but for his skill as a linguist and perfection as a pistol shot as well. From his father he had inherited an easy bonhomie, an appreciation of cultural elegance, and an unpretentious grace in facing circumstances—regardless of their nature. It was his mother, however, who had taught him the value of precision and the intrinsic worth of duty for its own sake. The result of this combination was that he could easily exchange tailor-made clothing and sterling flatware for a sarape and folded tortilla, but he would invariably wear the blanket with a precise elegance and use the flat cake with the grace of a Medici.

So, because he felt a certain obligation to his traveling companions, and because he understood both the mathematics of rhythm and the necessity for exact timing, he considered himself perfectly qualified to organize the interference necessary to allow the Pelzigs to escape.

As the train struggled up the last few miles to the central plateau of Mexico, Candenning explained the situation to Karen. Two men had boarded at Puebla. They were apparently intent upon doing some harm to Mr. Heinrich—who was really Dr. Pelzig—and his wife. If Miss Tait would be kind enough to delay the men in the event of their exit from the front of the car, he would do the same at the rear.

Karen asked several quesitons, all of which he answered with kindness and tact. As the train began to slow, however, he patted her almost patronizingly on the knee.

"Believe me," he told her, "it will be painless—absolutely painless."

As she stood up, her expression was not one of unbridled enthusiasm.

"Really," he said. "It might even be fun."

She pulled her valise from the luggage rack and struggled it forward along the length of the car. As he watched her progress, he could not help admiring her sense of timing. Just as the train wheezed its last few yards into the terminal at Mexico City, she passed forward of and between the seats occupied on one side by William Scofield, and on the other by the two men who had boarded at Puebla.

He watched her wait until the train actually stopped, saw one of the blond men rise and start forward, then heard her little cry of exasperation as she dropped the heavy suitcase sideways in the aisle and knelt down, ostensibly to pick it up.

The man who had risen stepped into the aisle just behind Karen and was moving with such inertia that, when she stooped, he almost catapulted over her. Had he not had superb reflexes, he would undoubtedly have soared forward to land face-down in the midst of discarded bits of food, spittle, and other unpleasantries which dotted the car's aisle.

He was, however, able to take a step sideways, grab the back of a seat, and thus regain his balance as his companion, now also on his feet, started toward the rear of the car.

Charles Candenning hastened the Pelzigs into the vestibule just to their rear then turned back into the car. The older couple dashed from the train as the second blond man started to the rear, pushing and shoving almost brutally against passengers who were barring his way in the aisle.

Candenning turned to the window, satisfied himself that the Pelzigs actually were gone, then, with meticulous timing, worthy, he thought, of Vaslav Nijinsky himself, turned at exactly the proper moment necessary to block the man with a force sufficient to recoil him several feet backward, almost into the lap of a very rotund and matronly woman.

"Oh!" Candenning thought he sounded like a completely untalented boy playing in some ghastly sixth-form play. "I am so sorry," he said in German. "So very sorry."

The man was obviously not amenable to apologies. "Swine!" he hissed. "Move! Out of the way!"

Candenning took a step forward. "Really," he insisted. "I am so terribly sorry."

"Bastard!" Suddenly the man's coat was unbuttoned. His hand darted within and, a moment later, returned holding a pistol.

Charles Candenning was staring at the muzzle of a very ugly Walther Military Model automatic.

"Move!" the German said again. "Out!"

Candenning lifted both hands. "Of course." He had been shot once twenty years before. He had no desire to repeat the experience. "Of course," he said again as he stepped out of the aisle.

The man darted past him to the rear vestibule.

At the forward end of the car, Karen seemed to be having more luck. Apparently quite flustered, she was still kneeling beside her valise blocking the aisle. Candenning had just started toward her when he saw the second German lean over, grab her by one arm, and drag her to her feet.

Domingo Portes also witnessed the scene. "*Momento!*" he called to the German.

The rest was almost a blur—a confused *pas de deux* which,

in his initial choreography, Charles Candenning had completely neglected to anticipate.

Portes pushed into the aisle, and as the blond man attempted to step over the valise, Portes slapped a hand on his shoulder.

"One moment!" he insisted again. "The lady—"

He said no more.

As the man spun around, his right fist seemed about to smash into Portes' face.

The physical threat, momentary though it was, became an eruptive catalyst. The menace of assault acted as a magic elixir. In the splinter of a second, Domingo Portes lost a decade. Within him, long-smoldering hostility erupted to fire. His blood pressure soared. He ignited to an exquisite intoxication. He was in combat again and loving the sheer beauty of violence with a totally vicious, absolutely abandoned sensuosity.

He parried the blow with his left forearm and, in the same easy, almost poetic, movement, slid that fist down to the man's clavicle.

The German grunted in agony, but before he could move, Portes looked directly into his eyes—the eyes of the machine gunner—and with all the power of trapezius and deltoid muscles, threw his right fist into the man's nose.

The impact was a flat wet snap—the sound perhaps of a damp tortilla dropped on a rock, yet amplified a hundredfold. The man flew backward, spattering flecks of blood right and left. Arms flaying wildly, he staggered but did not go down. Blood drenched his upper lip and mouth and flew in a great, partially coagulated clot as he shook his head to clear his senses. His eyes were wide with pain and fury, his voice inchoate as he, too, drew a pistol and leveled it at Portes.

The railroad car might have been a coffin. It contained no sound, no movement. An eternity passed, eon upon agonized eon—all compacted into four impossibly protracted seconds until suddenly the German replaced his pistol and, remembering some forgotten immediacy, dashed from the car.

The passengers remained silent a moment longer before each of them began speaking at the same time. Candenning again began forcing his way down the aisle, packed now with gesticulating passengers speaking a variety of languages and dialects, with varying tones of shock, panic, or hysteria.

He could see a tiny man slapping Portes enthusiastically on the biceps. "Not shabby," William Scofield was speaking

English. "Not half-shabby at all. Not Queensberry's best, but what the hell? You decked that son of a bitch good. He won't be sticking his nose in anywhere for a while now."

Candenning pushed himself another few feet to Karen. She stood absolutely motionless, obviously still shocked at what had happened, and the speed with which it had taken place.

"You all right?" he asked.

She nodded, but the movement lacked any conviction.

"I'm sorry," he said. "Here, sit down." He led her to an empty seat and eased her into it. "I should never have—"

"I'm all right," she said. "Really."

As she turned to him, he noticed the rich blue of her eyes made even more opulent by the pallor of her cheeks. Then, slowly, beginning as a tiny sparkle far in their depths and spreading almost casually to her face, he watched a smile begin to light her entire being. It reminded him of a Greek Orthodox Easter service he had once attended. In a packed and completely darkened cathedral, candles had been lit one by one until the entire building had been literally saturated with light.

The same sort of slow, but total, glow filled her face. It lifted her lips in a wide and beautiful smile until she finally chuckled. It was a deep, throaty, and very wonderful sound.

"Painless," she finally said. "Absolutely painless. Right?"

"Believe me, I never thought for a moment—"

She was still chuckling. "Go tell that to what's-his-name out there with the broken nose."

It was his turn to smile. "I guess the moral is—don't play around with chivalrous Mexicans."

As though his words had been some sort of cue, both of them turned to Domingo Portes. He was still standing in the aisle, absently inspecting the back of his right hand as he opened and closed the fingers.

"I saw that," Candenning said to him. "Very nice."

Portes stopped flexing and smiled. His teeth were very large and white. "I suppose," he said, "I'm just another Don Quixote—trying to right all the world's wrongs."

He turned to look at the little man with whom he had apparently been sitting.

In Portes' expression, Charles Candenning thought he saw something quite out of place. He could not be sure, but it seemed as if the Mexican's casual self-evaluation had, in actuality, possessed a very cold, dark promise.

The little man blinked and again Candenning thought he saw something out of place in his reptilian eyes.

The illusion lasted only an instant—unspoken threat and unexpressed acknowledgment. Then it was gone—like snow on the desert—as though it had never been.

The small man reached up to the luggage rack for what appeared to be some sort of knapsack, as Portes picked up a small suitcase.

Candenning felt as though he had somehow stepped in where he had no business being. He might have inadvertently invaded some sacristy of another's privacy. "Say," he said to Portes in an attempt to be as casual as possible. "Do you know the capital?"

"Slightly," the Mexican said. "I haven't been here for almost ten years. As I told you, I'm from the south. However . . ." He turned to the young woman who had remained calmly seated throughout the entire incident. "Perhaps Miss Inez . . ."

Candenning nodded. "Charles Candenning," he said. "And this is Karen Tait. We were thinking of touring the city tomorrow, seeing as much as we could."

"One cannot see Mexico City in a day."

"Maybe some highlights—"

The woman shrugged.

"And a good hotel near the station?"

"Most Americans stay at the Regis or the Reforma. But if you want to be close, there's the Biltmore. I'll be staying there myself."

"The Biltmore it is," Candenning said. "And for the information . . ." He turned to Portes, "and for the chivalry . . ." He turned next to Scofield. "And just for being a fellow American . . . you shall all have dinner on me."

"Really," Teresa said. "I don't think—"

"Nonsense," he insisted. "It's not every day one perpetrates an international incident, lets a fugitive escape, sees a punch like that, and gets free touring information as well."

Portes looked at Teresa. "Why not?" he said.

She shrugged.

"Done then!" Candenning said.

Bill Scofield had pulled his knapsack off the luggage rack and was now looking up almost pugnaciously at the illustrator. "Sorry," he said. "I've got business to tend to."

He pushed past Candenning and elbowed his way to the vestibule.

Candenning lifted his eyebrows. "Nothing personal," he said almost absently.

Almost as though he had understood the English, Domingo Portes nodded. "He is upset," he said. "He knows he has little time left."

"What's that?"

"*Nada*," the priest said. "Nothing at all. Yes, we'd be delighted to have dinner with you."

Nicholas Markoff made no attempt to be inconspicuous. He was well aware that his six feet four inches of impeccably tailored, athletic body topped by a leonine, obviously foreign, head was quite noticeable, and that any attempt to skulk or hide would not only be futile, but ludicrous as well.

Basically, however, he had no desire or need to hide. He had been paid to do a job, and he intended to perform his mission with the same high degree of professional efficiency he had always used. His proposed victim knew nothing of the plan and thus could be eliminated without any of the futile, annoying, cat-and-mouse maneuvers so frequent in these matters.

At the beginning he had been sure that his task would be relatively easy. Now, however, he knew it would be even easier. Juan Miguárdez had given him information which would make the assassination of Jesús Guerrero something close to child's play.

The president had just returned from one of his many trips to the heartland of Mexico. This time he had been to the north. He was concerned about Marcos Almidero's army, and the atrocities performed in the name of counterrevolution. But he had also traveled to many small villages to gather firsthand information necessary to aid his programs of land distribution, irrigation, and transportation reform.

According to Miguárdez, the president wanted to sever completely the Gordian knot of foreign control over Mexico's railroads. Hard facts had stopped him. Almost all the skilled railroad workers—engineers, switchmen, and executives—were foreigners.

Smashing foreign control of the National Railroads would cripple them. They simply could not be turned over to the workers until hundreds of Mexicans could be trained to take over the more responsible functions of operating the various lines.

Cárdenas, however, did plan an attack on the foreign interests controlling his country's transportation system. He intended to expropriate the railroads—to consolidate the bonded debt with the general obligations of the federal government—and thus deprive British and American creditors of millions of pesos. The accrued interest on the railroad debt had increased to such a point that it now exceeded the face value of the obligations themselves.

Miguárdez knew what the president actually intended to do. So, now, did Markoff. The problem was that hundreds of English and American railroad employees, possessed of the skills needed to operate the rolling stock safely and efficiently did not. It was almost public knowledge that Cárdenas intended something drastic, but what that would actually be was a matter of conjecture and rumor. The result was that most of the foreign railroad employees were playing a wait-and-see game, which had already crippled almost all scheduling and would continue to do so until the president made his plans known.

For Markoff, the transportation situation only meant that Jesús Guerrero and his family would be trapped in the very city they had intended to flee, and that if they didn't fly or take a bus north—unlikely choices at best—they would remain trapped for at least another day, perhaps longer.

His pale eyes scanned the passengers descending from the recently arrived Puebla train. He saw the older, obviously European, couple fairly jump from the rear of one car, then scurry through a group of passengers walking toward the main terminal. A moment later a blond man jumped from the same door and replaced what looked like a pistol beneath his coat. He glanced right and left before he, too, ran toward the main terminal. Several seconds later another blond man, his face and shirtfront covered with blood, jumped from the front of the same car. He, too, glanced this way and that before heading toward the terminal.

As he watched the little drama enacted before him, the Russian's facial features never changed. He was a man inured to the pain of others and completely unimpressed by the sight of blood. He was also capable of concentration so intense it might, in others actually be painful.

He was looking for one man, perhaps a woman or two

small children. He had seen photographs of them all. They alone comprised his mission. Middle-aged couples, men with pistols or bloody noses, jostling Indians, *metizos*, the sounds of wheezing engines or crying porters all were irrelevant to him.

His eyes might have been parts of a high-speed camera, clicking pictures of each departing passenger, then etching them into his brain, where each would be briefly evaluated, labeled, then discarded.

There were Indians who had come to the capital either to sell their wares or to petition the president about some local grievance or need. Along with them were the ever-present politicians, all easily identifiable by the pistols strapped to their waists. Although there were no horses, there were men in Charro suits, as well as a host of foreigners dressed either in business clothing or the rougher costumes which explained their reasons for exploiting Mexico as plantation overseers, miners, or employees of various oil companies.

Markoff saw a tiny man scamper from the same vestibule from which the bleeding man had jumped. Almost absently, his brain analyzed and labeled him "dangerous."

A moment later, a tall man descended the same stairs and turned back to offer his hand to someone else.

Gentleman, thought Markoff. *A tourist but upset about something . . . a man with personal problems.*

The first woman had hair almost the color of strawberries.

Very serious, the Russian thought. *Problems, too, but here on some business.*

The next woman was stunning. He knew he had seen her before. *At what party*? he wondered. *What gathering of the Mexican elite and their hangers-on*?

Finally came the Mexican in the ill-fitting dark suit. Markoff almost smiled. *A priest*. They never seemed able to wear ordinary clothes. *Bad one, too . . . Probably out to bomb some government building.*

He looked toward the rear of the train, then let his eyes wander all the way to the front. Most of the military escort was still on board. Some, however, had descended to the platform where they were smoking and idling until receiving their next orders.

He, too, decided on a cigarette, and as he lit it, wondered what had happened to the feral little man he had seen at the station earlier. The nondescript fellow was certainly waiting for someone or something on this particular train, yet he was nowhere in sight. He couldn't have stationed himself at another track. Since rumors had spread of Cárdenas's proposed move against the foreign railroad interests, this had been the only train to arrive at the capital from the southwest.

Again the dark-haired woman's face flashed in his mind. He turned toward the main terminal in hopes of getting another look at her.

A peasant woman with shoes? Walking with a barely disguised priest and an American tourist? Improbable.

Then, suddenly, he knew.

The actress!

He had never met her—had never seen one of her movies, yet several months ago there had been something in the news about the Hotel Regis Bar—something to do with Jesús Guerrero.

Teresa Inez . . . just one of Guerrero's many women . . . and on this train . . .

The platform was clearing now. Markoff remained immobile, quietly smoking his cigarette and looking at Teresa Inez' retreating back. Just as the actress passed one of the forward cars, he noticed a porter struggling with something in a vestibule. A moment later, the porter and a companion in the train lowered a woman in a wheelchair to the platform. Two little boys scampered after her.

Nicholas Markoff took a final deep drag on his cigarette, dropped the long butt on the platform, and ground it to dust. Jesús Guerrero was obviously hiding, waiting for an opportunity to depart unseen from the train. Still, he wouldn't leave both his mistress and family for long.

I have the goose, Markoff realized. *The gander cannot be far behind.*

He followed the porter, who pushed the wheelchair through the station, but in passing through the main terminal, was so intent upon Elodia Guerrero and her sons that he did not notice the man about whom he had previously wondered.

Victoriano Felix was also intent, but only on finding one man. He thought little of the woman and nothing of the tall foreigner who walked some ten paces behind her chair. His right hand gripped the razor in his coat pocket. He was annoyed that his palm was sweating.

Outside the station, Nicholas Markoff watched as the woman was helped into a taxi along with the children. He waited patiently as their two suitcases and the wheelchair were strapped

163

on top; then, after the car had turned into the stream of traffic, he walked casually to one of the porters who had helped the woman from the train.

"With your permission . . ." He was the soul of continental elegance as he slipped a ten-peso note into the man's hand. "Can you tell me to where that taxi went?"

"That one, Sir?"

"Yes."

"Hotel Biltmore, Sir."

"It's good," said Nicholas Markoff. "Many thanks."

Long before the train arrived in the city, Jesús Guerrero left the car in which he and his family had traveled and moved to the one just forward. There he waited until he was the only remaining passenger. Squatting on the floor so as not to be seen from the platform, he watched his wife being rolled from the train and waited until he was sure she was safely on her way to the hotel he had selected. It was American, cheap, and far from the social heart of town—the kind of place in which no one would suspect a wealthy politician to take rooms.

Finally, he had locked himself in the car's restroom. There, he had put to the final test the skills Teresa Inez had spent so many painstaking hours teaching him.

His tools were few—a razor, pencil, some coloring and flour—all contained in a small paper bag. Shaving his mustache had been the hardest part. It was both physically and emotionally painful. Something, it seemed, of his very manhood had been cut off with it. The rest, however, was actually easy. It took him less than a minute and a half to complete the entire job.

A pallid, gray-haired man with dark circles under his eyes hobbled from the train and, with a painfully infirm step, shuffled toward the terminal. There was little if any resemblance between this sick, almost pitiful, creature and the handsome young aide to President Cárdenas, who was known to be on some official mission in Chiapas.

Everything was working perfectly. It was true that Elodia had objected at first to continuing in the wheelchair, but he had convinced her of the necessity. He had also impressed upon the children the importance of playing the game seriously.

Now they were safe and, in a matter of minutes, he would be too. As he shuffled through the main terminal, Jesús Guerrero was barely able to suppress a smile at what he was sure was a superbly realistic performance. It took him the better part of an eternity to make his way outside and slide into a taxi there.

He allowed the driver to start before he mentioned his destination. Even when the cab was stopped for the routine police check to assure the proper licensing of the driver, Guerrero retained the image of a painfully sick, perhaps even dying, man. His cough was both pitiful and frightening. His voice was weak. His hands trembled, and his breath wheezed in and out like air through a broken bellows.

The policeman waved the car on.

Guerrero allowed himself to relax. His next performance would be at the hotel. There, he might have to be more careful. There was no way to tell how long he might have to hide in the capital. He would simply have to wait out the rumors until Cárdenas made his move with the railroads.

Bastard, he thought, *spitting on the very people who had actually built the country. The man's a dreamer of nightmares.*

For a fleeting moment, he wished he could be in the National Palace, privy to inside information, but he realized that any attempt to find out the president's plans or the proposed timing of his actions could mean immediate exposure. Cárdenas might have a reputation for leniency, but under the circumstances, even he probably would insist on a firing squad.

He leaned back in the seat and tried to relax. He was playing a dangerous game, but the ends were well worth any risk. Power was beautiful, simply and only for its own sake.

Because he did not look out the back window, he did not see the taxi traveling directly behind his own. He could not know that it had been hired by an enraged clerk harboring the ridiculous notion that he had been robbed of a fortune.

If he had, he would probably have given the matter little thought. Jesús Guerrero was concerned with great issues. The destiny of Mexico was in his hands. He had no time for the inconsequential pique of a minor clerk.

3

Hotel Biltmore

NEIL HAD BEEN preoccupied and hasty. Despite Margaret's efforts to manipulate his lovemaking, and tease him to heights of prolonged passion, he had approached the union almost as a mechanical chore. There had been no expression of affection. There hadn't even been the purely physical joy of lusting only after erotic delights. She had tried subtly to direct him along paths leading to her own pleasure, and to draw out their mutual enjoyment, but he had rushed to his own climax and almost abruptly withdrawn into pensive silence.

Margaret Whitley lay bitter and unfulfilled. She felt used and insulted, not merely as an individual but as a symbol of her entire gender. The taste of emptiness was absinthal in her soul. She was a woman physically and emotionally betrayed, and realizing this brought her close to fury.

She watched as Neil rose from the bed and, still naked, walked to the dresser. There, he pulled a cigarette from a flattened pack and lit it.

"I don't suppose I could have one as well?" She didn't even try to control the bitchy quality in her voice.

He ripped the pack apart, then crumpled it. "Last one." Absently, he removed it from his mouth and held it toward her.

"No, damn it!" She sat up on the rumpled bed. "The least you can do is give me my own bloody cigarette."

"You didn't bring any?" He sounded concerned.

"No I didn't bring any," she mimicked. "What's so bloody tragic about that?"

"Maybe I've got some." He walked to where he had discarded his clothing and probed the jacket and shirt pockets. "We're out," he said.

His voice was melodramatically helpless. He looked utterly naked and vulnerable, and his facial expression could have been the mask of Tragedy itself. Standing before her, nude and dejected, he almost made her laugh.

166

"Jesus Christ, Neil." She shook her head. "It's just a cigarette."

"Yes," he said. "But we're out."

"Well then, we shall bloody well have to get some more, shan't we?"

"We can't—"

"Can't? The damned things aren't the Hope Diamond, you know!"

"Goddamn it, Maggi! Don't you understand? I can't afford to leave the room."

"Oh, don't be so impossibly silly. I'll go down there myself—"

"You'll do no such thing!"

"Oh?"

"I absolutely forbid it!"

"Forbid it?" She almost laughed. "You're in no position to forbid anything, not after that last oh-so-masculine performance. Why it was worthy of any high-school sophomore fumbling in a rumble seat."

"Now, Margaret—"

"Oh, shut up!" She lifted her long legs, spun sideways to the edge of the bed, then reached for her clothing which lay beside it.

"Seriously, Maggi . . ." He was almost pouting. "It could be dangerous. I mean, you know the situation. Móndez knows about you as well as me."

"So what?" She put her brassiere on, clipped it in front, then slid it around before snaking her arms into it and adjusting it to her ample breasts. "I'm not the one who pissed away his money on cockfights and billiards."

"That's not the point—"

"Neil . . ." She looked him directly in the eyes. "I have no intention of hiding here like a sniveling craven simply because you think a bloody hotel lobby is dangerous. If you're too terrified to be a gentleman, I'll simply go down there myself."

"All right, Goddamn it! All right!" Almost viciously, he grabbed for his underdrawers and slipped into them. A moment later he was clothed in his shirt and trousers and slipping into his shoes as she ran a comb through her cinnamon hair. "You just stay up here," he told her. "I'll get your damned cigarettes."

"Not bloody likely!" She knew she was behaving like a

child, yet she was savoring something close to a sadistic thrill by exasperating him. "It's too late," she snapped. "I'm going."

"Maggi—"

She threw the comb on the dresser top, spun on her heel, and yanked the room's door open.

"Goddamn it!" he cried as she stepped into the hall. A moment later she heard the door close and he was beside her.

"This is silly," he told her. "Two grown people going for one lousy pack of cigarettes!"

"Then go back and hide under the bed!" She lifted her chin and, the picture of regal indignation, stalked to the stairs.

Only after they were in the lobby did she realize that, in her fury, she had neglected to bring her purse.

He bought two packs of Chesterfields, opened one, and offered her a cigarette.

The lobby was virtually empty. Except for the desk clerk and two bellboys absently waiting for possible arrivals, they were the only occupants. He struck a match and, as he extended it, glanced over her shoulder to the Ramos Arizpe entrance to the hotel.

"Jesus Christ!" he gasped suddenly. He dropped the match and grabbed her by the left arm.

"*Will* you stop this!" She jerked her arm free and turned toward the hotel's entrance.

Two women had just entered. The first was a redhead. She was slender and attractive, although obviously quite travel-worn. Behind her was an exquisite Latin beauty dressed in some sort of native costume. Two men came in behind them. The first was a Mexican in an ill-fitting, dark suit; the second, a tall, very handsome blond.

Margaret Whitley looked at Charles Candenning and instantly decided that, physically, he was one of the most attractive men she had ever seen. As he glanced at her, his eyebrows lifted in friendly recognition. Then she realized he was looking just beyond her.

He waved his hand. "Neil!" he cried. "Neil Oberon!"

"Jesus Christ," Neil said again. This time, it was barely a whisper.

Again he took her arm, and again she tried to pull free, but his fingers were like a tourniquet as he pulled her toward the elevator. Then, because the door was closed, he jerked her away and literally dragged her up the stairs.

By the time they reached the room of the honeymooning Mr. and Mrs. Noyes, her annoyance had built to the point where she could barely contain herself.

When the door slammed behind them, he finally released her arm.

"That was the rudest, the vilest—"

"Oh, shut up, Maggi!"

"Don't you tell *me* to shut up!"

"Goddamn it, can't you get it through your head? I'm trying to hide!"

"Well, you're certainly not doing such a bloody good job of it, are you? I mean what with your name being screamed across the lobby—"

"Christ!" He slapped his forehead with the heel of one hand. "I hardly know him. He's some magazine editor or illustrator or something. Met him in Connecticut. I knew his wife years ago."

"I'll just bet you did. Well, for her sake, I hope you knew her a bit better than you just finished knowing me!"

"Oh stop being such a bitch."

"And you stop acting like such a bloody lunatic."

"Look, Margaret . . ." He took a deep breath, held it for several seconds, then exhaled. "The situation is sticky. I mean really sticky. I wish you'd see that. Try to understand—"

"I understand perfectly. You're in trouble, but you brought it on yourself. I also understand that we are going to leave this wretched city and go to Texas, where we are going to get married. You are going to make me an American citizen. What you do after that with Mr. Móndez and your Mexican bandit generals and the rifles from America is no concern of mine."

"You're the soul of charity, darling."

"And you . . ." She picked up her purse, threw one of the new packs of Chesterfields in it, and turned toward the door. "You are a coward." She pulled the door open.

"Just where do you think you're going?"

"I'm going out for a breath of air that isn't stale. Who knows? I may even meet your old friend from Connecticut."

"Maggi! Don't—"

She walked into the hall and slammed the door behind her.

The man who had recognized Neil was not in the lobby.

Neither were the two women and the man who had come to the hotel with him. The only new occupants were a woman in a wheelchair and two small boys. Margaret thought little of the matter as a porter pushed the woman past her toward the elevator. Nor did she give a great deal of thought to the tall, exquisitely tailored gentleman who approached the desk. She did not see the ten-peso note he slid across the counter into the clerk's hand, but she did hear him ask the number of the crippled lady's room.

She sat in one of the lobby's overstuffed chairs.

The desk clerk said, "Two ten."

She opened her purse as the tall gentleman who had been at the desk passed her on his way to the staircase. Absently, she glanced up. The man had a noble, arrogant bearing and a military stride. He also seemed extremely pleased about something.

She took the cigarettes from her purse, lit one, and, in the smoking of it, tried to regain some of the composure she now wished she had not lost. She might threaten to blackmail Neil by telling the American authorities of his plans, but she knew she would never actually do that. There were many weaknesses to Neil Oberon, but she still felt a certain affection for him, as well as a sense of primitive loyalty. He might infuriate her at times but, all things considered, he had been good to her. Also, he had agreed to marry her so, ultimately he would be responsible for starting the career she had dreampt of for so many years in so many parts of an often hostile world.

At first, she did not notice the apparently sick man shuffle in from the street and make his painful way to the desk, but when she did, she was struck by a sense of familiarity. She was sure she had seen him somewhere before.

Her curiosity aroused, she snuffed her cigarette out and watched as he leaned over the desk and asked for the room number of a Señora Gonzales.

Again Margaret heard the clerk mention the number 210. Again she heard the sick man's voice as he thanked the clerk, and again she felt a very keen sense of familiarity.

It wasn't, however, until the man turned from the desk and their eyes met that she was sure of his identity. In the chipped fraction of a second, she saw his recognition of her and the flash of terror in the depths of his dark eyes.

Jesus! Her brain pronounced the name first in English only

170

as an exclamation, then again in Spanish—Jesús—the name of a man she had once loved and had once thought loved her.

By some standards, Margaret Whitley might have been considered immoral, even promiscuous. By others, she could be labeled "self-seeking" or even "ruthless." Still, no one who really knew her could deny that she had always played Cupid's game according to strict rules. She could threaten blackmail or use a man to better her financial or social position; she could argue or taunt, or even insult, but with love itself she was ultimately honest. She gave herself totally and exclusively to the man of the moment, and when it was over, she eased away as gently as possible before going on to her next romance. Her past lovers were never forgotten. Many remained friends and all, even those who had been forsaken years before, were individually cherished. Each would forever occupy a very special niche in the sacred catacombs of her memory.

Her affair with Jesús Guerrero had taken place over a year before. It had erupted like uncontained gunpowder, flashing white-hot and furiously passionate for but three short weeks, during which time Margaret—sophisticated, worldly wise, and supposedly far above such things—had, like a school girl, completely lost her heart and almost her very soul to the handsome Mexican.

Then—he had simply disappeared.

Margaret had tried to maintain her pride. She had struggled to remain aloof, but the agony of his absence had been a canker too excruciating to ignore. She had felt sure she would die without him, and because nothing in the universe mattered more than the sound of his voice or the reassuring touch of his hand, she had gone to him.

She had humiliated herself. She had broken down before him and begged him to return to her. She had no more pride. If she could not have him, nothing else could possibly be worthwhile.

He had listened to her pleas with a casualness that, although outwardly polite, was, in fact, almost contempt. Love, he explained, was an impermanent tide. One should be pragmatic and greet its ebb as one welcomed its flow.

She knew he meant only that he had taken from her all that he wanted. It was over. Love—all powerful, all consuming—was, in reality, no more than breath exhaled into winter's chill. It steamed briefly, then simply wasn't there any more.

171

She was that which she had never before been nor even thought she might be—a woman scorned. Her self-esteem had been sacrificed on the altar of Guerrero's ego. She had been loyal to him. In return, he had betrayed her. She had played by the English rules and had been a decent sport. He had cheated—and won.

Perhaps it had simply been a case of poetic justice. Logically, she could understand it as such. Still, her attitude toward being so casually and brutally spurned was bifurcated. As with her view of the United States' quota system, she at once understood yet considered the whole thing personally unfair.

Because Guerrero had played a perfidious game, she had been hurt, and because pain had been inflicted on her ignobly, her passion which had once been so positive, turned negative. She had suffered, not merely because she had felt more for him than for other men, but because she had also allowed herself to believe that he shared not just her feelings, but their depth as well.

Time, the ultimate physician, had allowed her wounds to heal. Her heart had convalesced, a cicatrix had formed over her lacerated emotions and the bile in her heart had neutralized. By the time she met Neil Oberon, she realized that a broken heart, like a hangover, is best cured by the very thing that causes it. Guerrero, if not actually forgotten, had been hidden under the poultice of Oberon's attentions.

The sight of her ex-lover now, as he tried to hide behind whitened hair, a made-up face, and shabby clothing, ripped that poultice away. Her scabs were torn off and all the raw agony of betrayal exposed again. Again, she was facing him with tears of rejection streaming down her cheeks. Again, she was hearing his casual voice speak of impermanent tides and pragmatism. She wanted nothing more than to exchange agony for agony, and humiliation for humiliation, until Jesús Guerrero was himself reduced to the begging, broken, sniveling and soulless wreck he had made of her so long ago.

Part of her wanted to cry out, leap from her seat, and, like a vengeful tigress, tear his very soul to scraps. Outwardly, however, she contained herself and merely watched as the tottering, made-up man shuffled toward the elevator.

Then her attention was drawn by a man who pushed in from Ramos Arizpe and walked rapidly to the desk. Dressed in an obviously inexpensive suit and old-fashioned buttoned shoes, he was almost completely nondescript, except that, in his eyes there was an intensity which was almost frightening.

Jesús Guerrero stepped into the elevator. The door closed. The needle above it began to climb.

The new arrival leaned over the desk. "That man . . ." His voice was tense—almost, but not quite, harsh. "That man in the elevator . . . To what room is he going?"

"Sir, I cannot give—"

"Here. Perhaps this—"

"Ah, of course, Sir. The room is 210."

"Many thanks." The nondescript man turned from the desk, took a few steps toward the elevator, then stopped. For a moment, it seemed he fought a brief but violent mental battle. Finally, his right hand thrust deeply into the side pocket of his coat, he almost dashed from the hotel.

Room 210, Margaret decided, was quite popular. A woman calling herself Gonzales and two children were already there, so, probably, was a tall and arrogant man. Jesús Guerrero, an important governmental official—disguised and obviously trying to flee someone or something—was also on his way there while yet another man was obviously quite interested in him or the other occupants.

Margaret, too, was interested. Room 210 of the Hotel Biltmore offered a perfect arena for revenge. The woman there might call herself Gonzales, but she could only be Guerrero's wife. The two little boys had to be her sons. Simply by going upstairs, Margaret could confront her betrayer, expose him as an adulterer, and unmask him in all his perfidy before his entire family.

First, however, she decided to put herself in the proper mood and state of mind for her planned performance.

She rose, walked to the desk, and asked the clerk to have a bottle of Schenley's brought to her room.

As Charles Candenning moved Karen's chair closer to the table and sat down beside her, he wondered why Teresa Inez had been so adamant about dining at the hotel. He had wanted to take a taxi to the heart of the city, see some of the sights, then either sample native food at the Mitla or Las Casualas, or dine at any one of a score of restaurants serving cuisine from all over the world.

The actress, however, had been firm almost to the point of unpleasantness. Traffic would be impossible, she had insisted.

Besides, it was late. Now, during the rainy season, there might very well be a sudden shower. *Cena*, she claimed, would be just as tasty and pleasant here at the hotel as at the Lady Baltimore or Manolo's or any of the other more famous restaurants. Besides, those eating places popular with the tourists—La Concordia, Pages and the rest—would surely be unpleasantly crowded.

It had been far easier to capitulate than argue. Karen and Portes apparently felt the same way. In the final analysis, the actress's insistence on a particular dining place was no more than an insignificant eccentricity. What really bothered Candenning was Neil Oberon's behavior in the hotel's lobby.

"Most amazing thing," he said almost absently.

Karen turned to him. "What most amazing thing?"

"Oh," he said. "Sorry. Just thinking out loud. It's just that I'm so sure of it—so dead sure. That Oberon fellow. He's a friend of Elizabeth's. Fellow Montaukers or something like that. I've met him in Connecticut and New York at least a dozen times. Granted, we're not exactly friends—not joined at the hip, mind you—but still to snub me like that . . ."

"Maybe he's trying to hide," she offered.

"Hide? Why would he? Oh, my God, that's right. That thing about Senator Dossier's daughter."

"What about her?"

"She's dead. That's about the long and short of it. He was escorting her. They were at some party. Pretty sordid really."

"Oh?"

"The case was quite similar to the Fatty Arbuckle scandal."

"Oh, how horrid."

"Of course, there was never any proof, but a lot of fingers were pointed his way."

"Well then, he must be hiding."

"From me? Preposterous. I've never for a moment thought he was guilty."

"There was a young lady with him," Domingo Portes interjected. "We do not know the situation. She could be married—there could be many considerations."

"Ah." Candenning took the menu the waiter handed him. "Intrigue! Wonderful!" He ordered a double Waterfill and Frazier and settled back to study the table d'hote.

Only when the drink arrived did he glance at Domingo Portes again. The man appeared quite ill at ease. He was staring at the menu with an intensity worthy of someone trying desperately not to fathom his own gastronomic desires, but rather all the absolute and eternal verities of the universe.

Teresa Inez was also looking at the menu, but with a wistful sadness ill-befitting one who had literally fought to dine at this particular restaurant.

Candenning turned to the waiter and was about to ask his recommendations, when Portes abruptly pushed his chair from the table.

"I'm sorry." He was obviously quite upset. "I must seem impossibly rude. Forgive me. I must leave."

"We've not even ordered."

"I can't explain. Really, it's a matter—a quite vital matter." He rose and, without bothering to replace his chair, left the restaurant.

Karen and Candenning exchanged glances. "Talk about intrigue," she offered.

"I'm afraid," Teresa said, "there's more to it than any of us know."

Again, they glanced at one another but confined their conversation to the ordering of dinner. Only after the waiter was out of earshot did Teresa lean forward. "He's a priest," she whispered. "An outlaw."

"Portes?"

She nodded. "It's difficult now in Mexico. Most of the churches are still closed. I'm sure he's running from something, perhaps the authorities, perhaps . . ." She shrugged. "Who can tell?"

"Well, well." Candenning took a long pull of his drink. "A fist-fighting Friar Tuck, an old acquaintance who snubs me, a fleeing physicist, and gunmen on a train. This has indeed been a day."

He finished his drink and ordered another with dinner. The three of them talked pleasantly over the meal. Teresa told them she would have been happy to show them the capital, but, unfortunately, certain obligations made it impossible. She did, however, mention some of the city's more interesting aspects, which tourists often missed or simply avoided.

The meal over, Candenning leaned back to enjoy a cigarette as Teresa told them the story of the Aztec Revolt—the Sad Night. She spoke almost as though she had been a part of the Spanish retreat that June so long ago. She had just finished explaining where they could find the very cypress tree under which Hernán Cortés had wept when their waiter approached the table, asked her identity, then handed her a note.

The actress appeared quite concerned, even afraid for a moment. She opened the note, read it, and her entire expression changed. Like a strange phoenix, she was transformed from a sad, ashen creature to a radiant beauty, ultimately confident and ultimately secure. She excused herself and stood up.

"But the Sad Night?" Karen pleaded.

"Another time," Teresa smiled. "I'm afraid I cannot dwell on sadness this night."

Candenning rose, wished the young woman a good-night and sat down again. "I suppose you realize," he said, "we are traveling with some rather strange people."

"The thought had occurred to me."

"That woman," he nodded toward Teresa's back, "is going to a lover. The priest, or whoever he is, certainly isn't hiding. He's a rough customer, and he's after something. And here we sit, you and I, completely unmysterious, frightfully ordinary—certainly unworthy of mention even in the pulps."

"I don't know." She smiled. "You haven't figured out yet why you're being recalled. That's still a mystery. And remember, we did have something to do with—what shall I call it?—'An Adventure on a Train.' Hardly an ordinary run from Oaxaca to Mexico."

"True." He exhaled pensively. "Perhaps we are worthy of some minor notice after all."

He finished his cigarette and the short brandy he had ordered, then called for the check. "Care to walk a few blocks?" he asked absently.

She drained the last of her coffee and looked at him. Her expression seemed somehow ambivalent, perhaps even troubled. She darted her focus first from his right eye then to his left, as if studying each in turn for his exact thoughts. Finally, after several seconds, she sighed. "Sure," she said. "Why not? Let's go down to La Reforma. I hear the monuments are spectacular."

Charles Candenning would never quite be able to explain specifically what made that evening so special. In fact, he could never quite remember what he and Karen had talked about or experienced or even seen. Certainly, he could describe El Caballito, the huge equestrian monument to Charles IV, and the statue of Columbus farther south, or even that of the

Aztec emperor Cuauhtemoc, about to hurl his spear into tomorrow's dawn. Still, his predominant feeling from the time of leaving the hotel was one of being totally at ease—completely at one with all of nature. He might have been an Arhat who had suddenly and miraculously attained nirvana. If anyone had asked him to, he might have described the evening as ultimately safe. It was one in which, it seemed, nothing could possibly go wrong.

Even when it did go wrong things still seemed to be all right. They might have walked forever had there not been the threat of rain. As it was, they found themselves lost when the first drops began to fall. They took cover in the doorway of a cantina until Candenning was able to hail a taxi to take them back to the hotel.

It was in the cab that the purely physical desire first touched him. It might have been an unseen passenger snuggled between them—invisible, intangible—but as real and alluring as her scent and presence itself. He wanted to touch her, to pull her body against his, and feel her femininity tightly pressed to him.

The thought frightened him, and the fear tightened not only his muscles but his conversation as well.

At the hotel, it was still there. He wanted almost desperately to kiss her but knew it would be wrong. He was married. To violate that would be shabby and somehow unclean.

At the elevator, he muttered a specious excuse and bade her good-night. She stepped inside and the door closed. For some time he stood immobile before turning toward the bar.

He had walked perhaps four yards before he realized that he really didn't want a drink. He turned around, returned to the elevator, and pushed the button.

Riding to his floor, Charles Candenning thought vaguely of all the values his parents and early educators had tried to instill in him. There was a thing called honesty and another called honor and, overriding them all—the great tarpaulin that contained and protected all gentlemanly virtues—there was duty. A gentleman always discharged his duty, no matter the cost.

Marriage, he realized as the elevator door opened, was a sacred institution. It involved total commitment with honor and honesty toward another. Marriage was a matter of duty, and duty could never be shirked.

But, as he turned down the hall, he wondered if there wasn't something more than naked duty.

He reached his room and placed the key into the lock. Wasn't there something else hidden in the great dungheap of life, he wondered. Wasn't there something that made all the other concepts worthwhile and really meaningful? Wasn't there something perhaps which made honesty easy because it took away the need to be dishonest—something that made honor a more real part of life because it made life itself honorable—something that made duty a pleasure because it made the obligation itself a pleasure?

There must be such a thing for outside, with Karen, under the Mexican night, he had almost touched it. Ghost or dream, it was gone now. He was alone, and reality was only this hotel, his recall to service, and his wife Elizabeth in Connecticut.

He opened the door and stepped inside. "Philosophy One" he muttered aloud. "And you're right there in Plato's cave with all the rest of the shadows."

He shut the door and, without bothering to turn on the light or remove any of his damp clothing, sprawled on the bed.

She finished her second drink and poured a third. She was beginning to feel quite mellow. Emotional hurt and hatred were being replaced by an almost completely dispassionate desire for vengeance.

"I swear to Christ," Oberon was saying, "I believe you actually do want to get me killed."

"Don't be silly, darling." She was quite calm. Her earlier annoyance with him had either been washed away by the Scotch or redirected toward Jesús Guerrero.

"Running to the lobby . . . getting booze sent up . . . You'll put this whole thing on the fritz."

"Nonsense." She sipped her drink. "You act as though I'm running up and down the Paseo de la Reforma screaming to everyone where Neil Oberon is. I'm simply having a civilized drink."

"You're drunk."

"A lady never gets drunk."

"You're no goddamned lady."

"You know, Neil, that's what I really like about you. You're so bloody direct . . . so admirably specific."

"Oh, lay off it, will you?"

"No, no, darling. I think we should discuss it. I really do.

I mean, you're direct and now I'm going to be direct as well.''

"Margaret, for Christ's sake!''

"Oh, not with you, darling. You're not a bad sort, actually. And I suppose I did get a bit more upset than I should this afternoon. No. I'm going to have a little talk with a very nasty man.''

"If you're thinking of leaving this room again—''

"But, of course I have to leave the room, darling. You don't really think I'd let a nasty man in here, do you?''

"You're drunk.''

"You said that before.'' She took a second sip of her drink, then put the glass on the night table. "Aren't you going to wish me luck, darling?''

"Oh, no you don't. You've skipped around this hotel for the last time. You're staying right where you are.''

"Oh, no I'm not.'' She smiled quite calmly. "I told you. I'm going to see a nasty man.''

"Don't bet on it.''

"You actually intend to stop me?'' She was quite surprised.

"Yes—if I have to.''

"But of course you have to, darling. I'm certainly not going to stop myself.'' She rose from the bed on which she had been sitting, steadied herself, and took a deep breath. "I'm going,'' she announced.

She managed to reach the door and open it before he grabbed her by the left wrist.

"You're not going anywhere!''

A moment before, Margaret Whitley had been quite affable, even mellow. Although it had not completely intoxicated her, the alcohol she had consumed had deadened the edge of her hostility. Now, with the grabbing of her wrist, her hatred was honed again. All her rancor toward Jesús Guerrero, her impatience to get north—her destination toward being confined in the room—erupted at once.

She spun around and slapped Oberon so hard across the face that he not only released her wrist but almost fell back against the open door.

"Fuck off!'' she cried.

He was stunned. Slowly, he raised one hand to his reddening cheek. There was an unbelieving expression in his eyes. "All right,'' he said. "Have it your way.'' Very deliberately, he closed the door.

The hall seemed empty, almost sepulchral. For a moment she even doubted the reality of her being there. It was almost a dream until she remembered her mission. Neil Oberon could wait. There was another man who owed the piper and she intended to collect.

At 210, she stopped to form some sort of strategy. She decided what she would say if Guerrero himself opened the door, then edited the script slightly in the event that his wife did.

She smoothed her skirt and knocked.

She was completely unprepared for the little boy with the puzzled expression on his face.

"I wish to speak to Mr. Guerrero." She thought her voice sounded stilted.

"This is the Gonzales' room."

"Look here, little fellow," she announced. "I'm not really stupid—just discarded. I still know Jesús Guerrero when I see him. So, you go in there and tell your not-so-nice papa that an old . . . an old friend wants to talk to him."

The boy seemed perplexed, then quite worried.

"Go on," she said. "Tell him."

The boy closed the door.

A moment later, it was reopened.

Jesús Guerrero stood before her. The makeup was gone. Except for the missing mustache he was the same, almost beautifully handsome, man who had, just a year before, thrilled her well beyond the limits of known rapture—the man who had taken her heart, caressed it for three short weeks, then tossed it in his special scrap heap of discarded mistresses.

At first his presence jolted her almost electrically. All her previous feelings of love and tenderness and physical yearning flooded through her. Then came the hurt—the callous rejection—and with it, total resentment.

"You bastard," she said quite calmly. "You absolutely unmitigated, self-made bastard."

"Maggi—por favor—"

"Oh stop the Latin-lover shit. I want to tell your family a little story. They really should hear about what a rotten, two-timing son of a bitch you are. I want your kids to know just how loyal their father is. And your crippled wife? Don't you think she should know what you do behind her back?"

He snapped his hand out and covered her mouth, then brutally drew her close. His eyes were very wide—their

180

expression almost deranged in intensity. *"Perra!"* he snarled. "I could kill you right here. You and your damned lost love. You think only with your genitals. The history of Mexico hangs on a thread, and you'd cut it to call me a bastard?"

As she stared into his very black eyes, Margaret Whitley was suddenly quite sober. With sobriety came understanding, and with understanding, fear.

"Go back to where you came from," he whispered through clenched teeth. "It's a kindness. I give you your life. Forget you saw me or—before God—I'll kill you."

She took a step backward as he removed his hand from her mouth. She stared at him for a second, saw his impassioned sincerity, and understood the truth of his threat.

Terror was a living, pulsating thing in her as she turned and ran along the hotel's corridor. Her hands were trembling and she wanted another drink.

She wanted Neil Oberon to put his arms around her and hold her tight.

Nicholas Markoff was, perhaps, among the luckiest of men. Circumstances, apparently, were all aligned exactly in his favor. What might have been a complicated and filthy affair, involving the risk of being seen with the rifle, getting soaked in the rain, and other unpleasantries, had turned out to be, all aspects considered, really quite effortless and, in fact, amazingly civilized.

He had followed Elodia Guerrero into the Biltmore, and once in possession of her room number and the knowledge that she had also taken the adjoining room, had gone upstairs to determine the position of the suite within the building.

Just as he was starting down again, an apparently sick old man had stepped from the elevator. From the concealment of the stairwell, Markoff had seen him look this way and that, then, with an alacrity ill-befitting his apparent age and health, almost run to the door of room 210.

Confident that he now had both the goose and the gander, Nicholas Markoff had left the hotel. Outside, he had done some mental mathematics and satisfied himself that the two rooms occupied by the Guerreros faced Ramos Arizpe and were near the south side of the hotel. Across the street, he had been pleased to note, was another hotel, which conveniently had only four stories.

Markoff had returned to his apartment, bathed, shaved, and

packed the belongings he intended to take with him from the city. Finally, carrying a valise and one other case, he had checked into the second hotel, where he had asked for a room on the top floor overlooking Ramos Arizpe. He was, he explained, a light sleeper who did not like the thought of other, possibly noisy, guests over him.

He had asked to be awakened at seven o'clock, then had followed the bellboy to his room. Once there, he tipped the young man nominally and waited for almost a full minute after he left before closing the door behind him.

Now the time had arrived.

Markoff took the smaller of the cases he had brought with him and laid it on the bed. A quite ordinary container covered in black leather, it might have been the carrying case for a musical instrument or perhaps photographic equipment. He unsnapped the two catches and opened the lid.

Within was a German Mauser—one of the short Gew 33/40 models made even shorter by its folding stock. It was equipped with a Weaver Model 330 telescopic sight but was otherwise unmodified. Ideally Markoff would have preferred another weapon, but there had been no time to have one made to his specifications. Juan Miguárdez had given him this, and he had accepted. It was adequate—light and easily concealed. The only problems were its exceptionally sharp blast and heavy recoil.

He took the carbine from the case, straightened the stock into position, secured it, then walked to the window.

It was dark now and the rain was still falling, but as he looked across the street, his visibility was not greatly impaired. He scanned the second story of the Biltmore Hotel, noting the windows which might belong to rooms 210 and 212. Only after he had made a selection with his naked eye did he lift the rifle to his shoulder and squint through the telescopic sight.

It was unfortunate that he was positioned just too high for an ideal shot. Although he could see quite clearly despite the rain, the angle of his vision was such that he could only view a little over three yards into any room and down to its floor. If Jesús Guerrero didn't come close to the window, he would have to be killed on another day.

The two little boys were in the room to Markoff's right. He watched through the scope as the woman he had first seen in the wheelchair walked back and forth, apparently seeing them

182

to bed for the night. The lights in that room went out, and a moment later he saw the woman's feet enter the room to his left.

At first he wasn't quite sure of the significance of her movements, for he could only see from her breasts down. She made a number of almost obscene gestures and several times drew attention to her hips and genital area. Then she began pacing back and forth. Each time she came near enough to the window for Markoff to see her face and upper body, he noticed that she was not only gesticulating, but talking quite rapidly and with obvious annoyance.

It was apparent that, for some reason, Mrs. Guerrero was quite upset with her husband, and was in the process of telling him so.

Markoff turned away from his window and snapped out the lights in his room. He returned to the window, opened the lower half and, standing just far enough away so that the barrel of the Mauser would not protrude and he himself would not get wet, watched Room 210 across the street.

Virtually without a sound, he lifted the bolt of the carbine, drew it back, and inserted a clip of the soft-headed sporting ammunition he had brought with him. He pushed one round into the chamber and gently snugged the bolt into firing position.

The woman walked back and forth waving her hand this way and that until, apparently both exhausted and exasperated, she turned her back to the room, stalked to the window, and looked at the street below.

Had Elodia Guerrero been his target, Nicholas Markoff's job would then have been done. As it was, he held the rifle in firing position, squinted through the scope, and silently wished that her husband would step into his sights.

A moment later Jesús Guerrero did come up behind his wife. He laid his hands on her shoulders and turned her toward him. Now Guerrero was facing the window, and the Russian's view of him was unobstructed.

Markoff adjusted the rifle so that his shot would hit exactly on the bridge of Guerrero's nose. The politician's final gesture would complement his entire life. His brains would be blown out while he tried to manipulate a beautiful woman.

Markoff squeezed the trigger with a very slow, almost delicate pressure. He did not want to jolt the weapon or have

183

his aim deflected in any way. Even he would not know the moment of firing until it had passed.

What happened could, perhaps, have been attributed to the slight blur of rain on the window of Room 210, or even to the paralax factor of telescopic sight and muzzle. In actuality, however, it was the result of a sudden movement made by the intended victim.

Jesús Guerrero had come up behind his wife in an attempt to soothe her anger. He had turned her around to face him and had placed both hands on her shoulders. His wife, however, had spit in his face. In fury, he had taken a step backward and to the side, jerking her around so that the instant the firing pin of the Mauser snapped into the loaded shell casing, her head was almost exactly where his had been but a second before.

Because the barrel of the carbine was so short and its weight so light, recoil was heavy. Nicholas Markoff did not actually see his shot hit. It took him a second or two to realign his eye with the scope in order to inspect the scene across the street.

What he saw was not gratifying. The window, of course, had been broken, but instead of a dead Jesús Guerrero, the politician's wife lay on the floor. The left half of her face was splashed into a pink slime. The eye, still attached to its optic nerve, lolled like an out-of-place white marble just beside her ear.

Elodia Guerrero was quite dead.

Markoff ejected the empty shell casing and, this time less cautious about the sound, slid another round into the rifle's chamber. He lifted the carbine to his shoulder, took aim, then stopped.

By all rights, Jesús Guerrero should either have been terrified for his own safety or grief-stricken over the loss of his wife. Apparently, he was neither.

He was acting like nothing less than a necrophilic pervert! He seemed interested only in the dead woman's genitals!

Although Markoff considered himself quite sophisticated sexually, perhaps even somewhat jaded, he was fascinated. No longer thinking of firing another shot, he watched through the telescopic sight as Jesús Guerrero lifted his dead wife's skirt and began to grope frantically in the area of her groin.

A moment later, Markoff realized that the woman had been wearing some sort of belt, and as her husband pulled it free, the Russian saw that it supported four leather pouches, each approximately the size of a man's fist.

Instantly, he grasped the significance of the situation. Juan Miguárdez had been willing to pay such a high price for the assassination of Jesús Guerrero because he knew of the belt. The pouches obviously contained something infinitely more valuable than a million pesos. Certainly, whatever was in them was enough to erase any trace of fear in Guerrero. It was also more than enough to intrigue Nicholas Markoff.

He lowered the rifle and shut the window. Almost methodically, he picked up the empty shell casing which had dropped to the floor, then refolded the stock of the carbine, and put the weapon back in its case.

Guerrero himself was the only witness to the murder, but he certainly would not report it. He was trapped for the night in the Hotel Biltmore with a dead wife and two sleeping children.

Slowly and deliberately, Markoff began to undress. He would enjoy a good night's sleep, then, at seven o'clock, he would resume stalking his prey. This time, however, he was sure the bounty on a dead politician would be considerably higher than a mere million pesos.

His actual strategy no more carefully organized than it had ever been, Victoriano Felix still knew he would have to move before morning. With day, Guerrero would undoubtedly leave the city—probably by air because of the nearly inactive railroads. Once gone, there would be no hope of seeing either the politician or the diamonds again.

He finished his dinner and, unmindful of the rain, walked back to the Hotel Biltmore. Because they offered more time to consider his tactics, he climbed the stairs instead of riding the elevator to the second floor. He was just about to place his foot on the last step when he heard what sounded like the backfire of an automobile and simultaneously the breaking of glass.

He stopped for a moment to reconsider his plans and was shifting his weight to climb to the very last step when he heard the click of a door opening. He pulled back, but curiosity overcame him. He peeked around the corner of the stairwell.

The door to Room 210 was open. Jesús Guerrero was looking out.

185

Victoriano withdrew the razor from his coat pocket. He wished his palms would not perspire so. He eased himself into the hall, then stopped.

Leaving the door open, Jesús Guerrero re-entered the room. He was gone for no more than half a minute before he reappeared, backing slowly into the hall dragging the body of a woman. Once he had pulled her feet clear of the door, he lifted the body, propped it against the corridor wall and steadied it there. Then he stooped to sling it over his shoulder in a fireman's carry.

Stunned into immobility, Victoriano watched as Guerrero trotted down the corridor with the body. Something terrible had happened to the woman's head. It was covered with blood and the left eye was hanging from the face, bouncing back and forth like a ghastly paddleball on a short string.

The woman was very obviously dead. Victoriano did not, however, associate the mutilated body with the sounds he had heard at the top of the stairs. He simply watched as Guerrero reached a door almost at the end of the corridor and knocked on it impatiently.

The door opened. Victoriano heard a woman gasp, then saw Guerrero enter. The door closed.

Because he was stunned by the scene and because he simply did not know what else to do, Victoriano waited. He knew where Guerrero was. He also knew that he could not remain there forever. It did not occur to him that the door to Room 210 had been left unlatched or that, in his haste to remove the dead woman, Jesús Guerrero might have left the diamonds behind.

Only a moment after Guerrero had taken the dead woman down the hall, the door there reopened and the politician stepped out. Peeking around the stairwell, Victoriano now saw another woman, this one as much alive as the other had been dead. Apparently she had been interrupted while performing her evening toilet. Her hair was disheveled and she was dressed in a bathrobe. Neither the looseness of her garment nor the disarray of her coiffure, however, detracted from her exceptional beauty.

There was something quite familiar about her. Victoriano was sure he had seen her someplace before, but could not quite remember where. Perhaps, he satisfied himself, she had been one of the passengers on the northbound train.

Guerrero and the woman exchanged hasty, whispered words.

Victoriano could only hear the tone, not the content, of the conversation. It was urgent, conspiratorial.

Suddenly Guerrero drew the woman into his arms and kissed her quite passionately. The couple embraced for several seconds until the politician pulled away, whispered a few more words, then started down the hall again.

Victoriano watched wide-eyed. He might have been the victim of some outlandish fantasy. For some time he was actually bereft of sensation. Then, as though by some sort of slow-motion process, the numbness seemed to dissolve, and he gradually became conscious of the still unopened razor in his hand.

The man who had stolen his diamonds was in the open. He was alone and defenseless in the hotel's corridor. It was the perfect time—the perfect place—to strike.

He opened the razor. He thought his breath sounded·like a hissing locomotive. His heart was pounding against his rib cage and his hands wouldn't stop perspiring.

Guerrero was walking quite rapidly, but was still some ten feet from his door when Victoriano stepped from the concealment of the stairwell to the middle of the hall.

"Thief!" he cried.

Guerrero stopped. His expression, at first, only one of surprise. Then he noticed the razor. He remained absolutely still for perhaps two seconds, then leapt for the safety of his room.

Victoriano was both closer and faster. He reached the unlatched door just before Guerrero, grabbed the politician's throat in his left hand and, holding the razor against his cheek, slammed him first against the door, then through it into the room.

"The diamonds!" he demanded. "Where are my diamonds?"

Guerrero seemed baffled.

"I'll kill you. I swear it by the Holy Mother. I'll cut your throat."

So single-minded had been his dream to regain the treasure which he had convinced himself was rightfully his own, that Victoriano Felix neglected to assess the man he held. He simply assumed that the expression in Guerrero's eyes was one of fear. As a dreamer, Victoriano might have understood Guerrero's ambition, but he could never appreciate the qualities of character that implemented that ambition. As a dreamer, he had thought only of diamonds. He had neglected all human emotions save his own greed. He had not considered that the dead woman recently carried along the corridor was his intended victim's wife or that now, the man he threatened was exactly on the level of any wild beast defending its cubs from attack.

Victoriano Felix was a dreamer. He was also a fool. He was quite shocked when both of Guerrero's hands suddenly flew up. The left knocked the razor away from his cheek, the right broke Victoriano's grip on his throat and the total gesture sent the diminutive clerk staggering backward.

Before he could regain any control of the situation, Victoriano saw his intended victim step forward. The clerk did not even see the fist, yet suddenly there was a great splash of pain in his cheek and his mouth was full of blood. Something red and black kept silently exploding behind his eyes. He tried to lash out with the razor, but another blow struck him in the solar plexus. He was sure he had been shot. All wind was sucked out of him. He was on his knees, blind, gasping, hearing himself beg for mercy from the bottom of some hellish pit.

He felt himself pushed forward to his stomach. There was a great pressure on his back. He felt Guerrero's hands slip under his chin.

His sensations were fragmented—kaleidoscopic. The razor was still miraculously in his hand and, in front of him on the carpet there was a brown stain. Near it lay a tangled mass of leather with three or four pouches in it. It was the kind of belt a soldier or policeman might wear to carry ammunition.

His chin was being lifted up and backward. He knew that Jesús Guerrero had his knee in his back and was trying to break his neck. He lifted the razor to the politician's hands, felt the blade cut into flesh and heard the sharp, pain-filled intake of breath behind him.

He felt—almost smelled—the flow of blood under his chin. He saw the tangled leather before him and, like a revelation, knew his diamonds were inside the pouches.

He reached for them as a great jolt of agony snapped his spine.

What had been but a dream in life was, at last, an actuality. Victoriano Felix was dead, but his right hand finally held a fortune.

In actuality, Teresa Inez was a contradiction to the sultry, often callous, women she played on screen. She enjoyed working in movies because it satisfied a need for romance, but that need was much better satisfied by the reality of Jesús Guerrero.

When she had read his note at dinner, she was sure she had blushed in anticipation. Their association was clandestined and adulterous. No marriage could ever result, yet she could not withdraw from it. She was a woman totally, irrevocably in love—one willing to endure almost anything in the name of love and for the sake of her lover.

The necessity for secrecy, the shame of her pregnancy, even the knowledge that her child would be born a bastard, could all be faced almost with ease as long as she knew her lover was near. No one had ever thrilled her the way he had. No one had brought her anywhere near the heights of physical and emotional ecstasy she had reached with him. She was somehow whole and secure only with him and, because he made her life complete, her devotion and loyalty to him were without bounds.

Since leaving the dinner table, she had dreampt only of the time she would soon spend in her lover's arms.

The dream had turned into a nightmare.

Guerrero had knocked on her door almost an hour earlier than his note had indicated. She had just stepped out of the bathtub and had not yet dressed or done her hair.

When she opened the door, she could not help gasping.

He was carrying the body of a woman. His expression was quite determined as he pushed into the room. "The closet!" he demanded. "Where is it?"

She had shown him the closet and even managed to open the door. Unceremoniously, he had dumped the body inside. Just before closing the door, Teresa had seen the pulped horror that had once been Elodia Guerrero's face. By some miracle, she had managed not to retch or cry out.

"You've got to hide her," her lover had insisted. "Just for the night. For the children."

"But, how?"

He had taken several breaths. "She was angry—having to wear the belt—some other things. She spat in my face. I jerked her around. I'm sure the shot was meant for me."

"Darling—"

"I'm going back."

"No! Whoever did that—"

"He won't be able to see me if I keep the lights off."

"Please, darling! Don't."

"I must. The children."

He had opened the door and stepped into the hall. She had followed. Then, almost impulsively, he had embraced her.

Twined in the protection of his arms—feeling the tenderness of his lips on hers—all had been almost well for a fleeting eternity. Danger seemed no more than a script-writer's concoction—the dead woman only a cinematic prop.

Then reality returned. The embrace ended. He was facing her, a frown clouding his handsome features. "Go inside," he had whispered. "I will return in the morning."

Obediently, she had re-entered the room and closed the door. She had glanced at the closet. Elodia Guerrero was dead—murdered by a bullet intended for her husband.

A chill scurried through her. Had it not been for an argument, a chance move, her beloved would be dead now. The full impact of the realization hit her with an almost physical force. Her hands began to tremble.

To steady her emotions, she had started pacing the room. It would be impossible for her to sleep. The body in the closet made her uneasy. She was desperately worried about Jesús. She wished she could do something—anything—to help him. Yet there was nothing to be done. She could only wait until he came to her in the morning.

A knock on her door made her gasp in alarm. She was suddenly very afraid. "Who is it?"

"I." He was back.

She jerked the door open.

He pushed two very sleepy young boys toward her and followed them into the room. Only after she closed the door and turned to face him did she notice the blood-drenched towel wrapped around his right hand.

"You're hurt!"

"It's nothing," he told her. "Teresa, listen to me. There are risks I had not foreseen. You must care for the children—"

"Your hand—"

"Never mind the hand!" he snapped. "Let them sleep here. No one knows of us but that man on the train. No one else must find out."

"There's a man sleeping on the floor," one of the little boys said.

"Hide these." Guerrero handed her two filthy, once-white pouches. "Use them if anything happens to me."

"Papa hurt himself," the second little boy said.

"Go to the station early tomorrow. You can't risk the airport, and a bus is too slow. Let's hope that Cárdenas hasn't completely ruined the railroads and you can get a train north."

"Jesús, darling, you're bleeding. You need a doctor."

He ignored her to kneel between the two sleepy-eyed boys. "This is Miss Inez," he told them. "She is going to take care of you for a little while."

"Where's Mama?" one boy asked.

"She had to go on a trip." Guerrero's voice was very calm and steady. "And so must I. You are my sons," he said. "I want you to be brave as men should be brave. Miguel, Roberto—no matter what happens, no matter what you may hear, remember, I love you and I love my country."

He rose again and looked at Teresa.

She glanced at his hand. "At least let me put another towel on it. Come . . ." She led him to the bathroom.

His index finger and thumb had almost been completely severed by the razor. They hung like dead things away from the larger part of the hand.

She tried to appear braver than she was but could not hold back her tears. Gently, she helped him wrap a clean towel around the wound and tourniqueted his arm with his necktie. Then she walked him back to the door.

A moment later, she was alone with two sleepy little boys and her own unborn child. With them, almost a specter in the room, lay the horrible empty sureness that she had just said farewell to a dead man.

4
Night

SINCE ARRIVING IN the capital, Domingo Portes had been preoccupied with thoughts of William Scofield. He was convinced that the little man was not what he claimed to be, and that what he was taking to the United States was, in fact, the treasure of Las Casas. Although his evidence was circumstantial, it was too coincidental to be ignored. Just after Christmas, two men with twelve burros had fled from San Cristóbal. Months later, twelve burros led by one man had descended from the highlands. Each burro carried two crates. Twenty-four crates of something had come from the southern mountains, and William Scofield claimed there were twenty-four crates belonging to him on the train from Oaxaca.

Portes had to see the contents. If, in fact, they were the Church's gold, he was sure he would have to kill Scofield to reclaim it.

Earlier, he had intended to finish dinner with Charles Candenning and the two women, then return to the railroad terminal and, posing as Scofield's employee, inspect the crates. His desire to see what the little man was transporting, however, had grown to such a compulsion that he had excused himself even before ordering dinner. He had dashed through the hotel, had run up Ramos Arizpe and across Puente de Alvarado to the railroad station.

At the terminal Portes made several inquiries and was finally directed to the outside yards, where he saw Scofield overseeing two men who were transferring the last of the crates from one baggage car to another.

Portes concealed himself behind a Pullman coach and waited until the transfer was completed. Scofield tipped the two men and turned to leave the yards. Only then did Portes step from his hiding place and walk along the tracks to where the men stood.

He greeted them affably. "This train . . ." He nodded toward the baggage car on which the crates had been transferred. "When does it leave?"

The men exchanged glances. Both pursed their lips and lifted their eyebrows noncommittally. "You ask us," the shorter one said. "You should ask the president."

"There's no schedule?"

Both men shrugged. The taller one pulled a crumpled pack of cigarettes from his trouser pocket. He offered it to Portes.

The priest shook his head.

"We hear rumors." The man lifted the pack to his mouth and extracted a cigarette with his lips. "Every hour something different. First he's going to give the railroads to us, to the union, then somebody tells him railhands and porters don't make switchmen and engineers." He lit the cigarette and inhaled luxuriously.

The short man spat between his feet. "Now it looks like he

won't be giving anything to anyone," he said. "He's just going to take over the money."

"Money," Portes said. "Always money."

"What difference?" the man said. "If it's just the money, maybe the foreigners will stay on. Maybe we'll have engineers and switchmen, and maybe this car will move—maybe."

"And when?" Portes asked.

"Who knows? Maybe tomorrow. Maybe Friday. I don't care. I'm going nowhere."

"But you must have some idea."

He shook his head almost sadly. "I don't make decisions for the railroad. The foreigners do that. The English say one thing, the Americans another. The trains come in and go out. I just do my job. It's better that way."

"But, this car *could* move out of here tonight?"

"Maybe. The National Palace is still open. The president's in there somewhere, deciding, you know—the destiny of the nation and other very important crap. Nobody but the president works at night. No. He'll make up his mind and then the rumors will fly again and, when the engineers and switchmen wake up, they can pick the one they like best. If they decide they still have their jobs, then they'll work. The foreigners will be happy and the trains will move. Otherwise . . ." He shrugged his shoulders.

"And, if the train does move—to where?"

"This one? If the train is put together tomorrow, it will surely be the last one before Cárdenas does whatever he's going to do. This one maybe will go to Piedras Negras or maybe Juárez."

"North then?"

"Oh yes, north. Certainly north."

"I'm with the police," Portes lied.

The men exchanged glances. Both were obviously in some doubt as to how to respond.

"I must inspect your cargo."

The smoker took a final suck on his cigarette and, as though fighting to appear casual, dropped the butt and ground it under his heel.

Not knowing how long he could baffle the two, Portes climbed into the still open freight car, then leaned down to help first one then the other man into the pitch blackness with him.

The shorter man snapped on a flashlight and let the beam

sweep the car. The twenty-four wooden boxes were neatly stacked in a corner.

Portes walked to them.

W. S. SCOFIELD CO.—IMPORTS & EXPORTS

Domingo Portes knelt and, with almost trembling fingers, gently touched the nearest box. Any one of the twenty-four could contain an emperor's ransom. There could be enough gold in the crates to support a man for the rest of his life.

For a moment the priest actually envied William Scofield. He felt greed and, with it, shame for the thought. Annoyed at his weakness, he tried with his bare hands to rip the lid off the case.

After a long and unsuccessful attempt, he felt a pressure on his shoulder and turned. The taller man handed him a jack-knife. Portes opened the blade and, using it as a lever, pried the lid off the box.

Inside, packed in what looked like dead jungle grass, were several bright objects. Portes separated the grass and pulled out a small statue. In the yellow beam of the flashlight, it looked exactly like thousands of others he had seen—a cheap, gilt reproduction of a pre-Columbian artifact for sale to tourists.

"Junk," the short man said.

Portes replaced the statue and recovered the crate. "Yes." He stood up.

The man was right. The crates contained exactly what William Scofield had said they contained. Domingo Portes realized that he had traveled almost half the length of Mexico for nothing. The treasure of Las Casas was gone. He had failed.

He looked outside the car to the bleakness of the railyards, gently haloed here and there by the ghostly glow of an isolated electric light. Rain had begun to fall. The scene was dreary—an impressionistic preview of purgatory.

"Junk," he repeated. "Nothing but junk."

Her hand held his wrist like a delicate talon. Blue veins stood out in stark relief, the brown spots of age contradicting the pale, almost translucent, flesh.

"Believe me, Jakob . . ." Hannah's eyes were quite level. "Sleep is all I need. Just a little sleep."

Tears welled into his eyes. For a moment they clouded his vision. "I can't let you suffer like this," he whispered. "Surely the hotel has a doctor."

She struggled to control her cough but failed. She hacked several times, then finally fell back exhausted. "No, Jakob. Your work . . . We can't risk it. There will be time for doctors in America."

"Darling . . ."

"We're safe here." Her voice was almost firm now. "Jakob, for the sake of all that is dear between us . . . Just a little sleep . . ." She coughed again and closed her huge brown eyes. "I'll be better in the morning, I promise you."

Her hand relaxed on his wrist. Gently, he placed it on her torso then, very tenderly, stroked her forehead. She didn't have a fever. Perhaps, he rationalized, she was just exhausted and didn't really need a doctor after all. Perhaps rest alone would be the best medicine.

He sat beside her until her breathing became more relaxed and regular. When he was sure she was at last asleep, he rose and crossed the room.

Once more he had escaped an almost certain capture. As he unwrapped one of the cigars he had bought in Vera Cruz, he wondered if any of it had really been worthwhile. There was nothing left for them in Germany, but what was there here? They were in a hotel in Mexico City. He didn't even know its name. The policeman who had inspected the taxi they took from the railroad station had been one of the many multilingual officers on duty in the capital. He had spoken German but had directed the cab driver in Spanish.

Dr. Pelzig lit his cigar, puffed it several times, then stepped out of the cloud of exhaled fumes to the room's window. He looked through the haze of rain down to the street.

Night in Mexico City, one of the world's most romantic, cosmopolitan cities! It was, in fact, quite wet and very dreary. He was about to turn away when something below made him squint.

Barely visible in the shadows of a doorway across the street was a man. He wore a fedora rather than a sombrero, and a belted raincoat instead of the conventional serape. Furthermore, he was standing rather than sitting hunched into himself.

Pelzig could not make out the man's features. He didn't have to. Individual physiognomies were unimportant to him. What mattered was the man's mission. That was virtually transparent. He was not an itinerant Indian camping hotelless in the capital overnight. He was a German—either one of the

195

two men who had been on the train from Puebla, or another working for the same master.

Pelzig turned from the window, glanced to where Hannah was sleeping, and sighed heavily. All his efforts had been futile. In Germany, Lisbon, Vera Cruz—on the train in the station, and now here—everything he had done to escape had ultimately proven absolutely useless. He was no more safe in Mexico now than he had been months and miles away in Berlin.

Jakob Pelzig sat heavily in the room's single upholstered chair. He was alone with God, and a stranger waited for him across the street. His entire adult life had been involved with time, yet he had never before realized how very precious a few minutes or hours could be.

Now there was little time left. He had pressed his luck too far. He couldn't escape again. Time had finally run out.

And—what difference did it make, really? The Germany he had once loved had been raped and destroyed. His children had been killed in the flower of youth, and his beloved Hannah was desperately, hopelessly sick.

He leaned back in his chair and inhaled deeply. "Time," he whispered aloud. He held the tobacco fumes in his lungs for a long, luxuriant moment before jetting them toward the ceiling. "It is only a matter of time."

Norm Henderson stayed with the Taylor Cub at the Oaxaca airport while his two passengers went about their business. For the better part of a full day, the pilot did nothing but smoke incessantly and watch every Mexican he saw with raw, unmasked suspicion.

The two younger men snooped unsuccessfully around the airport then hired a taxi north, through town, to the railroad depot.

Henderson continued chain-smoking. He remained intolerably suspicious of every movement within fifty yards of the plane.

At the railroad terminal, the agents learned only that a man had almost killed himself trying to catch the last northbound train. The stationmaster remembered nothing about Germans or Americans. To him, all foreigners were the same. He confessed that he probably couldn't tell one from another. He would even have forgotten about the baggage if that stupid fool hadn't started to race the train.

196

The agents decided to check the tourist hotels. At the Monte Albán, a clerk remembered.

"Yes," he told them. "There was a German couple. They were met by an American."

"American?" The two men exchanged noncommittal glances. Desmond had said nothing about anyone else on the case. "Are you sure?"

"Mister Candenning? Of course I'm sure."

"Not a German?"

"He said he was an American. Why would he lie?"

"And what did they do?"

"Do? What do Americans always do? He drank."

"Drank?"

"There was an earthquake—damage to the tracks. A minor delay, then they all took the train north."

"All?"

"The German couple—Heinrich I think the name was—and Mister Candenning, then the young lady. They're surely in the capital by now."

The two men thanked the clerk, left the hotel, and returned to their waiting taxi. Klein got in first. McMillan followed and slammed the door behind him. "*Aeropuerto*," he told the driver.

The car drove two blocks east, then turned right, and headed almost due south on Bustamante.

Klein pulled a pack of cigarettes from his shirt pocket and offered one to his companion. "Jesus Christ!" He almost spat the words. "Heinrich! We can't even be sure."

McMillan crimped a cigarette between the nails of his thumb and second finger and pulled it from the pack. "It's him," he said. "Don't worry."

"So what? Mexico City! Talk about a needle in a haystack!"

McMillan tapped the cigarette several times on the crystal of his wristwatch before he lit it. "It's not that bad."

"Oh? I suppose they issued you a crystal ball?"

"You're new," McMillan said. "Mexico isn't a city—it's just a front. Ever since old man Díaz was running this place, Mexico's been nothing more than a first-class facade."

"What's that got to do with our needle?"

McMillan spoke over exhaled smoke. "You can get shot by bandits in Chihuahua or cut to suet in Vera Cruz; you can get robbed in the country or beaten up in any city. It's par for the course, except in the capital. The capital is strictly for

197

foreigners. It's there to show everyone just how civilized this country really is."

"What's your point?"

"My point is simply that this whole stinking country is nothing more than a political, moral, ethical swamp. There's nothing faintly redeemable here—nothing. It's pure barbarism with a flush toilet or an automobile every one hundred and fifty miles."

"I heard Mexico City's very cosmopolitan."

"Of course. That's my very point. It's one little island. It's there to make the swamp look like the fruited goddamned plain. That's where the government tells the big lie. That is where, if you're not careful, you may start to think Mexicans are really civilized after all."

"Still . . ."

"There was an earthquake here. It delayed the train. As far as the railroads go, there's talk of big wheels and deals in the Palacio Nacional."

"So?"

"So, the last train out of here is probably the only one into the capital from this area in the last day or so."

"What difference—"

"In Mexico City most of the cops are bilingual. Not only that, there is a police inspection of every cab leaving the railroad station. The drivers are checked—all to protect the foreigners."

"I still don't understand."

The taxi turned southeast and headed toward the Oaxaca airport.

Richard McMillan took a last deep drag on his cigarette, then flicked the butt out the window. "Never mind," he said. "I do."

After overseeing the transfer of the twenty-four crates, William Scofield tipped the two men who had done the work, then wrote down the number of the freight car. He turned away and started through the railyards, completely unaware of Domingo Portes' presence a few yards away. His emotions at the time had been of relief. Had he been poetic, Bill Scofield might have likened himself that night to a scarf with one loose stitch. With the safe transfer of the gold, that stitch had finally been pulled. In one great jerk, the tightly knitted scarf had been transformed into a loose pile of gently kinked yarn.

His blood pressure sank to normal. The adrenaline in his system might simply have evaporated. His blood vessels expanded. His muscles relaxed, and he breathed deeply of the wet air.

The drizzling rain had soaked insidiously into his coat then through it to his shirt and skin before he had reached the shelter of the station. It didn't matter. The crates were safe. The freight car would be hooked into a northbound train the following morning. There would be no more problems, unless some baggage-smashing customs inspector did more scratching about than he was supposed to. Chances of that were slim. With Roosevelt sitting on the hard money, and the government in Mexico robbing the church and everyone else blind, no one but a clairvoyant would even suspect what was really in the crates.

He was almost smiling as he entered the railroad terminal. Exhilarated and wide awake, he considered for a moment checking into a hotel, then discarded the idea. If he let himself relax—lie down on a bed—there could be no way of knowing how long he might sleep.

He couldn't afford to miss the coupling of the freight car, or let the northbound train leave him behind.

He slammed his hands into his trouser pockets and sat down on a bench.

He awoke with a jerk, realizing at once that he had fallen asleep instantly and slept too long. Outside, a newspaper vendor was shouting something about President Cárdenas and the expropriation of some foreign debts.

Bill Scofield paid no attention. It was almost dawn and he couldn't afford to sleep again. He had more important things to worry about than Mexican presidential orders.

5
The Last Train

THURSDAY MORNING, the capital learned the news. As was his habit when there, President Cárdenas had worked late into the night. Before leaving the National Palace, he had announced that his government would expropriate the debt of the National Railroads.

The presidential decree, published in the Official Gazette, said that in the future the railroads would be administered by a new federal department yet to be formed. That department would be empowered to take any measures necessary to reorganize the railroads on a more profitable basis.

The announcement assured all foreign investors and bondholders that the Mexican government would reimburse them after the confiscated properties had been inventoried and evaluated by the Treasury Department. It then noted that approximately thirty-seven percent of Mexico's railroad bonds were held by British interests and another thirty percent by investors from the United States.

Domingo Portes read the news with no particular interest or enthusiasm. He had been up since dawn, had already packed his few belongings, then had decided to walk the streets. He had hoped the morning air might eliminate, or at least mitigate, the deep sense of depression and personal failure from which he now suffered. The morning was clear as crystal. There was no hint of the previous night's rain. Portes breathed deeply of the thin, mountainous atmosphere, but it did little to ease his guilt.

He was glancing through the newspaper as he walked, when a second item captured his attention. Portes stopped.

VILLA HERMOSA, Tabasco, June 23. Dispatches from the Medellin Ranch reported today the slaying of nine persons, including the Villa Hermosa police chief, in a gun battle that followed an attempt by police to arrest a group of Catholics attending religious services in a private home. Two other policemen and six civilians were said to have been killed. Federal troops were sent to restore order at the ranch.

As though in a trance, Portes folded the newspaper and started back to the hotel. His soul felt vacuous. After all the years of fighting and hiding, of secretly hearing confessions and administering the holy sacraments, he still could not totally believe the stark reality of which he was a part. Six more martyrs had joined the almost endless list of his countrymen who were guilty of no more than showing faith in the Supreme Being. Was this God's will, he wondered—the murder of the faithful, the imprisonment of priests, the defilement of all that was, and had been, sacred for centuries?

Portes entered the Hotel Biltmore. A sleepy clerk looked up from the desk, apparently convinced himself that the man in the ill-fitting, drab suit was no one of any consequence, then returned to studying his own morning paper.

Portes had failed. He had no idea what had happened to the gold. He only knew that he had followed blind intuition and hearsay reports. They had led him on a wild goose chase—a crusade to nowhere. The treasure of Bishop Las Casas might have been no more than worthless sand. Certainly, it had slipped entirely through his fingers.

There was nothing left but to make his way south again. The Church was beaten. The gold he had failed to track down represented Her last hope. All he could do was report his failure to his provincial and take the consequences.

Before he left the capital, however, he wanted to wish Teresa Inez farewell. Because of her own troubles, and the fact that she knew his secret, she had been a link to sanity for him over the last two days. He had done what little he could for her. Now he could do no more. He prayed she could escape the danger surrounding her lover, and that, somehow, she and her unborn child could find happiness and security north of the border.

Instead of taking the elevator, he climbed the stairs to her floor and turned toward her room. He didn't pay any particular attention to the several dark stains spotting the carpet for almost the entire length of the corridor, but he was somewhat surprised when his knock on Teresa's door was answered by a young boy.

Teresa stood directly behind him, her beautiful face shadowed by worry, her eyes hollowed by fear. It was obvious that she had slept little through the night. "Father!" she whispered. "Thank God!" She pulled him into the room.

Portes pushed the door closed behind him. Except for the two silent young boys, everything appeared to be in perfect order, yet there was a tension in the room which fairly crackled like a high-voltage electrical installation.

"Come," Teresa said. She led him away from the two boys and spoke in a conspiratorial whisper. "You must help me, Father. You're the only one I can trust."

He glanced back to the children. They sat beside one another on one of the beds. Their bodies were immobile, their huge eyes wide with curiosity.

"Their mother is dead," Teresa whispered.

"Dead?"

"And Jesús—badly hurt. I don't know where he is. I only know he told me to leave—to get to the railroad station and take the children north."

"You haven't heard?"

"Heard?"

"The president worked late last night. There are no railroads operating."

"What!" The air might have been sucked out of her by a huge unseen pump.

"He's expropriated the foreign interests. He's going to form some sort of federal agency."

"But, I must—"

"Wait." He laid his hands on her shoulders. "Perhaps there is a chance. I talked to some railroad men recently about another matter. They thought if the engineers still had jobs—were still going to get paid—they'd work. Cárdenas has hurt the investors with this, not the foreign employees."

"If only—"

"Don't get your hopes too high, but we can try. You get these boys ready, then come downstairs. I'll go with you to the station and see what can be done."

"And the trip?"

"No," he said. "I cannot go north. Six more Catholics were killed last night."

"Oh no!"

"Yes. In Tabasco."

"Holy Mother—"

"My duty is here." He stared for a moment into her very worried, very beautiful, black eyes before lifting his palms from her shoulders. "I'll meet you in the lobby." He turned toward the door.

It was still dark when William Scofield stood up and began walking through the terminal. The huge building was virtually deserted. He walked through to the passenger loading area and beyond. There were no trains on the tracks or people on the platforms.

He decided to make himself as comfortable as possible and wait.

He was quietly smoking a cigarette as dawn splashed the first pink glow into the crisp morning air. A few people had begun to dribble into the terminal. All seemed excited, even enthusiastic.

He overheard snatches of their conversation.

". . . Cárdenas fooled the gringos again . . ."

". . . Now we *really* own the railroads . . ."

". . . It's time those damned foreigners learned . . ."

And—as ever and always—the multi-significant cliche "*Viva la Revolución.*"

At first, all he was sure of was that General Cárdenas had done something that affected the foreign interests controlling railroad money, but as he listened to more and more snatches of conversation, he had become concerned. Finally, he had stopped a fairly well-dressed man and asked for the news directly.

Hadn't he heard? The man made absolutely no effort to conceal his national pride. "General Cárdenas has expropriated the railroad debts. As soon as the new department is established, Mexico will control her own transportation absolutely."

Scofield had grasped the situation immediately but with split emotions. On the one hand, he couldn't help admiring the sheer audacity of the Mexican president. On the other, he detested the inconvenience of having to wait days, possibly even weeks, until some bureaucratic department was established to run his train from the capital to the border. Anything could happen in that time. There could be cargo inspections, misplacements, losses—anything.

He was determined not to wait.

Bill Scofield had walked through the passenger loading

area to the railyards outside. The freight car in which the crates had been placed was exactly where it had been the night before. Several railhands were lounging nearby, but they knew nothing about schedules and obviously didn't care to learn. They did, however, point to a man some twenty yards away. He was, they told him, *el maquinista de locomotora.*

The engineer was a Frenchman whose Marseilles accent was so thick that Scofield could not understand his Spanish. They spoke in ruptured English.

The man knew his job was safe—at least for a few months. Still, at the moment, he had no idea what country or department or company intended to pay his salary. Until such details were made clear, he intended to do nothing.

Scofield tried to convince him that nothing had changed as yet, and wouldn't until the new department of railroads actually was formed. The Frenchman, however, remained cynically unreceptive until Scofield suggested forming a semiprivate train.

The plan was childishly simple. Some train had been scheduled in some way to leave for Juárez. In fact, the engineer himself had been assigned to run it. All that had to be done was to prepare it as planned, then have the porters collect an extra peso from each passenger in addition to the regular fare. The money could then be divided among the crew. Surely there would be enough people wanting to get out of the capital to make the plan practical, if not extremely profitable— and—if someone didn't want to pay, he could simply wait for the reorganization of the transportation system.

At first the Frenchman was skeptical, but Scofield knew he had generated at least some interest.

"Of course," the engineer warned, "such a train can be formed. But when it can leave . . ." He shrugged.

"Sure, I understand."

Goddamned onion. Want to make sure you squeeze out every last peso you can, don't you?

Scofield dug into his trouser pocket, peeled a ten-peso note from his rapidly diminishing supply of cash and handed it to the Frenchman. He nodded to the freight car containing the gold. "Just make damned sure that one there's hooked in."

The engineer glanced from the freight car to the money in his hand. He shrugged very Gallic shoulders. "Okay," he said. "I'll get your train."

Scofield reclaimed the knapsack he had checked the night before. Then, carrying it, returned to the passenger loading area, where he paced the platform and chain-smoked while waiting for the Frenchman to keep his word. More and more people arrived, some obviously expecting to find trains which were not there, others simply curious as to how the president's edict had affected the railroad system.

Most of the new arrivals were Mexicans, involved to greater or lesser degrees with the new law. Except for the singular lack of waiting trains, the crowded station soon appeared quite normal. Indians and clerks, police, peddlers, and heavily-laden women looking exhausted yet determined all jostled back and forth, busily going nowhere, as they discussed the expropriation of the railroad bonds.

Scofield had taken a last drag of a cigarette, dropping it to the ground underfoot, then glanced up to see a man who looked distinctly out of place. He was definitely not Mexican. In fact, he looked very much like the English actor Leslie Howard. What arrested William Scofield's attention, however, was the woman with him.

She had a face that might have been painted by Modigliani. It was crowned with cinnamon hair and adorned with pale eyes. Her breasts were grandly beautiful and her hips so magnificent he was sure her legs might be hinged in honey.

The anxious, furtive posture of the man made it clear that he wanted to get out of the capital fast. Scofield decided that inasmuch as the two people came as a unit—at least for the time being—he might just as well try to get them on the northbound train with him. He took a breath and, with the unbridled arrogance of the very short, walked directly to them and introduced himself.

The man was apprehensive, if not actually terrified, about something. The woman was calmer, far less concerned, and judging from her accent, English.

"Don't worry," Scofield assured them. "There'll be a train backing in here in no time. You folks going north?"

"No." The man spoke at the same instant the woman said, "Yes."

Scofield chuckled. "It sure doesn't matter to me one way or another, except the train coming in here's probably going to be the last one going out for some little time."

Because they had not read the morning papers or talked to anyone else, Scofield explained the railroad situation in general, then went on to mention his conversation with the French engineer. He had spoken for no more than two, or perhaps three, minutes when the train began to back into the terminal.

"That's it now," he had told them. "The last train north."

"What we should do—" Charles Candenning chewed very deliberately as he looked across the table at Karen. "—is go to the station, find out if this really has done anything to the scheduling, then plan accordingly."

"You don't seem upset in the least." She sounded genuinely shocked.

"I'm not." He lifted another forkful of eggs. "Should I be?"

"But it's grand theft!"

"Of course it's grand theft."

"But how can he do it? How—"

"He can do anything he likes," Candenning assured her. "After all, he's the president."

"Well!" She really seemed quite indignant, not merely at the decree of expropriation, but at Candenning's sincerely casual attitude toward it. "You certainly can't expect England and the United States to sit back and allow this sort of thing. Why, they've loaned millions."

"They won't do anything," he assured her.

Very deliberately, she laid her fork across her plate and stared at him. "You sound as though you actually condone this sort of highway robbery."

"No." He smiled. "Not at all. The rules are just different down here. The old school tie simply doesn't fit anymore. Besides, what's the good of complaining? You don't think General Cárdenas is going to change his mind for me, do you?"

"Let's hope Mr. Chamberlain and President Roosevelt aren't taking the situation so casually."

"Surely you don't expect warships and marines swarming all over the country just because of a few dollars, some track, and rolling stock? Besides—" He tossed his napkin on the table. "—what does it have to do with you and me and sightseeing? I mean, either there will be trains or there won't. If there won't, we'll just have to find some other way north—that's all."

"I suppose you're right," she sighed. "It just seems so unfair."

"Unfair?" He placed a few peso-notes on top of the check and rose to help her from the table. "Life itself is hardly otherwise. Most people here would probably call the whole thing remarkably fair—patriotic, in fact. I mean, it's Mexico for the Mexicans, and down-with-the-foreign-devils sort of thing. Cárdenas is a hero because he's telling England to fly a kite and thumbing his nose at Uncle Sam."

"All right," she said. "All right, you've made your point. Do you mind if we walk to the station? It's such a nice morning."

Gently, yet quite purposefully, he placed his palm under her elbow and led her from the dining room through the lobby. On Ramos Arizpe, they turned north toward Buenavista Park and the station beyond.

The air was thin and crisp. Breathing reminded him somehow of breaking crackers over soup. The sky was spectacular. He was sure that if he lifted his hand over his head, curled his second finger tight against his thumb then snapped it out, the dome of heaven might actually chime.

Instead, he moved purely by instinct and, without actually knowing in a fully conscious way that he had done so, clasped her hand in his.

Palm to palm, they walked toward the station.

There, the furor of activity seemed in no way unusual. The huge terminal appeared to be operating quite normally. People of every description scurried here and there, more like insects than human beings. Each seemed motivated not merely by his own individual circuit, but by another wired directly to Destiny's ultimate generator.

Right or wrong, Candenning knew, Lázaro Cárdenas had again captured the hearts of his countrymen. One way or another, he would *make* them believe in Mexico's greatness and independent power over foreign control.

The sounds in the station were a muted cacophony. Yet they, too, might have underscored the national hymn. People called to one another, the wheels of baggage carts sighed as though in relief as they moved and, far in the background, the incessant wheeze of engines threatened to move long trains over great distances. It was all like a discordant anthem—a tone poem prophesying the glory of total national freedom soon to come. Spain, the Church, foreign emperors, bankers and businessmen—all were finally to be ground under the wheels of the newly expropriated railroads. Every person, cart, and vehicle in the huge station seemed to know and delight in the fact.

Still holding Karen by the hand, Candenning made a few inquiries about departures to the north, but no one seemed to know which trains would run when or where. Indeed, no one to whom the illustrator spoke even seemed to know, or care, for what department he worked. As yet, nothing had been done about the new agency that the president had promised to create, but none of the railroad employees were concerned. President Cárdenas was a man who could and would work miracles for the workers. All would go well with them, regardless of titles or particular governmental offices.

Unable to gather any solid information in the terminal, Candenning decided to move to the tracks. He led Karen into a world smelling lazily of tortillas and chilies, animals, cigarette smoke, and, behind all else, the electrically invigorating snap of ozone. Soldiers and peasants, porters, men in business suits, and hundreds of black-clad women milled back and forth on the platform. No one seemed to be going anywhere, yet all appeared compelled to engage in some form of activity. Feet moved forward, then back. Arms raised cigarettes to their owners' lips and heads gestured sagaciously about some almost secret knowledge.

He and Karen stopped to inspect the crowd. At the same moment they both saw the three people standing some fifty yards forward on the platform.

Neil Oberon, the woman whom he had been with the night before, and the diminutive American, William Scofield, were having what appeared to be a somewhat animated conversation.

Candenning smiled. "Suppose I should risk another snub?" he asked.

"Risk away," she told him. "Just keep me clear of that obnoxious little man. He really—I mean, *really*—makes me crawl."

He grunted, remembering Scofield's abrupt rudeness the previous afternoon as he had left the train. "Come on," he said. "Maybe they know something the Mexicans don't." He started down the platform.

While still some ten yards away, Neil Oberon looked up, spotted them, and dashed toward Candenning. His facial expression—his entire posture and manner—was one of almost abject supplication.

"Look here." He sounded very sincere. "I'm really sorry about yesterday. I mean, dashing off that way and all. Frankly, I had—well, an appointment—one of those devil-waits-for-no-man sort of things."

"No matter," Candenning said. "Karen, this is Neil Oberon late of Connecticut or Montauk. Neil—Karen Tait."

"Delighted," Oberon said.

Both he and Karen nodded. Neither extended a hand.

"What's the story on scheduling?" Candenning asked. "Anything going out of here today?"

Oberon shook his head. "Don't know." He seemed not only disappointed but genuinely alarmed, even furtive. "That fellow I was talking to—Scofield's his name—seems he has pull with some of the people here. Seems to think they'll get this one train out before Cárdenas completely rehashes the whole system. C'mon. Let me introduce you."

"We've met." The edge was quite apparent in Karen's tone.

"Yes," Candenning said. "We were on the train coming up yesterday."

They followed Oberon down the platform to where Scofield was standing with Margaret Whitley.

"You know Karen Tait," Oberon said, "and Charles Candenning. This is Margaret Whitley."

The men nodded. Margaret extended her hand, and Candenning took it briefly.

Scofield looked from Karen to the illustrator. He was obviously less than pleased to see them together.

Candenning tried to break what he was sure would soon become thick social ice. "Neil tells us that you and *El Presidente* are the only two men in town who know what's happening," he said.

"I'll tell you this much." Scofield nodded as though imparting an important confidence. "Old Lázaro is one smart son of a bitch. Can't help but admire a guy like that—real guts. Here the limeys and Americans fund the whole stinking railroad system and once payment's due, he just ups and takes the whole thing. I mean, is that your old Mex machismo, or ain't it?"

"Fine," Candenning said. "But are the trains going to run?"

Scofield frowned slightly. "Sure they're going to run," he said. "Why wouldn't they run?"

"Because, whatever department Cárdenas is supposed to set up doesn't exist yet. That may look like a train behind you, but I'll bet you seventeen *centavos* there's no engineer, or if there is one, he doesn't have the foggiest notion who's paying his salary. In short, right now there's no system."

"Oh?" Scofield challenged. "Well, you listen to me, Bo. The Mexicans may have no system. Hell, that's par. But you can bet your seventeen goddamned *centavos* that I do. There's plenty of system for this train here, and that engineer knows damned good and well who's paying his salary. This one's northbound and it's probably the last one out before any newfangled agency takes over. You can bet there's enough bribe money in that engineer's pocket to buy the goddamned thing outright. If I was you, Mister, I'd check out of wherever you're staying and hop aboard. Believe me, you miss this one, what with the Mexican speed of things and, like as not you'll be hoofing it to the border."

Candenning didn't like Scofield's pugnacious, self-important attitude. Still, the truth of what he had said was apparent. The train beside which they stood could very well be the last one north for days—perhaps even weeks. There could be no way of telling what might happen to the railroads between now and the time when purely political wheels rolled sufficiently to reorganize the system.

He glanced to Karen. "Well," he smiled, "there goes a day of touristing."

"*Mañana*," she said. This time it was she who slipped her hand into his and led the way back to the terminal.

Because they had no idea how much or little time remained before the train's departure, they decided to take a taxi back to the hotel. They had just stepped outside when one stopped before them.

The young man who got out looked very much like an adult Tom Sawyer. He was neatly dressed, and although not actually handsome, certainly quite presentable—the kind of young Englishman or American commonly labeled "clean-cut." As he left the cab, he looked just an instant more than casually at Karen.

Candenning helped Karen into the taxi, then slid beside her, and closed the door. "Hotel Biltmore," he said, and then glanced out the window.

Something about the previous passenger bothered him in a vague, almost spectral way, yet he couldn't quite put his finger on it. Only when the cab turned south on Buenavista did he suddenly realize what it was.

Clean-cut, he almost whispered aloud. Yet there had been something almost filthy about the young man. Filthy—and, yes—obscene as well.

As he paid the driver and prepared to step from the taxi, the first thing Thomas Kemp had noticed was the woman's legs. They were long and lean—strong, but not unpleasantly muscular. They were legs designed for leisurely walks along winding country paths, and for twining in naked abandon over a man's hips before an intimate fireplace. These were legs of which erotic dreams are built—limbs that could and did bring life, albeit tentatively, to dead capabilities.

He allowed his eyes the luxury of dwelling on her calves, and crawling along the unseen firm swell of her inner thighs. He savored the succulent flair of her hips, devoured her flat abdomen and barely hinted soft convexity of Venus's mound. His eyes moved upward to the woman's torso, appreciated her slender waist and well-formed but modestly proportioned breasts. Finally, his glance rested on her level, azure eyes.

In that fleeting erotic moment, Kemp luxuriated in fantasy. What, he wondered, would she be like naked—writhing beyond control—screaming a high incohate wail mingled of agony and ecstasy? What would she do as his fingernails tore furrows into her firm buttocks and raked themselves down her long, slender thighs? What obscenities would she cry out? What forbidden acts would she beg?

Thomas Kemp stepped from the taxi. He walked past the woman and the tall blond man and into the terminal. Just inside the main entrance, he stopped.

He was both tired and annoyed, yet convinced that Mexico City's main railroad stations offered his last hope of finding Neil Oberon. Kemp had spent most of the previous afternoon and night and far too much money in cab fares riding from one hotel to another. He had asked a series of blandly unconcerned clerks about a young American gentleman and his English companion. No one had seen Oberon or Margaret Whitley or anyone faintly resembling them.

Not until he had heard rumors of President Cárdenas's intent to expropriate the railroad debts, had Kemp realized just how limited Oberon's options were. He had no car, and was entirely too much of a gold-plated snob even to think of taking a bus out of the city. The airport was being watched and Oberon was certainly smart enough to know it. He might get on a plane flying out, but he'd never come down with it.

Neil Oberon had exactly two choices. He could either remain in the city, waiting to be spotted and gunned down, or try to board one of the final trains out of the capital before the entire Mexican transportation system fell into a managerial limbo, awaiting formation of whatever new agency the president intended to appoint.

Kemp had returned to his own apartment. He had showered and shaved, then changed his suit and taken a taxi to El Estación de los Ferrocarriles Nacionales. Now, standing just inside the main terminal and watching an apparently normal scene, his primary emotion was one of infuriated frustration.

Kemp scanned the crowd. The terminal was bustling with people hurrying this way and that yet apparently going nowhere. Kinetic energy was being expended but to no real purpose, and in no specific direction. He did not see Oberon or the woman. Indeed, he saw no foreign face.

Kemp pushed his way through the terminal to the tracks. There, almost immediately, he saw them.

He also came face to face with exactly how wretchedly complicated a supposedly simple assignment had become.

Neil Oberon was standing on the platform with his mistress and a short, dark-haired man. At this distance, it would be easy to kill him—in fact, to kill all three of them. To do so, however, would be to plumb the depths of stupidity. Kemp was surrounded by soldiers, police officers, politicians, and other armed men, all of whom would delight in shooting down anyone on the barest pretext. Were he to fire at Oberon— were he even to draw the Luger—he could never hope to get off the platform, let alone out of the terminal.

Thomas Kemp drew a leather cigarette case from his inside coat pocket, snapped it open, and lifted a Camel. He lit the cigarette with a slowness that was almost theatrical, inhaled deeply, and began to evaluate his situation.

The irony of it was that he himself was as thoroughly trapped as his target. He simply couldn't shoot in the crowded terminal without sealing his own death warrant. Still, there was hope. Oberon obviously intended to board the waiting train when it left the station. Once aboard that train, Kemp would surely find some place offering privacy.

As he exhaled, he looked at Margaret Whitley. Her legs were also quite long, her hips wide, and her breasts high and large.

His assignment, he decided, would take a little longer. Now, however, there would be fresh compensations. He would board the train and would meet Neil Oberon's mistress. He would ingratiate himself with the long-legged woman and then, some place between Mexico and the border, he would find the time and the privacy to kill both Oberon and the woman who posed as his wife.

He inhaled again. The woman's body was slender but quite opulent. It could still be savored—tasted and bitten and scratched—in many ways.

Once the time came, Neil Oberon would die quite rapidly but, muffled by the noise of the moving train, the woman's final screams could very well last for hours.

Jakob Pelzig woke and lay for some time staring at the ceiling of the hotel room. He was quite calm and genuinely surprised at the fact. Carefully, so as not to wake Hannah, he drew the covers aside and placed his feet on the carpet.

Yesterday his soul had been reduced to the ashes of despair. During the night, or in the instant of waking, a metamorphosis had taken place.

He was not a man to analyze abstracts except in purely scientific terms, but he knew something had changed and changed radically. As he wiggled his feet into his slippers, he straightened his back and took a deep breath.

The diminutive professor of physics from the Kaiser Wilhelm Institute had, in fact, become a human incarnation of the phoenix.

Despair was gone. He rose and, in doing so, was again possessed of his old determination. There *was* hope. They *would* reach Princeton.

Leaving Hannah to sleep as long as possible, he shuffled to the window. The street was clear and dry. The city, stretching for miles, was low and hauntingly beautiful under the crisp morning light.

Most important, there was no one in the doorway across the street! In fact, there was no man—no one—on the street itself!

Perhaps, he thought, the man had been no more than a product of his imagination—an illusive trick of rain and shadow and the configurations of ancient Spanish architecture—created by an exhausted, traumatized mind.

Jakob shuffled from the window to the bathroom and there set about his morning ablutions. He ran hot water in his shaving mug, poured it out, then whipped the soap in it to a soft lather. The brush handle made warm, clicking sounds against the side of the mug.

He and Hannah now rested exactly at the pivotal point of a long and circuitous route of flight. From this moment on, he could no longer twist and alter his true course.

He daubed shaving soap under his chin and over his face in slow, circular movements. His hand might have been that of an artist applying wind-tufted texture to a gleaming snowscape.

From the capital, they had to go straight to the border. There was no other choice. He could no longer double-back by playing east for west, or south for north as he had since leaving Berlin so many weeks ago.

He opened his razor, then stropped it exactly six times, as he had every morning of his adult life. Gently, precisely, he mowed the first wide furrow through the shaving cream on the front of his neck and under his chin.

Danger now was in all probability nonexistent. He and Hannah had certainly escaped the two men who had boarded the train in Puebla. Also, the man in the doorway was gone.

Puckering his lips in a ridiculous grimace, he started to peel the shaving cream from his right cheek. The razor slid easily from temple to jaw.

One couldn't afford to be overconfident. It could mean a false sense of security. Still, there would surely be no attempt at violence on the train itself, and no chance for it once they reached the United States . . .

Jakob Pelzig leaned forward and inspected himself in the mirror. He was satisfied. He had not even nicked himself.

The only time he and Hannah might face any danger at all would be in leaving the hotel. Nothing could happen to them in a taxicab, and very little could go wrong while they were boarding the train . . .

He soaked one of the smaller towels in hot water, wrung it as dry as he could, and covered his face with the steaming cloth. Then, still moving more slowly than usual, he wiped

214

the last of the shaving cream from under his ears, replaced the damp towel, and dabbed his face with witch hazel.

Finished in the bathroom, Dr. Pelzig again walked to the room's window. He looked to the street, the doorway—then right—then left.

There was no sign of anyone below. If all the streets in Mexico were as deserted, the capital had surely become a ghost town.

He took a deep and satisfying breath, crossed the room, and laid a gentle hand on Hannah's shoulder. "*Liebchen*?"

Huge, beautiful eyes opened and looked lazily at him.

"Time to wake," he told her. "We must go now—leave as soon as possible. We can eat on the train."

Jakob Pelzig had neither heard the previous night's rumors from the National Palace nor read the morning paper. He believed that all was well with the nation's rail system, and that if he could only reach the main terminal, he could simply board any one of many trains traveling north.

As Hannah prepared for departure, Jakob enjoyed the day's first cigar. He went to the window twice more to check the street below and the doorway. Now more than ever, he was convinced that Charles Candenning actually had diverted the two men who had been on the train, and that at last he had escaped pursuit.

Still, after Hannah had finished in the bathroom and their scant possessions were again neatly packed, he took the precaution of going down the hotel's stairs rather than using the elevator. He also made a careful inspection of the lobby before walking to the desk.

It was there that he became finally and absolutely convinced that today of all days would be blessed for him with impossibly good luck. Mercifully the clerk on duty, although not really bilingual, did have a primitive command of German. He understood enough to instruct the doorman to call a cab and order it to take the Pelzigs to the main railroad station.

Jakob paid his bill and thanked the desk clerk for his kindness. Still, the habits of the hunted remained with him. He waited by the main desk until the taxi drove up and stopped and he held Hannah back as a bellboy carried their two bags outside and loaded them into the vehicle's trunk.

Only when he was absolutely sure of safe and rapid passage, did he cross the hotel's lobby, lead Hannah through the

215

revolving door, and start across the wide sidewalk to the waiting cab.

What happened next was a blurred montage.

It began with running footfalls just as Hannah stepped into the cab. Then it was her wide and frightened eyes—her baffled expression—as she gasped his name.

Shoes on the pavement pounded nearer . . . Sudden, heavy, talonlike pressure on both shoulders at once.

He was spun back and away from the taxi and knew instantly that, despite his tricks—his backtracking and subterfuge—they had him at last.

He couldn't escape, but maybe—maybe—Hannah could get free.

"Gehen!" he cried to the driver. *"Gehen Sie!"*

Somewhere from the bottom of a long, hollow infinity, Hannah screamed.

He was jerked backward . . . The world blurred as his glasses spun from his ears . . . There were forms around him, but no faces . . .

He was thrown against the taxi, then pulled roughly away.

"Gehen!" he cried out again. *"Oh, Hannah! Gehest du!"*

He was pulled backward along the sidewalk, his heels dragging against the concrete . . . A car's door opened behind him . . . he was pushed downward, then backward . . . His head struck metal . . .

The hard, unmistakably brutal impact of a clenched fist smashing against facial tissue . . .

A grunt . . .

Another blow . . .

One sibilant Tutonic obscenity . . .

And a lazy American voice . . . "Fuck you, too, Heinie!"

Impact! Flesh hard on flesh . . . Something wet snapping . . . A grunt . . .

The talons were gone . . . Someone moaned . . .

The lazy voice in English again, "Go!"

Hands, gentle now, under his elbows—leading him along the sidewalk . . .

Blurred images . . . He was in front of the hotel . . . The taxi was still there . . . Hannah was inside, one foot still extended to the pavement . . .

The lazy masculine voice again, "Go, Doctor Pelzig!"

He turned . . . looked down through bleared distortion

216

. . . A man on hands and knees . . . rocking back . . . reaching under his coat . . .

A foot . . . from nowhere—like a meteor . . . a human ballista . . . smashing the face like a soccer ball . . .

Blood flecked his trouser cuff and ran stickywarm through his sock as an impotent pistol clattered to the pavement. Then, miraculously, through the jellied aspic of vision, glasses.

He stooped, picked them from the pavement.

"Go!" Another voice in English, then the same in Spanish to the driver. *La estación de los ferrocarriles! Apresura!"*

He was eased into the taxi. The door slammed.

It was over.

Acceleration pulled him backward into the seat. Very slowly, he lifted his glasses and, with an habitual gesture, wiped them clean. He replaced his handkerchief in his breast pocket and, very precisely, hooked the glasses over his ears.

With clarity of sight, the world became sane again. He was a traveler. He was sitting next to his wife in a taxi and they were going to the railroad station.

He squeezed Hannah's hand. *"Schön gut,"* he said. "It's all right. It's over now."

Still, there *was* blood, cold now and crisply flaking as it clotted on his sock and someone he didn't know lay on the pavement behind them with his face kicked as concave as a soup bowl.

No, he told himself. *It was a dream. Such things simply do not happen.*

"It's all right," he said again.

But he knew he was lying.

The train huffed and wheezed. It jerked several yards forward, then backed again. The engine made important, but not quite imperative, sounds.

William Scofield, Oberon, and Margaret Whitley decided to board and wait. There could be no telling how soon the train actually might leave the station. That depended entirely on the greed of the engineer.

They found seats together and secured their luggage. Scofield had just relaxed and was happily contemplating several hours of enjoying the woman's face and torso when a young man came up the aisle from behind him and stopped.

"Say," he said to the woman. "You're Maggi Whitley, aren't you?"

She seemed momentarily confused. She turned to her companion, then back to the stranger, but didn't speak.

"I heard you sing at the Largo months ago. You made me one of your biggest fans."

She smiled. "How very nice—"

"Yes." He sat down next to Scofield. "I really think you have one of the finest voices I've ever heard."

The man looked like a rustic in an expensive suit. Still, he was obviously no farmer. He annoyed Scofield. Not only had he butted in—sat down without even asking—but he was talking to the woman as if he'd known her for years.

Scofield turned and was about to speak, but something about the man arrested him. He was sophisticated—apparently friendly—but there was something else.

The man was cold—bitter cold. His chill came through the expensive suit like a blast of Minnesota wind. It sawed between Scofield's ribs and laced his viscera with ice.

As William Scofield listened to Thomas Kemp's easy banter, he realized that for perhaps the first time in his life, he was afraid.

No. He was actually terrified.

As Karen Tait snapped her valise shut and secured the two leather belts around it, her thoughts were far from travel and luggage. They were dominated by Charles Candenning.

She had spent a scant few hours in his company, yet the attraction had been more than merely alluring. It had been electrically magnetic. She was amazed at her rapport with the man and surprised at herself not merely for relaxing with him, but for her almost desperate enjoyment of that relaxation. When she had allowed him to take her hand on the walk to the railroad station, it had been such a natural gesture she hadn't even been fully aware of it until they were almost a block from the hotel. Then it had been too late. She hadn't wanted him to release her. She hadn't wanted to draw her hand free.

She stood erect, pulled the heavy valise, from the bed and dragged it to the door. She then checked the room a final time for possible unpacked belongings.

On the walk to the station, and during the ride back, she had opened up to Candenning in a way which now embarrassed her almost to the point of humiliation. She had told him about her husband's embezzlement and flight. She had confessed her feelings—first of betrayal, then of relief—once the divorce was final.

He had listened with such tolerance that his cynical veneer disappeared completely. It seemed as if he could actually feel what she had gone through because of some similar experience of his own. Because she had sensed, rather than known, of some hidden suffering within him, she had told him her doubts concerning her planned book and her fears about her new life as a teacher at Vassar.

Only with a great deal of difficulty did she manage to get the valise and the rest of her luggage out of the room. Her various postures were almost ludicrous as she struggled her way to the elevator.

In a matter of no more than a day, she had allowed herself to feel not only an appallingly strong and decidedly indecent physical attraction for Candenning, but an unnerving emotional one as well. She was quite amazed at how she had allowed him to manipulate her on the train. She could have been hurt badly, perhaps even killed—all because of her willingness to do Candenning's bidding.

The elevator door opened. The operator helped her put the luggage inside.

She knew that any association with a man like that—wealthy, secure in his career and, above all, married—could only be dangerous, if not actually disastrous. It would surely destroy all the plans she had made for herself.

Luckily, they would be out of Mexico in a matter of hours. She could go to New York and he to wherever the army wanted him. It would be over—a brief meeting of two travelers who would never see each other again.

He was waiting for her in the lobby. As their eyes met, her heart seemed to leap within her. She was sure she actually blushed.

During the short ride back to the station, they again discussed the expropriation of the railroad debts. He was cynical almost to the point of fatalism. Yet as she looked at him, she saw beyond the facade.

He would probably always insist that nothing could ever be done about the irregularities of life, the indecencies of people, or the inhumanity of the so-called system. Yet beyond the blue eyes, the slightly graying temples, and the strong jaw

219

lay something she could understand quite clearly, possibly only because she was a woman.

Charles Candenning was a man of both compassion and purpose. He was a man who had almost, but not quite, succeeded in hiding from himself.

At the station they went directly through to the passenger loading area. The scene was as they had left it. The platform was still crowded—the train still waiting.

Also waiting on the platform was the German couple with whom they had ridden north. Both the man and his wife appeared to have just awakened from an identical bad dream.

A small contingent of soldiers marched toward the front of the train. She watched them enter the first passenger car, then moved her glance backward.

William Scofield was sitting at one of the train's windows. At the next window was the English woman who had been on the platform earlier.

She was looking directly at Charles!

Impulsively, she reached for his hand, but before she touched it, arrested the motion. She was jealous, she realized, and because she was, she was also quite ashamed.

She had lied to herself. It wasn't simple attraction. It was more. In some inexplicable and horrid way, and because of some instant and nasty magic, she had been tricked by an unkind Fate.

Karen Tait had fallen in love.

"Well." He turned to her and again she was amazed at how handsome he was. "We might just as well get on board. There's nothing to do but wait."

"Yes," she repeated. "Nothing but wait."

The thought made her quite sad.

On the station's platform with the children, Teresa turned to Domingo Portes. "Please," she whispered. "Come with us. I'm so afraid."

He looked at the woman who had stirred his emotions so dangerously. He wanted to take her hands in his and explain the maelstrom of his emotions. He stood, he knew, on a scale's fulcrum. With her, he might be able to capture some of the temporal world's uncertain joys. With those joys, however, he knew he would have to live with the constant reminder that he had deserted his God, his duty, and his companions in faith.

It was a choice between all the beauty and joy possible on a worldly plane and everything he had dedicated himself to on a spiritual level.

"I want to . . ." It was difficult for him to speak. "I can't. I cannot run from duty."

"But, you've come this far—"

"I know. Just far enough to touch failure."

"I don't understand."

"It is of no matter," he told her. "I've been chasing intuition, nothing more. Now I must return. It is not possible to go north. To accompany you would only compound my sin."

"You know, Father . . ." She laid a very gentle, feminine hand on his forearm. "I think you are too demanding of yourself. I think you follow duty so strictly you see only what is before you. Oh, I know we live in a time of martyrs, and there is much reason for hatred—even in a man of God. But I also know there are things other than those directly in front of you—things best seen from the corners of the eyes."

He didn't understand. He only knew that being with her in the last few minutes before the train's departure was an agonizing joy. "I must go," he told her.

"With your permission . . ."

They both turned to see a tall man of military bearing. His accent, dress, and posture all marked him as a foreigner.

"This train . . ." He nodded to it. "It *is* traveling north?"

"Yes," Portes said.

"Good, then." He turned away, took one step, then turned back. "Forgive me," he said. "Are you the actress, Teresa Inez?"

She nodded.

"Your children are quite as beautiful as you."

She lowered her eyes.

"My name is Markoff." He extended his hand to Portes. "Shall you be taking the train?"

"Portes," the priest said. "Domingo Portes. No, unfortunately." Then, because the man was obviously of aristocratic breeding, "I wonder," he essayed . . . "I wonder if you could do us a service?"

The Russian frowned slightly.

"The lady shall be traveling alone with the children. If you could watch over her—just until Juárez . . ."

The Russian looked from Portes to the two boys to Teresa,

then back. "But, of course. I'd be honored." He seemed the very soul of chivalry.

"Thank you," Portes said. "You are most kind." He turned to Teresa. "Until another time." His mouth was dry and his throat constricted. He wanted to take her in his arms and pull her tightly to him. Instead, he turned and began to walk back toward the main terminal.

Behind him the train huffed a great warning of impending motion. A bell rang and someone called, "*Vamonos! Vamonos!*"

He entered the main terminal feeling sad but thankful that Teresa at least had someone to protect her as she traveled north.

He had almost reached the street exit when a private automobile screeched to a halt. Two young men in business suits leapt out and rushed into the terminal past him toward the boarding platform.

A taxi stopped immediately behind the abandoned car. Another two men stepped out. One tossed a handful of peso notes to the driver, then both dashed into the station past Portes.

Behind him he could hear the train begin to move.

He dreaded what lay before him. It would be a long journey south. He would have much time to think, not merely of his personal weaknesses, but of his responsibility for the ultimate failure of the Church in Mexico. The treasure—millions, which could have been spent on education, medicine, even weapons—was gone simply because, somewhere along the line, he had turned left instead of right.

The treasure, the meaning of his faith, his duty, and his feelings for Teresa all swirled in his thoughts. He felt too strongly for the woman. He didn't want to form the words in his mind, yet he knew love was but a thread's breath from the truth.

Maybe . . . just maybe she had felt some little bit of the same for him. What was it she had said?

There are things other than those directly in front . . .

The train huffed.

He was a weak priest, unworthy to be a soldier of the Cross. He had allowed a woman to dominate his thoughts and, in trying to trace a fortune, had found but cheap gilt which any tourist could buy for a few pesos.

Things best seen from the corners of the eyes . . .

But . . . what if . . . what if somehow, the real gold had been packed beneath the gilt . . . perhaps even plated over simply to look cheap?

From the corners of the eyes . . .

Portes stopped. As if the Almighty had actually whispered to him—he knew. In an instant, the truth came to him. William Scofield *was* one of the men he was after. The treasure of Las Casas *was* in those twenty-four crates in the train just pulling out of the terminal.

Like a madman, he spun around, dashed through the terminal to the platform and, as he had done in Oaxaca, raced after the train.

He reached the last car and pulled himself aboard. This time it wasn't so difficult. Perhaps, after all, there was Someone who answered prayers—who would help him do his duty and reclaim the gold.

So intent was he on catching the train, that Portes did not notice the man in dark glasses who pulled himself painfully aboard as he had been running along the platform. He did not see the man's heavily bandaged hand or wonder why he was wearing an overcoat.

Nicholas Markoff was more observant. As he sat opposite Teresa Inez and admired her flawless beauty, he spotted the man in dark glasses and overcoat. Absently, he wondered what had happened to his hand.

Absently too, he hoped Teresa would not be a witness to Jesús Guerrero's death. It would be a pity to have to kill a woman so beautiful.

He sighed—a sound mingled between great contentment and a foreboding of unspeakable tragedy.

Such thoughts, he knew, were purely academic.

Still, it *would* be a pity.

6
Predators

PUEBLA, ANCIENT SPANISH "City of the Angels," boasts a magnificent view, good hotels, and fine restaurants. Known as "the Rome of Mexico" because of its many magnificent churches, it is also famous for its Talavera pottery and tile work. *Powers' Guide to Mexico* that year called it "a splendid place to spend a few days . . ."

The editors had not, however, taken into consideration the impatience of a man intent upon murder.

Ian Conrad had long before inured himself to the impression he made on people. He had seen his scarred and broken face in more than one mirror. Now, the embarrassed discomfort of the station master did not bother him in the least. What was annoying was the news.

The last northbound train had gone through the previous day. There would be no more until a new federal office was established to administer the presidential fiat.

Conrad heard the same news at both railroad terminals. He then limped the short way to the *Paseo Nuevo* and, in the neatly laid-out park, sat down to collect his thoughts.

Scofield, he was sure, had come through either on yesterday's train or the day before. There could be no doubt that he had already reached the capital. In Mexico City he would have to transfer the treasure either to another train or to a truck. Again Conrad discarded the possibility of a truck. If Scofield wasn't already far to the north, chances were that he was trapped because of the railroad situation.

Either way he was traveling too fast for Conrad. Even if the trains had been running, Scofield had the advantage of at least a six-hour lead.

Ian Conrad did not linger in Puebla to appreciate the climate, the churches, or the spectacular view from the Hotel Colonial's roof garden. Instead, he changed his pattern of pursuit.

He hired a private airplane and pilot to fly him to the capital. There he drove to the railroad terminal, where he learned of the train which had left for Ciudad Juárez no more than hours before.

Conrad spent the rest of the morning buying mining supplies. Just after noon he arrived at the airport, where he personally oversaw the loading of his baggage.

It consisted of one case of dynamite, a box of blasting caps, several hundred yards of fuse, and three rolls of electrician's tape.

As he boarded the 12:15 flight to Chihuahua, Conrad was annoyed that he had been unable to find an electric generator. Moreover, he was furious at the necessity for having to purchase a new miner's knife. His had been lost in an unfortunate accident some months ago in the Chiapas mountains.

The loss, however, would soon be avenged. Somewhere far to the north that revenge would be sweet—and thorough.

Napoleon's armies may, as their leader later claimed, have marched on their stomachs. The forces of Marcos Almidero depended on something a bit more abstract than food. A bandit masquerading as a patriot dedicated to freeing his country from oppression, relies not merely on information, but on the right information at the right time.

It had just arrived.

The Scorpion hitched his gunbelt around his expanding midsection, then scratched his groin. He was still smarting from a recent encounter with federal troops near Rio Ramos. He had lost seven good men and had almost been surrounded and annihilated. He was convinced that the trap into which he had fallen was a result of the president's recent visit to Durango. He knew Cárdenas from the old days. The man was a fox. Almidero was convinced that the visit had nothing to do with land distribution, but had simply been an excuse to form a plan that would eliminate his own private army.

Now the tables had turned. Not only had he escaped the trap, but he was listening to information that might very easily lead to the overthrow of the entire Cárdenas regime.

The president had expropriated the foreign railroad debts. Although the rail system was virtually paralyzed as a result, a single train had been routed out of Mexico City to Ciudad Juárez.

It would have to pass through Durango!

Regardless of what that train carried, it would have to be destroyed. Such an action would prove to the Mexican people that their leader had acted irresponsibly. The country might very well be thrown back into the chaos on which Almidero thrived.

Aside from its political importance, the train would undoubtedly be carrying items of value in its baggage car. The passengers would have some money and there would, as usual, be women.

"The military escort is small," the courier said. "A token force—one sergeant and six men. It is the only train routed north. It will be an isolated target."

The Scorpion grunted. "Good." He scratched his groin again. "Such a prize is too beautiful to miss."

Juan Miguárdez looked from one to another of the several photographs which appeared to have been scattered at random on his desk. They were police photos of two corpses showing each from several angles—as when first discovered and later, naked front and back, when laid out prior to postmortem examination.

The chief of Metropolitan Police, a middle-aged man with a disproportionately large mustache and an even more substantial abdomen, stood before the secretary's desk. He was obviously ill at ease.

"Ordinarily, Mr. Secretary, I would not bother you with such a matter. The circumstances, however . . ."

Miguárdez looked from one picture to another. He realized that he undoubtedly knew far more about the two crimes than the chief or any of his detectives. Still, he wanted to know exactly how much the police had discovered in the few hours since they had been called to the Hotel Biltmore. "You did the right thing," he said. "You say the maids found them?"

"Yes, Sir."

He picked up the photo of Elodia Guerrero lying naked on her back. He frowned slightly as he inspected what appeared to be bruises or scratches on her thighs and the mark of a belt around her waist. "Any indication of theft?" His voice had a casual, almost absent, quality.

"Perhaps from the woman, Sir. But we don't think so. The

man had his papers and some money with him. Robbery may have been a motive there, but if it was, he cut his attacker too severely.''

"I see. What about a link?''

The chief shook his head. It was an almost tragic gesture. "I would say, rather, certain . . . peculiarities.''

"Oh?''

"He wasn't registered, but he was in her room. She was registered but found in another room. Also, she came in a wheelchair, but apparently she didn't need it to reach that second room.''

"And that room?''

"Rented to an actress. Teresa Inez. She's fairly popular.''

Miguárdez had by now pieced the entire puzzle together. Not only was he able to reconstruct the two crimes almost exactly as they had, in fact, taken place, but he was sure of the various motives involved. "You have, of course, identified the bodies?''

"He's a clerk for the National Bank,'' the chief said. "Victoriano Felix. Married . . . four children . . .''

"And the woman?''

"A Mrs. Gonzales. Registerd with two children. They may have been kidnapped. The duty clerk told us two men wanted to see her. One older—rather sick, the other a foreigner. Also, the dead man himself, Felix, inquired about the sick man.''

Juan Miguárdez made a slow and very deliberate inspection of the photos. Finally, after almost a full minute, he looked up. "This woman . . .'' He tapped a photograph with his knuckles. "She is not Mrs. Gonzales.''

"Oh?''

"She is the wife of Jesús Guerrero.''

"What?''

"And Guerrero is a traitor to Mexico—to the revolution!''

"Señor Secretary, I can't believe . . .''

"What I'm going to tell you, Chief, must not leave this room. I need certain information. In turn, I'll give you enough to solve this little matter quite easily. First of all, did any trains leave the capital today?''

"There was one,'' the chief told him. "Headed north—to Juárez.''

"Guerrero is on that train. I'm sure of it. So are his

children. There is no doubt they are being cared for by your actress, Teresa Inez. She's Guerrero's current mistress.''

"A train is an easy thing to stop, Señor Secretary.''

"No. I need proof. If the train's going to Juárez, it must make at least ten stops on the way. I know it's out of your jurisdiction, but we need to keep this as confidential as possible for now. Get a man on that train—simply to verify that this Inez woman and the two boys are aboard. Once I know that, we'll notify the Americans and get Guerrero at the border.''

"The Americans?''

"There are political issues at stake, Chief. Any favors we can do them now will aid the president's future plans for Mexico.''

"I see.''

"Once they know that Guerrero intends to enter their country as a revolutionary, I'm sure they'll be delighted to help.''

For the first time that afternoon, the chief smiled. Then he cleared his throat. "And this investigation, Señor Secretary?''

"Ah.'' Miguárdez leaned back in his chair and tented his fingers. "Two very serious murders—a key employee of the National Bank and the wife of an important presidential aide. You see these marks here?'' He indicated the scratches on Elodia Guerrero's thighs. "Clearly the woman was molested in a very perverse way. Surely no Mexican would do such a thing.''

"A foreigner?''

"I think, chief, you will find that he's a Russian—a man named Nicholas Markoff—and still very much in your jurisdiction right here in the capital. One thing, though. Once you get him, I'm sure Markoff will try to escape.''

"I understand perfectly, Señor Secretary. Is there anything else?''

"Else? No. I've told you everything I know.''

Except, he thought, *about four bags of diamonds*.

228

Book V

DURANGO

1
Querétaro

ON THE MOVING train, Charles Candenning tried, for the first time since the previous evening, to analyze his emotions. Karen Tait was an exceptionally attractive young lady. He could not deny his affection for her. Neither could he refute the purely physical desire she generated. Still, he admonished himself for allowing his feelings to take such a strong hold. His duty was clearly to his marriage. Despite his feelings for Karen or hers for him—despite the possible depth of those feelings—adultery could never be anything but a shabby business.

He looked from the young woman sitting opposite him to the scenery outside the train's window. They were already almost a hundred miles north of the capital. Eventually they would be in El Paso. There, he and Karen would separate, undoubtedly never to meet again.

He was considering the parting with bittersweet fascination when his mood was interrupted by a cheery ''Hello.''

Neil Oberon's attractive English companion was standing beside their seats. ''I just thought you two would like to join us back in the club car.''

The thought was appealing, yet for some reason he couldn't quite explain, he looked to Karen for confirmation. Both her expression and posture seemed negative.

''Oh, do come.'' Margaret smelled of subtle, very expensive, perfume and was obviously quite aware of her magnetic femininity. ''I feel like I'm in a men's club. Besides . . .'' She turned directly to him. ''You and Neil are such old friends.''

''Well, I know him . . .''

''And it is *so* refreshing to speak English for a change. Come on now. Actually we have quite a little colony back there.''

''Really?'' There was no enthusiasm in Karen's voice.

"Oh, yes. Neil and I, of course. Then there's Mr. Scofield and young Mr. Kemp. Do you know him?"

Again Karen and Candenning exchanged glances. "No," he said. "Never met."

"He's a bit strange, that one," Margaret said. "Very charming and attentive, really. Still, there's something a bit off about him."

"Off?"

"Not dangerous. I don't mean that. Just, well—odd—that's all."

"Sounds charming," Candenning said.

"Interesting, really. And besides, Neil wants to apologize properly. I mean for running off like that in the hotel. He's the one who suggested I find you both."

Candenning could actually feel Karen's reluctance. He was just about to offer a polite refusal when the train began to slow.

"I say!" Margaret bent to look out the window. "What now?"

"Offhand," Candenning said, "I'd say we're in Querétaro."

"Oh?"

"It's where they shot Maximillian, you know."

"What a perfectly charming thought." Margaret Whitley smiled. It was an expression completely lacking in humor. She looked from Candenning to Karen, then turned, and walked back to her companions.

Because Domingo Portes found it easier to think standing up, and because he was confident of Teresa's safety with Nicholas Markoff, he had spent the hours after leaving Mexico City strolling up and down the length of the train. Although seriously pondering the execution of his mission, he was also thankful to be going north on a tourist train instead of south. The absence of animals, baggage, and other annoyances in the aisles made his movements, if not his thinking itself, far easier.

Virtually at the end of his task, he leaned on the observation deck railing at the extreme rear of the train and there watched the flight of railroad ties soaring into a diminutive distance. He pondered his final options and began to realize the awesomeness of the task his provincial had assigned him. Scofield would be, of course, a problem, but a greater obstacle

231

involved getting the treasure from the train back to San Cristóbal.

Portes stood erect and looked one last time at the track, which seemed to fly away from the train. He sighed heavily and turned back into the club car. He had just opened the door when a possible solution came to mind. Private possession of gold had been illegal in the United States for three years. It was a gamble, but he might be able to have the Americans confiscate the treasure, thus preventing the Mexican authorities from appropriating it until the Church could reclaim ownership.

The thought pleased him so much that as he passed the three Americans sipping cocktails in the middle of the car, he nodded to them and smiled pleasantly.

Two of the men returned his greeting. Bill Scofield, however, merely stared at the priest with expressionless, reptilian eyes as the train slowed.

Portes made his way to the vestibule and was almost to the next car when he heard snatches of conversation from the station platform. The train had apparently sustained some minor damage. It might take an hour or more to repair it.

His basic plan made, he decided to sit down, relax, and evaluate the details. He made his way through the diner to the one Pullman car. It was not particularly crowded and, after the announcement of a possible delay, most of the passengers had decided to stretch their legs outside. Portes soon found himself in an almost deserted car.

The German couple who had come from the south sat to his right in the middle of the car. Both the man and the woman looked as if they were awaiting the fall of a headman's ax.

At the far end of the car, behind the German couple, two men were seated together. Both were young, quite ordinary-looking foreigners—probably Americans. They were only vaguely familiar until Portes remembered them as having rushed past him in the Mexico City terminal.

The only other occupants of the car were two other men sitting across the aisle, but somewhat forward. Their backs were to him, but he was sure they were also foreigners. Both had blond hair.

While the train was delayed in Querétaro, Domingo Portes tried to work out the details of his plan. Although he saw almost every movement made by the people in the car, he attached little significance to any of them. Had he been told that the fate of the civilized world sat with him in a very ordinary Pullman car, he would have thought the notion ridiculous.

The two men at the far end of the car exchanged a few words, then one of them rose. Absently, Portes watched him leave the train, then cross the platform, and enter the terminal building.

The blond men, too, whispered a few words to one another. Then one of them rose and walked past Portes. The man left the car, walked along the station platform, and re-entered from the rear. Portes looked up just in time to see him enter the men's lavatory. He did not give any thought to the man's strangely circuitous route.

His speculations were interrupted again when the second blond man rose and walked past him. A moment later the man spoke briefly to a woman on the platform and handed her some money. He then returned to the train and took his seat.

A minute or two after that, the woman entered the car from the rear. She spoke to the single man sitting there.

At first he appeared perplexed. He glanced down the length of the car to the single blond man, then to the German couple. He frowned, then, with a somewhat annoyed reluctance, rose. He turned past the woman and walked the few paces to the men's lavatory.

Portes returned to his speculations but was soon arrested by another movement. He looked up to see the first blond man coming from the lavatory. He was apparently self-satisfied about something.

Then, for a moment—perhaps it was only the priest's imagination—it seemed as if the two blond men intended to converge on the German couple. The one who had been seated rose and stepped into the aisle. For a fleeting moment the car was filled with a crackling tension. It was there, then, like an electrical shock, gone so fast one wondered if in fact it had ever really been at all.

The man who had gone into the terminal building entered the rear of the car at the same moment as Charles Candenning and Karen Tait stepped in from behind Portes. The arrival of the three seemed somehow to deflate whatever plan the two blond men may have had. One stepped from the aisle and sat down again. The other passed the German couple without so much as a glance and rejoined his companion.

Candenning touched Portes on the shoulder. "*Que pasa*?" he said.

The priest looked up and shook his head. "*Nada*," he replied—Nothing.

The wire from Querétaro had, at first, been telephoned in, but Sidney Desmond had insisted upon immediate confirmation. Now, it lay on his desk, telling him in succinct telegramese that Dr. Jakob Pelzig and his wife had escaped would-be abductors in Mexico City and were now aboard a northbound train, which had stopped for repairs at Querétaro. Once those repairs were made, the train would travel through Zacatecas to Torreón, then on through Chihuahua to Ciudad Juárez. Two men, undoubtedly German agents, were also on the train.

Between first hearing the message, and its actual delivery some twenty minutes later, Desmond had given the matters of Jakob Pelzig, Cordell Hull, and Mexican-American diplomatic relationships a great deal of almost painful thought. As was invariably the case, he had come to two conclusions: First his assignment of the moment was his most important consideration. Second: the ends always justified any means necessary to achieve them.

Sidney Desmond decided that to achieve any success at all, a few Mexican feathers would have to be seriously ruffled.

The duty officer of the day at Randolph Field was Captain Leslie Noores, USMA, Class of '22. The call was put through to him from the message center. The voice at the other end of the line was definitely southern, but Capt. Noores could not pinpoint the accent.

"I want to talk to the commanding officer!"

"At the moment, Sir," Noores said, "you are."

"All right, then, listen to me," the voice said, "and listen damned carefully. I'm Sidney Desmond and, at this point, you might say I represent the entire foreign policy of the United States. I want you to get me some planes and intercept a Mexican train."

Noores was immediately convinced that he was listening to a lunatic. His cadet training, however, coupled with fifteen years of active service, all in company grades, had disciplined him sufficiently to keep his voice level. "I'm afraid, Sir, that's imposs——"

"Listen to me, Boy! You'd better hop ass on this, or you won't be having any ass to hop with. I want those planes in the air right now if not sooner on a route to Querétaro. There's a train coming up and on board there's a man named Pelzig."

Suddenly Captain Noores found the situation quite amusing. His caller was actually ordering him to take full personal responsibility for invading Mexican air space. "You're making a serious mistake, Sir," he told Desmond. "This is Randolph Field—"

"Goddamn it, Boy! This is not baked wind! I'm Sidney Desmond and I want some planes—"

The amusement changed to annoyance. "This is not a vaudeville stage, Mr. Desmond!"

Gently, but firmly, Captain Noores, USMA, '22, hooked the earpiece on its cradle and replaced the telephone on his desk. There were more maniacs in the world, he decided, than any one man could ever count.

"Okay, Noores . . ." Desmond sighed heavily as he tapped his right fist several times on the desk. "Guess I'm just going to have to burn your little old barn right on down."

He pressed the phone's cradle for a second or two to clear the line, then dialed the long-distance operator. After an exasperating wait, his call was answered by the honeysuckle-sweet voice of Cordell Hull's private secretary.

"I've got to talk to the Secretary," Desmond said.

"Why, I'm sorry, Mr. Desmond, but Mr. Hull is gone for the day."

"Oh . . ." He paused for a moment to collect his thoughts. Then said, "Listen to me now. I'm not joking one bit. I want the president's number."

"Why, I can't do that, Mr. Desmond. You know . . ."

"All right." He hated red tape. He had devoted most of his life to cutting, shredding, or mutilating it. Now, faced with what he was sure was an insurmountable dedication to bureaucratic regulations he tried to keep his tone level and calm. "All right," he repeated. "You do it then. You get on through to one or the other of them. Right now, y'hear? You tell them I'm right on top of this Pelzig thing, hear? You tell them we've got one chance in a thousand of getting that boy out. If he's still alive, you can bet your pajamas he won't be for long. You tell Mr. Hull or the president—I don't care

235

which—to get on back to me just about lickety-split, hear now?''

"Why, I'll try, Mr. Desmond. You know that."

"You better do a lot better than just try," he told her, " 'cause, if I don't get my boy safe out of Querétaro, it's surer than gravy on grits you won't be bringing home any more bacon—leastways not from Mr. Hull's office anyway. Hear now?''

"Yes, sir, Mr. Desmond. I hear you."

"Hop now, honey. Go on and hop like a bunny in a forest fire!''

In the ancient Aztec city of Querétaro, the train's engine wheezed, then huffed several times. The engineer rang his bell and a station hand cried, *"Vamonos! Vamonos!"*

Passengers who had been idly strolling on the station's platform reboarded, and after several minutes the train again started to travel north.

2
Rails North

DOCTOR PELZIG WAS both relieved and thankful that Charles Candenning was sitting opposite him again. The mere presence of the man made him feel a great deal safer. Now, however, he was doubly grateful for the American's company. He needed to relieve himself, but until the arrival of Candenning and Karen Tait, he had been reluctant to leave Hannah.

Pelzig was convinced that the two blond men sitting about four yards in front of him were intent either upon abducting or killing him. Just before excusing himself, he mentioned the fact to Candenning.

The illustrator seemed at once skeptical and apprehensive. His manner almost bordered on the timorous. "Don't you think," he forced a smile, "we've upset enough apple carts for one trip?''

236

"Mr. Candenning," Pelzig leaned forward, "I am not an alarmist. I am a realist. I'm quite sure Mr. Hitler has more than two men working for him in Mexico."

He went on to tell of the man in the doorway outside the hotel and of the abortive, but nonetheless horrifying, attempt at kidnapping mere hours earlier. "Please," he said finally, "I must excuse myself. I really must. If you would just keep watch over Hannah . . ."

He squeezed his wife's hand and tried to give her a reassuring smile as he rose and turned toward the rear of the car.

The single foreigner seated at the far end glanced his way, then looked out of the window. The man was young and almost nondescript. He was apparently quite concerned about something. Pelzig, whose back had been toward the lavatory during the train's stop in Querétaro, had seen none of the movements witnessed by Domingo Portes. He had seen only those of the blond men in front of him. Wary now almost to the point of paranoia, he simply assumed that the young man was another Nazi agent. He almost turned back toward his seat, but his need for relief, coupled with a deep commitment to propriety, forced him to quicken his pace and dash into the lavatory.

There, he immediately locked the door. He turned past the sink and opened the door to the toilet compartment.

Unfortunately, it was occupied.

The train swayed and Jakob Pelzig took a step backward. Bile rose in his throat as his stomach churned. He lifted a trembling hand to his lips. The taste of vomit was in his mouth, the smell of stale urine in his nostrils, but what he saw was most offensive of all.

The bowl was filled with blood, which had overflowed to the small compartment's floor. It had partially coagulated on the rim and sides of the toilet. The man whose face was submerged in his own gore lay crumpled like a ghastly travesty of an aborted fetus. Although Pelzig could not see the entire wound, he was sure the man's throat had been slashed so deeply that both carotid arteries and the internal and external jugular veins had been severed. The spinal column alone connected the head to the torso. The blood in which he was partially submerged had clotted in his hair, making strangely obscene designs in his right ear.

"Gott," Pelzig gasped. He fought the vomit back. *"Oh, mein Gott."* He swallowed again, but the taste remained. *"Mein Gott."*

He had no idea who the murdered man was. He knew only that he and the corpse shared something in common. The thought was terrifying. He was shocked and sickened, yet withal, still suffering from the need which had initially brought him to the lavatory.

Jakob Pelzig became the victim of his own particular upbringing as well as subject to long centuries of tribal civilization. He could neither bring himself to remove the corpse nor to use the bowl while the man's head was partially submerged in it.

Feeling somehow like a naughty child, he turned away from the toilet compartment and relieved himself in the sink. Then, both ashamed at the hygienic offense and nauseated by the brutally slashed corpse, he rebuttoned his fly, unlocked the door, and stepped out.

Pure animal reflex cannot be predicted with any accuracy. Cowardice and courage are often definable only in terms of directions taken. When Doctor Pelzig saw the man standing there, he did not analyze his options. He could have returned to the lavatory and locked himself in with the corpse or done what he actually did. He reacted without conscious thought.

He leapt forward, knocked the younger man off balance and scampered back to his seat.

"Mr. Candenning . . ." He tried to keep his voice calm. "Believe me. I'm absolutely sure of it. Those two men behind you and that other one—behind me—they're Nazis."

"Dr. Pelzig . . ."

What was it, he wondered, in the American's eyes. Then he knew. Charles Candenning was actually afraid.

"Don't you think you're painting the devil on the wall?"

"On the wall, Mr. Candenning?" He was suddenly quite annoyed. "No. Not on the wall. But on this train. Of *that* I can assure you!"

Nicholas Markoff considered himself the recipient of marvelously good luck. Not only did he find Teresa Inez a beautiful and charming traveling companion, who obviously had no idea whatsoever of his actual mission, but in the short time since leaving the capital, he had been able to capture the attention and admiration of the two little boys with his stories of the Bolshevik Revolution and his own fight against it. The bloodier the accounts, the more heroic and grisly, the more Jesús Guerrero's two sons appreciated them. Markoff did not, however, neglect the woman or go so far as to offend her with unnecessary accounts of war's brutality, nor did he touch on political issues of any sort. He remained attentive, but quite formal, and as the miles slipped by, became more and more self-satisfied with his performance as a platonic companion and protector.

The height of Markoff's fortune, however, came some eighty miles north of Querétaro, just after crossing the Santa Maria River. Somehow, even before it happened, he anticipated it.

Teresa Inez glanced past him and, for the smallest part of a second, an expression of recognition flashed in her eyes. It was followed by an almost imperceptible nod of her head. Behind him, he knew, someone was signaling unspoken questions to her. Because Domingo Portes had recently passed from that direction, Markoff knew that person could only be Jesús Guerrero.

Markoff knew the politician had entered the car, seen Teresa sitting with a stranger and, in some sort of dumb show, asked her about that man. Fortunately, he had played his part well since leaving the capital. Although no fool, Teresa was apparently trusting enough to believe that he was no more than what he claimed to be—a tourist returning to Europe by way of the United States. As for his command of Spanish, he had told her that he had lived in Spain for some years prior to the outbreak of war. Now he had seen far too much of war. He no longer knew or cared for the problems of nations or the political issues that stirred their citizens.

Jesús Guerrero came to the seat and sat down next to Markoff. He was pale and unshaven. His overcoat smelled dank. It was apparent that he had spent the previous night without sleep or shelter—that he was not only quite weak, but still in great pain. He tousled his son's hair with his left hand, then leaned back and delicately placed his towel-wrapped right in his lap.

Teresa started to introduce the two men, but Guerrero interrupted. He gave his name as Gonzales.

"Much pleasure." Markoff looked at the injured hand, then simply nodded.

"An accident," Guerrero said. "It's nothing. I'll have it looked to later." He turned to Teresa. "I've been the length of the train. It's all right to ride together. I'm sure."

As the train crawled north, Markoff engaged in friendly

conversation with his companions. The Russian used all the social charm he possessed and carefully studied the effects of his performance. This was a monumental seduction, not of a beautiful woman, but of the confidence of a man well-used to political infighting.

Only after crossing into Durango did Markoff decide to test the effects of his performance.

"I think I'll stretch a bit," he announced to no one in particular. Then, as casually as if he had been offering the time of day, he glanced to Guerrero. "Care to join me for a cigarette, Mr. Gonzales?"

Guerrero seemed to hesitate. Although Markoff fought to keep his expression and posture casual, his insides were kinked by tension. For an instant he tasted the agony of defeat, then subjugation swelled to victory.

"Good," Guerrero said. He turned to Teresa. "We'll be back shortly." He rose and followed Markoff through the car to the vestibule.

In the clattering steel emptiness between the cars, Markoff offered the Mexican a cigarette, lit it then his own before snapping his case shut and replacing it in his inside coat pocket. He inhaled deeply. "I didn't wish to offend the lady," he said.

"I understand." Guerrero sucked smoke into his lungs, then removed the cigarette from his mouth between the first two fingers of his left hand.

Markoff inhaled again, then looked directly at the politician. "Mr. Guerrero . . ."

Horror of understanding leapt into the Mexican's eyes. Otherwise he did not move. He was trapped between the vestibule's outside door and the Russian.

"What's in the belt?" Markoff's voice was disarmingly calm.

Guerrero's mouth opened slightly, then closed. He was obviously fighting desperately to appear puzzled. "What?"

"For a favor." Markoff might have been reasoning with a naughty child. "Let's not fence. Your wife is dead. She wore a belt."

"You!"

Markoff nodded. "Of course. But you avoid the issue. What's in the belt?"

Desperation was livid in Guerrero's haggard face. He was weak, beaten—obviously in debilitating pain. Still, Markoff knew he was dealing with a man whose gift for survival was monumental.

"Listen." Guerrero's licked his lower lip, "I'll tell you, but you must understand. We're dealing with history—the entire fate of this country. Here . . ." He dug into his overcoat pocket.

Markoff poised, ready to grab a possible knife or pistol, but the Mexican only extracted a filthy bag which might once have been white.

"Here," Guerrero said again. "Take this, but let me go. I must get to the United States. The entire future of Mexico depends on it."

Markoff took the bag and started to untie the knotted string which secured the top. So intent was he that he didn't see Guerrero reach behind himself for the door's latch.

What happened next took but seconds. The Russian opened the bag and saw the contents as he was hit by a blast of hot moving air. He looked up just as Jesús Guerrero leapt from the train.

Instantly, he realized that the Mexican was far more desperate than he had previously thought. He also knew that the belt once worn by Guerrero's wife contained a great deal more than merely one bag of cut diamonds. The man who had just jumped from the train was probably carrying wealth sufficient to assure Nicholas Markoff's entire future, and in a style he had not enjoyed since before the Russian Revolution.

He thrust the bag into the right pocket of his coat and, without hesitation, jumped from the moving train.

Pain shot through him like a barbed assegai. He crumpled to the rocky ground, rolled twice, then started to rise. His right leg collapsed in an inferno of agony, still his dominant thought was of Jesús Guerrero and of how many more bags of precious stones he might be carrying.

He tried to stand, but again excruciating pain shot through him from foot to knee. He saw the contortion of his right leg and almost absently noted that his shin had broken. Having nothing on which to brace his hands, he was unable to rise and hop to the Mexican. His only choice was to crawl the several painful yards along the tracks.

An agony later, he reached Guerrero's crumpled body. Apparently, the man had instinctively tried to arrest his fall with his injured right hand. The towel had come unwrapped. His split palm was bleeding profusely. There was also blood

241

in his hair and on his forehead. Although his eyes were partially opened, he was unconscious and, Markoff was certain, dying. If the blow to his head hadn't injured his brain sufficiently to kill him, he would surely bleed to death.

Viciously, Markoff dug through the dying man's pockets until he found the second bag of diamonds. He pulled it free and weighed it in his hand. Despite his pain, he smiled.

Somewhere in the northern distance, the train had now disappeared. Its only trace was a fading stain of smoke, now but an unclean smudge on an otherwise cloudless horizon.

Markoff opened the bag and inspected the contents. Pain shot through him again. He retied the bag and decided to examine his leg.

Gently, he reached down and lifted the cuff of his tailor-made, but now torn and dirty, trousers. He eased it over the break and past his knee. A splintered fragment of tibia protruded from the twisted leg like a strangely white stalagmite. It had punctured the flesh of his shin which now surrounded it with a raw circle of bleeding skin.

Cynical to the very last, Nicholas Markoff looked from his leg to his companion. Jesús Guerrero was indeed dying. He could neither help pull the leg straight nor make a primitive splint. Even if he could, there was nothing with which to make such a splint.

Markoff lay on a vast and arid plain thousands of leagues from the ravished land of his birth. He was miles from even the most primitive medical aid, let alone the sophisticated attention that a compound fracture required. In the distance in any direction he saw only horizon. There was no hint of humanity, life, food or water.

Perhaps the lessons learned in a soldier's training are never forgotten. Perhaps, too, there is a sternness of character reserved for those of certain bloodlines. Whatever the reason, there are men who refuse to be demeaned by fortune.

Nicholas Markoff propped himself to a sitting position next to his intended victim. He looked up to the relentless fury of the Durango sun and accepted the specter of his own death.

There was but one consolation. He would, at least, die as a gentleman should—Wealthy.

William Scofield remained with them until the train passed Fresnillo. When the little man left, Thomas Kemp acted.

He removed the Luger from his shoulder holster and held it unseen just above his right leg under the club-car table.

It pointed directly at Neil Oberon's groin.

"I suppose you should know," he said almost casually. "I'm from Móndez."

Oberon glanced from the table to Kemp, then to Margaret, and back to the table. "Look," he said, "we can work something out. I mean—I'm going to get the guns."

"On a train?"

"There are ways. Believe me. I mean it. Let's at least talk about it."

"Oberon, you've already stepped in more with your right foot than you and Móndez together can kick off with your left. Right now you couldn't get yourself out of a pay toilet if I loaned you the nickel."

"You can't do this." Margaret was barely able to contain herself.

"Oh?" He glanced at her without turning his head. "Listen you big-titted bitch . . ." His voice was very low. "I *am* doing it. Now—we are going to get up like good friends, and we are going to walk forward all the way to the baggage car. And, you know what? You are going to do wonderful things for me—perhaps even wonderful enough so that I'll let you live. As for Mr. Oberon over there, I'm afraid he's already parboiled his own goose."

"Wait," Oberon said. "You don't understand—"

"Oh, I do understand. I really do." Kemp was speaking so slowly, so intently, that he actually sounded deranged. "You did wrong, Oberon. You blew away a lot of Mr. Mondez' money on cockfights and other shit, and now the talley's due."

"But I'm on my way to get the guns right now. Don't you understand?"

"I understand this," Kemp said. "If you don't shut up, I'll plug you right here."

"You wouldn't dare." Oberon's bravado was obviously counterfeit.

"Wouldn't I? It's you who don't understand. See, Oberon, I don't really care. I don't have too much to care about. Now, you two get up and just as friendly as cereal and milk start walking forward."

He could see he had made his point. He waited until they

243

both rose, then slipped the pistol into his coat pocket. Covering it with his hand, he stood up and followed them forward toward the baggage car.

Near the village of Yernanis, some twenty-odd miles northeast of the lava beds, Marcos Almidero wiped the last bits of food from his plate with a folded tortilla, rose to his feet, and hitched his gunbelt around his waist. He had just enjoyed a prolonged and elaborate belch, followed by a loud flatus, when he spotted the galloping horseman.

The man was riding as fast as he could spur the animal. When he arrived, he vaulted from the saddle and was already running toward the Scorpion before his horse could stop its own forward movement.

"General! General!" he was screaming. "The train!"

Almidero waited until the man regained some of his breath.

"It's just south of the river—"

El Escorpión grunted. He knew the area intimately. The train could be attacked just after it crossed the Aquanaval River basin. It would be a perfect spot. There would be no problem killing whatever troops guarded it. Then, passengers and baggage could be robbed in a matter of minutes. By the time the train was able to move again and start for Torreón some twenty-five miles north, he and his men would be long gone and, hopefully, far richer.

What was perhaps more important was that as soon as the train did limp into Torreón, the entire country would know about the ineptitude of its president. The Cárdenas regime would be seriously injured. It might even be toppled completely. There was even a chance that he, Marcos Almidero, might one day sit in the Palacio Nacional.

He belched again. "Good," he said. "Let's go."

3
The Raid

IT BEGAN WITH the insidious slowness of all unadulterated horror. The first sharp report forward sounded like a distant truck's backfire. Three more followed at irregular intervals. Finally, there was the unmistakable pocking of small arms fired in macabre seriousness. Shots were punctuated by the cries of men hit and by others shouting orders. Horses occasionally screamed in blind, uncomprehending agony. Glass broke, men swore—the train gradually slowed.

Long before it stopped, Candenning realized it had been attacked by a mounted troop using transparently obvious tactics. The attackers intended to overpower the federal troops riding behind the engine, then take over the train. They would rob all the passengers, probably kill the men, then abduct the women they found attractive. Regardless of his love for the people of Mexico, the beauty of the old churches, and the seemingly tranquil style of life, Charles Candenning was well aware of the Indian savagery coiled just beneath the patina of Latin culture.

With awareness came the old fear, and the remembered agony of being wounded in France during the Great War. Again, the fingers of his right hand were completely paralyzed. Panic that he would never paint again surged through him. A vision of the man he had stopped in the train's aisle in Mexico City flashed in his mind. Again he saw the pistol— knew somehow that it would utterly destroy him.

Before Candenning could react physically to his almost mindless terror, the train stopped completely. Almost immediately, he heard a Mexican voice behind him at the far end of the car.

"Keep your seats," the man said. "No one will be hurt. You serve the cause of freedom."

A male voice, this time speaking German, insisted, "This is an outrage!"

Candenning turned to see one of the blond men behind him stand and begin to reach inside his coat.

The Mexican who had entered the car from the rear vestibule was a medium-sized man dressed in a charro suit. He stood no more than a yard from the German and held a large pistol in his right hand. His face, a mixture of the blood of many tribes showed perhaps another drop, but no more, from somewhere in Renaissance Spain. It bore no expression. He' seemed to move in slow motion. He even managed to call the German an incestuous goat before firing three rounds into his torso.

Great holes plashed out of the German's coat. Blood erupted from within as he was smashed backward by the lethal impact of three lead, .45 caliber bullets. He was literally thrown to and over the back of the next seat forward. He lay there, arms wide, mouth open in the acute amazement of the thoroughly dead. Candenning saw his eyes staring at the ceiling as though in utter disbelief of this, the ultimate insult.

A woman stifled a scream.

Dr. Pelzig whispered, *"Mein Gott."*

The Mexican smiled. Two of his front teeth were gold. They had probably never been brushed with anything more abrasive than a corn tortilla. He started to chuckle as another pistol report smashed through the hushed car.

The Mexican seemed startled. He took a step backward but otherwise did not react. A little ooze of crimson began to stain his left side. He started to lift his pistol to fire toward the rear of the car, where the nondescript young man had crouched behind a seat for cover and was aiming his small handgun for another shot.

The young man squeezed off three more rounds. Then, before anyone could shout a warning, another Mexican entered the rear vestibule and, at close range, literally riddled the young man's body with the entire cylinder load of one revolver.

When the first round hit him, the young man leapt as though stung. He tried desperately to retain his footing as round after round smashed through him. Bits of gore and bone chips spattered the seats' upholstery and the wall of the car as some wild and unexplained reflex emptied the last three rounds of his small automatic. Finally, long dead, he fell face downward between the seats.

The first Mexican staggered another step backward and

fell, as the more recent arrival announced, "Do not resist like fools. You will not be harmed. You serve the revolution and General Marcos Almidero."

A moment later Candenning heard a slipping sound under his seat. Immediately he looked down to see a small, pocket-sized 7.65 mm Mauser. He realized that the second German behind him, whether in panic or as a result of some logical thought had disarmed himself—probably to avoid his companion's fate. He had kicked his weapon forward under the seats without realizing that it might stop exactly where it had—almost directly in front of his intended victim, Dr. Pelzig.

Karen, too, saw the weapon. She looked from it to him. "Take it," she whispered. "At least . . ."

Fear was like a living thing in him now. "Don't be a fool," he told her. "That's all the excuse they'll need."

Obviously annoyed, Karen leaned forward, quickly picked up the pistol, and sat on it. It was while watching her make this rapid movement that Candenning glanced to Hannah Pelzig.

The older woman's mouth was slightly open. Her eyes were wide in surprise.

Without seeing any sign of blood, Candenning knew. Hannah Pelzig had been shot—probably by one of the last three, unaimed rounds fired.

He started to speak, but her expression arrested him. She was literally ordering him to remain silent—not to let her husband know.

Two more Mexicans entered the car and very systematically, using their sombreros as church ushers might use alms' plates, robbed each passenger of money, jewelry, and watches. As they worked their ways down the aisle, they insisted they were merely collecting contributions to the cause of Mexican freedom—to the overthrow of Lázaro Cárdenas.

Charles Candenning was trembling as he emptied his pockets. Yet, strangely, when he pulled his wedding ring from its finger, he became suddenly calm. He felt what he knew to be a ridiculously foreign emotion, under the circumstances.

He was actually quite relieved.

Neil Oberon had just entered the baggage car when he heard the first shot and the three that followed. Thomas Kemp pushed Margaret into the car, stepped in behind her, and closed the vestibule door. He had taken his Luger from his pocket and was now holding it in his right hand.

The three were alone in the car for only a few minutes as the train's military guard was overpowered. Oberon watched what happened after that with something close to hypnotic fascination.

Several shouts came from outside. Then, with a sudden grating slide, the door of the car was wrenched open. A man in a charro suit leapt from his horse into the car.

Kemp shot him twice at point-blank range.

The Mexican gasped in agony and amazement, staggered back, and fell panting on some storage crates stored forward. He was propped there, apparently quite shocked and surprised at his sudden misfortune, when one of his companions, still astride his horse outside the car, fired a pistol three times.

Oberon saw the left side of Kemp's jaw disappear in a grisly splat of blood, flesh, and teeth. Kemp dropped his Luger and, with twitching, desperate fingers, reached toward his chest, collapsed on his knees, then fell forward on his mutilated face.

Margaret screamed, clutched her right biceps, then began sobbing.

The Mexican dismounted and, still holding his pistol at the ready, stepped into the car.

Oberon had his hands high above his head. He was thinking not so much of his fate as of its irony. His would-be assassin had been killed, only so he could wind up exactly as dead as planned—but at the hands of bandits instead.

While contemplating this somewhat cynical speculation, he happened to look beyond the man pointing a pistol at him. Outside, several riders were shouting and waving their weapons. They all looked much the same, but he recognized one of them. *El Escorpión* himself was no more than fifteen yards away.

"*Hey, amigo!*" he cried. "Marcos!"

Almidero reined in his horse, looked toward the baggage car, and squinted.

"Marcos! It's me! Neil Oberon!"

With an almost maddening slowness, the Scorpion walked his horse to the baggage car and looked inside. He inspected Oberon, then turned to the gasping man slumped on the crates. He noted Kemp's body on the floor and saw Margaret standing just slightly away from the car door bleeding profusely from her upper right arm. Finally, he looked back to Oberon. When he spoke, his tone was quite jocular. "Ho, Oberon," he said. "What're you doing here, man?"

Oberon glanced at the bandit still leveling a pistol at him. "Tell him I'm a friend," he said. "I was coming to see you. Didn't you get my message?"

"Message? I got no message. I've been busy with the Federals. Bastards almost got me too. Now I'm busy with a train. What message?"

"We must talk," Oberon said.

The Scorpion shrugged, then turned to the man with the pistol. "What's in those crates?" he said to no one in particular. "Manolo, go see."

"That's nothing," Oberon insisted. "I've got a plan to make you rich." He had never been more desperate. "Maybe even president."

"This train can do that. When I finish with this, Cárdenas will look like the biggest idiot of the generation."

"It's nothing," Manolo said. Apparently unmindful of his gasping companion, he had opened one of the crates and was holding a gilded crucifix in his left hand. "It's junk—for tourists."

The Scorpion grunted. "Leave it then. Go through the train," he said. "Kill the men. Take the women you want."

"Wait!" Oberon glanced from Almidero to Margaret. She was clutching her wounded arm, struggling to hold back sobs of physical and emotional anguish. Perhaps, in that moment, some of the gentility he had been exposed to as a boy rose slightly from the grave to which he had so long consigned it. "Wait," he said again.

"For what?" Almidero seemed genuinely puzzled.

"This train . . ." Oberon was clutching at any straw available. "It's the last one out before the railroad takeover."

"Of course," Almidero agreed. "That's why I'm here. Cárdenas is responsible for this train—for losing everything, everyone on it."

"Yes, but if you kill everyone . . . take all the women . . ."

The Scorpion chuckled. "Only the young ones, the beautiful ones."

"Even so, it will not look good. You will not look like a benefactor, not like a president."

"Ah!" Marcos Almidero pursed his lips as he pondered what Oberon told him. He looked from the baggage car, then right and left along the length of the train. "Still . . ." He seemed hesitant. "I cannot let the soldiers live. If I set them free, they'll come back to fight again. If I take them with me, I'll have to feed them."

"They're soldiers," Oberon insisted. "But the passengers—passengers don't fight."

"It's true."

"And, if you let them go—spare the men and leave the women—you'll be a hero, a benefactor. Besides, I must talk to you. I have a plan."

Again, the Scorpion looked right and left along the length of the train. He glanced again at Oberon. "You want to talk? Come with me. You ride?" He looked at the gasping man who was slumped against the crates clutching his abdomen. "Take his horse. Manolo, tell the men. Just the money."

"You bastard," Margaret gasped.

"Oh, shut up," Oberon told her in English. "You're hurt. Serves you right. At least this way, I'm saving you for the doctors in Torreón."

"Bastard," she said again, but this time her voice held no conviction.

"No women?" Manolo stood erect. He seemed quite baffled and stricken.

"For the revolution, Manolo," the Scorpion said. "Tell them. I wish to be a man of mercy—of compassion—for my people. It's for politics."

Like a surly child balking against discipline, Manolo stuck the crucifix in his gunbelt. He walked to the door of the car and remounted his horse. As he spurred the animal forward, Oberon heard his disgusted mutter: "Politics! How can a man fuck politics?"

Teresa Inez was terrified. She huddled in her seat, her arms spread protectively like the wings of a mother bird around the two Guerrero children as two of the bandits moved closer and closer along the aisle. Where, she wondered, was Jesús—or the Russian, Mr. Markoff? What about Domingo Portes? She was alone and terror-stricken—a cravem trembling woman absolutely sure that in no more than minutes she would be ruthlessly and contemptuously defiled.

Outside her open window, the Scorpion's men had already begun the systematic execution of the pitifully few federal soldiers who had survived the attack. Those not involved in actual executions were riding back and forth, joking, or whooping their elation at having won another battle.

The two bandits inside the car came closer. Their sombreros were nearly filled with paper bills and metal coins, watches, and bits of jewelry. Then, what she had dreaded from the beginning happened.

One man looked up and saw her. His lips curled in a wide, leering smile. As he stared at her, he nudged his companion with his elbow. "Hey, Pasqual," he nodded toward her. "There's one beauty, eh?"

More terrified of her own rape and possible harm to the children than anything else, Teresa had completely forgotten the two bags of diamonds her lover had entrusted to her in Mexico City. They were now in her purse. It was tightly pressed between her and Roberto Guerrero on the seat.

The Scorpion's men came to where she sat. She could not keep from trembling. The one named Pasqual lifted her chin between his thumb and forefinger. His hand smelled of horses and leather, unwashed manhood and gun oil.

"Yes," he said. "A real beauty, this one."

"No," she gasped. "Please—"

"No?" He smiled. Both incisors were missing, probably as a result of a long ago fist fight. "For why, no?"

"Please," she begged. "The children . . ."

Both men laughed. They might have heard an uproariously funny story. Finally, his sense of humor satisfied, Pasqual grabbed her by the wrist. In one brutally swift jerk, he pulled her to her feet.

Roberto Guerrero jumped from the seat and kicked the man in the shin. "You leave Aunt Teresa alone," he screamed.

The bandit grunted in pain. He released Teresa, stepped back, frowned, then smiled. "Little soldier, eh?" He grabbed the boy by the hair and held him at arm's length.

Teresa retreated to the seat. She huddled there, hovering over little Miguel Guerrero.

"Come, little one," the bandit said. His voice now had a hard, sinister quality. "You come with us."

"Please," she said again.

Pasqual handed his sombrero to his companion. Again he pulled Teresa erect.

She was struggling against his grip, trying desperately to pull back and away when a horseman rode up just outside her window. Out of the corner of her eye she noticed the incongruity of the gilt crucifix stuck into his gunbelt.

"Hey, Pasqual!" The horseman seemed remarkably unhappy. "Leave her."

The hand still gripped her wrist like a manacle. Now the man's expression changed from one of animal expectation to shock. Clearly, he thought the horseman was joking.

"Leave her alone," the rider said again.

"You crazy, Manolo?" the man asked. "A beauty like this?"

The rider shrugged. "I only bring the general's orders."

"Orders?"

"No women."

"No women?"

"And leave the men alive."

"Alive?"

"It's for the revolution," Manolo said. "For politics."

"Politics?"

"He said so."

"I don't like politics," Pasqual said. "I want this woman." Again, he pulled her wrist, this time jerking her into the aisle.

"Hey, man . . ." The rider outside the train window was now holding his pistol. "I do what the general tells me. You do the same. Leave her here—or I leave you here. Understand?"

Reluctantly, Pasqual released her wrist. He grabbed his sombrero from his companion and together they stalked the few paces to the car's nearest vestibule.

Teresa Inez was shaking as she slumped back to her seat. Her eyes were filled with tears of near-hysteric relief. Her hands trembled, her heart hammered against her ribs, and her breath came in short, irregular gasps.

She barely heard the soft rumble of hoofs as Marcos Almidero's men rode away. Only when the train jerked forward was she pulled partially back to reality. Even so, she could not know that three dead men now rode with her, or that a fourth and two women had been seriously wounded.

She only realized that she had been incredibly fortunate. She still had the diamonds and her life. Most important, the children had not been harmed.

*　　*　　*

The man responsible for the change in the general's orders rode between the Scorpion and a man named Manolo. He paid no attention to the shiny crucifix stuck in Manolo's gunbelt. He was too intent upon convincing Marcos Almidero of the feasibility of making a raid in the United States.

4
Torreón

WILLIAM SCOFIELD WAS in the club-car's lavatory when the Scorpion's men attacked. Luckily, he had not locked himself in. From the toilet compartment, he heard the outside door open and one of the bandits satisfy himself aloud that the room was empty.

Throughout the raid, Scofield remained in the tiny, evil-smelling compartment. When he finally heard the whooping horsemen ride away, he was so concerned about his crates of plated gold that he didn't even rebutton his fly.

He pushed and shoved his way forward through the diner and three passenger cars, paying no attention to the near-hysteria of the people he jostled. He did, however, notice Domingo Portes's expression as he passed. For a moment, their eyes met and held, like gladiators in a deadly battle of wills.

Scofield was convinced now that the man in the ill-fitting suit knew about the contents of his crates. Portes, he decided, would have to die, and the sooner the better. First considerations, however, had to be seen to first.

He pushed his way through the last passenger car, into the vestibule, then through to the baggage car.

The side door was still wide open, allowing a wide shaft of light to illuminate what otherwise might have been total darkness. The first thing Scofield noticed was a man at the far end of the car. He was sitting, slumped forward, on the crates. His forearms cradled his abdomen. The man was semi-conscious, gasping painfully, and apparently dying.

Scofield took a step into the car, but whirled like an attacked animal when he heard Margaret Whitley's first sob.

She was leaning against the side of the car, standing in the shadow just beside the open door. Her left arm was stretched across her chest, the hand holding her right bicep. She was covered with blood almost from her shoulder down the length of her arm. It was melting in grisly red icicles from her fingertips.

"Help me," she whispered.

Ignoring her, he took one step toward the body just in front of him. Thomas Kemp was huddled on his knees—a macabre Moslem genuflecting on a puddled crimson prayer rug.

Scofield nudged the body with his toe.

Like a sleeping fetus, it rolled to its back. The chill was gone. It smiled up to Scofield through half a missing jaw.

He walked to the crates where the Mexican Kemp had shot still sat. He jerked the Mexican's pistol from its holster, and pushed him from his seat. The bandit cried out in sharp agony as he hit the floor, but made no sound as Scofield shot him twice in the chest.

Margaret screamed.

He glanced toward her. "What's your trouble?"

"You killed him!" Her gasp was incredulous.

He only grunted as he turned to inspect the crates. Relief surged through him. Only one had been opened. The bandits had apparently thought exactly what he wanted the American customs' inspectors to think—that the merchandise of W. C. SCOFIELD CO.—IMPORTS & EXPORTS consisted of nothing more than worthless gilt junk.

He resealed the crate, hammering the nails back with the butt of the dead Mexican's revolver.

"Help me," Margaret begged. "I'm hurt."

The treasure secure, he could afford to relax. He crossed the car and looked from her face to her shattered arm. "I'm no doctor." It was a flat, compassionless statement of fact. "Get some of the women to tend you."

He slipped the revolver under his belt and, as he did, noticed for the first time that his fly was open. Slowly, without embarrassment, he rebuttoned it, then reached outside the car to pull the side door closed. It grated shut, enclosing him in stygian darkness. He groped his way toward the rear of the car, tripped, but did not fall over Thomas Kemp's corpse, and finally he reached the door.

He opened it then turned back to the sobbing Margaret. "Come on," was all he said.

Slowly she came toward him, stumbled through the door, and staggered toward the next car.

He sighed as he watched the fluid movement of her hips, then snugged the pistol in his belt, and covered it with his coat tail. It felt good. With the gold secure and the revolver loaded, it would be duck soup taking care of that nosy bastard Portes.

The truck stopped some thirty miles below the American border. It was surrounded by the rolling, barren sand dunes just south of Samalayuca. For sheer isolation and stark loneliness, it was a perfect spot for murder.

Ian Conrad pulled the hand brake, turned off the ignition, and wiped his face with an already sweat-soaked handkerchief. He made a sweeping inspection of his bleak surroundings, scarred only by a single line of railroad track, then, he opened the door. He struggled from the open cab to the running board and finally to the ground.

The sun, an inferno, had given his face a nasty burn, turning the concave cheek a raw pink and thus making his dead eye look like a tiny gray egg being fried in a sea of rhubarb. Physically, Conrad was absolutely alone and completely miserable. His shirt was sticking to his body, and the back of his pants was uncomfortably dank where he had perspired against the driver's seat.

Emotionally, however, he was quite pleased. The terrain was in his favor and, most probably, so was time. Still, he had much to accomplish before his ex-partner's arrival, and he wanted to be sure it was done with meticulous care. Not only did he want William Scofield dead, he wanted few witnesses to the killing. He wanted the gold as well, for he now had formed a plan to get it across the American border.

As Conrad limped to the bed of the small truck, his twisted leg made strange designs in the sand. He grunted and sighed many times as, slowly and painfully, he unlatched the tailgate and began to unload his equipment.

He had landed in Chihuahua several hours earlier, after having spotted the train once from the air. At that time, it was traveling quite slowly and was still far south of Torreón. Although he didn't know its exact schedule, he knew trains from the capital to the border took anywhere from forty-odd hours to over two full days. He was sure this last train would make one stop in Torreón, then, one more in Chihuahua before starting the last leg of the trip to Juárez. He was confident he would have just about enough time if he worked with maximum rapidity.

He knew nothing of the Scorpion's attack which, in fact, had given him at least one, possibly two, extra hours.

In Chihuahua, Ian Conrad had bought a small truck. He had loaded it with the supplies he had collected in Mexico City, as well as with certain other items that would be necessary for the success of his venture—lanterns, lumber, a hammer, saw, nails, and a tape measure.

After filling the tank with gas and adding the necessary oil, he had only twenty pesos left. He didn't care. He had climbed into the cab like a crippled tank commander preparing to do battle, and had headed north.

He had passed through Gallego almost two hours earlier. Now he was doing what he had set out to do.

First he unwound three feet of fuse, marked it in one-foot increments, then lit it. He timed the burn-rate twice, not only to determine its speed but to satisfy himself that it was absolutely consistent. Because he had been unable to locate or afford either an electric generator or a pull-type fuse igniter, he was forced to rely on matches. They would make the job's timing far more critical, not only in terms of his own physical movements but because of the number of separate fuses he would need.

The exact sites for his charges were the fish plates at the junctions of individual rails along one track. There, he crimped a cap to each fuse, then, with the spiked end of his miner's knife, made a diagonal incision in a dynamite stick and inserted the activated fuse. Although he was sure that one stick per charge would be sufficient, he wrapped two together for good measure. When the one with the fuse blew, it would discharge the other. After digging a tunnel under the track for the fuse, to avoid the danger of the train's wheels cutting it, he placed one charge on the inside fish plate holding the two lengths of rail together. On the outside, he placed two more charges, so that the three bundles with two dynamite sticks each formed a neat triangle.

He did this at three junctures of rail, working his way south, unwinding and burying his fuses beside the track as he moved from one joint to the next. For each junction, the three fuses would have to be lit at exactly the same time. Then the charges would blow with sufficient force to snap the joint and lift the nearest wheels of the train from the track. He was sure they would be raised high enough so that when they came down, the various cars would fall on their sides. If the train was not completely derailed, at least it would be incapable of moving forward.

As he worked, he became more and more annoyed at his inability to locate a generator. It would have made the job so much easier and neater. With a generator, he would simply have to depress the plunger in order to blow all three sets of charges at once. Without it, he would have to light three different sets of fuses and hope that the individual blasts would accomplish his purpose.

When all the charges were laid, he ran the nine lengths of fuse south along the track, covering them loosely with sand. Some thirty yards from the nearest charge, he angled away from the tracks and finally stopped at a sand dune forty or fifty feet east of the doomed rail.

Leaving the fuses there, he returned to the truck and moved it south, so that he and his equipment were exactly opposite the place where he intended to stop the train. He stopped for a moment exhausted, but knew he could not afford the luxury of a respite. His last two, most important, tasks were still unfinished.

From the truck's bed he removed a small box, nailed a cross to the top of it, then inspected his handiwork with satisfaction. Although the wooden device was actually quite harmless, it looked exactly like an electric generator with the plunger ready to be depressed. Certainly, it would fool anyone seeing it from a stopped train fifteen yards away.

The last thing he did was build a barricade across the track and hang lanterns from it. When the train stopped there, the military escort in the first car would be exactly opposite his position and clearly able to see not only his truck but his prop generator with the plunger primed.

His plan was simple: the train would stop at the barricade. He would tell the military guard they were poised over enough dynamite to kill them all several times over. If they did not throw down their arms, he would depress the plunger, thus blowing them to eternity.

It was a desperate gamble, but it was the only way he could think of to overpower an armed escort, which he was sure would outnumber him by at least ten to one. In fact, his scheme was totally unnecessary. Because he knew nothing of the Scorpion's raid, he had no knowledge of the soldiers all having been assassinated near the Aquanaval River.

The second step of the plan was to have the soldiers transfer Scofield's crates to the truck, remove the barricade, and finally deliver Bill Scofield to him personally.

Once in possession of his ex-partner, he would let the train proceed north and light his fuse. While it burned, he would enjoy the luxury of killing Scofield, then return to the truck. He estimated that, by the time the burning fuse reached the first charge, the entire train would be in a perfect position to be completely derailed. The dynamite might not kill all the passengers, but it would certainly keep any of them far enough from a telephone or telegraph operator until he could be safely over the border.

The truck still had plenty of gas. He was sure he could cross into the United States just west of Las Palomas without being spotted. He knew he would never be whole again, but at least there would be some compensation. Great wealth could ease a great deal of pain, and the final agonies of Bill Scofield might very well ease a great deal more.

Long before they reached Torreón, the ache had changed from a sharp agony to a dull, insistent throbbing, similar to what she already knew so well, albeit more intense. Hannah Pelzig had not wanted anyone, particularly her husband, to know of her wound. Unfortunately, there had been no way to hide it.

The bullet had entered just below the right scapula. It had punctured her right lung and lodged there. The blood from the intial wound ran down the back of the seat to form a viscid puddle between her and Jakob. When she had finally been unable to contain her cough, a great clot of bubbled gore had smeared her handkerchief.

Someone had pulled the Pullman seats across the aisle into a lower berth. They had carried her across. Now she lay on her side, her head propped slightly by a pillow as Karen Tait held a cool towel to her forehead.

She thought the situation incongruous. She was badly hurt, yet somehow able to accept both the pain and the presence of impending death almost easily. She had lived with pain for so long and had seen the dark angel so many times that this final, sudden wound had been almost expected.

The young woman she could not understand, and who could not understand her, had placed a small pistol on the berth just beside her head, then, from somewhere, she had produced wet towels to bathe her brow. The two things—the pistol and the towels—seemed so incompatible.

From where she lay, she could see Candenning. The handsome American was watching her. He appeared quite concerned. It was as though he was not only sorry for her discomfort, but somehow deeply ashamed of himself as well. She saw him glance to Karen, his expression one of regret, perhaps even of responsibility for all that had recently happened.

It was Jakob, however, sitting beside her on the berth, for whom she felt the deepest concern. She could feel his own pain—knew he was suffering far more even than she.

"It's all right," he kept saying to her. "We'll soon be in—Torreón." The statement was really a question, and he turned to Candenning for confirmation.

The American nodded. "Yes," he said. "Torreón."

"There will be doctors and a hospital there."

She took his hand in hers. "Jakob . . ."

She coughed and the pain stabbed her again. Again blood frothed onto the pillow. She was ashamed of making a mess even though she could not help it. She could feel the bullet in her lung. It was throbbing as though with a pulse of its own.

How could she make him understand? She had watched him deny the truth for so long, refusing to accept the obvious. Now, he *had* to understand. A stray bullet had simply outrun the tubercles. What mattered now was not her own life or death. That had been ordained. All that mattered now was that her beloved reach the United States and his friend Albert.

He leaned forward. "Yes, Hannah?"

"I can't leave you, Jakob. I won't."

"I'll be with you, darling."

"No, Jakob." She could not control her coughing. "You must not do this."

The train began to slow. They were nearing a terminal. She gathered her strength. She pulled him closer.

"Jakob—don't you understand? There is still one man."

She saw him turn and knew instantly that he had spotted the last Nazi agent. She also saw him try to keep the knowledge from her. He was simply not actor enough.

259

"You must get north," she told him. "I won't let this stop you."

"There are doctors here—"

"Jakob, there is nothing a doctor can do."

His eyes were anguish itself. She knew he was fighting in any way he could to avoid accepting the truth.

Beyond him, the English woman was holding her shattered right arm and sobbing quietly. Hannah looked again to Jakob, but did not speak. The effort was too painful.

Karen Tait leaned forward. Again, she wiped Hannah's forehead with a damp towel.

With a final, almost excruciating scrape and sigh, the train stopped. Almost immediately, the normal noise and snatches of conversation on the Torreón platform changed to mindless, agitated babble. Like scattered tongues of fire in dry, wind-lashed grassland, news of the raid crackled from the train through the city.

Karen removed the towel, glanced out the window, then over her shoulder. Her expression was a mixture of compassion and anxiety as she slid the small pistol forward and under Hannah's pillow.

Suddenly, the car was a flurry of motion and harsh commands. Several Mexicans in non-matching uniforms scrambled aboard. Some wore white arm bands with red crosses on them, others merely wore pistols. From where she lay, she could not see all that happened. She could, however, see the man across the aisle bandaging Margaret Whitley's arm as another man, unseen, made a long and apparently very official speech.

Margaret was helped to stand, then led beyond view just as a man with an almost perfectly round face leaned over the berth. Although not Oriental, his eyes were quite narrow and his lips amazingly thin. The impression was that of a brown ball that had been stabbed three times, then equipped with a dispro-portionately large nose.

As he leaned over Hannah, he smiled a sad little lifting of his lips and touched her forehead with the back of his right hand. In the simple gesture she felt a world of genuine compassion. He started to talk to her, but Candenning interrupted in Spanish.

This would be her last chance. She summoned all her strength. Strangely, she never thought of herself as in any way courageous or selfless. It was simply a thing that had to be done.

"Mr. Candenning," she said in German. "You must tell him that I won't go. I won't be taken off this train—taken away from Jakob."

"Hannah," Jakob told her. "It's all right. I'll go with you."

"We can all go with you," Candenning said.

"No," she insisted. "You must understand. If we leave the train, Jakob will be killed or abducted. I know it. He must reach the United States."

"Hannah—"

"No, Jakob. Don't you see? It makes no difference. I'm dying. On the train or here in Torreón. It makes no difference. I don't want to die here, away from you, or put you in even more danger. No. I want to be with you, Jakob. I want you safely in the United States."

Finally, she could see him begin to understand. He had known from the beginning, but had doggedly refused to accept the truth. He had pushed it away—tried to cover it with a brightly colored carpet of false hope and rationalization. Now, at last, she had torn the sham away and made him face the fact.

With final acceptance of that with which he had lived so long, there came to Jakob's eyes an anguish beyond tears. He looked down to her and, so close were their hearts, his hurt became her own.

She tried to smile as she squeezed his hand. "It's the only way, Jakob," she said. "The only way."

After that, there was a long interchange in Spanish between Candenning and the round-faced man. Finally, the doctor shrugged his shoulders. He gave her an injection in the right arm, bandaged her back, then stood up and looked down at her. Again, she could almost touch his compassion, so tangible was it between them.

He sighed. *"Amor,"* he said. *"Es lastima!"* He stepped out of view.

For some time, officials stalked up and down the aisle, interrogating passengers and barking orders. Easily and quite effortlessly, the injection began to take effect.

She did not know how long they stayed in Torreón, but by the time the train made its first monumental lunge forward, the pain was entirely gone. She was really quite comfortable.

261

The bullet in her lung had stopped pulsating and her back no longer ached. Even the pistol under her pillow did not bother her.

It was true, there was still one Nazi agent aboard, but he was alone. Certainly, he would not dare do anything with so many people near.

Hannah Pelzig rested easily, for she knew she had done the right thing. At last her beloved Jakob was safe.

Alvaro Sánchez was an illiterate peasant. As a boy, he had attended a church school for a few months before it was abolished and the nun executed. Still, he had never quite mastered reading, let alone writing. He had worked hard all his life except for the short time he had served in the army. That had been good. There had been much to drink, and many different women to enjoy, but the army was no way to spend a lifetime.

Now there was only Maria and she was getting older and more tired with the children. He supposed that one day he might marry her if he could ever afford to pay the necessary fees to the church. But then, these days one could never find a priest anyway. It was just as well, for if there were a priest in his village, and Sanchez could not pay for the marriage, the priest would talk of sin, and sin was relative. To live with a woman out of wedlock was a sin, but so was to kill a sin. Yet hadn't the priests themselves been telling everyone to kill back when General Calles had been president?

No, just to live was enough. A man tried to get through life with enough luck so he could eat at least once a day.

Alvaro Sanchez was a simple, ignorant man living a very typical life and destined to die long before his fortieth year. He accepted his lot, because he knew no other. Still, he allowed himself the luxury of one great dream. One day, he hoped, the president of Mexico would do what he had promised and reapportion enough land so that Alvaro could have his own plot. Then those six of his little sons who were still alive could grow up to raise enough food to feed themselves.

These speculations, however, were not heavy on his mind as, some several miles south of the Rio Aquanaval basin, he walked along the railroad tracks leading north to Torreón. In fact, his only thought was surprise, when, in front of him, he saw the bodies of two men who were both apparently quite dead.

Immediately fearful that their killer or killers might be nearby, Alvaro whirled in a complete circle, then crouched slightly as though anticipating attack. A viewer might have thought the movement ridiculous, even comic, but there was no viewer. Alvaro was completely alone. There was nothing within miles but the railroad tracks and rocky barren land, stretching for what seemed like eternity in every direction.

Cautiously, with the care and stealth of the very superstitious, Alvaro took one hesitant step toward the bodies, then another. He did not wish to be abrupt or rude to two immortal souls, even though he hoped that their less permanent bodies might be carrying some scraps of food or a few coins which might be of benefit to him or his family.

He stood for some time looking down at the two bodies. He was sure they had not been dead long. There was none of the smell of putrefaction in the hot air, and the animals and insects had not gotten to them, even though he did notice three vultures circling anxiously overhead.

Finally, he took a deep breath and leaned over, deciding first to search the shorter man in the overcoat. Strangely, his pockets had already been turned out. More strange, their contents had not been stolen. They lay scattered on the ground beside him. There was a handkerchief, a comb, part of a package of cigarettes, a wallet, a few coins and a strange little golden box with a lever on top.

Fascinated by the tiny box, Alvaro picked it up and depressed the lever. He was so shocked by the small flame which leapt from it that he immediately dropped it again. A moment later, braver and more curious, he retrieved it and depressed the lever again. Although ignorant, Alvaro was not a stupid man. He realized on the second pressing that what he held in his hand was an automatic fire-maker. The very thought that such things actually existed was nearly stupefying.

Carefully, he laid the cigarette lighter on the ground and picked up the man's wallet. It contained some apparently official cards which Alvaro could not read and several hundred paper pesos.

Alvaro Sanchez could hardly breath. He pinched his lower lip painfully to prove that he was not dreaming. He had suddenly become rich beyond his most irrational, riotously demented fantasies—maybe even rich enough to buy his own piece of land and not have to wait for the president to move in his favor.

There was some other money in the wallet, but the pictures on it were of strange men and unfamiliar buildings. Alvaro knew it was foreign, and because he also knew he would never travel to a foreign land, he considered it worthless.

He extracted a cigarette from the pack, again picked up the lighter, and with infantile glee set fire to a twenty-dollar bill, waited until it had burned almost in half, then lit his cigarette with it.

Alvaro Sanchez squatted on his heels and savored the luxury of the cigarette. He could not believe his good fortune. He had just found more money than he had seen in his entire life! The implications were staggering. Perhaps he didn't need the land after all. Perhaps there was enough money there to let him live without toiling. He could buy food like rich men did and have many women to enjoy and much pulque to drink.

Dreams of abandoned luxury swirled in his brain as he quietly sucked on the cigarette. It was good, and he enjoyed it until the butt was so short it began to burn his lips. Only then did he flip the shreds of paper and tobacco away and turn his attention to the second man.

He was quite tall—obviously a foreigner. His right leg had been badly broken and had bled profusely. Once his suit might have been fashionable, but now it was filthy and torn. The strange part about the man, however, was that, even though dead, he was holding two little sacks, one in each lifeless hand.

Gently, almost to the point of reverence, Alvaro lifted one sack from his limp fingers and opened it. Inside there were several little glass chunks cut so that they caught the light of the sun and sparkled. He poured three of them into the palm of his left hand, and immediately satisfied himself that they were really quite pretty but entirely worthless. Still, instead of throwing them away, he replaced the three stones in the bag and again secured the string.

Absently he removed the second bag from the man's inert fingers, saw that it too contained no more than sparkling chunks, and laid both bags aside.

He then began to go through the man's pockets with exactly the same luck he had experienced before. There was a handkerchief, a comb, a case containing several cigarettes of a different sort and a little fire-making machine—this time silver.

There was also a thin little book with an elaborate coat of arms on the cover, many official stamps inside, and a somewhat unflattering picture of the dead man. Finally—a perfect reward at the end of long labor—there was the wallet. This, too, contained several cards of an apparently official nature and a great many peso notes in a variety of denominations.

Alvaro Sanchez was so exhilarated over his newfound wealth that he actually jumped up and down several times as he chuckled to himself and, again and again, muttered the single word, "Rich."

Only after several minutes of this near-hysterical ecstasy, did he allow himself to calm sufficiently to consider the pathetic aspects of the situation. Two men were dead. Their bodies lay far from their homes—far from their friends and families and loved ones. Aside from the murderers, only God, the Blessed Virgin, and he himself knew of them. It did not seem right that they should remain there only for the animals and the vultures.

Still, he could not carry them to his village, and there was no way he could bury them. He felt helpless yet compelled to offer something, if only some last prayer or sacrament, to the dead men.

"For a favor," he finally muttered, "be good to their souls, Blessed Mother, for they have been good to me and I wish to acknowledge the kindness."

There was no more he could do. He stood looking down at the bodies for a long moment, then returned to the reality of his own life. He had long kilometers to travel before he reached his village. Again, he stooped and began to pick up the items he thought of value.

He left the wallets and their strange cards. He left the wristwatches because, for him, time was not measured that way. He left the foreign money, but he took the peso notes and the coins, the cigarettes and the two little flame-makers. He even pulled the shorter man's arms out of his overcoat. Nights could be quite cold and a little dried blood inside a right sleeve could do a man no harm.

Satisfied that he had collected everything of value, Alvaro Sanchez stood up. He glanced once to the three vultures still patiently circling overhead. Then, with a heavy sigh, began to walk along the tracks.

He had moved some ten yards from the bodies before he

stopped, thought for a moment, then nodded in agreement with himself. He turned back.

They were worthless, he knew, but the shining chunks in the two bags would make wonderful playthings for his children.

He picked up the two bags and again started his long walk home.

Book VI

CHIHUAHUA

1
The Chase

THEY CAMPED IN the mountains near Gómez Palacio. There the men counted the meager fruits of the robbery and grumbled about their leader's decision to spare all victims but the train's military escort. He had never done such a thing before. It had not been good. They had lost two of their companions, had collected virtually nothing of any value and, worst of all, there were no new women.

El Escorpión listened to both the muted grumblings of his men and Neil Oberon's dramatic pleas. He affected a bored, almost painful, expression.

In the mountains, against a magnificence of primitive scenery, the well-dressed American looked shorter than he actually was. In contrast to the sweating horses and hardened men of action, Neil Oberon seemed quite emasculated and thoroughly out of place. His expensively tailored suit, his sophisticated bearing, even his voice which, from time to time took on a slight whine, all added to the impression of ineffectual weakness.

Still, it was a feasible plan, one which could not only acquire many new weapons and much ammunition, but might even be instrumental in overthrowing or, at the very least, shaking the present government. For a man like Marcos Almidero, the weaker the government, the better the opportunities life offered.

It was, however, always wise to appear doubtful and unconvinced. That way, one's opponent would feel insecure and perhaps even unworthy. The Scorpion enjoyed making people feel insecure and apprehensive about their immediate futures. He particularly enjoyed seeing foreigners squirm. Now Neil Oberon was squirming like a rabbit on a knife's blade.

"But the *real* beauty of it," he was saying, "is that when we go over, we'll make it look like we have Cárdenas's backing—like he's the one behind the raid."

The Scorpion grunted but was careful not to nod.

"I mean, they're probably already pissed to the teeth about the railroad bonds. And who the hell knows what he's going to do with the oil companies?"

Almidero scratched his groin with elaborate thoroughness. He looked casually to his second in command.

Manolo still had the gilt crucifix stuck in his gunbelt, the intersection of the cross just over his navel. The dying Christ gave the ridiculous impression of being in the pouch of a slightly overweight humanoid marsupial. Manolo sucked something from between his teeth with a long and scabrous hiss. He shrugged without commitment or negation.

"San Antonio is not good," Almidero said. "We would have to cross at Piedras Negras or Laredo—much too far east for me. Then too, it's almost 200 kilometers into the United States."

"Fort Bliss, then," Oberon urged. "It's right across the border. There should be plenty of weapons there."

The Scorpion pursed his lips and partially closed his eyes. Oberon must be made to believe he was giving the matter some very serious, very negative consideration. He liked the American, but he liked the game even more. Oberon had helped him on several occasions. Chances were good that he was actually helping him now. Still, the squirming was a pleasure to watch.

"It's a risk." He scratched himself again, this time redressing his parts before adjusting his gunbelt. "A big risk." He looked to Manolo again.

Obviously unwilling to be drawn into his leader's game, Manolo only lifted his eyebrows and cocked his head slightly to one side. Then, retreating from the game entirely, he removed the crucifix from his belt and appeared to give his entire attention to it.

"Think of it!" Oberon insisted. "The Americans will think Cárdenas sent you. You'll have enough guns and ammunition to do what you like. They'll be after Cárdenas and will surely back you. Hell, they might even set you up as president. Tell you what, Marcos. I'll even just take half of what I'm supposed to get off to Spain. Just enough to get Móndez back on my side again. Now, where can you get a deal like that?"

"Interesting," the Scorpion said. Once again, he looked at Manolo

Still isolating himself from the play, Manolo had begun to

269

toss the crucifix absently up and down. Perhaps he had seen an American gangster movie in which one of the characters flipped a silver dollar in a similar manner.

The game was taking its toll of Oberon. Over the past several minutes he had become progressively more nervous and transparently concerned about the outcome. "Hell," he announced with obviously false bravado, "Pancho Villa did it."

"Ah," the Scorpion sighed. "Doroteo."

"What?"

"Doroteo Arango. That was his real name. I knew him, you know. I once rode with the Golden Ones."

"Then you went over the border?"

"Neil—friend—Columbus, New Mexico and unarmed Americans is not the whole United States Army."

"It'll be easy, I tell you. The army's asleep at the switch forty-eight hours a day. Believe me, I know my own people. They're never ready for anything until after it's walked over them and half-way back. Hell, you'd be in there and loaded and halfway to Durango before they even got a bugle to their lips."

"I don't know."

"Hell, if Pancho Villa can do it, so can you."

"And have the whole damned American army down here?"

"So what? They never got Villa, did they? You're twice the cavalryman he was. There's no chance they'll get anywhere near you."

"Listen, Neil, friend—I have Cárdenas after me. The man is a fox. I have the Federals. I don't want the Americans as well."

"Think of all those beautiful rifles, Marcos! Think of all the nice, fat banks in El Paso—the jewelry stores!"

"It's tempting, Neil. I will think of these things. I will let you know."

Throughout the short conversation, Manolo, although listening intently, had continued to affect a casual disinterest. He appeared bored and somewhat juvenile as he flicked the gilded crucifix higher and higher, letting it spin like a glittering boomerang above his head, then down to be caught at waist level. Despite his feigned apathy, however, his attention was momentarily, yet thoroughly, captured by Oberon's mention of banks and jewelry stores. Such were the things to which Manolo's mind related most intimately. The moment he heard

270

them mentioned, he was unable to divide his concentration sufficiently between lust and cross-tossing. The result was that the spinning rood slipped through his fingers to clang against a rock at his feet.

Although jarring as the single hit of a bell's clapper, the sound of the impact did not affect either Oberon or the Scorpion. The former was too intent upon convincing the latter who, in turn, was too involved in his own game of pretended detachment. It did, however, disrupt Manolo.

Marcus Almidero had turned slightly away from Oberon when mentioning that he would consider the proposition. He saw Manolo kneel, inspect the cross, then frown. Slowly, almost painfully, he rose again to his feet. For a moment he appeared childishly puzzled. Then, just as childishly, it seemed as though he might even cry. Almidero saw his companion try to peel something from the shaft of the cross. The gesture intrigued him. Ignoring Oberon completely now, he walked the three paces to where Manolo stood and took the cross from his hands.

El Escorpión had matriculated in the School of Revolution and Counterrevolution. He had been educated on a campus of theft and death. Constant fighting and the need to be relentlessly alert both as hunter and hunted had been his entire curriculum. *El Escorpión* did not know how to read or write, but he had graduated *summa cum laude* from the University of Animal Survival.

A crude and illiterate peasant, he was still eminently qualified to author a definitive treatise on ruthlessness. He also knew 24 karat gold when he saw it.

He inspected the chipped cross from which Manolo had already peeled away almost a square centimeter of cheap plate which had been sufficiently cracked by the impact with the rock to allow a thumbnail's leverage. He remembered the several crates in the train's baggage car and recalled Manolo's contention that they contained nothing but tourist trinkets. More than that, however, he remembered Neil Oberon's insistence that the crates were absolutely worthless.

El Escorpión turned around and smiled to Oberon. Almost casually he held the cross up for the American's inspection. "Hey, friend," he said, "it's pretty, eh?"

Oberon was tense—obviously feeling trapped. He shrugged, but the gesture lacked any semblance of casualness.

"There are many crates on the train, eh?"

271

"How would I know?"

"Ah, Neil—you are the clever one. You talk of guns, but you think of others things, eh?"

"I told you about Móndez."

"Yes, Móndez. Very clever. But it's not clever to play with scorpions."

"Marcos, what are you saying?"

"I wonder—you think maybe the Scorpion will ride into the United States for you . . ."

"Of course! That's what I've been saying—"

"And maybe get into big trouble with the gringo soldiers?"

"I told you before . . ."

"That would make big news. Maybe they even would kill me for you."

"Ridiculous!"

"But, it *would* take attention from you—from you and the gold."

"Gold? What gold?"

"Everyone would be after the Scorpion, so that you and the gold could slip right over the border with much ease."

"I don't know what you're talking about!"

"Ah—" The Scorpion's voice was deceptively soft. "You don't know. You're going to tell me you're ignorant of this—that you come to see me because we are good friends—that you want to make me strong with foreign rifles. Ah, my good friend Neil Oberon, I have known you for much time, eh? We know one another well, you and I. We must face the truth together, eh?"

"What truth? What are you saying?"

"The truth, nothing more." The Scorpion chuckled. "I'm a general. It's true. But really, I'm a thief. That's most important. You—you are a businessman. But what is your business? I'll tell you your business. You're a liar. And now—now, you are lying to me. It's not good, Neil. You are trying to take all the gold, not to share with your good friend Marcos. It's very bad."

"Marcos, believe me. I don't have the foggiest idea—"

"Silence! Son of a mother who fucks goats! You have tried to divert me—to cheat me. It's I—I'm the thief, yet you try to rob from me?"

"Marcos, for a favor—"

"A favor, you say! No! I urinate in the cunt of your father!" The Scorpion drew his pistol.

272

"Marcos! In the name of God—"

The pistol buckled in his hand. The shot hit Oberon an inch above his navel. It made an entrance hole approximately the size of a five-cent piece, but pulled visceral tissue in a horrible inertia through Oberon's abdomen with such force that, when it hit the top lumbar vertebra, it smashed the pedicel as well as the transverse and articular processes and threw the chipped parts a full two yards behind the body. The hole in Oberon's back was bigger than a grown man's fist.

He was thrown a full yard, tried with legs that no longer moved to retain his footing, then sprawled on his back. He lay on the rough ground clawing at the agony of his abdomen, staring up at Almidero in wide-eyed, open-mouthed disbelief.

El Escorpión had never seen anyone look so completely shocked and surprised. Certainly, Oberon of all people should have known what would happen. It was always unwise to trick an old friend. He walked to where the American lay.

The dying man still had enough life in him to gasp, "Marcos . . . for why?"

The Scorpion did not answer. He looked down at Neil Oberon for several seconds then, almost absently, aimed the pistol at his face.

The first round hit just to the left of Oberon's nose and smashed out scattering chips of the occiptal and lower parietal bones. As the head jerked against the impact, bits of cerebellum, corpus callosum, and nermis were splashed from it to form a grisly pillow.

The second round was completely unnecessary, a waste of perfectly good lead and brass. It contributed immeasurably to the anatomical mess, but Neil Oberon was quite dead.

The Scorpion turned to Manolo. He returned the crucifix, then holstered his pistol. "That train probably made an extra long stop in Torreón, but it'll go north again. We must reach it before Chihuahua."

Manolo frowned. It was a puzzled, but noncritical expression.

"Get the men," Almidero said.

"But we already—"

"Idiot! That crucifix! That cheap bit of tourist junk—is gold! Those crates in the baggage car are full of it!"

Manolo started to turn away.

"A moment—" The Scorpion said.

Manolo stopped. "You wish?"

273

"Yes," the Scorpion mused. "This time, tell them they can kill anyone they like and take all the women they desire."

Manolo smiled. He actually skipped as he ran to tell the rest of the men.

The manila folder containing both reports lay open on the huge desk. Beside it, in meticulous formation, were Nicholas Markoff's passport and wallet, as well as Jesús Guerrero's wallet, two wristwatches, and a neat stack of one hundred and twenty-three United States paper dollars lashed together with a rubber band. Both wallets contained a number of identification papers. The money was in various denominations.

As he reread the first report, Juan Miguárdez was both puzzled and displeased. A troop of cavalry on a routine patrol had found two bodies and had carried them to Fresnillo. Because of Jesús Guerrero's importance in the government, the chief of police there had telephoned the presidential secretary immediately.

Miguárdez had ordered the bodies kept in Fresnillo. The commander of the cavalry patrol was flown under guard to the capital, along with all the possessions taken from the two dead men.

Captain Henrico Mendoza had been escorted into the huge office only minutes ago. His guards had placed the wallets, watches, and identification papers of the dead men, along with the money and reports' folder, on Miguárdez' desk. He had ordered them to leave the two bundles of clothing on a corner table then had dismissed them.

Miguárdez had read Captain Mendoza's handwritten report as well as the one from the police chief of Fresnillo. He was now reviewing Mendoza's account of the discovery. It was penned in a precise hand—couched in succinct, articulate language.

He pursed his lips, closed the manila folder, and looked up. For the first time, he allowed himself the liberty of inspecting the cavalry officer standing before him.

Henrico Mendoza, like many of his companions in arms under the Cárdenas administration, was a new breed of Mexican soldier. Although apparently somewhat young for his rank, he was absolutely dedicated and thoroughly professional. Also, unlike many officers serving under previous presidents, he was honest.

That, Miguárdez knew, was the trouble. Because he

knew, he also realized that he had no reason to doubt the accuracy of the captain's report. What lay on his desk represented everything that had been found with the bodies, as well as a truthful account of the circumstances under which they had been discovered.

It was not difficult for him to reconstruct what had happened. Markoff had apparently been dedicated enough to his assignment, or to his own greed, to follow Guerrero from the capital. The men had fought and fallen from the train. Already severely weakened by his wound, Guerrero had actually been killed by his head injury. Markoff had died of exhaustion and loss of blood, his death hastened by the trauma of a compound comminuted leg fracture.

There remained only one mystery—the whereabouts of the missing diamonds.

He stared at Captain Mendoza.

The young man was a perfect picture of military discipline. Despite not having been changed for two days, his uniform was still neat. He was clean-shaven except for his neatly trimmed mustache, and his posture was erect.

Miguárdez swept his hand, palm up, over the reports' folder and other items on his desk. "And this," he asked. "It's the total?"

"Yes, Mr. Secretary."

"You were present when the bodies were disrobed?" He nodded to the two bundles of clothing on the corner table.

"Yes, Mr. Secretary."

"Anything in the clothing?"

"Combs, handkerchiefs, no more. These things are wrapped with the clothing."

"No small bags? Nothing in the lining—in the shoes?"

"The police did a thorough job, Mr. Secretary. The linings have been completely removed."

Miguárdez pursed his thick lips. He stared at the closed reports' folder, thought for a moment, then looked up. "And you?" he said. "You searched?"

"No, Mr. Secretary. I ordered my men to give me the wallets. I realized the political importance of Mr. Guerrero, so I personally delivered both bodies to the Fresnillo police. What you see, Mr. Secretary, is all that was found except the clothing."

"Captain, your report states that wallets were found beside the bodies. Doesn't that strike you as unusual?"

"In what way, Sir?"

"Had you considered robbery?"

"Yes, Sir, but only briefly. There is a considerable amount of currency on your desk, Mr. Secretary. Also both men were wearing wristwatches. I'm not a jeweler, but I believe both watches are quite valuable."

Juan Miguárdez sighed as he leaned back in his chair. What the captain said did hold a ring of validity. A stack of one hundred and twenty-three American dollars was on his desk. The police report had detailed the specific amount found in each wallet, but that was unimportant. What was important was that a thief would have taken that money. If he did not intend to go to the United States, he could easily exchange it for pesos. It was apparent that Markoff and Guerrero had themselves changed pesos to dollars with the intention of crossing the border and staying there.

Had the diamonds been with the men, surely a thief would have taken them, but any thief aware of the value of the diamonds would surely know the worth of the two gold watches as well.

Finally, Miguárdez knew that Jesús Guerrero was anything but stupid. From the very beginning, he had known the risk he was running. He would most probably not carry the diamonds himself. Still, his wife had not had them, and Victoriano Felix had not managed to get them. Somehow, they had simply vanished.

He looked up to Mendoza again. "Thank you, Captain." His voice was entirely lacking in gratitude. "You will remain in the capital with your escort until further notice."

"Yes, Sir." As though on parade, Mendoza made a smart about-face, marched to the door, and left the office.

Juan Miguárdez looked up to the elaborate baroque ceiling, then down to the various items on his desk. He tapped his fingers several times on the desk's top, then pursed his thick lips. Slowly, his dark eyes widened as he nodded. By the time he reached for the telephone, his round, toadlike face was almost smiling.

After some delay with various operators, he was able to reach a man in Ciudad Juárez who was in his debt for the political power he enjoyed. The man was an effective minion—unthinking, unprincipled—but always blindly obedient.

"There will soon be a train arriving from the south," Miguárdez told him. "Aboard will be two children—boys named Miguel and Roberto Guerrero, although they may be traveling under the name of Gonzalez.''

"I understand."

"Caring for them will be a woman—probably quite beautiful, but trying to hide the fact. She is the actress Teresa Inez. She, too, may be traveling under a false name."

"I understand."

"You will board the train in Juárez—before it crosses the border—arrest them, and hold them under maximum security until I can personally supervise the interrogation."

"I understand, Mr. Secretary."

"And, Juan—understand this as well. This time, keep your hands off the woman. I want her alive when I get there."

The hours long wait had rivaled any tour through Hell personally conducted by Signore Alighieri. Although he had remained in his office, Sidney Desmond had given up hope. He was contemplating an elaborate revenge for Cordell Hull's secretary when the telephone finally rang. The harsh sound at once paralyzed and electrified him. Still, he was able to whirl from the office's window and grab the earpiece before the instrument could ring a second time.

"Desmond!" It sounded more like an order given during a bayonet charge than a name.

"Mr. Desmond . . ." There was no mistaking the voice or the accent. "This is Franklin Roosevelt in Warm Springs."

The conversation between the two men was terse—exacting. Although the president never lost the easy charm and effortless manners for which he was famous, the tense situation, the element of diminishing time and increasing hazard and, most important, the vital significance of the knowledge possessed by Doctor Pelzig, allowed for few amenities.

The president's final words were, "Mr. Desmond, I am hardly being a bit melodramatic when I say the future of civilization may very well depend entirely upon you."

"Don't worry, Mr. President." Desmond started to hang up, but arrested himself. "Oh, Mr. President . . ."

"Yes?"

"I wonder if you'd do me one favor?"

"Of course. What is it?"

"Just tell that little old girl who handles Captain Hull's office that I'm mighty grateful—mighty grateful indeed."

He made one more call to Randolph Field and again spoke

to Captain Noores. This time he didn't allow the duty officer an edge. He simply ordered him to stand by the teletype for a direct presidential order.

"You hand it over to your post commander toot goddamned sweet," Desmond told him. "If you can't get him, comply yourself. You got any questions or doubts or who-struck-Johns, do it anyway or, surer than hogs rolling in goose shit, you'll be standing in front of a court-martial within a week and, like as not, a firing squad 'fore the month's out."

During the few minutes it took him to race to Randolph Field the executive order had been received on the teletype and the post commander notified. Sidney Desmond had received *carte blanche* from the president of the United States.

Captain Noores, a somewhat baffled expression on his still youthful face, met him on the steps of the Administration Building.

Desmond took in at a glance the polished, ready-made boots, the precise angle of the Sam Brown belt, and the complete absence of medal or campaign ribbons.

"I want three planes," he said. "Two seaters. Shrikes will do, but P-30s are better. Hell of a lot faster. Won't need but one gunner—him and three of your best pilots."

Captain Noores's mouth opened slightly. Framed against the arch of the building's central door and overshadowed by its huge tower, he seemed both insignificant and confused.

"Hey, Boy!" Desmond snapped. "Let's pull clear of the meadow muffins and get hopping. We got us a train to catch."

Inside the building, Noores made the necessary telephone calls. Within minutes the two men were marching across the main landing strip. In the distance, three pursuit planes were being wheeled from their hangars.

"You're lucky we have them." Noores seemed almost apologetic as he nodded toward the planes. "Ordinarily, we don't station combat assignments here. They came in just last week for the flight-training program."

Built at the Consolidated factory in San Diego, the PB-2A was the only two-seater monoplane fighter to reach operational status with the various air corps between the two great wars. A final evolution from the original Lockheed Altair or XP-900, it had an all-metal design on low wings with just under a forty-four-foot span. It boasted a retractable undercarriage and a long, enclosed cockpit to accommodate a pilot and gunner in tandem. The 700-horse-power V-1570-61 piston Vee in-line engine had a cruising speed of 215 miles per hour, but could be pressed to a maximum of 275 mph at up to 25,000 feet.

Its armament consisted of two fixed, forward-firing 0.30-inch guns and one flexibly mounted 0.30-inch gun in the rear cockpit. Desmond had told Noores to have the planes fueled for their full range and loaded with a maximum of ammunition.

As the two men neared the aircraft, a high-wheeled command car raced across the landing strip. Before it stopped completely, three pilots and an enlisted man leapt from the doorless vehicle. They were waiting at the planes when Noores and Desmond arrived.

The military men exchanged salutes. Noores introduced Desmond and mentioned his authority.

Desmond waited until the command car had driven out of hearing distance before he drew a deep breath. When he spoke, his voice was deep and serious.

"First of all," he said, "I want you boys to understand there's not one particle of shit in what I'm about to say. Second, is after you do what I tell you, none of us here is going to know doodilly fuck about any of it. What I mean, boys, is you are about to do something that, officially anyway, is never going to happen."

The men exchanged skeptical glances, then looked to Noores for confirmation. He nodded. The youthful quality had disappeared entirely from his face.

"There's a train coming up from Mexico," Desmond said, "heading for Juárez and El Paso. I figure right about now it's somewhere in the Torreón-Gomez Palacio area—maybe as far north as Jiménez. There won't be any trouble spotting it. Hell, with Cárdenas fucking all over the railroads down there, she's probably the only train running."

He took another breath and glanced at the four men, looking directly into the eyes of each for a brief second. "You boys are going to stop that train."

The pilots glanced at one another. The gunner's expression was professionally noncommittal.

"I don't care how you do it," Desmond went on. "Try to be kind, but if that doesn't work, do anything you need to. You can strafe the tracks—kill the engineer—just make damned sure you don't hit a passenger car. Once the train stops, the plane with the gunner and one of the others will

279

land. One of you will be aloft at all times just in case. The gunner will cover the military escort. If they get to feeling patriotic, kill them. You . . ." He turned to one of the pilots. "You'll leave the other grounded plane, board that train, and find a man named Pelzig—a little guy, German, wearing glasses. Get him and his wife off. Load him in your plane, take off, and replace your pal in the air. He'll land, then pick up the wife, and the three of you'll hop ass back here."

"Jesus Christ!" the aviator said. "That's armed combat, international—"

"Hey, Boy!" Desmond's expression was suddenly as hard as dried Tennessee clay. "You just go fly your plane. I'll worry about the interfuckingnational complications. I told you, didn't I, nobody's going to know chigger shit about it."

"Go ahead," Noores told them. "The post commander knows. I saw the presidential order myself."

Like men dazed, the pilots and gunner climbed into their aircraft. A moment later, Noores and Desmond watched them taxi into the wind, rise from the tarmac, then bank to the south.

Eight minutes later, the planes were out of sight, headed southwest at an altitude of 15,000 feet. Sidney Desmond was once again outside the main entrance of the Administration Building, facing the flagpole and the upside-down letters labeling Randolph Field.

Before he started toward his car, he turned around to Captain Noores. He smiled and, for the first time, extended his hand. "Say . . ." He was the picture of Southern affability. "I was just thinking. Next time I call, wanting a vaudeville stage, it might be one hell of a sight easier just to give it to me first time around."

Without waiting for a reply, he turned and walked down the few steps to his car.

As Captain Noores watched the older man round the hood and slide behind the wheel, he reaffirmed, for the second time that day, his belief that there were more maniacs in the world than any one man could ever count.

2
Battle

As MILES OF rail clicked away to the south, a sense of anticlimactic emptiness settled deeply into Charles Candenning. In a few short days, everything humanly possible had happened. Nothing more could go wrong or be in any way upsetting.

His first vacation in years had been shattered by a government which, for no apparent reason, had insisted he return to uniform. He'd almost been shot by one man, had been robbed of all his money and jewelry by another. Somehow, the simple act of translating for what at first had appeared to be no more than a couple of middle-aged tourists had swept him into a mysterious international maelstrom. The woman was now seriously injured, the man was still being stalked, and he himself might very easily wind up in a premature grave.

Worse than anything else, however, was that he had come to a painfully upsetting emotional conclusion. Charles Candenning finally accepted the fact that he had fallen in love.

To any other man, such a realization would undoubtedly have come as a joy. To Candenning, however, it represented the nadir of an ill-spent, worthless life. A man motivated since childhood by a concept of duty, he had convinced himself that his career, although necessary and monetarily successful, was in fact no more than a cheap sham. He had married because he got along with Elizabeth, and marriage was the thing to do. He maintained a house in Connecticut. He discharged his obligations both fiscal and conjugal to his wife and, until he had met Karen Tait, had considered his life quite like that of most men he knew. It was even. It was ordered and, when measured by the standards of society, quite normal. Had anyone asked him if in fact he was happy, he would have considered the question ridiculous.

Only since meeting Karen—since sharing their evening in the rain and being with her afterward—had he realized how utterly empty everything had been without her. Worse, he now understood how vacuous a future lay before him.

The entire trouble was rooted in his attitude toward duty. It was on this level that he was most obsessed. A married man simply did not fall in love with another woman. It was just not the thing to do. More immediately, he had convinced himself that he had played the coward during the bandits' raid. Thus, his self-applied masochism had satisfied his insecurity, not only with the knowledge that he was an adulterer but that he was unmanly as well.

Just as another man might have accepted his newfound love with a sense of happiness, he might also, if beset with Candenning's doubts, have kept them to himself, borne his own company north through Chihuahua to Juárez and departed in El Paso muttering something about ships passing in the night, or some other metaphoric platitude equally as inane. Candenning, however, believed he had a duty to confess his thoughts and emotions to the woman responsible for them.

Hannah Pelzig was sleeping peacefully. The injection she had been given in Torreón apparently had been quite effective. Her husband was sitting with Candenning across the aisle staring at her frail, sleeping form so intently that Candenning could almost feel the man's agony. Karen still sat on Hannah's berth, a damp towel in her hand.

Gathering the shreds of something close to adolescent courage, Candenning rose, stepped into the aisle, and tapped her gently on the shoulder.

When she turned, what was it he saw in her eyes? Contempt? Hatred? Or was it just his own self-deprecation? Could it be no more than exhaustion and mild surprise?

"I wonder . . ." He sounded like a boy torn between the safety of ice hockey and the peril of a girl he had suddenly found amazingly attractive. "I mean . . . could I have a word with you?"

She glanced to Hannah Pelzig, satisfied herself that the woman was resting comfortably and, without speaking, rose to follow him through the deserted car. Most of the passengers had left in Torreón, apparently convinced that another catastrophe would surely beset them if they remained aboard. Those who had stayed had gathered in other cars out of respect for the wounded Frau Pelzig.

In the vestibule, they both moved as if on cue. She turned to him and looked up, a quiet question in her eyes.

He wanted to touch her, knew the thought was wrong, and fought it away. "I don't quite know how to begin . . ." He drew a breath and tried to collect his thoughts. "I suppose an apology might be as good a start as any."

She frowned.

"I behaved like a perfect ass back there—I mean during the robbery."

She smiled. Her teeth were very even and white. "You didn't have much choice, did you?"

"I should have taken the pistol. At least . . ."

The smile was still there as she reached for his hand. "I like you much better alive."

"Look, Karen . . ."

Her eyes were quiet lagoons covering a strange mystery in their depths. As though drugged, he stared into them, forgetting the train, his cowardice, his very life itself. He looked to her lips and could fight no longer. Slowly, as though sinking through a sea of fragrant oil, he leaned toward her.

She rose to meet him, pressing her body warmly against his to welcome the embrace. Her arms looped around him and pulled his body close to her own as her lips parted in eager acceptance.

Her breasts were warm and firm against his chest, her thighs almost hungry as they pressed his, and her mouth eager and wet as desire itself. Only after an insane eternity of clasping her—of devouring the nectar of her lips and tongue—did any sense of sanity return.

Like a rough hand clawing at his shoulder, guilt pulled him away. "I'm sorry," he managed. "I should never . . ."

She pressed one finger gently but firmly to his mouth.

"I told you . . . I'm married. I just couldn't help . . ."

Suddenly, he understood the secret in her eyes. It was wisdom—the accumulated, inherited knowledge of women throughout all time. She knew what he might never know, yet because of it, he realized that somehow, some way, nothing was really wrong. No matter what else happened everything between the two of them would be all right.

His guilt, self-doubts, and recriminations—even duty itself—dissipated like the mist of breath against a crisp December dawn. Again, he leaned forward and lowered his lips to hers.

She came to him easily, willingly, as though she had always belonged to him. Her body—lithe, long, and feminine—

molded exactly to his—the missing part it was and had forever been.

Like a man blind from birth suddenly blessed with sight, he was whole and grateful beyond the ability to thank. The train's swaying motion, the clack of wheels on rails, might have been a tango played for them alone. In each other's arms, there was now total acceptance. No doubts or shams hung between them. Without words, they spoke to one another, each giving in total honesty, each accepting in total commitment.

Finally, after what seemed hours, even centuries, they drew apart.

"We'd better get back." He knew it sounded stupid.

"The soul of good form." She smiled as she gripped his hand.

He was still looking at her when they entered the car. There, her smile might have been slapped away. "My God," she gasped. "No!"

He glanced forward. Because he couldn't see Hannah Pelzig's berth, the entire car appeared deserted except for two struggling men. Apparently the remaining German had found an opportunity to dispose of Dr. Pelzig. The car was deserted except for the German, the physicist, and his sleeping wife. The German had attacked the diminutive man and was now arched over him, arms extended downward, thumbs depressed viciously into his throat.

Pelzig was gasping, clawing frantically but without effect at the hands choking his life away.

Candenning started toward the two men, not quite certain what he would do when he arrived. He had taken only three steps when the first shot interrupted the combatants.

The blond man's left shoulder jerked, sagged, then slowly began to turn crimson. He released Dr. Pelzig and stood erect, a shocked, yet infuriated, expression on his face. He turned first to look at Candenning, then to where Frau Pelzig lay.

A second shot hit him in the chest, jerking him a half-turn, much like a badly handled marionette.

"Jew bitch!" He almost spat the words from between clenched teeth as he regained his balance and moved toward Hannah. He had extended both hands, apparently to grasp her throat or hair when three more shots were fired in rapid succession.

The German might have been no more than a mannequin

held erect by a single string. The shots severed that thread. He was dead before he hit the aisle.

Candenning walked the few steps to where the man lay, glanced briefly to his crumpled body, then to Dr. Pelzig. The tiny man was sitting almost primly, a baffled expression on his face, as he rubbed his throat with one hand and readjusted his spectacles with the other. He was in mild shock but otherwise uninjured. Candenning was sure the worst injury had been to his own sense of academic dignity.

He turned around to where Hannah Pelzig lay. The wounded woman still held the pistol Karen had slipped under her pillow. "Jakob?" She coughed. "Jakob?"

Gently, Candenning lifted the weapon from her limp fingers as Karen smoothed a wisp of dark hair back from her forehead.

"He tried to kill Jakob," Hannah said.

"I know," Candenning said.

"I had to . . ."

"It's all right," he told her. "It's over now."

Dr. Pelzig stood up and crossed to his wife's berth. His throat was somewhat redder than usual, the only hint that anything unusual had happened. "I'm fine, Hannah," he told her. "You rest now."

"Jakob . . ." The effort seemed almost supreme as she reached out to grasp his hand. "Oh, Jakob . . ."

A fleeting little smile, faint perhaps as a memory of youth's violins, touched his lips. "Thank you," he whispered. "Sleep now."

Once more, Candenning looked at the body on the floor. "We can't leave him here," he announced. "He'll be a final straw for the authorities in Chihuahua. First the bandits, now this. There'll be enough red tape to keep us in Mexico forever." He glanced from Karen to Dr. Pelzig. "Try to clean up as much blood as you can," he told her. Then, in German, "Here . . ." He handed the little man the pistol. "Next time someone tries to strangle you, shoot him yourself."

Careful to keep his own clothing from being stained, Candenning slipped his hands under the dead man's armpits and dragged him toward the car's nearer vestibule. There, he opened the outside door and tipped the German's dead weight through.

The body hit at a grotesque angle. Leaning out, Candenning saw the inertia of its fall make it flip twice like a huge ragdoll, then lie still and appear to shrink as the train left it in the distance covered by afternoon's long shadows.

He was about to reclose the door when, through the twilight, he saw the horsemen. Instantly, he realized they were the same riders who had attacked the train south of Torreón. The knowledge swelled in his viscera like a sharp-edged block of dry ice, for he also knew why they had returned.

The money was already gone. Now they had come to kill the men . . .

. . . and rape the women.

If it hadn't been for some wild-eyed brass hat's scrambled-brain notion, Christopher Fulton probably could have been celebrating his thirty-first birthday in a San Antonio Bar or perhaps even the officers' club at Randolph Field. As it was, he found himself in the cockpit of a P-30 pursuit plane high over northern Mexico. That was bad enough. What really smarted was the fact that because of his rank, he had been blessed with the dubious distinction of commanding a mission certain to be disastrous. Captain Fulton was flight leader of three, armed United States' aircraft which, he was absolutely convinced, would shatter every vestige of diplomatic relations between his country and Mexico for years—perhaps for decades to come.

Still, whatever the reason—whatever was known at headquarters and unknown here—the mission had at least broken the regimented monotony of ten years' service with the Army Air Corps. Even though Captain Fulton realized his orders had been issued by a madman, he was also somewhat happy for them. His sense of logic may have whispered forebodings of an international catastrophe, but his emotions were eagerly excited as he looked forward to intercepting the train.

During the flight south from Randolph, Fulton had outlined the operation and assigned each of the men specific duties. As flight leader, he had volunteered to board the train and get Dr. Pelzig and his wife off.

In the radio exchanges it had all sounded simple, except for the purely diplomatic complications—but then no one had mentioned anything about armed cavalry.

It was almost twilight when they spotted the train below the hills south of Chihuahua city. It was already being stopped by Marcos Almidero's horsemen. Captain Fulton realized immediately that the train had been attacked and was about to be boarded. If he allowed that to happen, it was certain that some passengers, Jakob Pelzig among them, might very well be injured or killed.

His mission, which had been insane from the beginning, now seemed nothing short of maniacal. Still, he *was* a soldier. As he gave the orders to dive for a strafing run, he wondered exactly how many tenets of international law he was violating.

Fulton led the attack screaming down from 5,000 feet out of the setting sun, leveling off almost over the horsemen's heads and hammering into them and their horses with controlled bursts from both forward guns. Pulling back on the stick, he almost left his stomach behind as he climbed then banked for a second run.

Next, Anderson dove into them. His forward guns flung them from their mounts, spattering parts of men and horses over the flat plain. When he swept up, his gunner continued to smash well-aimed destruction into them.

As Fulton came around for his second dive, he could see at least fifteen dead or wounded men, along with several animals scattered beside the train. Those who remained mounted were in obvious disorder. Only a scant few of them had the vainglorious presence of mind to aim weapons at his aircraft. When he began firing, even those turned to flee. His last impression, before easing back on the stick, was of a man's left hand and a horse's eye smashing simultaneously into crimson eruption.

Demoralized, routed, the horsemen scattered from the train. Anderson made one final sweep over them, cutting down men and animals with his forward guns, then, as he turned back, his gunner almost completely decimated the now frantic riders.

Circling the still immobile train, Fulton gave his final orders. He and Anderson would land. Collings would remain airborne. As Fulton boarded the train and brought the Pelzigs out, Anderson's gunner would threaten and, if necessary, fire upon both the military escort and any wounded men still willing to fight.

The landing was as rough as any he had ever experienced. Three times he actually believed he might crash. Somehow he managed to land the plane, swing around, and taxi to within yards of the train. Anderson was already in position, his gunner grim and ready to fire.

Fulton slid his cockpit cover back and pulled himself out of the plane. There was no sign of a military escort. He jumped to the wing then down to the ground. With the heavy weight of his pistol slapping against his hip, he ran through groaning, screaming men and wide-eyed, wounded horses to the first passenger car.

"Pelzig!" he called as he came in from the vestibule. "Jakob Pelzig!"

The car contained only Mexicans, all baffled and terrified. In the second car he encountered a short muscular man.

"You Jakob Pelzig?" he demanded.

The short man shook his head. He pointed over his shoulder with his thumb. "Back there," he said. "Wife's been hurt."

Fulton ran through one more coach, pulled its rear vestibule door open, and entered the Pullman car. "Pelzig!" he called again. "Jakob Pelzig!"

"Ich bin Doktor Pelzig."

He saw a small man with thinning hair and spectacles standing in the center of the car. Behind him was a slender attractive woman and a tall blond man.

"Oh, Christ!" Fulton said aloud. "You don't speak English?"

The taller man came from behind Dr. Pelzig and extended his hand as though at a garden party. "My name's Candenning, Captain. I'll translate for him."

"Right," Fulton said. "Chris Fulton. Thanks. Tell him I've come to take him off—him and his wife. I've orders to get him to the States pronto."

"Good luck," Candenning said.

"What do you mean?"

"I mean," the tall man said, "that your chances of getting him off are about as good as lighting a match on a piece of soap."

"I'm afraid there's no choice." Fulton felt suddenly angry. "I have my orders."

Candenning shrugged. "I'll tell him." Quite casually, he turned to Dr. Pelzig and spoke quietly in German. It seemed to Fulton that his tone held a certain cynical humor.

The German nodded several times. Each time his head moved up then down he seemed to be progressively more infuriated until, like an enraged Mr. Hyde, he addressed Candenning in a fury of Tutonic invective.

Only after the better part of a full minute did he stop long

288

enough to allow Candenning to turn to the pilot again. "He says . . ." The tall man was smiling as though at some mysterious joke. "I mean, without the unnecessary adjectives, he says that you are . . . How should I put it? A final straw to break his camel's back. He says his wife cannot be moved. He says he's not going to leave her. Essentially, he says he doesn't really give a damn about your orders."

"What!" Christopher Fulton, the lone representative of the sovereign power of the United States of America, was totally baffled. "Come on," he pleaded. "He's making this whole thing ridiculous. We've already ruined diplomatic relationships with Mexico. Just let me take the old guy off. Hell, it's for his own good."

Candenning shrugged. Again he spoke a few words to Pelzig.

The smaller man was still thoroughly infuriated. His face had turned quite red. Fulton heard him say *"nein"* several times as he shook his head from side to side.

For the first time since boarding the train, Captain Fulton realized that the man he thought he would be saving was anything but grateful for the rescue. Jakob Pelzig would not fly out of Mexico without the application of force. "All right," he said. "If you're going to play it that way, you don't give me much choice." He unsnapped his holster's cover and reached for his forty-five.

Pelzig was a blur as he sprang forward. Captain Fulton felt a cold and annoying pressure hard against his nostrils and looked down almost cross-eyed at the Mauser in the doctor's hand. A spray of German fury rang in his ears as his own pistol was jerked from its holster. He waited in dismay, possibly for death itself, as Pelzig continued to pelt him with unintelligible, but naked, fury.

"What he's telling you," Candenning said quite calmly, "is basically that he's not going."

"I kind of thought that." Unarmed now, Fulton took a pace backward.

Dr. Pelzig still held the pistol leveled at him.

"You see . . ." Candenning's voice was sympathetic. "He's gone through quite a bit in the last few days. His wife's received a bullet and can't be moved."

Fulton glanced to his right and noticed the frail, dark-haired woman who had previously been lying out of sight on the extended lower berth. "Look . . ." he was almost desperate. "I've got orders . . ."

"I don't know where they came from," Candenning said, "and frankly, I don't care. I'm just sure—"

"They're from the president," Fulton announced. "Right from F.D.R. himself."

"Oh?" Candenning was clearly unimpressed.

"Now, will you tell him to come along?"

"I'm not his keeper," Candenning said. "I just translate. He doesn't want to go. Don't you understand? He doesn't care figs for you or Roosevelt or anything else. He wants to stay with his wife. Try to change that and I'm sure he's been pushed just far enough to shoot."

"He's crazy," Fulton said.

"Maybe." Candenning lifted his eyebrows in acknowledgment. "But not crazy enough to violate foreign air space, machine-gun a lot of Mexican nationals, and attempt to kidnap two people from a train."

"Oh, Christ!" It was the ultimate gasp of desperate exasperation.

"Besides," the tall man went on, "there's no danger here. It was kind of dicy for a while, but whatever problems he had are gone now. Believe me, he's perfectly safe. I'll personally see to it that he reaches the border safe and sound. As for his wife—you can see for yourself—it's touch and go." He turned to Pelzig and extended his hand. *"Bitte,"* he said.

Now, more like a contrite, obedient child than the enraged madman he had seemed a moment before, Dr. Pelzig handed Candenning Fulton's pistol. Obviously intimately familiar with weapons, Candenning pressed the release, pulled the clip free of the handle, then slid the receiver back to eject the single round lodged in the chamber. "Here." He handed the impotent weapon to Fulton. "Best thing for you is to hop into your flying machine and get home before the Mexicans get the notion you've started another war."

Fulton took the pistol, replaced it in his holster, and shook his head. "Christ!" he said again. "Jesus Sweet Christ on a bicycle."

He was beaten. Dejected and petulant, he turned and stalked through the car. The mission was the catastrophe he had known it would be from the beginning. He had personally been responsible for killing or wounding at least a score of

290

Mexicans, but his goal, the unreasonable maniacal Jakob Pelzig, was still on the train.

Visions of court-martials and hangmen's ropes danced in his mind as he left the train and picked his way back through the blood-soaked, moaning remains of men and horses. He waved to Anderson to follow him and climbed into his cockpit.

Aloft, he could barely see the train moving forward again. He hoped Candenning had been right. He couldn't imagine any possible danger Pelzig might face. The man was armed and the train itself had been virtually deserted. Besides, there were only a few hundred miles left before it reached El Paso.

He had no choice but to return to Randolph and report. He banked to the right, glanced at the train a final time, then headed into the darkened east.

Although he could understand most of the tirade, Sidney Desmond assumed a posture of ignorance. *"Despacio,"* he said several times into the mouthpiece. *"Despacio, por favor."* Then, grasping the futility of his pleas, he yelled, "Goddamn it, Carlos! Speak American, will you? What in hell are you raving about?"

"You know fucking well what I'm saying." The Mexican Consul in San Antonio had lost all semblance of diplomatic veneer. "You two-faced son of a bitch! And you know who's responsible. You! You're behind the whole thing and you know it!"

"Hey, Carlos. Carlos, *amigo*!"

"Don't *amigo* me, you goat turd. This is war! War, I tell you!"

"Hey, Carlos—planes fly over all the time. Hell, yours are coming into Randolph every week."

"Fly. Sure, fly! But they don't shoot up unarmed trains. Don't you give me a lot of double-shit, Sidney. You sent them down there. I know. And don't try to squirm out of it. I've got the reports from Chihuahua right here. Engineer, passengers—everyone confirms it. Yesterday three planes—United States planes, clear markings—strafed the train and killed we don't know how many."

"Killed?" Desmond was suddenly worried. "Killed who? Soldiers or passengers?"

The Mexican's voice became suddenly uncertain. "There were no soldiers aboard. Apparently . . ."

"Passengers then?" Desmond was as afraid as he had ever been. "How many?"

"That's not the point." The consul was trying to remuster a tone of authority. "Apparently the train was being . . . being stopped."

"Stopped? Stopped by what?"

"It's immaterial, Sidney. The point is that your airplanes strafed and killed citizens of Mexico in an act of unprovoked and infamous armed aggression. And you—you, goddamn it—are responsible. You're not with customs. You sent those planes down there. A clear violation of every principle of international law . . ."

"Who was killed?" Desmond persisted.

"I told you." The authoritative tone eased slightly. "The train was being stopped."

"By who? Come on, Carlos. You can level with ole Uncle Sid."

"Frankly, there were some bandits . . . ."

"Bandits, eh?"

"Beside the point, Sidney. They were Mexicans. Subject to Mexican authority not American guns!"

"Couldn't have been Almidero's boys, could it?"

"How did you know?" There was a definite uncertainty in the voice.

"Hell. South of Chihuahua. The Scorpion's been fiddling around down there and in Durango for years. Had to be him." Desmond chuckled. "So they shot up ole Marcos, eh?"

"It's not funny, Sidney. You are up to your chin in one big heap of international shit. You and your entire meddling country. President Cárdenas will hear of this within the hour. You know how he feels about American interference."

"I know how he feels about Marcos Almidero!"

"What do you mean by that?"

"I mean, Carlos, that somebody should tell him what a big favor we've done. How many of Almidero's boys did we get?"

Now the voice was definitely peevish. "Fifteen dead so far and another twenty-two wounded."

"And no passengers, right?"

"Sidney . . ."

"Right?"

"That's right."

"What about Almidero?"

"Dead."

"Aha, Carlos! *Esta muy bueno*! Bet that gets one rotten, egg-size burr right out from under ole Lázaro's saddle, eh? Hell, way I figure it, you should be thanking me instead of—"

Abruptly, the line died. Sidney Desmond realized that the Mexican Consul had hung up in humiliated exasperation. He also realized the the the death of "General" Marcos Almidero, *El Escorpión*, would undoubtedly be more than exchange enough for official Mexican silence.

Slowly, he recradled his own earpiece and lay back in his bed. The pilots not only had done exactly what they had been told to, they had even given him something extra. By now, Doctor Pelzig and his wife were probably safe at Randolph Field. With Almidero dead, the world would be no wiser.

Sidney Desmond sighed in monumental satisfaction. He closed his single eye in hopes of another hour's sleep, knowing that things just naturally had a way of working out for the best.

3
The Border

DESPITE THE PREDAWN HOUR, Charles Candenning was wide awake when they reached Chihuahua. Sleep simply had not come. A man trying to probe for untimate truth rarely enjoys the luxury of sound slumber.

Candenning had expected a long delay. Reports regarding Marcos Almidero's second attack and its rout by the American planes would have to be filed, individuals questioned, accounts compared. Fortunately, the stopover took less than an hour. The authorities were as sleepy and lacking in enthusiasm as the passengers they interrogated. Quite obviously, three o'clock in the afternoon in Torreón and four o'clock in the morning in Chihuahua made a world of difference to the efficiency and spirit of Mexican officialdom.

Candenning had expected Hannah Pelzig to refuse to be moved. Because her husband and Karen Tait were both sleeping in bone-weary exhaustion, Candenning himself had asked for a doctor to come aboard. The quiet and very serious young man couldn't have been more than five years away from medical school. He had changed Frau Pelzig's dressings and given her another injection. Finally, he had moved a discreet distance from the semiconscious woman and told Candenning what the illustrator already suspected.

"Her chances are slim," he had said. "I don't really think she'll make it to the border."

"Couldn't we force her to a hospital here?"

He shook a sad face. "She's been terribly weakened by tuberculosis. Without x-rays I can't tell the location of the bullet or the exact damage it's done, but I'm sure she's bleeding internally. She's beyond a hospital's help now."

He had stepped to the station's platform, a shy, dedicated young man, and lifted one hand in an almost hopeless gesture of farewell as the train started forward again. He was still standing there, arm uplifted, as Candenning turned from the vestibule into the car.

Dreary, exhausted, yet still wide awake, he had returned to his berth and, still fully clothed, laid down. He was shocked no more than an apparent second later to open his eyes to morning's bright light.

His watch had been taken in the robbery, but he sensed by the position of the sun that it was sometime around nine or ten o'clock. Outside his unshaded window, sand stretched for miles.

When the train began to slow, he thought it might be making a stop at some small village. When it actually did come to a full halt, however, he was somewhat surprised to see no station—no sign of civilization whatsoever.

He looked as far forward as he could, spotted a truck and then, some twenty yards east, a badly disfigured, white-haired man hunched over a dynamite plunger.

"You're resting on enough explosive to blow you all to hell!" the man shouted. Although he cried out in Spanish, his accent was vaguely British. "Do what I say," he called, and you'll live. Resist—and I'll kill you all!"

Candenning rolled off his berth and crouched in the aisle. "Stay down," he told Karen. Then, to Doctor Pelzig, "Let me see the pistol."

294

He took the small weapon and inspected it thoroughly before returning it to the physicist. "I'm going forward," he said. "If you have to use that, do a good job. You only have two rounds left."

Pelzig nodded. There was no confidence in his expression.

Karen touched his hand. "Charles . . ."

He tried to smile, but felt he only looked ridiculous. "I'll be fine," he told her. Then, almost on his hands and knees, scurried as fast as he could along the aisle, through the two forward vestibules, into the next car.

Although most of the remaining passengers were still in their seats, William Scofield and Domingo Portes were hunched below window level. He almost bumped into them as he dashed into the car.

"You can bet your ass he means it," Scofield was saying. "And he knows what he's doing, too."

"What's he want?" Candenning asked. "We've already been robbed of everything."

"It's a long story," Scofield said.

"Now hear me!" The crippled man was screaming at the top of his voice.

Candenning crawled between two seats and lifted his head just high enough to look out the window.

The lone man was still hunched over the dynamite plunger, an expression of ultimate fanaticism on his mangled face. "I want everyone—every single man and woman on that train—to get out on this side. No tricks. I can see through under the cars. Slowly now—out you go."

"He must be bluffing," Candenning said. "There's nothing—"

"He's not," Scofield said. "Believe me, he's dead serious."

Candenning glanced to Domingo Portes.

The Mexican nodded his head but did not speak.

"Move!" the man called. "Get off that train.! All of you!"

"Look," Scofield said. "I can't go out there. I know what he wants." He pulled a pistol from his waistband. "I'm going to kill the son of a bitch once and for all."

"And risk everyone on the train?" Candenning was appalled.

Domingo Portes smiled. His expression was smug as he looked directly at Scofield. "And," he said very softly, "all the gold as well?"

"You bean-eating son of a bitch!" Scofield swung the pistol toward Portes and cocked the hammer.

Candenning grabbed his wrist, forcing the barrel away. "Don't!" he said. "We can't afford to fight ourselves. Not with him out there."

Reluctantly, Scofield lowered the pistol. He gave Portes a truculent glance then turned to Candenning. "His name's Conrad," he said. "Ian Conrad. And he's dead serious. That's the whole trouble. He knows explosives inside and out. He's a very goddamned efficient pain in the ass."

"I'm counting to ten!" Conrad screamed. "I want all of you off, and off right now. One!"

"Come on," Candenning said. "We'd better do what he says."

"Go," Scofield told them. "He's not going to do anything until he's sure I'm here."

"Two!"

Candenning and Portes rose and turned toward the car's rear exit.

"They're thieves," Portes whispered as they neared the vestibule. "Conrad and Scofield—both of them. Believe me. There's still a fortune on this train."

"What?"

"It's true," Portes said. "I've seen it. I know."

They entered the vestibule and turned down the steps.

"I'll tell you the story if we live. For now, let me say that there are millions of pesos worth of gold aboard and these two—the fellow with the dynamite and Scofield—will do anything to keep it."

They were on the ground now. Portes fell silent as they aligned themselves with the rest of the men before the train. They stood uneasily awaiting the worst.

"Scofield!" The white-haired man was still hunched quite low over the plunger. He was almost entirely covered from view by sand. "I know you're in there, Bill. What's it to be, lad? Do I press it? Shall I blow you to hell where you belong, or do you come out with the rest?"

What happened next occurred with such rapidity that neither Portes nor Candenning, both ex-soldiers, had time to fling themselves to the ground. They heard the scrape of a footfall in the vestibule behind and above them, then the shot fired from there.

No more than a foot from Conrad and the dynamite plunger,

the sand puffed in a tiny explosion where Scofield's first bullet hit.

"You lime-sucking pain in the ass!" Scofield fired a second time.

Conrad was prone, his revolver clasped in both hands. His first bullet spanged into the steel railroad car and whined in agony as it ricocheted away. The second made the unmistakable flat thump of lead hitting flesh.

Scofield grunted. "Bastard!" he gasped. He fired again.

Another round hit. Leather soles slipped on the metal flooring. There was a strange, final gasp of air totally exhaled. Then William Scofield pitched forward. He fell face down into the sand, a tiny crumpled mass of flesh, muscles, and strangely twisted bones.

Only after the six shots had been fired, did Candenning start to fling himself forward. Then, with the silence of death itself hovering over the dunes, he realized it was over. He was standing no more than a yard from the remains of William Scofield, feeling both terrified and somehow foolish as well.

"You!" Conrad screamed in English. "You, the blond chap!"

Candenning looked up again.

"Take his pistol," Conrad called. "And be careful. I want no tricks."

Slowly, Candenning walked to Scofield's crumpled body. He knelt beside the man and turned him over.

William Scofield was holding the pistol loosely in his right hand. He was still alive, definitely in shock, perhaps even paralyzed.

"Take his pistol!" Conrad screamed again.

Candenning removed the pistol from Scofield's limp hand. It would be a desperate gamble, but he just might be able to swing and fire accurately enough to kill Conrad, or at least wound him sufficiently to get off a second, better-aimed round. The thought lasted but an instant. It flitted through his consciousness like a half-remembered dream, then swirled to nothing. He thought of the dynamite under the train and tried to convince himself that his duty was to the women and children still aboard. In fact, he knew he was afraid.

"Kill him!" Conrad cried.

Scofield blinked his eyes. They were very flat and black. Even when facing death, they showed no more expression than they ever had. Candenning couldn't know if the man was begging for life or merely staring at him contemptuously.

Candenning turned toward Conrad. "He's dead!" he lied.

"Kill him again!" Conrad screamed. "Empty that gun into him!"

Candenning stood up and, holding the pistol pointed toward the ground, looked down to the little man for several seconds. Then, very deliberately, he thumbed the hammer back, aimed very carefully and quite methodically, shot the weapon's last round into the sand an inch to the side of Scofield's head.

The little man refused to acknowledge the favor. His expression didn't change. Mortally wounded, he remained impossibly arrogant—even pugnacious.

Still aiming at the sand, Candenning let the pistol's hammer snap on three empty chambers before looking back to Conrad.

"Now!" the cripple cried. "Throw it away!"

Candenning tossed the empty weapon into the sand.

When Ian Conrad gave his next order, Candenning realized that Domingo Portes had told the truth. He and the Mexican opened the baggage car's side door and, with the rest of the men, removed the crates. Portes and Candenning worked as a team, hauling one of the heavy crates out of the car and over the sand to the waiting truck. Silently, they slid it into the truck's bed, then turned back toward the train.

"We must stop him," Portes whispered. "That gold—it belongs to the Church. You must help."

"Help?" They were trapped. The train had stopped on enough dynamite to kill them all. The crippled man hovering over the plunger was armed with a revolver as well. "Impossible."

The truck loaded, Conrad told them to remove the barrier and proceed north again. It was only then that Candenning realized the truth. As he and Portes started around the engine to help lift the heavy timbers from the tracks, he saw a bare few inches of exposed fuse. He slipped his toe under it and raised it just enough to see that it extended forward—northward along the track.

Instantly, he knew they had been tricked. There was no dynamite under the train. It was yards ahead, waiting to be exploded after they began moving forward again.

With the knowledge, fear left him. The old sense of duty clarified itself. He had a personal obligation to the passengers. Portes, the engineer, and the rest of the men who had helped move the crates could really do nothing.

He could. Because he could, he realized that the fate of every person on board rested exactly in the palms of his own hands—specifically in his skill as a pistol shot.

As they walked in front of the engine, he glanced back to see Ian Conrad stand as erect as he could. The white-haired man started to turn from the plunger.

Candenning turned to Portes. "Wish me luck," he whispered and, without waiting for a reply, ran around the engine and started back on the far side of the train.

As his legs pistoned backward past the engine and tender, Conrad saw them. A shot hammered the hot air. Sand erupted no more than just a foot from him. At the first passenger car, Candenning found the forward door closed. He had to risk the run to the rear. Another shot smashed against the morning. This time a jet of sand leapt up a yard to his right. He reached the rear entrance to the car, swung himself up to the vestibule, and started through the train.

Outside, Conrad was limping from the plunger, dragging his crippled leg grotesquely as he made his way south.

Candenning understood now. The plunger was no more than a prop—a cheap theatrical device to intimidate and insure cooperation. The dynamite was actually going to be set off not with an electrical charge, but with a cigar or match. Conrad was making his way toward his fuse ends lying some distance from the mock plunger.

The train jerked forward as Candenning entered the Pullman car. The movement almost sent him sprawling. He regained his balance and ran to Dr. Pelzig.

"The pistol!" he gasped. "Give me the pistol."

The train jerked again as Pelzig fumbled in his coat pocket, pulling ineffectually at the weapon caught on the fabric there. After what seemed like an eternity, he handed it to Candenning.

He pushed past the physicist to the car's rear vestibule. The train jerked again. In the shadows he tried to steady himself against the acceleration.

Conrad was limping frantically now—a crazed and crippled Pheidippides desperately racing the train to get to his fuse ends.

Candenning clasped the pistol in both hands. Two shots, he remembered—and of a ridiculously small caliber as well. He knew nothing about the weapon's sighting peculiarities—nothing about its trajectory.

He took careful aim, leading slightly, trying to compensate for both the train's momentum and Conrad's movement.

Then, gently as a mother's caress, he squeezed off one precious round.

The tiny pistol hardly recoiled in his hands. Still he blinked. When his eyes refocused, he saw that Conrad had dropped. He sighed but too soon. The wounded man pulled himself to his feet, scrambled behind a sand dune, and disappeared.

There was no way to stop him now. The only thread of hope lay in stopping the train itself.

He wrenched the door open and ran into the car, pushing past Karen and Doctor Pelzig as he dashed through the train like a man amok.

As though intentionally fighting him, the engineer was pressing the train's acceleration as fast as he could. It rolled faster and faster forward, gaining momentum, as though it were trying to outrun not merely the devil, but all his demons as well.

Candenning tore through the final coach, then into the baggage car. He raced toward the forward door.

"Stop!" he screamed. "Stop!"

Then it didn't matter.

The explosion was dull. The engine squealed to an agonized, struggling stop—like an animal desperately trying to claw itself forward after its hind legs had been blown off.

Conrad, he knew, had won. The engine was unharmed, but the rear cars had undoubtedly been derailed, and their passengers killed or maimed as the explosion's impact hurled them from the tracks.

He turned as though in a daze, then clamped his teeth tightly together. The Pelzigs were back there. So was Karen.

Again he rushed through the train. The coaches were absolutely level and stable. So was the Pullman car. Miraculously it was exactly as he left it. Karen was kneeling beside Frau Pelzig. The doctor was standing above her, a shocked and puzzled expression on his face.

Satisfied that they were unharmed, Candenning made his way through the car to the diner behind it. Although some of the chairs were overturned, and the one steward there was quite shaken, there was no real damage.

Only when he stepped into the observation car did he

realize what had happened. Conrad's wound had apparently slowed his movement considerably. That fact, coupled with the engineer's frantic desire to race from the dynamite he thought he had first stopped over saved most of the train. The dynamite fuses had been lit seconds too late. The train itself had almost completely passed the explosive charges. Unfortunately, it was now immobilized. The rear wheels of the observation car had been blown from the tracks. Damage was limited to a few glasses and bottles behind the bar. No one seemed to have been hurt.

Candenning started to turn back to the Pullman car. As he did, a movement outside caught his eye. A man was running across the sand.

"Portes!" he gasped aloud. "My God!"

The Jesuit had leapt from the train and was running at a furious pace toward the truck.

Candenning noticed something else. Ian Conrad had risen from behind the sand dune that had previously concealed him. He glanced to the immobile train, then started toward the truck. He had dragged his crippled and wounded leg almost three yards before he saw Portes.

There was one round left in the pistol Candenning still held. It would be an impossibly desperate shot. The weapon was of a low caliber, the target small, and the distance great. Still, he had no time to consider alternatives. He ran to the vestibule where he could command the best field of fire.

Conrad had already lifted his own pistol to aim at Portes now zigzagging across the sand. Candenning extended his arms, steadied his weapon in both hands, and aligned the sights as carefully as he ever had done in his life. Slowly, deliberately, he squeezed off his last round.

Conrad jerked as though he had been kicked in the solar plexus. His pistol arm still extended, he looked toward the train. Slowly, he turned, his single malific eye stared directly at Candenning as he swung his arm around, deliberately aimed his pistol at him, and fired.

Candenning blinked, sure that his eyes would never open again. The single round spanged against the train and whined off.

Ian Conrad took one agonized pace closer, aimed for a second shot, then crumbled to the sand.

Candenning jumped from the train, ran to Conrad, and grabbed the pistol from his limp fingers. There was no need.

The man was dead. Candenning's shot had caught him just below the heart and had probably been buffeted back and forth against his ribs and spine to chew his insides apart. Hate alone had made Conrad able to fire the one round he had.

Candenning rose and walked to the truck. Portes was standing beside it.

"You are an excellent shot," the priest said.

Candenning shrugged. He felt embarrassed, as though he had suddenly been placed naked on a stage before a packed audience.

"This gold . . ." Portes nodded toward the truck. "It won't save the Church. It won't destroy Cárdenas or the government. Such men are inevitable—patriots—believers in temporal destiny. But maybe—maybe, it can help educate some children—let them see the real meaning of God." He made the sign of the cross. "You're a brave man, Mr. Candenning. May the peace of the Lord be with you."

He still felt embarrassed. "Thanks," he said. "I need all the help I can get."

Portes smiled—a fleeting, bittersweet illusion of nostalgia on his face for but an instant. "We are all sinners, my friend. Hope is only in knowing the fact." He climbed into the truck and started the engine.

Candenning rode the running board as they swung around to the more solid ground near the tracks. By the train, he jumped down and waved to Portes.

"Go with God." He didn't even think of the humor in the Spanish expression.

"And you, my friend . . ." Portes smiled. "With God."

For some moments, he watched the receding truck as it moved south along the empty tracks—a tiny moving dot in a vast, inert wasteland. Finally, he climbed aboard, surprised to see Karen waiting for him in the vestibule.

They looked into each other's eyes for a long time before shock overcame them both. Then, she was in his arms, sobbing softly, and whispering his name.

It was over and they were together. Nothing else in the entire world mattered.

It had taken no more than minutes to uncouple the observation car. Ian Conrad's body had been carried aboard the train along with that of his dying ex-partner. Ironically perhaps, they had been placed side by side in the same lower berth.

Again the train moved north.

Candenning, Karen, and Doctor Pelzig sat in silence across from the physicist's wife. All were beyond speech. Too much life had been crammed ruthlessly into too small a package of time. There was no room left for words.

As the train moved through the outskirts of Ciudad Juárez, Teresa Inez entered the car, gently pushing the two Guerrero boys before her. She came to where they sat and leaned over Karen. "Would you mind watching the children," she said, "just while I freshen myself. I'm still afraid . . ."

"Of course." Karen rose and, with the two little boys, moved across the aisle to seats just ahead of Hannah Pelzig's berth.

Candenning remained with the doctor. He was staring out the window, pondering exactly how he would ask for a divorce, when the train slowed for its last stop in Mexico. Preoccupied with all that had happened and with the depth of his newfound feelings for Karen, he barely noticed the two well-dressed men who entered the car, glanced this way and that, then started down the aisle.

He was reevaluating duty, realizing that, for forty years, he had been living in absolute dishonesty. Elizabeth, the house in Connecticut, perhaps his entire career, were no more than shabby lies simply because they were all based on a false sense of duty. Real duty involved commitments that were honest, and now the honest truth was inescapable. He loved Karen Tait.

He glanced over his shoulder, surprised to see the two men taking seats opposite where she sat. The one nearer the aisle removed his hat, placed it on his lap, and leaned forward to whisper a few words. Then Candenning noticed the pistol under the hat.

Strangely, there was no fear in him at all. Like a tangible thing, it had simply been left behind in the sand dunes some thirty miles to the south. His mind was clear—absolutely unfettered by any emotion whatever. Karen was in danger, and he had a duty to her.

He still had the empty Mauser with which he had killed Ian Conrad. He palmed the pistol and rose as casually as he could. He turned, took three paces, and stopped just beside the Mexican with the pistol. He leaned over the man and spoke quite softly.

"With permission?"

The man looked up. "Sir?"

Candenning placed the muzzle of the empty automatic firmly against the man's temple. "We have had much trouble on this train," he said. "We don't wish more. For a favor, you and your friend need to leave. I would not like to kill you in front of the children and the lady."

The man's mouth opened an inch, but he did not speak.

"Give me your pistol," Candenning said, "and go with God."

Meekly, the man handed his revolver to the illustrator. Both men rose and, wearing expressions of stunned surprise, walked down the aisle and sulked off.

The train started forward.

On the platform the two men still seemed quite baffled.

Candenning turned to Karen. "It's all right," he said. He sat down across from her, laid both weapons on the seat beside him, and leaned forward. He took her hands in his. "We're only yards from home now."

She squeezed his fingers, then shook her head. "They thought I was Teresa. They wanted me and the children off."

"It's all right," he said again.

"My God!" Her eyes were quite level, but she was smiling. "What a trip!"

No more than seconds after the train stopped in El Paso, the car was invaded by an army colonel flanked by two company grade officers and a florid, one-eyed man in a rumpled suit. The colonel asked for Doctor Pelzig and, as he had done with Captain Fulton, Candenning stepped forward.

"He doesn't speak English," he said. "I'll translate for him. I'm Charles Candenning."

At that moment, hell erupted.

"Candenning!" the colonel screamed. "You son of a bitch! Where the hell have you been? You've disobeyed a direct order—absent without leave—"

"Hey now," the florid man interjected, "get off this boy, Mannas."

"Like hell I will!" He turned back to Candenning with absolute fury in his hard eyes. "I am going to personally throw the entire book at you, Candenning. Hell, I may even put you right in front of a firing squad."

"Hey, Mannas . . ." The southerner's voice remained

304

soft, but the edge was unmistakable. "If I was you I'd button that regular army lip before it got itself into some real serious political trouble."

Whatever retort Mannas might have made was interrupted by the two men who pushed into the car. One opened a canvas litter as the other leaned over Hannah Pelzig. He touched her eyes, lifted her left wrist, and pressed his fingers to her pulse. He frowned, turned to the colonel, and shook his head.

"She's dead, Sir."

Candenning was standing beside Doctor Pelzig. He laid a gentle hand on the man's shoulder. "I'm sorry," he said.

The words sounded absolutely useless—completely empty and ineffectual.

Pelzig looked up to Candenning. "Sadness is selfish, really. I should think of her instead." He sighed. "For her it's a blessing. I have my work. She . . ." He shook his head. "Both our boys were killed in the war. Our country has gone mad. For her, there was nothing but me, and look—I'm just a little old man. No . . ." He lifted his lips in a fleeting, almost ironic smile. "She's happier now. Don't be sorry, Mr. Candenning."

Very formally, he shook Candenning's hand, nodded farewell to Karen, and followed the litter bearers as they carried his wife's body from the train.

Col. Mannas was but one pace behind the physicist. Almost at the vestibule, he turned and looked directly at Candenning. Although he did not speak, impotent fury was stark naked in his eyes for almost five full seconds before he spun around and scampered off the train.

"Never mind him." The florid man extended his hand. "Poor guy's never come around to realize politics is more important than guns. Desmond's the name. Sidney Desmond. You want anything, just let me know."

"What?" Candenning chuckled. "How about an all-expense-paid vacation to Bellevue?"

"I got your orders canceled," Desmond said. "You're a civilian again. No problem getting through customs. Hell, I *am* customs."

"We'll need money," Candenning told him, "I'd like to wire Connecticut."

"No problem. Just see me on the other side of the station." He slapped Candenning affectionately on the upper arm and, like a little boy on some privately important mission, left the train.

His suitcase and easel, along with Karen's luggage and bundle of notes, sketches and undeveloped film had all survived the robbery. They collected their possessions, and struggled out of the car and down to the platform.

Teresa Inez and the two little Guerrero boys were there.

"Mr. Candenning," the actress said, "I want to thank you. You saved their lives."

Just as with Domingo Portes, Candenning felt suddenly embarrassed.

"I want you to have this." She handed him a small bag.

He took it, untied the string securing it, and almost whistled as he saw what was inside. "Why," he managed, "this must be a fortune."

"It's little enough," the actress said.

Candenning retied the bag. "I can't take this," he told her. "Besides, you'll need them yourself."

"I have another." She smiled. "And, like all Mexicans, I have relatives here in El Paso. I just wanted you to have something."

Candenning looked from the actress to Karen. "Wait." He opened the bag again. Very carefully, he inspected the diamonds, then reached inside and removed one beautifully facetted stone. He retied the bag and returned it to Teresa. "A token," he said. "For remembrance."

"Go with God," she said.

"With God." He nodded.

She turned and, with the two little boys, walked away.

He and Karen were alone.

"Well," she said. "I guess—"

"No!" He turned on her. "It's not good-bye. We have the whole trip east and . . ." He felt like a mischievous youth embarking on some critical adventure. "I know it's presumptuous, but I thought this . . ." He held the diamond between his thumb and first finger. "Well—it just might look good in a ring."

She frowned slightly, then lifted her eyebrows as full understanding came to her. Her expression was quite serious as she questioned him with somber blue eyes. "Are you sure?" she asked.

He placed the single diamond in her palm and closed her

fingers over it. "Yes." He clasped her hand in both his own. "Absolutely sure."

As they started toward customs inspection, the train's engine sighed behind them. It was a sound of monumental relief after much effort—an auditory symbol of his own feelings. He felt totally relaxed. He had journeyed philosophically and emotionally to the land of Ultimate Truth while traveling physically through storms and earthquakes, intrigues, plots, and gunfire.

He knew a complicated adventure was at last over.

He also knew another had just begun.